# MY

# THIRTY-FIRST

# YEAR

## (And Other Calamities)

# MY
# THIRTY-FIRST
# YEAR

## (And Other Calamities)

*a novel by*

# EMILY WOLF

SHE WRITES PRESS

Published 2022
Printed in the United States of America
Print ISBN: 978-1-64742-082-6
E-ISBN: 978-1-64742-081-9
Library of Congress Control Number: 2022904056

For information, address:
She Writes Press
1569 Solano Ave #546
Berkeley, CA 94707

She Writes Press is a division of SparkPoint Studio, LLC.

*Book design by Stacey Aaronson*

*For Josh, for his steadfast belief, support, and calm*

"[Women's] ability to realize their full potential . . . is intimately connected to 'their ability to control their reproductive lives.' Thus, legal challenges to undue restrictions on abortion procedures do not seek to vindicate some generalized notion of privacy; rather, they center on a woman's autonomy to determine her life's course, and thus to enjoy equal citizenship stature."

*Gonzales v. Carhart,* 550 US 124, 171-172 (2007) (Ginsburg, J.,[1] dissenting, quoting *Planned Parenthood v. Casey,* 505 US 833, 856 (1992)).

"[T]he month of *Av,* which occurs in July or August, is the unhappiest month. 'From the beginning of Av,' the rabbis teach, 'we diminish happiness' (*Mishna Ta'anit* 4:6)."

—Rabbi Joseph Telushkin[2]

"[I]f your partner is broken, or impatient, or has darker needs— is unknowingly trying to build you in the shape of another woman he once knew, and lost; is trying to lean into your foundations to make his own stronger—you will build something with rotten walls, and impossible angles, which will, one day in the future, collapse."

—Caitlin Moran[3]

---

[1] "Ginsburg, J." = Ruth Bader Ginsburg, the Notorious RBG, The Shiznit, My Idol. Even in death, she continues to kick all kinds of ass.

[2] From *Jewish Literacy* by Joseph Telushkin. Copyright© 1991 by Rabbi Joseph Telushkin. Used by permission of HarperCollins Publishers.

[3] From *How to Be Famous* by Caitlin Moran. Copyright© 2018 by Casa Bevron. Used by permission in the US of HarperCollins Publishers and in Canada of HarperCollins Publishers Ltd.

## Author's Note

Although I resemble Zoe Greene in some ways (I too grew up in a semi-Jewish home, loathe the Cardinals, and run very slowly), this is a work of fiction. My life is not Zoe's life, as she is a fictional character many years my junior. Zoe's supporting cast are also all fictional characters—minus U2, who by some heavenly miracle, are a real band.

# TABLE OF CONTENTS

---

# PART ONE

---

# Shit Smithereens

# One

"Zoe. You need new dating panties."

I blinked, still foggy from the anesthesia, and tried to focus on the ancient pair of Jockeys my mom was holding at the foot of my gurney. I couldn't help but smile before giving in to the temptation to close my eyes. Only she could make me laugh *maybe* ten minutes after I'd had an abortion.

"Sure," I whispered hoarsely. "I appreciate your optimism."

I heard her sigh and drop the undies back into the hospital-issue plastic bag. *Dating panties.* Although I was, at that moment, minutes removed from being pregnant with my husband's baby, Mom and I both knew that my marriage couldn't be salvaged. But living any kind of normal life after this moment, much less one that involved dating, seemed impossible.

My nerves began to fire too fast. The moment was surreal and ridiculous. Crazy! Because *none of this* was supposed to be happening. I tried to arrest the physical manifestations of panic that were already taking hold: I slowed my breath. Released my jaw. I attempted to be present in the tiny, curtained recovery cubicle. To concentrate on the blood pressure cuff on my bicep—its squeeze and release. On the plastic pulse thingy affixed to my pointer finger that lit up blood red. I forced my breath in and out, even though it kept getting stuck in my chest.

"Well," Mom said with a decisive nod. "I'll take you shopping when you're ready. For the panties."

I studied her. She was working so hard not to lose it. But as usual, her huge green eyes betrayed her. In them swam sympathy, concern about how (if?) I'd manage to put my life back together after this radically un-Zoe-like shitstorm of a disaster, and rage at Rob, all at once.

*Rob.* The very idea of him startled me. Strangely, despite pushing me to this moment—and being the center of my universe since high school—he had become a nonentity. Not even a void, because something has to have had a presence before its absence can be felt. No. After deciding to have a baby together and then, nine weeks into my pregnancy, reneging not only on his decision to become a father, but also to be my husband, it became as though he didn't exist and never had. I couldn't recall what it felt like to touch him, eat with him, or watch TV with him. I couldn't conjure an accurate picture of his face. He left only vapors of a scent you're not sure was ever really there. You know—like a fart.

I didn't have the energy to explain this to my mom—to tell her that I didn't care about Rob anymore, and she shouldn't either. Nor to share with her the intensity of my relief about carrying out a decision that was not just the right one, but the only one. Yes, that choice coexisted with a sadness and loss that were bigger, heavier, and scarier than I could have imagined. But I had anticipated this. I knew, from the second I'd decided to abort, that I was about to know real grief and shame. The sense of relief, though, was a welcome surprise, even in its nascent form. My heart rate was steady, and I drew full breaths for the first time in days.

The even bigger revelation I had while lying there was that, After The Abortion, I was, somehow, still *me*. This, I had been certain, could not be. I was sure I would awaken from the abortion not only devastated but a totally different person. That the very core of my being would be removed along with the contents of my uterus, my DNA would be scrambled, and I would be, from then on, unfixable and incomplete. Isn't that what we're taught to believe? But now, to my inarticulable joy, I knew that I'd been wrong. Even After, I remained at my core the same Zoe Greene I had always been—albeit a Zoe Greene whose once-perfect life had been pulverized into a heaping pile of shit smithereens.

IT WAS A blindingly sunny, July Chicago day. The sun penetrated the multiple hanging curtain dividers between the windows and me, lending my spare recovery cubicle an odd cheeriness. I couldn't quite grasp that I was no longer pregnant; it's amazing how quickly you fall in love with the idea of the baby growing inside you. Now it was gone. I let the tears fall. My mom squeezed my feet. *But I am still me*, I reminded myself. *I am still me.*

A nurse came to inspect the contents of my "maternity pad."[4] She nodded, satisfied, and left a box of apple juice and package of graham crackers on my tray before wordlessly moving along. I rested some minutes before eating and drinking. Mom was still standing at the end of my gurney, deep in thought, occasionally patting my toes through the blankets. The

---

[4] "Maternity pad" = euphemism for "enormous adult diaper for uterine blood and goo."

abortion was done. My goo had been checked and rechecked. The apple juice and graham crackers had been consumed. Now I needed to go.

"Get me the fuck out of here," I whispered. I felt the corners of my mouth turn up into a smile. "Would you please slap a clean diaper on those gnarly underpants and tell them I'm leaving?"

Mom smiled and nodded. "Done."

# Two

As I was wheeled out of post-op, I felt pinpricks of guilt creep up my arms and legs—and the occasional goober bubble into my diaper. I felt sure at the time that every other woman in the recovery unit had lost an unhealthy pregnancy. I knew that they hadn't chosen to abruptly remove embryos from *their* wombs that were, by miracle of nature, growing into healthy babies. But their partners were patting their feet, not their moms. This didn't put even the tiniest dent in my guilt or enable me to meet a single pair of their eyes.

We drove out of the Chicago Women's Hospital garage into Friday afternoon rush-hour traffic. The sun leapt off the glittery glass-and-steel surfaces of densely packed buildings. It felt more like early September than July: The breeze was crisp, the sun was warm but not hot. Lake Michigan sparkled crystal blue and boats of all sizes bobbed, motored, and sailed just beyond the skyscrapers. It used to baffle me how many Chicagoans own boats. But I came to appreciate their chutzpah as part of the city's identity. Not only will you see runners on lakeshore paths in sub-zero temps and sideways-shooting snow, but in a city with sixteen weeks of decent boating weather in a *good* year, the competition for dock space is cutthroat. A few lawyers at my

firm disappeared by three o'clock every summer Friday to dash
to the lake. I thought about those lawyers, and about my colleagues and friends who were probably gathering at bars and
cafes to kick off their weekends. It looked and felt, ironically,
like the perfect Friday afternoon.

As Mom navigated ever so slowly through Streeterville, I
rested with my eyes closed. Whenever my anxiety began to surge
—about my decision to terminate, the demise of my young marriage, why I hadn't realized that Rob was as fucked up as he obviously was, when and how I'd get him out of our apartment,
how to split up our stuff, whether our pets (my cat, Frankie, and
our French bulldog, Basil, whom we'd inherited from a law
school classmate of Rob's who couldn't care for a plant, much
less a puppy) were managing without me, or how I'd put one foot
in front of the other for the fifty-four more years the actuaries
predicted I'd live—I'd say something stupid about nothing, and
Mom would say something equally distracted back.

She managed to cut through the traffic zooming west on
Ontario to drive through McDonald's for a Coke. (Despite being
pumped with endless bags of IV fluids, I was desperately thirsty.)
As we approached the speaker to order, I considered the weird
food Rob preferred from McDonald's: Quarter Pounders with
Big Mac sauce, Chicken Nuggets with a side of American cheese,
and, when "in season," McRibs. How did I not realize there was
something seriously wrong with this guy?

I reached for my phone, ignored the voicemail Rob had left
hours ago, and typed out a text: Done. Why I felt any sense of
obligation to Rob at that point is a good question, but one I
wasn't prepared to answer yet. I hit SEND, shoved the phone
deep into my bag, and hoped that the half-eaten Balance Bars

and receipts lurking within would bury both Rob and the glaring fucked-uped-ness of my life.

"I want a divorce," I heard myself announce with gusto as my poor mother handed two one-dollar bills to the drive-thru attendant. He, a twenty-year-old kid with long, blond eyelashes, gave Mom her change and closed the window in record time. She sighed in solidarity.

"I know," she said before catching herself. I could practically hear my dad's voice in her ear: *Of course she needs to divorce. But Zoe has* got *to get there on her own, Rachel. On. Her. OWN.* "What I mean is . . . I understand why you might feel that way."

I smiled. Mom, bless her, was never one to keep her (strong) opinions to herself. So I waited, silently, watching her grip on the wheel tighten, her lips purse, and her round eyes narrow. Five, four, three, two. . . .

"Dad-and-I-already-started-a-list-of-who-should-take-what," she spewed. "Last night. When we couldn't sleep." She looked both sheepish and relieved upon sharing this information. My blood began to boil at my family's anguish.

"Of course you did," I replied. "Because even though *he's* the one who said he 'couldn't' be a father, and even though *he's* the one who says he 'can't' be a husband, *we're* the ones who will have to do *ehhhhh-ver-ree-thing*. Or, *un*do everything, I guess."

My escape valve blew open.

"Rob just gets to say, 'Oopsie, I don't want that baby after all!' before assuming the fetal position—irony duly noted—and checking out. But *I'm* the one who had to decide to have, and then actually have, the abortion. And *you're* the ones who have to start facing all the logistical *crap* of getting a divorce—which, Rob knows full well, is what 'can't be a husband' means—because you're too kind to let *me* face it right now, because, let's be honest, none of us knows if I'm going to survive having my baby vacuumed out of me. So, while Rob gets to perfect his *'poor me, I'm so fucked up, I can't do ANYTHING!'* routine, you and Dad are spending sleepless nights dividing up your nearly thirty-year-old daughter's marital assets, and I'm wondering how to get Rob out of my fucking apartment, all while bleeding into a fucking diaper!"

Mom opened her mouth and closed it again, tears welling up in her eyes. "I. . . ." she whispered. I should've stopped—for her sake—but couldn't.

"He'll find someone new, you know," I continued, my voice hoarse and phlegmy. "Some gullible, not-too-smart-but-capable-enough-to-take-care-of-him type. Someone who'll feel sorry for him and believe she can help him 'reach his potential.'" I made air quotes. "*He'll be great someday*, she'll tell herself. She'll marry him, and carry him, until one day she wakes up and realizes he'll never be the man he promised he would be. That he's sucked her dry and, oh, by the way, stolen her twenties. Just watch. You'll see."

I exhaled the air that hadn't escaped during my tirade.

"Well," Mom eventually said quietly. "Won't that be a relief—not to be sucked dry anymore."

I began to sob. "Yeah," I managed in the drooly, ugly way of an adult having a real cry. "It *will*." And it would, if only I could picture my life doing anything other than grinding to a screeching halt.

We didn't talk for the remainder of the drive. We were too busy struggling with exhaustion and reality. By the time Mom pulled up to my parents' Lakeview townhome, I was treading water in a pool of humiliation; I needed babying when my adult life was supposed to be gelling according to meticulous plan! Done with Yale Law, positioned at a top-notch firm, living in the just-right neighborhood in my all-time favorite city . . . but I was mired in mess. And yet, there they were, my family, diving into the toilet with me without giving it a second thought. Tears—of anger and gratitude—popped from my eyes. I willed my shit to come together while Mom retrieved her purse and my discharge papers and pills. She helped me from my seat.

"Tonight is for recuperation," she said, tired but resolute, as she walked me to the front door. I nodded as if recuperation were possible. "We're pressing PAUSE on the heavy stuff," she explained, holding the screen door open with her butt while sliding her key into the lock. "Because we need to."

She was right.

"Dad was going to pick up Hecky's. He and Zach should be waiting for us. And for a few hours at least, we're just going to. . . ." She couldn't think of the word but smoothed the air with her hands.

Smoothing anything seemed hopeless—until the door closed behind us, and we stood in the cool, airy foyer. I inhaled mesquite. Hecky's made my favorite baby back ribs, which came with my favorite fries (frozen and crinkle-cut). Zach, my twenty-four-year-old "baby" brother who, thank God, was spending a couple of weeks at home before moving to New Haven for his master's in architecture, bounded down the stairs, enveloped me in a bear hug, and whispered, "*Tenenbaums*[5] is queued and ready." When we parted, I noticed that my dad had quietly

---

[5] *The Royal Tenenbaums* is perfect and, therefore, my favorite movie.

joined us; he hugged me firmly, last but in no way least. I looked at them all. An emotional ceasefire, even if artificial—plus ribs, fries, and *Tenenbaums*—appealed to every fiber in me. I let the four of us move together as a pack, wordlessly, away from the door and into the house.

A HALF-RACK and some hours later, Zach was gently shaking me awake on my parents' sofa. I touched the wetness at the corner of my mouth—a mixture of drool and barbecue sauce. It was dark, and Zach and I were the only ones left. The TV screen was blue.

"Goddammit," I whispered. "What'd I miss?"

"You were out by the time A.B.[6] finished his opening mono-logue, I'm afraid," he said, strumming his ever-present acoustic guitar and cocking his thick left eyebrow in the comical way only he could. "Mom and Dad didn't make it five more minutes. I woke them first and think they're up to bed." He strummed, and we sat for a moment before he grinned. "I watched the whole thing and enjoyed it immensely."

"I never fall asleep during *Tenenbaums*!"

"Well," he sighed, scooching next to me, "it's been . . . a day."

"Yep," I agreed, becoming aware once again of the oozing thickness between my legs. "But you'll watch with me again to-morrow, right?" If I could schedule every foreseeable moment of my future, then perhaps I'd be too busy to confront my shattered life!

"Of course," he nodded graciously, cocking his eyebrow again.

At twenty-four, Zach's maturity and calm amid the

---

[6] Alec Baldwin, *The Royal Tenenbaums*' flawless narrator.

smithereens amazed me. He'd spent his school years in a near-constant state of boredom until an Intro to Architecture class piqued his interest in college. He then adopted a laser-like focus we'd never known he had: He attended tutorials, crushed every math, engineering, and design-related course in his path, and even audited courses at the grad school. Thank God he wasn't leaving for another week; I would miss him mightily. I made a mental note not to let Rob take *any* of the models Zach had built and let me keep. Zach and I would rather die.

Zach strummed *Dirt* by Phish almost inaudibly, shaping the lyrics with his lips but not singing them. I was wrapped in a lap blanket on the chaise end of the sofa. My hair was a mess and I smelled of Hospital. The contents of Zach's oversized backpack, out of which he would live until he left for *his* stint at Yale, were strewn about the remainder of the couch. The piles of change he always left in his wake, and which drove me nuts, littered the coffee table. Poor Zach had moved out of the third-floor guest room and onto the den's pull-out sofa when the smithereens brought me to my parents' doorstep. Mom and Dad's two rescue mutts, Phats and Daphne, snoozed happily in a pile of Zach's clothes.

"I guess I should try to go to sleep," I said. I was exhausted but couldn't fathom achieving unconsciousness.

"Yeah," Zach agreed. "I'll walk you."

"Oh, please," I dismissed him. "I'm fine." My words rang hollow the second I uttered them; we could both tell how unsteady I was. Zach said nothing while he followed me, vigilant—the way my husband should have. That I was counting on care not from Rob, but from the little brother whose spelling homework I used to correct, seemed apropos of the parallel universe in which I was living. We paused for a breath on the second floor before continuing slowly to the third. We turned left into the guest bedroom/office where "my" bed sat waiting, neatly turned down, even though I'd left everything in a tangle that morning. My nightshirt was laid neatly across the pillow closest to the bathroom. Déjà vu whisked me back to elementary school during which my mom—while I was otherwise engaged and oblivious—would ready my room for bed each night, like magic. A loving, everyday gift I had taken for granted then but not now.

We heard my dad snoring when Mom opened the door from their master across the hall. I was so happy he'd fallen asleep; he'd worn the gray pallor of exhaustion at dinner. Mom padded in wearing her robe.

"Everyone OK?" she fretted.

"Totally." I managed to smile. "Goodnight, guys." I hugged Zach and then my mom before turning toward the bathroom. But they sat on the bed.

"Go," I insisted. "I'll be OK."

They stared at me.

"*Seriously*," I added.

Zach stood up. We locked eyes in understanding: Nothing was OK, everything was fucked up, but sitting around the guest room all night wasn't going to help. It was time to engage in ritual, put toothbrush to teeth, head to pillow. I wanted to give my family permission to ditch the smithereens and rest.

"'Night, Zodo," Zach said, hugging me sideways one more time.

"Goodnight, Sweetie," Mom said, standing up and kissing me on the head. She hesitated in the doorway before leaving.

I heard the master bedroom door click shut and Zach's

enormous feet plod down the stairs. I washed my face, flossed, and brushed my teeth, all while avoiding my reflection in the mirror. I changed my maternity pad after peeing and flushing some bloody chunks down the toilet, carried the Ambien I'd begged off Dr. Fine, my wonderful OB/Gyn, to bed, and burrowed under the covers. It was The After, and I was alone.

♡

July 27, 2007

Dearest Bono: Today I aborted my first pregnancy. And Rob is a monster. (Why bury the lede?)

You watched your mother collapse from an aneurysm, at her own father's funeral, when you were only 14. And yet, you survived. You evolved into a partner, father, artist — a citizen of the world. You took care of yourself by taking refuge in your friends, and in Ali, your high school sweetheart turned wife. You had children. Four! You grew and charted your family's course together.

Rob's parents are assholes. Your mom fucking died. And yet Rob is broken, and you are BONO. Why?

Today was the worst day of my life. But now I appreciate you even more, which I'd never thought possible. Love, Zoe

PS: And I feel/Like I'm slowly, slowly, slowly slipping under/And I feel/Like I'm holding onto nothing. . . .[7]

---

[7] Yep, that's right—I journal letters to the members of my favorite band, U2, and have since I was fifteen. No, I don't know them, and no, I'm not crazy. I'm in love with their music—their *magic*. I make no apologies.

# PART TWO

---

# This Was Not Supposed to Be My Life

# Three

I met my first boyfriend (finally!) when I was fifteen.

I grew up on Chicago's tony North Shore, where six suburbs feed into one huge public high school. By eighth grade, I was *really* ready to get to high school because I had been with the same kids since kindergarten. And every single one of the boys in my class knew that I was (a) very tall, (b) burdened by troublesome Jewish hair, (c) wont to trip over nothing (and everything), and (d) smart. All of this forced them to the conclusion, it seemed, that I was undesirable and un-kiss-worthy. I accepted this. It felt like they had a window not only into my insecurities, but into who I really was.[8]

But I had a plan for high school: The new crop of boys wouldn't know that I'd been five foot eight for two years. They'd never know, now that I could French braid my hair, what it looked like when left to its own devices. My brain had gotten the memo from my body, so I wasn't tripping (quite) as much. They didn't know *the real me*. If I could just keep it that way, I might get myself kissed!

These were big dreams. But I spent freshman year doing the

---

[8] Of course, I never questioned whether *they* were desirable or kiss-worthy. This mindset is a woefully common affliction amongst adolescent girls.

same things with my same friends from grade school (i.e. watching Must-See TV, making phony phone calls, and not hearing about, much less attending, parties). Which is why I nearly spontaneously combusted when Parker Owens approached me sophomore year. The bell had just rung to signal the end of geometry and, happily, the day.

"Hi! I know we haven't met yet," he said with confidence. "I'm Parker." He extended his hand and flashed me a grin. *Wow.*

My face turned eggplant as I struggled to jam textbooks into my Eddie Bauer backpack. Did he really think I didn't know who he was? Of *course* I knew who he was. He'd made both the varsity swim and tennis teams as a freshman—unheard of—and was state-ranked in both. There were already plaques bearing his name in the school's athletic wing. He seemed totally at ease in his body, sports, and all things high school. He always moved with an entourage, got invited to parties, *and went.* Could this really be happening? COULD THIS BE MY MOMENT?

"Oh. Hi. I'm Zoe."

"Listen, you seem to really know this stuff." He lowered his voice as we walked past the teacher. "And I kind of . . . don't."

"HA!" I laughed. Parker stared at me as though I had an entire stalk of broccoli stuck in my teeth. "Ohmigod, sorry," I stammered. "I'm not laughing at you—I'm laughing because math is usually my worst subject. Geometry's the only math I get."

He laughed. "Well, my practice schedule's pretty tight the next couple weeks, but then I'm chill for the holidays. Wanna get together? And maybe go over some of this stuff?" My heart sank. He didn't want me—he wanted a math tutor. But then he flashed another grin and added, "And get something to eat?"

*YARSE!*

"Yeah! Totally." I beamed like the North Star.

By the time we'd eaten personal pan pizzas over our homework, killed an hour walking around the mall, and kissed in front of the Cinnabon the Sunday after Thanksgiving, I probably knew deep down that Parker was using me. He wasn't terribly bright and *did* need help with his homework. And like so many superstars, he basked in my admiration—he seemed to actually *need* it. I was an easy mark. But Parker was undeterred by my height, hair, or intellect, and his desire to touch my boobs appeared genuine. I wasn't about to let his dimness or calculating personality overshadow this.

The single worst experience of my pre-abortion life occurred after watching Parker set the Illinois high school record for the hundred-meter freestyle. The meet was held ninety minutes away and involved hours of waiting around in a dark, dank natatorium, so I'd undertaken a real labor of love even before walking into the team party, armed with balloons and a bag of Sour Patch Kids (Parker's favorite). As soon as I entered the party house, which was crawling with a veritable who's who of upperclassmen, the place went quiet. Parker's teammates stared at me, then averted their eyes. Some animal instinct told me to turn and leave, but I couldn't. So I ventured farther down the hall, only to find Parker tongue-deep in Eileen Connors, a freshman swim-groupie. I shrieked, sent the balloons flying into a ceiling fan, burst into tears, and ran from the house in abject humiliation; I hung onto the Sour Patch Kids, every last one of which I shoved into my face while waiting for my mom to pick me up. My homeroom teacher signed me out of PE for two weeks—to give me time to cry privately after enduring math with Parker—

after even *she* heard about this fiasco. My high school dreams were, apparently, dashed.

So, back to phony phone calls I went for a long while. Until I met Robert Baros.

Our high school was so big that we didn't cross paths until senior year, when we finally met in Social Service, the school's community outreach program. Rob was cute—big blue eyes, thick dark hair, chiseled bone structure, thin but strong—and had not so much a sweet, but a gentle aura about him. He was studious and seemed to have nice friends, including lots of other Greek American kids. And he liked me! Whenever I spoke during Social Service meetings, he'd blush. My friend Elise noticed this and contrived a way for Rob and me to work together. From then on, we watched movies, went to dances, made out, and did normal, teenage stuff. Rob wasn't obsessed with perfecting his serve and spent zero time in dank natatoriums. He seemed, in a word, lovely.

But there was always a sadness behind Rob's eyes. Eventually, I learned that, when Rob was seven, his father, George, stunned Chicago's tight-knit Greek community by leaving in the middle of the night. It took a private detective five years to find George at a resort in Big Sur, where he taught the yoga and Reiki healing he'd studied on his extensive travels. The heir apparent to his father-in-law's (and, before that, grandfather-in-law's) successful Greektown restaurant—an institution known for business lunches, special events, and everything in between—George left behind not only financial security but several families: the Greek community for whom the restaurant was a hub; his family-of-origin, which left Chicago in George's turbulent wake; his furious in-laws; and his own nuclear family—his wife, Arianna, and son, Rob. That both Arianna and Rob were hard-fought miracle babies (only children conceived and delivered after much struggle) did not help matters.

Rob never expressed interest in his father. How much of this stemmed from Arianna's inextinguishable anger—she made clear that, like Voldemort, George's name was not to be spoken—I could never tell.

"Would you ever call him?" I asked Rob more than once.

"No," Rob would say firmly. "He left."

One time, when I was on the verge of suggesting that talking to his father might at least provide closure, Rob headed me off.

"He *left*," he repeated, trying to master his tone. "He betrayed our trust. You don't understand."

He was right—I didn't. My family remained intact. I couldn't imagine my father abandoning me. And, unlike Rob's, my grandparents weren't Greek Orthodox or devoutly religious. Divorce didn't carry the same stigma in my world as it did in the Baroses' (Arianna had legally changed her own and Rob's last name back to "Baros" once George's whereabouts were confirmed). Who was I to say what was right or wrong in another family or culture? Plus, Rob seemed resolute about forgetting his dad and devoting himself to his mom. I didn't know then that you can't ignore foundational fissures without consequence; that you must unearth them, examine them in the daylight, and either patch the cracks or build anew. I erroneously thought that Rob's ability to forge ahead, seemingly unscathed, was a sign of strength. It also made it easy for both of us to see only our happy teenage relationship, which gave each of us exactly what we thought we needed.

# Four

'll never forget the first time I met Arianna. Rob and I had been dating for a few months. He had already met my family several times, but Arianna was a single mom and practically lived at the restaurant, which was forty-five minutes away. She was never home when I went to Rob's house, a McMansion on the edge of the school district into which Arianna's parents refused to move because they preferred to walk to the restaurant. I figured that Arianna bravely decided to leave Greektown because she thought the suburbs would make a better life for Rob. But the McMansion had a flimsy quality about it, despite its largesse, and cold, high ceilings. It ticked all the boxes but never felt like a home.

Rob finally brought me to the restaurant the Sunday before prom. It was ten thirty in the morning, and the restaurant, with its warm wood floors, gleaming glassware, and crisp linen tablecloths, all awash in sunlight from both the floor-to-ceiling windows and multiple skylights, couldn't have been more inviting. It was the antithesis of the McMansion.

Rob's grandparents and a gaggle of their fellow octogenarians were parked at what was clearly "their" table, which was strewn with the remnants of fluffy pastries, thick Greek coffees, and smoldering cigarettes. Due to fertility struggles, Rob's grandmother and mother had become parents later than their peers, so Rob was this group's youngest grandchild. They fussed mightily over Rob in Greek—I caught the word "Penn," where Rob had decided to put in an application after I told him I'd applied early, and happily accepted admission—and then fussed over me in broken English. Their joy upon seeing us was contagious, and I loved commiserating about our shared affection for Rob by smiling wide and clasping each other's hands.

Honestly, I was surprised when Rob got into Penn—it was a reach for him. I was ashamed that I'd ever doubted him after watching the way in which he animatedly engaged his many *yia-yias* and *papous* (in fluid Greek, no less). It was at that moment, I think, that I fell in love. And was thrilled to have won the table's stamp of approval.

My gaze went immediately to Arianna when she emerged from the kitchen with a tray of clean espresso cups. So did everyone else's. She had the kind of performative energy that commanded attention. I immediately noticed her immaculate posture, assured demeanor, and fuchsia-lipsticked smile. Although she was short and squat—just the right amount of plump for a restauranteur—there was something almost glamorous about her. She dyed her hair dark pepper because she preferred youth and drama over her natural salt streaks. Her beige shirt-dress had been perfectly pressed and cinched with a thick brown belt to give the illusion of a waist. Gold knots dotted her ears; gold chains pooled above her ample bosom. Sturdy, pristine block heels clicked beneath her as she strode across her kingdom.

That Arianna's entire presentation was a facade would never

have occurred to me. If I had looked closely, I might have noticed the cracks: the puffiness in her face from too much drink, the tightness in her jaw, the advanced wrinkles around her blue eyes—that her fuchsia lips twitched upon seeing me. But back then, the way she threw her shoulders back, stuck her chin out, and took up space captivated me. I just wanted to be near her. And I was in luck: She zipped out from behind the coffee bar, cupped Rob's face in her hands—*"Agapi mou,"* she whispered ("My love" in Greek)—before summoning every one of her sixty inches and grabbing my shoulders.

"Zoe, what a beauty! Finally, Robert brings you to me."

She pulled me down into an embrace. "It's so nice to meet you, Mrs. Baros. Thank you for having me to your beautiful restaurant."

"To *my* beautiful restaurant!" Arianna's father said in heavily accented English. Everyone laughed. This time, I did notice Arianna's jaw clench, almost imperceptibly, before reassuming her lively smile.

"And yet you are the one drinking the coffees and I am the one making them!" she replied. This elicited chuckles from the elders and a loud "What did she say?" from her father. Arianna winked at me. "Sit. Have a coffee," she said.

We sat.

"Did I hear you tell my mother that you're also going to Penn?" Arianna asked.

I'd assumed she'd known. Her eyes narrowed; Rob blushed.

"Oh. Yes!" I said, blushing too.

Arianna recovered quickly. "How nice. Boys tell their poor mothers nothing!" A large party walked in the door bearing a baby in a christening gown. "Ah! Sophia!" Arianna smiled and waved. "Please excuse me—make yourself at home." Arianna went to welcome her guests.

The next thing I knew, it was eleven at night.

"Is it always like that?" I asked Rob as he drove me home.

"Like what?" He stifled a yawn and checked his rearview.

"Cheerful. Bustling. Lively!"

Rob laughed. "Yes. Always."

"It's amazing," I marveled. "I loved it."

"I'm glad." Rob smiled at me.

I waited a minute before asking why he hadn't told Arianna that we were both going to Penn and that it had been my idea. A vein popped at Rob's temple.

"Oh." He drummed the steering wheel for a moment. "Mom's just old-fashioned."

Ah. Fair enough. Her son was off to another city with his girlfriend. I hoped this wouldn't sour her—I really wanted Arianna to like me. Not only because I loved Rob, but because I respected and admired her. While raising a son alone, she ran a thriving, important business. She managed the books, did the purchasing, oversaw the staff, taste-tested every wine and recipe on the menu, and was an uncommonly skilled mistress of the house. She knew exactly when to suggest another bottle of wine or produce a complimentary dessert. But her real skill was spending just enough time at each table to make every patron feel special. That—in addition to the spectacular food, beautiful decor, and cheerful ambiance—was what made the restaurant tick. I often heard that Arianna had inherited her charisma from her father and grandfather. But they were not single mothers. While Arianna may not have initiated the restaurant's sterling reputation, she sustained it. I was totally enamored of her.

# Five

I never needed much. That was my weakness. I never really considered why Arianna didn't invite us around more during college. And when I began sensing competition and dislike—Arianna tended to call Rob to the restaurant whenever we had important plans, for instance, to celebrate my mom's birthday—Rob dismissed my concerns. Arianna was a single, hardworking mom and daughter (who would lose her father our sophomore year) with a lot on her plate, Rob would remind me, shaming me in the process. But then he would fill me up *just enough*—with a sweet gesture, a kind word, a well-timed kiss. Rob was very good at *just enough*. And for a very long time, *just enough* was good enough for me.

Like when we stood tearfully on my doorstep days after high school graduation. I was heading to Mexico with Social Service the next morning; Rob would work at the restaurant for the summer.

"Hey, Greener," Rob said softly after our sixth or seventh "last" kiss. He had his arms linked behind my back, patiently abiding my outpouring of teenage angst about our imminent separation. "I have something for you."

I pulled away to let him reach into his back jeans pocket. He retrieved a smooth, brilliant-green piece of sea glass.

"That," he said, putting his arms back around me, "is a good luck charm my great-grandpa gave me. It's from his favorite beach in Santorini. I've kept it with me every day since he died. It's probably the most important thing I have. So." He stared at the faded orange "C" on his Chicago Bears T-shirt.

"This is for me, Baros?" I asked, unsuccessfully blinking back tears.

"Well, not to, like, *have*," he teased. "But to borrow. While you're away. I thought you could, you know, give it a little rub whenever you think of me, and know that I'm thinking about you too."

I kissed him again. He tasted like Wintergreen Certs. When Rob finally left, he waved to me out of his car window the whole way to the corner at which he had to turn.

Everything felt perfect. Everything *was* perfect. But Rob would never rise above this moment. Looking back, that was Rob at his very best.

June 9, 1995

Dear Bono: I don't even know what you mean right now, With or Without You. I've met a boy and I for <u>sure</u> need him all. The. TIME! We have to be apart for the whole summer and I think it may literally KILL me. Why can't you write about <u>this</u> feeling? Even on Boy, when you were . . . oh, my God, you were basically my age. I've done nothing, and you

were already on the fast track to World
Domination. But anyway, even on Boy, the love you
sing about is so sad. Where's your song about <u>bliss</u>?
About wanting to just, like, kiss all the time? I
think you should write about <u>that</u>. Love, Zoe

# Six

My college roommate, Maddie, and I only ever had one fight.

It happened just after we'd arrived on campus for our senior year. Maddie was trying to camouflage our Yaffa Blocks with decorative fabric when Rob and I walked into the apartment's cramped kitchen. He pilfered an apple from the fridge.

"Looks good, Mads," I said.

She surveyed her work. "Well, it's not the Ritz, but at least it's not so former-Communist-bloc."

"It's perfect."

"So? How'd it go?" Maddie asked.

My face reddened. Of course, I *was* going to tell Rob about my meeting—eventually. But why rush? Maddie looked at me quizzically.

"How'd what go?" Rob asked.

"Oh. Umm, this weird meeting," I said with a wave of my hand. "It's no big deal. You're so busy today—buying books, settling in. I was gonna mention it tonight."

Now *Rob* looked at me quizzically.

"I have a minute. What meeting?" He leaned against the counter to eat his apple.

"It's no big deal," I repeated. "But this man who coordinates

fellowships and stuff for the university called me last week—
when we were still in Chicago—and asked me to meet with him
when I got back to campus."

"About what?" Rob asked.

"Oh, he wants me to apply—to *consider* applying—for a
couple of . . . scholarships."

"Uhhhh," Maddie said. "Not just *any* scholarships. The
*Rhodes* Scholarship. And the Marshall." She beamed at Rob.
"That's right," she told him. "I've spent three years living with
someone who continually makes me look bad, and it's about to
get worse."

I tried to laugh, but nothing came out. I awkwardly avoided
Rob's narrowing gaze and wiped the sweat from my upper lip.
Even then, I knew this wasn't how I was supposed to feel when
my boyfriend learned of my success. But I told myself that Rob
had come to depend on me in a special way and just didn't want
me moving across the ocean.

Maddie waited for Rob to say something. Eventually, he did.

"Don't you have to be an athlete to get the Rhodes?" he
asked.

"Yeah," I coughed. "I guess my occasional twenty minutes on
the Stairmaster doesn't count. . . ."

"Uh, no." He laughed before taking a loud bite, which grated
on my ears like grinding bones.

"But didn't the guy tell you—" Maddie began.

I interrupted her with my eyes. Yes, the scholarship dude
had made clear that athletics had become less important to the
Rhodes and meant nothing for the Marshall. But I didn't want
to get into it. Maddie assumed her This-New-Yorker-Is-Pissed
face. Rob managed not to see it.

"And don't those scholarships send you to England?" he asked.

"Umm. Abroad, yeah," I said.

"For an entire year, right?"

I nodded.

"And we missed each other when we were abroad last year," Rob said casually as he dropped his apple core in the trash and picked up his backpack. This was not actually a casual subject, as Rob had spent the entire year in Greece, while I spent one semester with Maddie in Rome instead. He kissed me on the forehead and lowered his voice. "Scholarship applications are a lot of work." (I wondered how he knew this.) "I'd hate to see you miss out on your senior year, grinding away on apps for things that, statistically, you're so unlikely to win."

I looked down. He had a point.

"Plus," he said, smiling, "I'd miss you."

I couldn't bear to look up until he walked toward the door.

"Off to overpay for books," he announced. "Good luck with the decorating." The door clicked shut.

I felt vaguely shitty, but Maddie was fuming. I'd seen her like this before, but never as the object of her ire.

"That was total bullshit," she said as soon as Rob's footsteps fell away.

"What?" I asked shakily. I knew it *was* total bullshit, but wasn't exactly sure what the "it" was yet.

"You can't be serious. He totally dismissed these amazing opportunities for you!"

I trusted Maddie, and she knew Rob well, so the fact that she was openly criticizing him was hard for me to ignore. But I was determined to try.

"He . . . just really gets me," I stumbled. "I'm a homebody! He knows I can't be an ocean away. Again."

"You loved our semester abroad," Maddie said with a level stare.

"Well—yeah, but that was only for, like, three months. And I was with you."

"Mmm."

"And Rob has a point about the athletics. He *does*," I added, before Maddie could interrupt. "Even if they're not as big a thing, they're still a thing."

Maddie flopped onto our futon, exasperated.

"Oh, please. Your grade point is, like, a million. You *know* you have as good a chance as anyone."

"But I'm a history major. Not a nuclear physicist. A good GPA isn't enough. . . ."

"Jesus!" Maddie said. "Your GPA isn't 'good.' It's *sick*."

I should never have told her my GPA.

"Dude," I pleaded. "I *don't* want to spend our senior year on applications, and they *are* super-competitive, and all I've wanted to do since I was sixteen is live in my own real apartment in Chicago."

Maddie wasn't having it.

"Well, maybe you *won't* want to go to fucking Oxford for fucking free, or pop to Dublin to visit U2, all while making your resume fucking frame-able. But don't you owe it to yourself to *try*?"

I shook my head.

"You're not even listening to me!"

"Mads," I ventured, "is not wanting to be away from my boyfriend really so terrible?"

"That's not the point," she said quietly, "and you know it."

"Whatever," I mumbled before going to set up my computer. I decided to be angry that Maddie didn't understand me in order to avoid the other feelings percolating within. I did a good job of this. But it was exhausting. When Maddie woke me up for dinner, her anger had morphed into a resigned sadness. I spent the next two nights at Rob's and none of the three of us discussed scholarships again.

Only after Rob and I divorced, when I was circling the drain, did I allow myself to consider the opportunities I'd thrown away in Philadelphia what felt like a lifetime ago. If I'd taken a chance, won the scholarship, and mustered the gumption to accept it . . . would I have realized that I was, actually, good enough, just as I was?

# Seven

Things started to get tricky with Arianna as college graduation approached.

Most of us were getting more buoyant by the day. The pressure was receding; the freedoms of semi-adulthood awaited. My mom's good friend Lila, who was opening a charter school in Chicago, offered me an amazing job. "I need someone organized who can help me jumpstart this thing," she'd said. "The pay sucks, but you'll be part of a great project from the start. And you can have my garden apartment for free. All I ask is that you give me a year." I gratefully accepted. I was excited to go home.

But Rob grew increasingly gloomy.

"My mom's leaving me daily messages about starting at the restaurant," Rob finally spilled.

"It's just a one-year trial run, right?" I asked. I thought Rob and Arianna had reached a detente over Christmas.

Rob smirked. "You and I both know that Arianna Baros has no intention of letting me go. Every conversation involves me 'taking over.'"

I laughed. "Can't blame her for dreaming."

"She also thinks I'm moving back into my childhood bedroom."

Yikes. Rob's bedroom was more like a shrine: trophies, diplomas, awards, and framed pictures of Rob with Arianna at the beginning and end of every school year covered every surface area. (Rob didn't seem to notice that, the couple of times we'd had sex there, I'd kept my eyes shut the entire time.)

"You knew she was going to want you home," I said. Arianna went to church most mornings and found co-ed colleges suspicious. "You're her baby. She loves you."

"What she loves is controlling my life."

Rob had never said anything like this before. Arianna's every wish had theretofore been Rob's command. But her past summonses had been at my expense. This one was at his.

"The restaurant *is* a successful business," I countered. "You'll learn a ton." Rob had been talking about getting an MBA.

"I'll give it a year. But I won't be left behind at that restaurant. Not like she was."

I couldn't help but wonder whether Rob's father had ever said something like this. Rob looked momentarily defeated; then he straightened up and rearranged his face. If he'd been wearing fuchsia lipstick, I could have been looking at Arianna herself.

THE NEXT YEAR was rocky. I loved working for Lila, whose patience amid interminable bureaucratic bullshit amazed me. Rob was a different story. The amount of behind-the-scenes work the restaurant required surprised him; the long hours wore him down. Arianna scrutinized every sigh and scowl he made as though each one threatened to thwart her plans.

Rob and I did have plans of our own, and they were gelling

nicely. Lila, a recovering lawyer, inspired me to go to law school. "But it's a *drag*!" she'd insisted. Maybe so, but I'd watched her use many of the skills she'd acquired and connections she'd made practicing law to build a beautiful school. So I would go to law school and Rob would go to business school in Chicago. We'd enjoy successful careers, marriage, babies, U2 concerts, good pizza, ketchup-free hot dogs, and Cubs games, and live happily ever after.

"You know," Rob said in bed one Monday night when he swung by on his way home from work, "I think I'm gonna go to law school too."

I propped myself up on my elbow to search his face. "Really?"

"Yeah. Running a business sucks."

"But I thought you were gonna get your MBA and, ya know, Do Capitalism."

Rob shrugged. "Nah."

"*Nah?*"

"Nah."

I blinked. "This is . . . new."

"I think law's a great fit. Numbers, the business grind . . . not for me."

"Are you *sure*?" I asked.

Rob looked back at me, annoyed. "Yes, I'm sure."

"Sorry—it's just a big change."

"A lot of twenty-three-year-olds change their minds."

True. But I still laid awake that night, on edge, and not entirely sure why.

$\backsim$

"JESUS CHRIST, SHE'S in the hospital," Rob said breathlessly into his phone one cold February night. We were supposed to be going to my new work friend Jimmy's birthday party in Lakeview—it was the first Saturday night Rob had taken off in nine months. But that afternoon, at my urging, Rob had finally told his mom he was going into law.

"WHAT?!" Back then, I could go from zero to one million on the panic scale in a snap. I was certain we'd killed Arianna all because Rob had decided to go to law school, all because *I* had decided to go to law school.

"They think it's a heart attack," Rob said, holding back tears. "We shouldn't have done this. You shouldn't have made me tell her."

My lip trembled. Now, Rob had ultimately agreed that quitting the restaurant the night before law school began wasn't the best idea. He would have had to tell Arianna eventually, and she was never going to love the news. I didn't *make* him tell his mother; he'd realized that he had to. But I automatically went to my I-am-responsible-for-all-things place and whispered, "I'm so sorry" before grabbing my purse to meet Rob at the hospital.

When Rob finally rejoined me in the waiting room, he did not sit down, and he looked as though he knew something I did not. I stood.

"She's fine," Rob said. "Not a heart attack."

"Oh, thank God." I clamped a hand over my mouth to keep my tearful relief at bay.

"I think you should go home. I'm going to stay with her."

"Oh—OK. You were in there so long—I was so worried it was. . . ."

Rob nodded with pursed lips and put a grave hand on my shoulder. "Go on home, Babe."

"I can stay with you," I offered.

"No, no. Get some rest."

"Is something going on?"

"She just wants some privacy. She's embarrassed. It was a panic attack. From when I told her about law school."

The truth was written all over his face: *She doesn't want to see you because this is all your fault.* "Oh." My lip trembled.

"I'll wait with her while her blood pressure comes down; then I'll take her home," Rob assured me, looking stoic.

"OK," I managed. "I'm really sorry." For going to law school, inspiring you to do the same, making you tell the truth, almost killing your mom. "Give your mom my best?"

"Absolutely." Rob kissed me on the forehead before sending me back out into the night.

ROB AND I WERE thrilled when we were both admitted to Northwestern Law: We could finally share that grown-up Chicago apartment. (Rob couldn't abide his twin bed any longer and was therefore willing to stand firm on this point.) So I understood why Rob was furious when I considered ditching Chicago for New Haven. Perhaps The Great Scholarship Imbroglio of 1998 gave me the strength to accept my spot at Yale Law School over Rob's strenuous objection; that my dad would have had a coronary had I turned it down was also persuasive. When I didn't acquiesce to Rob's guilt trip—"staying in Chicago was *your* idea!"—even after four days of the silent treatment, he knew I was serious. And that he could use my abandonment as leverage.

Arianna had become mysteriously unavailable whenever I stopped by the restaurant. So I was surprised when she intercepted me during Rob's last night on duty. "Zoe," she said brightly through her fuchsia smile. "Be sure to see me before you leave. I have something for you." My body flooded with relief. Maybe she'd just been busy.

When the crowd finally dispersed, and Rob was helping the staff close up, Arianna beckoned. I followed her to her office in back. She looked tired and wan, and I noticed that in her coffee cup was not coffee, but port.

"For you, my dear." She proffered a box expertly wrapped in fancy gold paper and festooned with swirling white ribbon. I accepted it gratefully and thanked her; she resumed her chest-up-chin-out stance. "Open it!" she urged, gently clicking the office door shut as I did so. It was a white espresso cup and saucer bearing the *Baros* logo. The restaurant bought them by the gross.

"This is so thoughtful. Thank you," I said.

"Well. Please remember us when you're off conquering the world." Her face changed as she retrieved the gift, put it on the desk, and took my hands in hers. "You must also remember," she said quietly, "that this restaurant is a part of my son. It is in his blood and at the center of his heart. So whoever loves Robert *must love this restaurant.*" Her eyes turned to ice. "And understand sacrifice."

Nothing was ever the same between us again.

# Eight

My only flicker of wanderlust came during my first year at Yale. About five minutes into orientation, I realized that I was surrounded by the most accomplished and interesting people I'd ever walk among. One of the men in my section, John Hutton, also happened to be dead sexy. And smart. And kind. He wanted to be a public defender. Maybe because he was quiet, he slipped under many women's radars, which seemed crazy to me. Though I had none of John's understated confidence—his intellect stuck out even at Yale, while I was intimidated on an hourly basis—he was my friend.

As had been the case in college, Rob struggled more with law school's learning curve than I did. This is not to say that I didn't struggle, because I SURE AS HELL DID. I just didn't pull out every single one of my eyebrow hairs during my first semester. Rob looked like he'd been either burned in a fire or waxed by a sadist during 1L winter break.

One Thursday in February, I nearly pissed myself in Criminal Procedure.

"Miss Greene," Professor Milken said. And then, *"Miss Greene!"*

Boone[9], my best and undeniably weirdest friend from Yale, elbowed me so hard that he bruised my triceps. In a class governed by the Socratic method—when the professor calls on students to answer lengthy questions without warning—there is only one thing more terrifying than the sound of your own name: the sound of your own name *twice* because you were too busy daydreaming about sex with John Hutton to hear it the first time.

"Huh? I mean, yes?" I stammered.

My young professor's eyes narrowed—the young ones were always the worst. "Miss Greene," he repeated. "Please recite for the class the legal definition of sodomy."

*Awesome.*

After I sweated my way through that particularly pleasant line of questioning, I ran into John at the campus coffee bar.

"That was intense," he said in his soft-spoken way. I blushed.

"Good lord. I'm so embarrassed." I blushed, more because of John's proximity than the subject matter.

"Nah. Milken was an ass."

We went to doctor our coffees. John poured half-and-half into his cup with abandon—"I've never been able to keep weight on," he used to say—while I carefully rationed skim milk into mine.

"You need whisky in there," he said.

"Seriously," I agreed.

"Actually, Boone and those guys were talking about hitting Rudy's for drinks tonight. You should come."

"In." I smiled. John had the longest, dreamiest eyelashes I'd ever seen outside a Maybelline ad. "Thanks."

---

9 Boone's given name was Adam, but he'd gone by Boone since high school due to his uncanny resemblance to the *Animal House* character.

"Great. See ya."

I ignored the adulterous butterflies in my stomach.

But I did hang out with John for most of the evening and drank *way* too much. We all did. It felt like our entire section was at Rudy's, blowing off steam. At last call, John and I found ourselves alone, laughing over very unnecessary millionth cocktails. He walked me home.

Our friend-vibe morphed into a date-vibe the minute we left Rudy's. Even in my drunken haze, I couldn't believe that John was actually attracted to me. (I'd seen pictures of his last girlfriend—she looked like Keira Fucking Knightley.) But I could feel that he was. When we got to my doorstep, we stood face-to-face.

"Thanks for walking me," I said, feeling unbearably awkward. Was I drunk enough to do this?

"Yeah," he said, starting to look nervous. "No sweat." He bit his lip. Neither of us moved. I wanted to kiss him so badly. Finally, he said, "Rob's a good guy" and sighed.

"Totally," I said, and then, quickly, "Goodnight!"

I ran inside just in time to cry in private, drunken frustration.


WHEN I SAW John in Property the next morning, he immediately asked how bad my hangover was. He was so gracious about everything; he made small talk just to squelch any weirdness between us. I wanted him even more.

While I focused on not throwing up into my laptop, John managed to ace a ten-minute grill session on adverse possession. I could never have hung like that when I was in top form; John did it with a splitting headache.

I guiltily put off talking to Rob until that night.

"Hey, Babe," he said.

"Hey! How was your day?"

"God," he sighed. "It was the most brutal week—Civ Pro[10] was making me nuts—"

"It's the worst. Did you get the—"

"*Until*," he interrupted loudly, "I got home and found your package waiting for me. Your Civ Pro outline and treatise *and* brownies. Zo, I wouldn't be able to do this without you."

Rob was relieved and grateful. I felt like a letch.

"Aww, you're welcome," I said.

"I didn't really get what you were talking about with Civ Pro last semester, but now that I'm in it. . . ."

"Ignore your prof—jut stick to the treatise and outline."

"I will. I feel *so* much better." He sighed again. "I love you, Babe."

"I love you too."

Rob's voice transported me out of my Yale bubble and back to the person I really was. I never knew what I was doing at Yale; everything felt out of reach. No one there needed me. But Rob did. And always would. If only I'd understood what a weak foundation need makes.

♡

---

[10] Civil Procedure AKA my least favorite 1L class. Everything I knew came from the treatise I bought during reading period.

February 8, 2002

Dear Bono, Edge, Larry, and Adam: Who do I think I am?! Please don't tell anyone about yesterday. As I learned in Criminal Law, just <u>thinking</u> about doing something wrong doesn't make me guilty — legally, anyway. Love you gobs, Zoe

PS: And your heart beats so slow/Through the rain and fallen snow/Across the fields of mourning/Lights in the distance/Oh don't sorrow, no don't weep/For tonight, at last/I am coming home/I am coming home.

# Nine

After nearly two years of long-distance dating during law school, people started asking when Rob and I "might get engaged." These questions were always rapidly followed by "just curious!" and a don't-shoot-me gesture. I'd been so focused on getting through school in one piece and moving back to Chicago that I didn't contract Wedding On The Brain Syndrome until the summer after 2L year. My mind began to drift to tulle and hydrangeas when it was supposed to be focused on important things. I surreptitiously bought bridal magazines the way I imagine people bought hardcore porn pre-Internet. That my rational brain couldn't overcome the narrow-minded fantasies our society forces upon women and girls was humiliating. Paying Martha Stewart $6.99 to ogle photos of unattainably perfect weddings made me feel filthy. But I did it (repeatedly) and silently obsessed about becoming a bride.

Finally—FINALLY!—when we were packing up my car to return to Yale for my 3L year, Rob asked me what kind of ring I might "theoretically" like, if I were interested in "that kind of thing." I stopped to look at him, feeling embarrassed and unprepared.

"*Theoretically*," he toyed.

"I . . . I. . . ." was my eloquent reply.

"And I know. As long as we're together, here in Chicago, you don't care about a ring or piece of paper," Rob dutifully recited.

Listening to him parrot the clichés I'd repeated over the years was like a punch to the gut. Why did I always run my mouth off like that? Because I didn't mean it! I *did* want a ring. And the piece of paper. I wanted all of it, OK? ALL OF IT.

Rob gave me a sideways glance, so I felt obligated to nod and mumble, "Paper, pffsh."

"Buhhhhhhht," he continued, "if we *were* going to go the traditional route, I know better than to try to surprise you with —well, anything."

"Umm." I willed myself not to hyperventilate and slammed the trunk of my Jeep shut while trying to compose myself. I stuffed some sweaty hair back into my ponytail.

"So *if* you wanted a ring," he pressed, "what kind would it be?"

*OMG. Holy shit.*

"Uh. Well?" I coughed. "Not gold. I mean, not yellow. So, white gold? If we—umm. Did that. . . ."

Oy.

"See, I didn't even know there was non-yellow gold. I'm glad I asked," Rob chirped with a glint of something in his eye—conspiracy, nerves, both?

"And I do not, I mean, *would* not, want some big diamond. That's so embarrassing," I blurted.

"Couldn't agree more." He grinned. We stared at each other until I looked away.

"So are we ready, Greener?"

Rob was driving to New Haven with me since Northwestern

didn't start until the following week. He would borrow my dad's miles to fly home.

"Yeah," I said, trying to switch gears. "Just let me run inside to pee and say good-bye to my parents."

Going back to Yale for 3L year with my friends was exciting, but looming separations from Rob were always difficult. When I came out of the bathroom, Rob was leaning against the wall in the foyer. (My parents had ditched the 'burbs and moved to the city by then.)

"Do you need to go too?" I asked.

"Actually," he said, looking odd. He rummaged in his pocket. "Would something like this work—theoretically?"

I was for *sure* going to die. There in his outstretched hand lay a plain platinum band topped with a 1.5-carat round solitaire diamond. To my simultaneous delight and self-conscious horror, I watched, open-mouthed, as Rob dropped to one knee.

"Zoe Greene, I've loved you since we were kids. Will you marry me?"

"YES!" I screamed, waving around like a crazed banshee as tears dripped down my face. We kissed and hugged.

My parents trotted down the stairs wearing a complexity of emotions on their faces: joy, disbelief that their daughter was old enough to get married, excitement, a sense of loss of me. We all hugged. Dad patted Rob on the back. Mom teared up, smiled, and hugged me. Rob and I agreed to start discussing wedding details (WEDDING DETAILS!) on our drive. As we climbed into the Jeep, I felt so proud. Rob had done this all on his own: He got me a gorgeous ring, despite being told he didn't need to, because he wanted me to have something beautiful. He loved me and wanted to be with me forever. I was so lucky.

♡

August 23, 2003

Dear Larry: Are you cool because you're principled?
Or principled because you're cool? It doesn't matter.
You and Anne have made a life together without
legal formalities because marriage is paternalistic
and arcane. Changing one's name is a vile vestige! I
agree with you. About everything.

But I am not as cool or principled as you. I'm a
hypocrite. An ardent feminist who wants to share a
last name with my husband and kids. What's worse
is that I've been reading wedding porn — MARTHA
STEWART — and taking notes. I just got ENGAGED
and I'm so excited that I keep peeing. In fact, I'm
writing to you from the bathroom of a Super 8
Motel on the way to the school while my FIANCÉ
(!!!) sleeps. All I want is not just him. I do want
diamonds on a ring of gold. I told him I didn't, but I
fucking DO. I hate the thought of disappointing you
but feel that good relationships are based on
honesty.

Also: RBG took her husband's last name and she's a
revolutionary. Oh, and also-also: I'll never forget
that you four were my first loves. Even when I'm
MARRIED! XO, Z

# Ten

During the entirety of 3L year, Arianna seemed fine with the engagement. After her emergency hysterectomy, that is; Rob had shared our big news with her from the motel, and by the time we arrived in New Haven the next day, she was being rushed to the hospital with a strangulated ovary. But after her (slow, painful) recovery, she seemed to accept the situation.

Sure, there was the occasional awkward moment, like when Arianna suggested we move into the McMansion, because why pay rent? But nothing major. My parents graciously offered to pay for the wedding, which would occur just after The Bar Exam, and Arianna offered to close the restaurant for the ceremony and reception—unprecedented for a Saturday night—and send us on a Grecian honeymoon (as long as we spent a week with her family there, which we were happy to do). Lila's husband, Gary, owned a beautiful event space that he insisted we use for the rehearsal dinner. I couldn't believe how lucky I was; I figuratively pinched myself every other minute.

By the time we went underground to study for the bar, I was euphoric. My adult life was unfolding precisely on schedule: Rob and I had graduated from law school and moved into a great Lincoln Park apartment; he had a tux; I had a dress; the deejay knew to load up on U2; our best friends were all coming to the wedding. What could *possibly* go wrong?

ABSOLUTELY EVERYTHING.

One afternoon, precisely four weeks before the bar, I was communing with my flashcards in our sweltering apartment, waiting for the A/C repair guy to call me back. Rob was at the (nice, cool) library. The landline rang. I raced to grab it, thrilled by the speed with which Ace Heating & Cooling responded to my SOS.

"Hello?"

"WHAT HAVE YOU DONE TO MY SON!" a barely familiar voice screamed.

The flashcards slipped through my fingers and onto the floor.

"Wh—what?"

"HE ISN'T HIMSELF. YOU'VE TAKEN HIM FROM ME."

It was Arianna, whom I had never seen lose control. Over anything. That she was screaming and slurring her words before the lunch rush had even cleared out was a lot to process. I tried to steady my voice.

"I can tell you're upset—"

"HOW PERCEP-TIVVVVVE."

Had she lost her mind? Had someone died? There had to be an explanation.

"Please, I'd be happy to talk if you'll just calm down—"

"CALM DOWN? *CALLLLMMMMM DOWN*?! YOU'VE STOLEN MY SON! AND I WON'T BE PAT—, PAT—, PA-TRONIIIIIZED BY A BRATTY LI'L BITCH."

With that, the line went dead.

I didn't get any more bar studying done that day. Rob was my next call. I was hysterical; he went cold.

"What was she talking about?" I cried into the phone.

"I really don't know," Rob said in a sterile tone that hurt almost as much as Arianna's vitriol. "There must be a reason—I'll go to her."

"OK," I blubbered. He was long gone before I wondered, *who was going to come to me?*

IT FELT LIKE forever before Rob called me back. "She's fine," he said drily.

"She *is?*"

"Yeah. She was lying down—said she had a migraine and would talk to me tomorrow."

I had no words.

"I think we should get back to studying," Rob said.

"N-no!" I stuttered. "Because *I* am decidedly *not* fine!"

Rob seemed surprised.

"Look," he finally said. "She's totally out of it. She took a pain pill for the headache and doesn't even remember calling. She's just whacked out. That's all."

"Oh," I said, sniveling. I briefly considered hanging up but couldn't. I knew deep in my belly that Arianna was full of shit. She'd never done this before, despite the multiple surgeries that necessitated prescription pain pills. "Rob. She *screamed* at me."

"Screamed? My mother? Come on."

"Excuse me?" I snapped.

"Zo! You're stressed, she has a migraine. Can we please just chalk this up to bad pain meds and move on? I don't wanna be the first person at my firm to fail the bar."

"Uh, I'm supposed to be studying too, and don't want to fail the bar either. But your mother got wasted and berated me!"

Rob broke the excruciating silence that followed. "Don't talk about her like that," he said quietly.

"I'm sorry," I immediately apologized. After losing his dad, Rob couldn't bear to lose his mom too. Maybe this *was* just a bad pain pill—that inappropriately amplified understandable, even sympathetic, emotions. Maybe, if I could move past this gracefully, I'd finally earn Arianna's favor. Maybe this was a *Father of the Bride* style freak-out that we'd laugh about later.

My bullshit detector was still screaming. I imagined that most single moms managed not to abuse their only children's spouses, even under challenging circumstances. But the beleaguered tone in Rob's voice wore me down. I resolved to order Art of Pizza and open a bottle of wine that night; to light some candles and have everything ready when Rob got home. I was determined to make it all better.

"Baby, let's not fight," I offered. "I'm really sorry I said that."

"Thanks," he replied. "But, Zo? I really do need to study."

"Of course. Go. I love you."

"Same," he said and hung up.

I rested my head in my hands for a minute, replaying Arianna's rant in my mind. The phone rang.

"Hello?" I answered cautiously.

It was the HVAC guy telling me he'd have to get to us tomorrow.

# Eleven

Alas, things continued to devolve. The next week, I received a similar phone call from Arianna complaining about how I'd brainwashed and stolen Rob not only from her, but from his "birthright," which I soon realized meant "the restaurant." This time, Rob was home. I made him listen. Even after hearing Arianna for himself, he seemed eerily dissociated; I had to insist that he go see his mom the next morning, when she would (hopefully) be sober. Rob returned ashen.

"What happened?" I asked, picking mercilessly at my cuticles.

"It's these migraines," he said helplessly. "The pain pills are the only things that help. She denied making the call."

"But you told her you'd heard it, right?"

Rob paused. "Of course."

"AND?!"

"Zoe, please. You freaking out doesn't make this any easier for me."

My face must have exposed my inner monologue: *easier for YOU?*

"Look. I know this sucks, but we've turned my mom's life upside down. She said the migraines are from running a business by herself for decades with no end in sight." He lowered his voice. "Please remember . . . she's all I have left."

My head was a jumble. *Had* we really turned Arianna's life upside down? Rob was getting married and practicing law—not moving continents or joining a cult. And as sensitive as I was to George's absence, Arianna was *not* all Rob had left. He'd forgotten his grandmother, his papous and yia-yias, my entire family (who treated Rob like one of their own), and *me*. What were we, chopped liver? I considered saying this, but Rob looked defeated. So I hugged him instead.

His temple vein remained visible. "What is it?" I asked.

"I'm just worried about her. She's never been like this."

*This* meaning *evil*?

"She's obviously having a hard time seeing you move on." I took a deep breath before adding, "And she's blaming me for it."

Rob shook his head. "She wouldn't do that. Not consciously."

I couldn't hold it together any longer. "But, Rob—" I whimpered.

"I know," he said softly, pulling me close. I cried into his shoulder for some time. "We just have to get through the bar and then the wedding. She'll come around."

I nodded. "Getting through" the wedding my parents were so busy planning (Arianna had disengaged after proposing a menu), and to which so many friends and family were going to great lengths to attend, didn't seem fair. But what else could we do?

My parents did try inviting Arianna to dinner, and I wrote her a note promising that I would always try to do right by Rob and by her. Both olive branches were rebuffed. Arianna studiously avoided us. She wouldn't even return Rob's calls. His temple vein got so bad that I began to wonder whether it was a tumor *masquerading* as a temple vein, and I began to poop, like, constantly. It's a miracle either of us managed to study at all.

And then The Bar Exam was upon us. Perfect! I packed lunches and snacks the night before and assured Rob we'd feel leagues better after getting it over with. My dad drove us to the test both days so, naturally, we arrived forty-five minutes early. Twice. The girl seated next to me started hyperventilating immediately before the test began, but immediately after we were warned not to speak, so I couldn't even ask if she was OK. The whole thing—including the sleepless night between test days—was ace.

Rob and I had big plans to celebrate the end of the bar with friends, deep dish, and many, many beers. But, when the time came, we weren't in the mood. Instead, he and I ate slices and drank half a Heineken each at some dive near the test site.

"Let's promise never to talk about the bar again. OK?" Rob said through clenched teeth.

"Sure," I replied.

I tried to make conversation (*I can't wait to sleep in tomorrow! No more library!*), but he wouldn't make eye contact. He just stared straight ahead and kept his jaw locked. I resisted the urge to pry it open. We cabbed home, put the Cubs on, and attempted to fall asleep—something that had become increasingly difficult for me to do.

♡

July 28, 2004

Dear Larry: You were right. (You're probably always right, aren't you?) You're not only the conscience of the band, but also of life. I, however, am nothing but a wedding-porn-addicted idiot who ignored your voice in my ear. I <u>don't</u> need the diamonds on a ring of gold! Not the dress, the flowers, the deejay — any of it. And all I want is <u>not</u> just Rob. I want to sleep without Nyquil. Be free of diarrhea. Is that too much to ask?

In other news: I noticed that none of you responded to the wedding invitations I sent — to the four of you individually, and to the band collectively, via your record label and via your manager. WTF? An intern should have sent us <u>something</u> — a photo, whatever — that's just good manners. I've been lining your pockets, not to mention showering you with unconditional love, for 16 years.[11] The least you could do is send a loyal fan a token of encouragement on her execution — er, wedding — day.

Anyway. You were right, I was wrong. Mating for

---

[11] U2 released *Joshua Tree* when I was nine years old, and I was hooked for life. I invited U2 to my wedding not because I expected them to come, but because it felt like the right thing to do, and because I wanted to receive a stock photo in an envelope covered in Irish stamps.

life: good. Weddings: bad. I'm not sure my colon will survive. XX, Zoe

PS: Sorry for being rude about your failure to RSVP. I _do_ think you should have responded. But I shouldn't have been rude about it.

# Twelve

The morning after I (barely) survived The Bar Exam, I crept out of the apartment for coffee. I was thrilled to get a call from Zach right after paying for my giant latte; we hadn't talked in a few weeks. I walked aimlessly with my coffee so as not to disturb Rob, who was still sleeping, and to enjoy the fresh air.

"Hey," he began. "Just confirming that you're still alive."

"And which potential cause of death might you be inquiring about—my fiancé's crazy mother, or The Bar Exam?"

"Let's start with the bar. How was it?"

Zach was spending that summer waiting tables to support an Italian architecture tour.

"Actually, way worse than I expected."

"Yikes," he said.

"Yeah. Like, I may honestly have failed the multiple-choice part—that's the first day. There were subjects I didn't even recognize. The essays were pretty OK, though. Except for one, which bore no relationship to anything I learned in law school or during bar prep—or, I'd wager, to practicing law. The test is basically a giant scam."

"That good, huh?"

"Rob won't even talk about it. He's convinced he'll be the first at his firm to fail."

"Oh, for fuck's sake. What do you need to pass?"

"That depends. Illinois usually passes about sixty-eight percent."

Zach was stunned. "Wait. You just need to do better than thirty-two percent of thousands of test-takers? You need a D-plus—on a curve?"

I considered this. "Huh. I guess so."

"You'll pass," he said firmly. "So will Rob."

I waited. "Wow, I for sure thought you'd bring up high school," I eventually said.

Zach cleared his throat before assuming his high-pitched-young-Zoe voice. "*Ohmigod you guys! I* totally *failed that test!*— Fast-forward two days—*Ohmigod, I can't believe it, I got an AAAAAAAA!*"

"Feel better?"

"Yes. Yes I do," he said.

"Well, I fucking hope you're right. Because I did everything one could possibly do to prepare for that test."

"Of course you did," Zach said, kindly. We enjoyed a moment of comfortable silence before he continued. "Now, dare I ask about your other *petite probleme*? How is that crazy witch?"

"Oh." To my surprise, I teared right up. "Actually? Really bad. The wedding's gonna be a disaster."

He exhaled audibly. Zach had picked up smoking in Italy. It made him smell like a neglected ashtray and me worry he'd get lung cancer.

"No it won't," he said. "You're not the first bride to butt heads with her mother-in-law."

I sniffed.

"So many people will be there to support you. What's-her-name will be way outnumbered."

Zach's astute distillations always comforted me.

"Is she still screaming at you?"

"Nope. Arianna is giving us the complete, grade-school style silent treatment—as is her mother, who has apparently taken Arianna's side in a dispute that still eludes me. It's killing Rob. No one even wished him luck before the bar."

"Mom mentioned that," he said. "Un-fucking-real." I could picture him shaking his head while flicking cigarette ash in his building's courtyard. "So I assume the liquid-hot-magma diet is still in effect."

"Oh yeah." I'd abused Zach with the gruesome details of my bowel movements all summer. "I've lost ten pounds. My dress fitting tomorrow should be interesting."

"Ten pounds? Shit."

"Exactly," I couldn't help but respond.

"Touché."

"Jesus. Scheduling a wedding ten days after the bar was lunacy even *without* the evil mother-in-law."

"I'm really sorry, Zo."

The sip of coffee I'd taken turned bitter in my mouth; I was already feeling guilty about the question I was going to ask. "Zach? You've known Rob a long time—and, obviously, me."

"Yep."

"And you're one of the few who knows Rob's backstory."

"Right."

"So. What do you think? I mean. What I'm trying to ask is—" I couldn't bring myself to speak the words. They practically *tasted* disloyal.

"Are you making a huge mistake marrying this guy?" Zach finished.

"No! I mean—well, kind of. Yeah."

He took a drag of his cigarette before responding. "That's something only you can really know." This was not what I was hoping to hear. There were plusses and minuses to Zach's straight shooting. "But I will say that a few of my closest friends have crazy parents."

This was a great point. "Like Maddie's! They're bananas," I said.

"Exactly."

"But Maddie would be able to take her parents' psychosis into consideration if she decided to get married. Advance notice of psychosis is helpful," I said, mostly to myself.

"Riddle me this," Zach continued. "Does Rob agree that Arianna's behavior is unacceptable?"

"Oh, definitely," I replied. "He's crushed."

"That's what matters. That you're on the same page."

"Totally."

I winced. Because, actually, I never *really* knew what Rob was thinking. He was dealing with Arianna's lunacy so internally that it was hard to know whether we were in sync. But we would be, eventually. When we were married. Because we'd have to be. Right?

"Wanna grab a drink later?" Zach asked.

"Immediately."

"It's a little early, but ASAP. OK?"

"Sounds great. Thanks."

"But Zo? You can't talk about your shit—like, your literal excrement—anymore. I can't deal."

"Fair enough, Zachy. Fair enough."

# Thirteen

The Big Weekend finally arrived. It was so good to see my friends and family that I was finally able to be excited about the wedding again. While Rob braved the restaurant (and Arianna's icy silence) to welcome the family who'd flown in from Greece, I met my favorite cast of characters for lunch.

Boone and his girlfriend, Brooke, rolled their bags right into my go-to restaurant, Hot Chocolate. Boone hailed from Long Island, had just taken the New York bar, and was poised to start a law firm job in Manhattan. His mannerisms were those of a prototypical New York Jew. Brooke and Boone met during his summer clerkship—on Brooke's *fortieth* first jDate. She worked in her family's high-end furniture business, which, incidentally, neither of her parents referred to as her "birthright," and was pursuing her MBA.

"Bump Face," Boone said, smiling, before hugging me. "Mazel tov." Brooke elbowed Boone; ever since I'd wiped out at the diner by campus my 1L year, Boone had called me some version of "Bumpy." (I hadn't stopped tripping over nothing *altogether*.)

"We're so excited!" Brooke said. "And starved."

"You've come to the right place. The food's amazing," I said, hugging her. "Let me introduce you guys." I brought them to our table. "Boone and Brooke—"

"It's Adam, actually—"

"I will give you that this weekend," I conceded.

"Bumpster gets a little confused," he whispered to the others.

I rolled my eyes. "Adam and Brooke, this is Jimmy, who worked with me at the charter school. He's practically running it now."

"OHMIGOD *HI*," Jimmy yelled as he unfolded his six-foot-three frame from his chair. He never could modulate the volume of his voice, even when he *wasn't* excited. "I'VE HEARD LEAGUES ABOUT YOU!"

"Likewise," Boone said, extending his hand.

"OH, DUDE. DON'T EVEN. BRING IT IN." Jimmy's long, chocolate-colored arms easily enveloped both Brooke and Boone in the same hug. He stepped back to admire Brooke's blow-out, maxi-dress, and designer bag. She was always impeccably styled. Jimmy made a show of pushing Boone aside and took Brooke's hands in his. "THIS GORGEOUS WOMAN GOES WITH *YOU*?" he asked after letting out the round, deep laugh I loved best.

"Can you believe it?" Boone beamed.

"HONESTLY, NO," Jimmy deadpanned. Everyone laughed. "IF I WEREN'T VERY GAY, I WOULD INTERVENE."

"Boonie and Brooke," I interrupted, "this is Alex."

"Alex!" Brooke yelped. They hugged.

"We've certainly heard lots about *you*," Boone added.

Alex—short for Alexandra—hugged Brooke and then Boone. She and I had clicked immediately when we met as summer associates the previous year. She was in great spirits, despite making clear on many occasions that she was suspicious of weddings in particular and marriage in general. Even though we'd only known each other a few months before I asked Alex to be a bridesmaid, it was a no-brainer; when our third year of law school took her back to the University of Chicago and me back to Yale, we talked on the phone every day. She and Jimmy had become close friends since meeting through me the previous summer and, in fact, Jimmy had become Alex's perma-date to Democratic political functions. She and I were karmic magnets; there was no pulling us apart.

"Last but certainly not least are Maddie and her boyfriend, Daniel," I said, winking at Mads.

Maddie, never a hugger, shook hands with Boone and Brooke. Daniel, a soft-spoken photographer who'd lived with Maddie for three years by then, stifled a yawn; they'd left Philly at an ungodly hour.

Just then, a waiter came over with a fancy pink bottle. "I understand we have a bride here today," he said as he prepared to uncork the bottle. Everyone—even Alex—whooped, cheered, and rapped the table. A server stood by with a tray of champagne flutes. Suddenly, I *did* feel like a bride.

Jimmy clapped his hands; that he was so large but had the mannerisms of an imp always cracked me up. "IT'S THAT CUTIE RIGHT THERE!" he hollered, pointing to me.

"What's this?!" I asked, now clapping like Jimmy.

"A beautiful bottle of brut rosé, compliments of one Aunt Steffi," the waiter said.

"Aww, Lady!" Alex said as she squeezed me. I said, "Oh, my gosh!"

Aunt Steffi was my mom's awesome younger sister who, despite working her ass off, never missed an opportunity to celebrate her people.

"She's amazing," Alex smiled. Like nearly everyone, she loved Aunt Steffi.

"Schmancy," Boone said as the waiter passed out glasses, and then, "*AHEM.*" He unnecessarily clinked his flute with his fork. "I'd like to propose a toast to our bumpy friend."

"Adam," Brooke said.

"What?"

Brooke answered him with a glare.

"Oh, come on. She's not *that* bumpy. Anyway, I think I just wanted to say that we're all really excited to be here. We're excited for you and Rob and to be aunties and uncles as soon as is convenient . . . for us. We promise to love and spoil your children but return them to you when they poo. Cheers!"

What a weirdo. But everyone cheers-ed and laughed. We had a wonderful lunch, and by the time I bounced off to the nail salon with the girls, I'd practically forgotten about Arianna and was wearing a smile fit for *Martha Stewart Weddings*.

"OH, LADY," ALEX said in the bathroom after the wedding rehearsal, which we'd had at the event space. I had just put on my dinner dress which, on account of the liquid hot magma, was huge. I held it up with both hands. "When's the last time you tried that on?"

"At the store when I bought it over spring break," I lamented.

"Let's see what we can do," she said evenly as she began to move seams around.

Maddie frowned in my direction on her way out of a stall.

I'd bought a flowery strapless dress that cinched at the waist, but now it wouldn't stay up, and the cinch didn't cinch.

"Oh, Lady," Alex said again.

"What should I do?" I asked. "I don't have time to run home!"

"Here," Maddie said as she climbed out of her dress. "It's not bride-y, but it's five years old and tight as shit. Try it."

I shimmied my dress down to my ankles and handed it to Mads. The gods smiled upon us: Our dresses fit each other.

"Bless you!" I hugged her and then squished my feet into her shoes while she stuffed toilet paper into mine.

"Sorry it's black," Maddie said of her dress.

"Sadly, I think black fits the occasion."

Alex and Maddie exchanged a glance. After Rob and I split, I asked Maddie and Alex if they'd sensed, during the many hours we spent together that weekend, that I was about to make a gargantuan mistake. But they were fixated solely on what Arianna might pull and how I would handle it—none of us had put the puzzle pieces together yet. Rob's collapse took us all by surprise. There are some things from which even our best friends can't protect us.

Soon, Maddie said, "I need a drink. Let's go!"

I took a deep breath and followed them out of the bathroom.


TWO PEPTO BISMOLS later, people started rolling in. Lila and Gary had used all their favorite vendors to make the place sing: sparkly lights, votive candles, bud vases, and ambient music all worked their magic. I got to enjoy this for approximately three minutes before Arianna's mother, wearing a plain gray dress (nun's habit?) and somber expression, led the confused-looking Greek relatives to a table in the back. When I saw Rob move toward them, I followed; I hadn't yet met the Greek Baroses. At their table, Rob introduced me in Greek. I smiled and thanked them profusely for coming. They double-kissed my cheeks, nodded, and smiled back. A pretty girl about my age answered in perfect English. "I'm Penelope," she said, and squeezed my hand as if to wish me Godspeed. The pity in her eyes made me uneasy. Rob bent down to kiss his joyless yia-yia on the cheek. She stopped me from doing the same with a surprisingly strong grip on my shoulder: "You," she whispered in labored English when my face was four inches from hers, "look like widow in mourning." She released me before reengaging her family in Greek.

Cocktail hour passed in a blur. Personally welcoming each guest and encouraging them to mingle is never easy, but it's particularly challenging when simultaneously watching your back. Arianna's failure to appear was making me twitch: She had informed our wedding coordinator that none of the Baroses would attend the rehearsal, seeing as how they all knew how to walk and sit, thank you very much, but had RSVP'd "yes" to the dinner. I decided to regroup in the bathroom. As I dabbed the sweat off my face, smoothed Maddie's dress, and tried to breathe, it occurred to me that Arianna had not a single friend. Her restaurant's patrons adored her, the staff respected/feared her, and the vendors were unflinchingly loyal; they could always count on her to pay in full and on time, ask after their families, and tuck crisp one-hundred-dollar bills into their holiday bonus baskets filled with baclava and ouzo. But, despite spending nearly sixty years in Chicago and accounting for half the wedding invitations sent, her chosen wedding guests were all business associates, blood relatives, or her parents' friends. My skin prickled at the thought.

When I stepped back into the twinkle lights, I froze. Although there were a couple dozen people between Arianna and me, I could feel her presence—like a black hole incarnate. She too wore a gray nun's habit accessorized with puffy skin and a matching gray pallor. I watched her move wordlessly, like a specter, to her mother's side. If I hadn't been wearing shoes one size too small, I would have run straight out the door. But I could only shuffle gingerly toward a waiter.

"Sir? May I please have a vodka?" I asked.

"It's beer and wine this evening, miss."

"Oh. Umm, that's OK. I'll buy it." I snatched a twenty from my purse. I knew Gary kept booze in the back.

Between the black dress and all the blood having drained from my face, I probably looked like Morticia Addams. The waiter shook his head and declined the twenty.

"This one's on me," he said kindly.

"Bless you," I whispered as Rob walked up.

"Hi!" I said shrilly. He kissed me on the cheek.

"Everything OK?" he asked.

"Sure!"

"My mother made quite the entrance." Rob nodded toward her, clenched his jaw, and popped his vein.

"What do we do?" I asked.

Rob could barely shrug before the elders were upon us. Julia, one of Rob's restaurant yia-yias whose dementia had advanced substantially during law school, grabbed Rob's cheeks, kissed him sloppily, and then asked his name. My great-aunt Elizabeth slipped an ancient sleeping pill into my hand with a knowing glance; she too had a nervous constitution.

"You look very thin, dear," my bubbe said.

"It's her wedding—she'll eat when it's done," Zayde admonished.

The meal passed in a whirlwind of schmooze and booze. I regretfully declined my knight in shining armor's offer of a second vodka and made sure to get down one entire dinner roll. The next thing I knew, my dad was crouching by my ear.

"Sweetheart. We're doing toasts, right?" I looked over at Boone, who was studying a piece of paper while mouthing words and making hand gestures.

"I guess," I said.

"OK." Dad smiled determinedly. "Is Arianna speaking?"

"I seriously doubt it."

He waved his hand and made a "pish" face, as if Arianna's determination to ignore our wedding was no big deal. I was about to say something untoward, but Rob was approaching.

"Rob!" My dad shifted gears. "Why don't I start off toasts? Might be nice for Rachel and me to thank your family for coming all this way."

I waited to watch Rob's temple vein dance in the candlelight, but to my surprise, it didn't.

"You know what? I'd like to start the toasts," Rob said. He held me near to him and kissed my cheek.

"Even better," Dad smiled.

I took a moment to study Rob. He'd enjoyed ouzo and cigars with his Greek family and plenty of wine at dinner. He looked happy. My stomach settled. We held hands as we walked to the front of the room and Boone, again, clinked his glass with a fork.

"Hi," Rob began. "Hi, everyone!"

Conversations decelerated, and chairs turned toward us. I couldn't help but notice that Arianna glared at me.

"Zoe and I just wanted to welcome and thank everyone—for traveling, giving us your weekend and," Rob cleared his throat, "your support. It means the world to us."

(Almost) everyone clapped.

"Thanks to Lila and Gary for hosting this great dinner." I looked over to mouth my thanks and blow them a kiss, which they returned. "And really, most of all, I want to thank Zoe." Rob turned to me. "We started our journey years ago, but tomorrow we start our lives as husband and wife."

His voice broke and everyone *awww*-ed. When I saw his eyes pool with emotion and his cheeks dimple in smiling response to the *awwws*, my throat caught, and I forgot for one blissful moment about Arianna. "No matter what comes up, you always have my back. And that gets me through everything," Rob finished. He even gave me a big, public kiss, which he was not prone to do. His lips were soft, and his arms were strong. I only took my eyes off Rob because everyone's attention had turned to Arianna. She was making a dramatic exit stage left, her mother not far behind.

♡

August 6, 2004

Dear Adam: Tomorrow I'm getting married, and I'm a mess. I'm afraid I'll spend the entire day on the crapper. Which is why I'm writing to you — not because I associate you with crap in any way, but because you are the King of Cool. You personify confidence and not giving a fuck. I give way too many fucks. And while my current situation is arguably fuck-worthy — given my impending, permanent legal relationship-by-marriage to a psychopath — I've gotta survive my wedding. So I need to borrow some I-don't-give-a-fuck-ness ASAP. I thought, naturally, of you.

I'm not a rock star or a millionaire. I've never had sex with a supermodel. (Great move not marrying Naomi Campbell, btw. Not to say, "I told you so," but several volumes ago, in this very journal . . . well. I told you so.) And I don't have an enormous dong. (Of course I looked at the European Achtung Baby album cover — which did not place a very large "X" over your naked crotch — when I was a teen. Good lord, man! How do you stand upright?) But I'm hoping you can lend me some of your swagger. I think I'm going to need it. Also, I love you so much and would even if your penis were of regular size. Zoe

# Fourteen

The wedding exceeded all of my wildest dreams. Just not in the ways I'd hoped.

I'd spent the night at my parents' house, and the day began with a call from the florist. I could tell that all was not well but actually dropped my bagel when I heard Mom say, "Oh, my God. She double-booked it."

"WHAT?" I shrieked.

Mom plugged her free ear and took the phone into the next room.

"Mom. What," I said when she was finally done. By now, my dad had stopped unloading the dishwasher and looked at her expectantly. But she could only blink.

"Rachel, honey. What is it?" Dad asked.

"I'll find out eventually," I said.

"Well," Mom began, "Julie called because another florist was delivering at the same time. For another event. At the restaurant."

"WHAT?" Dad and I asked, although I louder than he. I opened the Pepto Bismol.

"And unfortunately," Mom continued, "the other flowers . . . are for a funeral." Mom leaned on the counter and hung her head. "Someone at the restaurant confirmed that the funeral starts at two o'clock and the wedding at five."

"Ah! So the funeral will be done!" Dad said.

"Dad. Zero Greek funerals conclude in three hours."

"And weddings take time to set up," Mom explained.

"Oh."

After downing my own, I handed two Peptos each to my parents.

"SHE HAS ANOTHER migraine," Rob growled into the phone from the golf course, "and won't take my call."

I sat silently. My mind screamed with competing strategies. Courthouse? Cancellation? Elopement? *My wedding is a literal funeral.*

"Zo?"

"Yes," I said in a tiny whisper. "I'm here." (Was I?)

"What do we do?" He covered the receiver. "Play through— I'll catch up."

I gathered myself. "Go—golf. Maddie and Alex are on their way . . . we'll figure it out."

"Listen," Rob tried, "I love you. If my out-of-town family weren't there, I'd go straight to my mother's. And probably kill her."

The doorbell rang. "Fuck. Rob—they're here. I gotta go." *And find my passport,* I thought.

"Wait! I totally forgot—Penelope wanted to hang out with you guys today. Can I give her your number?"

"Sure." I remembered Penelope squeezing my hand the night before.

"What a shit show," Rob murmured.

"Total."

We hung up.

"Hey, Lade—" Alex and Maddie stopped in their tracks in my parents' kitchen.

"Who died?" Maddie asked.

If only she'd known. I explained everything.

"Fucking asshole," Maddie said. "Ooh—sorry, Mr. G."

Dad waved her off. He didn't seem to be listening anyway—he was probably calculating the money he was about to spend on my premature funeral. My cell phone rang; I reflexively reached for the Pepto, just to hold its reassuring pink bottle in my palm, when I saw Arianna's home number on the screen. I answered but no words came out.

"Allo? Zoe?"

I sighed with relief. "Penelope! Hi. I'm so sorry I didn't invite you earlier. But. Umm . . . something's come up."

"I know about funeral," she whispered. "I have idea."

While Alex drove to the burbs like a bat out of hell to retrieve Penelope a block from Arianna's home, my mom called Celine—we were all due at her salon imminently—to explain our predicament.

"Jesus fucking Christ!" I heard Celine exclaim through the phone.

"Right," said Mom.

Maddie and I spun in circles, gathering things as though there would be a wedding. My parents whispered and brainstormed. Alex reappeared in the driveway after making unfathomable time —without a speeding ticket, and without getting lost, which made me dare to believe in miracles. She honked. We all ran outside.

"Get in," Alex said to Maddie and me. "Mr. and Mrs. G., we'll be in touch."

"Do we bring our—"

"Yes, bring all," said Penelope impatiently. We shoved our things into Alex's trunk; my hands shook when I realized we were burning rubber to the restaurant.

"Closed today," the valet said.

"Not to us. This is the bride," Alex said. He looked surprised. Who could blame him? I wore pajama pants, a U2 Zoo TV concert tee, and pure terror. Alex threw him the keys; we rushed toward the door to survey the damage. I stopped at the threshold.

"Come," Penelope said kindly but firmly.

"I'm afraid," I whispered.

"Arianna is not here! She is very drunk in her bed. My family hopes she comes to the wedding, but I doubt."

I was overcome with relief. Was it ideal that my impending mother-in-law might be too fucked up to attend my wedding? No. But her absence seemed less complicated than her presence. As I stepped inside, I thought about how beautiful I'd once found *Baros*, about how it was once just a lovely restaurant—not a Birthright, not a symbol of divided loyalty or broken dreams. The thought of getting married here had thrilled me mere months ago. Now it was literally death.

Maddie and Alex looked around, wide-eyed, while Amanda, our wedding coordinator, beckoned the florists. Dmitri and Christos, a couple of old-guard restaurant staff who knew me, shyly returned my wave before looking at their feet. Others were nearly done transforming half the restaurant into a funeral parlor. "OH, MY GOD, THERE'S GONNA BE A CASKET," I accidentally said out loud.

"And it'll be *open*," Alex said. Her parents were religious Albanians. Penelope nodded her agreement. Eventually, all eyes rested on me.

"I guess we'll set up here," I heard myself say.

Penelope negotiated with Dmitri and Christos to condense the funeral parlor. We sweet-talked the rest of the staff into helping us divide the remaining two-thirds of the restaurant into ceremony and reception areas. The florists went to work as did Amanda's people—hanging lights, arranging place cards, directing the wedding cake to the kitchen. The girls and I lugged tables and chairs while Penelope created an aisle between the funeral parlor and us. When I saw her helping Amanda to hang a large, sheer cloth (that someone must have frantically procured moments prior) between the funeral and wedding areas, I wanted to kiss them both.

"Hi," I panted into my cell.

"I'm at the house," Rob panted back. I'd so hoped we'd be out of breath much later in the day, and for different reasons. "She's locked herself in her bedroom."

I rubbed the Pepto bottle in my pocket.

"Christ!" I yelled before waving my apologies to the staff.

"Brad ordered a car to bring the rest of the family to the wedding just in case. . . ." Brad was Rob's smartest friend.

"Well, things are coming together at the restaurant," I said as cheerily as I could.

"You're there?!"

"Yeah. Just to check on Amanda and—well, it's working out. It'll be . . . fine."

"The woman double-booked our wedding with a funeral. 'Fine' is a miracle."

For lack of anything else to say, I repeated the mantra I'd always offered Rob when he was stressed: "Nothing to do but laugh. Right?"

"Right," he said. But he didn't laugh. "Love you."

"Love you too. You're the only one I really need to show up."

"My RSVP is a definite yes." I smiled into the phone before reluctantly hanging up and staring into space.

"You are good person." Penelope startled me.

"Uh, *you're* the good person. You're spending your vacation saving our wedding!"

She shrugged. "I enjoy. People are complicated, but it makes life interesting, yes?"

"Man, you're wise. Thank you." I hugged her.

"Arianna is—" Penelope stopped herself. "She is wrong to be this way." She plucked a dust bunny from my hair and went back to her work.

Christos and Dmitri tossed sandwiches to us as we dashed from The Birthright minutes before the funeral was set to begin. We piled into Alex's car.

"Umm," Maddie said, consulting her watch.

"My gym is close by," Alex said and peeled away from the curb.

Shortly thereafter, we'd commandeered the gym locker room to prepare for the wedding. Ladies in various stages of undress scurried out of our way. Alex, a true Renaissance woman, declared that she'd do makeup and instructed us to shower. We reconvened in our skivvies; after twisting her thick, wet, black hair up in a clip, she did the same to mine, whipped out her makeup bag, told me to sit, and sent the others to blow-dry. My jaw dropped when I looked in the mirror: In fifteen minutes, she'd transformed my face from Pepto addict/sunless vampire to camera-ready bride. Alex's childhood friend, Geneva, a professional hairstylist, burst through the locker room doors with tools blazing. "Outlets!" she commanded. "Weddings. Always an adventure!" Her laugh filled the room.

Thanks to the magic of female friendship and teamwork, we found ourselves styled, dressed, and ready on time—even my mom visited the locker room for a makeup retouch and moment with me.

"Eat these." She pulled a row of Saltines from her tote.

I stared at them with trepidation. This was unnerving for someone who had always loved food. When friends dieted in college, it never occurred to me to join them. Not because I didn't feel the same ridiculous pressure to lose five pounds, but because I knew I'd never succeed. Missing even one meal reduced me to a hangry toddler, and the thought of foregoing Cap'n Crunch seemed absurd. That anxiety prevented me from consuming a *cracker* without consequence spoke volumes. (That multiple guests complimented my gaunt frame also spoke volumes, but about a whole different problem.)

I nibbled, distracted by my mom's beauty.

"You look amazing," I told her. She wore a silk, mint-green dress with a silver belt and silver sandals. She looked stunning and also like herself—the special-occasion gold standard.

"So do you. You *are* amazing." I let her hold me and tried not to cry off my mascara. "I have something for you." She handed me her mother's ivory handkerchief; she'd had *Zoe Ellen* embroidered on it in blue. My mascara didn't stand a chance.

"Mom, I don't know what to say. Thank you for *everything*. I'm sorry you've gone to all this trouble and expense for a funeral."

Mom laughed and took my hands in hers. "Zoe. Life is unpredictable. Celebrating our daughter isn't 'trouble'—it's our pleasure." I hugged her tight.

"Now," she said, "let's have an adventure."

We dabbed tissues under our eyes and left.

Suddenly, the wedding party was lining up. Our guests were already seated—I was glad to have missed their reactions to the funeral, which was still in full swing behind the scrim Amanda and Penelope had hung. When the processional music began, my stomach leapt into my throat. I froze.

"Babes, you're stunning," Alex said.

I smiled gratefully. "So are you."

We all really did look good. My simple-but-elegant ivory satin gown was only slightly too big and had turned out beautifully. ("You girls!" the seamstress had scolded. "Bridal dieting is out of control!") Maddie rocked her natural dark curls and a lemon chiffon dress. Alex went boho with a flowy, floor-length, baby-blue number and perfectly undone bun. They both wore the pearl earrings I had gifted them.

"You really look gorgeous," Maddie added quietly.

"Are you *crying*, Mads?" I teased.

"No. I mean, maybe a little." She added, "Someone *did* die."

We laughed but stopped suddenly when it was Arianna's turn to walk down the aisle. She wore the most elaborate funeral attire I had ever seen. Black starched fabric covered her from head to toe, and a black lace overlay dotted with small black buttons ran from her chin to her black belt. Black sleeves that dead-ended in black lace cuffs barely encased her sausage-like arms. Black lace-up boots—the kind that Laura Ingalls Wilder's school teacher might have worn—revealed themselves when she stepped.

A short, black-lace veil hung from her bun; she'd wrapped a matching black hankie around her colorful nosegay bouquet, which she held away from her body as though it were a turd. Her expression was a swollen combination of hangover and grief. I noticed that her fuchsia lipstick was, for the first time, uneven.

When she finally sat, having sucked all the air out of The Birthright in the process, I looked helplessly at Alex. She grabbed my hand.

"Listen," she said. "There are a hundred people who love you in there, and only one cunt with a death hanky. OK?"

I nodded.

"And Rob is just a few feet away," Maddie added.

"Thanks," I whispered.

Alex squeezed my hand, produced a tissue from inside her bra, and dabbed under my eyes one last time. After my dad helped my grandparents down the aisle, he hustled back to me.

"Ready, Kiddo?" he asked as he took my arm. He looked dashing and proud in the tux my mom made him buy. "You look wonderful." He smiled wide with glistening eyes.

"Thanks. So do you. I'm ready."

I smiled back at him and snapped a mental photo of his face. As Maddie and Alex walked down the aisle before me, I stared straight ahead and let everything in my peripheral vision blur— even the beautiful flowers and lights—to focus on the picture of my dad in my mind's eye.

The doors to The Birthright closed and the music paused. Just as I was thinking, *I really, really should have shat before putting my dress on,* the doors opened again. Thousands of people, it seemed, stood, and the "Wedding March" played. I saw Judge Smythe, Lila's friend, in front of me at the bottom of the long aisle. And then I saw Rob. When we locked eyes, he smiled openly for what felt like the first time in forever. This gave me the strength to let go of my dad's arm at the top of the aisle. *I love this guy*, I reminded myself. *And look—he loves me too.* Boone flashed me a thumbs up, presumably for not tripping. Rob whispered into my ear that I looked beautiful, causing me to mirror his grin.

The ceremony exceeded expectations: short but sentimental, and Rob and I forgot for a few blissful moments about the funeral, despite the incense wafting up our noses. Since Arianna was behind me, I could only feel her darkness, which was demonstrably better than seeing it. Rob gripped my hands with confidence; while I had to consciously try not to pass out, standing in front of all those people (plus one corpse) didn't seem to faze him. When we made it back up the aisle and out onto the patio, I was dizzy with relief. We'd made it.

Amanda had cordoned off a table and was waiting for us with two plates. "No one eats at their wedding unless they do it now," she said, and left us. But in what seemed like a blink, she returned. "Time for pictures!" Her stress was palpable—an understandable reaction to Arianna's hungover-Victorian-sailor's-widow vibe. We needed a Plan B. "Should we just take pictures of . . . us?" I offered.

"No," Rob said, and pulled me determinedly away from our spanakopita, olives, and dips to march down the block to the small park our photographer had chosen in Normal Times. Alex, Maddie, Daniel, Brooke, Jimmy, and Boone—the last two of whom had read during the ceremony—were gathered on one side of the park's fountain near my parents, Zach, and our extended family. Rob's groomsmen were draped on a park bench, cocktails in hand. In contrast, Rob's family was huddled over Arianna, who was splayed on the other bench, moaning faintly and fanning herself with her hanky. Poor Yia-Yia Julia stood off to the side, smiling into the distance. I asked Daniel to make sure she didn't walk into traffic. Our photographer, Holly, gulped.

"Umm, Greene family, maybe . . . over here?" She tried to distance us from the Baros melee.

Rob was ghostly white. I tugged his hand. "We could just leave now," I half-joked.

"No," he said, not taking his eyes off Arianna, who had successfully drawn everyone's attention. "We're taking pictures."

As we approached, my family and friends all tried to offer congratulations, but they were distracted by the increasingly loud Baros kerfuffle. Arianna had apparently fainted—or pretended to. One of the relatives ran back to The Birthright for a glass of water while the rest of the family tried to revive her. Yia-Yia Julia succeeded by slapping Arianna hard across the face and cheerfully instructing her to "WAKE UP!" in English. Penelope steered Julia to the farthest corner of the park, where she haplessly pointed out birds.

"Should we keep going?" Holly asked. I was going to suggest not, but Rob said, "*Yes.*"

We got through precisely one full Greene family shot before Arianna's moaning, which had morphed into sobbing, could no longer be ignored. Rob marched over to his family, temple vein ablaze. His grandmother threw eye-daggers, Arianna had entered a kind of fugue state, and the rest of the family seemed equal parts aggrieved and confused. Rob got in his mother's face. Hand gestures flew. Even Rob's groomsmen—at least two-thirds of whom were already buzzed—watched with rapt attention.

Rob stomped back to Holly. "Ready," he said.

To our collective amazement and horror, two of Arianna's male cousins hauled her to her feet. She swooned before they dragged her, each holding one of her arms over their shoulders, much like a down-but-not-yet-out prize fighter, to the fountain. She reeked of liquor even from several feet away.

"Fuck," Alex whispered.

"She's tanked!" Boone said.

Arianna looked vomitous. Her family fretted around her.

"Daniel, why don't you take Brooke and. . . ." Maddie motioned up the sidewalk and away from what we all feared would soon become a crime scene.

"Uh, right. Brooke, let's. . . ." Daniel and Brooke began to walk speedily away. They stopped on The Birthright's patio to share a cigarette and monitor the action from neutral ground.

My parents winced. Zach eyed Arianna warily, wondering what to do if something needed doing.

"What are they saying?" Bubbe pulled on my arm.

"They're speaking *Greek*," Zayde, who was terribly hard of hearing by then, told her.

"NO, THEY'RE IN ENGLISH NOW," Jimmy said.

"*Shh!*" I snapped. I realized I had picked the polish off one entire fingernail.

Arianna was, somehow, both languid and hysterical. I kept thinking about Liberace as she waved her hanky around. Rob's grandmother wore a determinedly neutral expression.

"Mom," Rob pleaded. "What's going *on*?"

She wailed and thrust an arm toward me.

"Shit, Bumpster. That hanky's pointing right at you," Boone said.

"I can see that," I muttered.

My stomach churned beneath my Spanx.

"*WHAT IS IT?*" Rob snapped.

"Sheeeee's havvvvvving an affairrrr!" Arianna slurred before hiccoughing and collapsing back onto her human supports.

Silence.

Rob, eventually: "*What?*"

"Oh, for God's sake!" my mom said. Dad grew crimson—Zach, more eggplant.

"Is true 'n' I've been sick abud it."

"WHAT IN THE ACTUAL FUCK?" Jimmy blurted.

With great effort, Arianna swiveled her head toward Jimmy. "With himmmm!"

The silence lasted for eons. Holly disappeared.

Finally, Jimmy began to laugh. And then howl. My parents, Rob, and I did not.

"No, no," Yia-Yia Julia said to Arianna in a happy sing-song. We all startled; we'd forgotten Julia was there. "That boy is *homosexual!*" That the lady with dementia was the most lucid *Baros* in attendance seemed apropos of the day.

"What?" asked Zayde.

"He's *homosexual*," Bubbe answered.

Rob stared at Arianna. She avoided his eyes and was soon led ever so slowly back to *Baros*. Only Penelope stayed behind; she had chosen sides. I wrapped my arm around her waist in thanks.

"I'm going to get Holly," Rob said. "We're finishing our pictures."

And somehow, silently, and sans a couple key Baroses, we did.

EVERYONE WHO'D WITNESSED Arianna's performance was in a trance by the time the deejay announced our entrance with U2's "Beautiful Day." Rob and I awkwardly swayed through our first dance (to a shortened version of U2's "All I Want Is You") while looking at, but not seeing, each other. We didn't *experience* our wedding—we survived it.

Most guests were rather remarkably oblivious to the strain of the day, thanks in part to the full bar and Arianna remaining on the patio. That said, the dance floor only *really* lit up when (1) the funeral finally ended and (2) Arianna had barfed into a potted plant and been removed to her mother's apartment. Attracted to the patio by a macabre curiosity, I gingerly retrieved a black lace hanky, smeared with fuchsia lipstick, and threw it away before going to dance.

When we were about to leave via limo, Christos came rushing out to tell us that Arianna was in an ambulance. Again. Everyone who'd come to see us off gasped; they were not used to these episodes. (This time, the doctors would sober Arianna up and remove her gallbladder.) I looked helplessly at Rob, who looked helplessly back at me. His eyes went dead while his temple vein sprouted anew.

I wasn't strong enough then to ask Rob not to go. To choose me on this one night that was supposed to be ours. He wouldn't have—he couldn't have—stayed, but at least, if I'd asked him to, I would have known. He pecked me quickly before running into the street for a taxi.

"Take the limo," I said quietly. He hesitated for a brief second before nodding and accepting my offer. Through the limo's open window I watched Rob's face settle into the tight, blank repose he would wear for the duration of our brief marriage.

# Fifteen

When our bar results posted—WE PASSED!—we were finally able to celebrate. But after an epic happy hour with our fellow elated associates, and even some drunk sex (any sex had become something of a novelty since the wedding), the pall quickly returned to our home. By Thanksgiving, I felt like one more day spent under Arianna's cloud would kill us, so I convinced Rob to see a therapist—Pam. Pam was apparently not one for pulling punches. She kicked off the third session, to which I was invited, thusly: "Rob's mother infantilizes and wishes to control him. She would like you to die, Zoe, and for Rob to remain a child—to live in his childhood bedroom, work at the restaurant, and play by her rules. She feels entitled to be the primary woman in his life forever."

Yikes.

"But what if Arianna came to see you too? Could you help her?" I asked. I was still so far from understanding that some problems—and people—cannot be fixed. Pam softened with pity.

"She's self-medicating, experiencing serious psychosomatic illness, and hasn't owned any of her behavior. I strongly suggest that you focus on your own marriage and creating your own rules and boundaries."

We both remained lost in our own thoughts until bedtime. By the next morning, I was determined to "get working." Arianna had been torturing us for years. The wedding was over. It was time to move on. Make those rules. Set those boundaries. We. Could. DO IT!

And maybe *we* could have, if we'd both been willing. But Rob said therapy wasn't for him—that he just needed "time to think." Of course, this was not a one-person job. I wish I could have seen that.

♡

December 15, 2004

My Loves: You guys had faith in Adam when alcoholism threatened to end him, and the band. He missed a huge concert. Instead of being angry, you rallied around him, and by all accounts, never wavered. He did the work and got well in order to do right by you and, also, himself.

I'm terrible for not having that same faith in my poor husband, who's now been abandoned by <u>both</u> his parents. I'm terrible for worrying that Rob won't do the work he needs to be happy. And that if <u>he</u> can't be happy, I can't be happy. I wish you could tell me that everything will be OK. Love, Zoe

♡

December 16, 2004

Guys: Ignore yesterday's message. Rob deserves time
to think. I just need to be patient, have faith, and
help him through this. That's what marriage is
about, right? It's what I vowed to do. I should start
writing in pencil. Love, Zoe

# Sixteen

P enelope remained the one shining Baros in our lives. We spoke regularly by phone after spending an entire weekend with her on our honeymoon. She said the extended family thought Arianna was beyond help and, after witnessing her behavior at our wedding, decided to keep their distance. Rob's temple vein went haywire during that particular conversation, and he seemed only marginally buoyed by the relationship we forged with Penelope.

Rob was constantly and excessively stressed about work. He logged too much time on the couch and too little time anywhere else. It took everything he had just to get through his workdays. It took everything *I* had to fulfill my own obligations while picking up the slack at home. I bagged Monday night yoga and started bringing work home every night so that Rob always had a hot meal waiting for him and never had to walk Basil. I spent Saturdays running our errands while Rob slept in, and I felt guilty whenever I stole away with Alex for much-needed breaks. I felt certain that Rob wouldn't be able to do his job—which he was convinced was exponentially more difficult than mine—if I didn't devote all of my non-working time and energy to propping him up. I also felt certain that all of this was nothing more or less than my marital duty. It's amazing what you adapt to when circumstances shift incrementally over time.

I'll never know why, in the spring of 2007, Rob seemed the best he'd been since our wedding. Maybe it was the tincture of time. Maybe Rob was learning to separate his mother's problems from his own. Maybe he had Spring Fever. (This is a very real thing in Chicago.) Maybe he, too, had a biological clock. Maybe it was none of these things.

But after Rob survived the flurry of 2006 year-end closings and had a few weeks of normalcy under his belt, I shared with him what I'd bottled up for months: I wanted to have a baby. I wanted to move forward, to enjoy a bond like the one I'd hoped to have with Rob—to bring warmth into our home. I wanted to draw Rob closer to me by making our own family. I wanted to force his attention into the future—for him to see the possibilities I could see. I succumbed to my body's ancient, primal call.

"I'm there," Rob said, but he wanted to use the entire first quarter to properly recover from his hellish fourth quarter, and take one last vacation before launching into baby life. I was thrilled and booked two tickets to Cabo. I silently pledged not to talk about babies despite thinking about them all the time. I did a decent job of this. But if *Martha Stewart Babies* had existed, I would have subscribed.

Rob was uncharacteristically buoyant when we returned home from a Saturday night out with friends shortly after Cabo. I was about to fall asleep when he snuggled me from behind and said, "So, that baby thing. Do you wanna?"

*YYYYYYEEESSSSSSSSS!* We *were* going to be a non-depressed couple! I was beside myself with joy. I finished the last couple birth control pills in my pack, had my period, and called

Dr. Fine. He said that "three times a week should do it" and to call back if I wasn't pregnant in six months.

"More sex? I like it," Rob enthused when I relayed Dr. Fine's advice. "But let's not over-plan. That takes the fun out of it."

"*Totally*," I lied.

Oh please. I loved plans. I *lived* for plans. I plotted three, evenly spaced sex slots per week the second I hung up with Dr. Fine. But I was so punch-drunk on the idea of getting pregnant and moving on with our lives that I *told* myself I was going with the flow. I just *coincidentally* initiated sex exactly three times per week. Rob was happy to participate in this sex, knew full well that no barrier stood between his DNA and mine, and enthusiastically approved of the reemergence of my honeymoon lingerie. He assumed a confidence I hadn't seen in ages: *I can have a healthy sex life. I can be joyful. I can move forward.*

"My boobs hurt," I told Rob the Friday night after I was due for my next period. "Like, bad."

"Hmm?"

"Yeah. It started when I was sitting in Chip's office—a dull ache." Chip was the eccentric, difficult older partner who, despite being constantly irritated by me, demanded that I work on nearly all his projects and reduced me to tears approximately once per week.

"Weird," Rob said absentmindedly as I served up Thai takeout.

"But I took a pregnancy test two days ago and it was negative."

He shook his head while taking a bite. "Isn't it too soon?"

"Yeah. This would be the very first month I could get pregnant."

We ate and binge-watched *24*. My breasts throbbed.

"Rob," I said, annoyed, when he turned out his light. "Do you even care? I might have breast cancer."

"You don't have breast cancer," he mumbled before drifting off.

The next morning, I got up at six to pee. While shuffling to the toilet, my brain clicked on. I had *never* been late. My boobs killed. Either I was pregnant, or I was dying (from the breast cancer). The pregnancy test kit came with two sticks. I'd used one and now decided to use the other. I crept into the guest bathroom so as not to wake Rob. I was about to do what I'd done the last time—do my whole pee on the stick—when it occurred to me to read the directions. I was only supposed to hold the stick in my urine stream for a few seconds; that way, the watery end of my whiz wouldn't dilute the pregnancy hormone.

I think I knew right then that I was pregnant—that I'd just screwed up the first test. But I wouldn't let myself believe this because I wanted to be pregnant *so badly*. I peed on the stick for four seconds, removed it, finished peeing, and set the stick on the sink. My heart raced as I paced the tiny bathroom, willing myself not to look at the stick for the requisite three minutes. I caved after 10 seconds. A pink plus sign was already beginning to appear. It shouted, "You are *super* pregnant, you idiot!"

Hands shaking, I double-checked the instructions. Plus meant pregnant. I was *pregnant*. A *baby*. I was gonna be a *MOMMY*. I would grow a big belly and waddle to work. At some point in the not-too-distant future, I could give up sucking in my stomach. Alex would be sure it's a girl. I'd sneak down the back staircase when I felt nauseous at the beginning or too tired to work a full day at the end. I'd pawn Chip off on somebody else during my *six-month* maternity leave, three of which were *paid*! I pictured my desk decorated with crayon artwork, infant photos, and one of those homemade paperweights with a tiny handprint in the middle. I inhaled the imaginary scent of baby lotion. Maybe it was TWINS!

I grabbed the stick and wondered how to give Rob the news in some adorable, novel way. Should I cook a meal comprised solely of baby carrots and baby corn, like Aunt Becky did for Uncle Jesse on *Full House*? Nah. I couldn't contain myself. So I ran past a grumpy Frankie, my beloved cat whom I'd gotten right after college graduation, and threw open the bedroom door.

"Rob."

Nothing.

"ROB!"

He woke up—barely—and lifted his head. I held out the stick.

"I'm pregnant!"

He squinted at it. I brought it closer to his face. He saw the plus. He smiled.

♡

June 23, 2007

Dear U2: I'm PREGNANT! Can you even?! I think it's a girl. And she'll be born a U2 fan, having listened to so much of you in utero, so this does, technically, involve you.

I hope I can protect her. But also that she has spirit. "Wild Horses." And if my daughter (!) tells me she's ditching college to join a rock band, I hope I'll have the wisdom to let her try. I want her to take the world by the ovaries and the patriarchy by the balls. I'll root for her every step of the way. Mine is a blind kind of love/Oh oh oh the sweetest thing! Love, Zoe and Her Little Bean

# Seventeen

"Obviously, we don't want to get ahead of ourselves. It's so early," Rob cautioned my parents when we told them about the pregnancy.

"Right," I dutifully seconded. "Please stay mum until I'm three months along."

*Three months along.* I loved talking like a pregnant person!

"Of course," they said. My mom had two miscarriages. They understood.

I asked Rob if I could tell Alex and Maddie because, *come on!*

"Babe," he said sternly. "I don't want you getting your hopes up."

I guiltily told both women shortly thereafter and swore them to secrecy. Rob refused to discuss my pregnancy. Whenever I pressed, he'd repeat his miscarriage mantra. So I relied on Maddie, Alex, and my mom to share in my excitement (Zach and my dad were excited too, but in a dude-type way), and held fast to my conviction that a baby's joyful energy is exactly what Rob needed.

Rob stared at me blankly when I said it was customary for husbands to come to the first prenatal appointment, which happened to fall on my first day of morning sickness. It was hot and muggy by seven fifteen. But I walked Bas and made our break-fasts anyway.

"Can you drive?" I asked. Rob had reflexively walked to the passenger side of the car because, when we drove to work, I always dropped him off first. "I'm really not feeling well," I told him—again.

"Sure."

His clenched face, reminiscent of our unhappiest time, upset me. *He just really doesn't want to get our hopes up*, I reassured myself. While I knew in my bones that my pregnancy was healthy, Rob couldn't experience that sixth sense. I wasn't showing, and our lives hadn't changed. *Rob's* boobs weren't sore. *He* didn't feel nauseous. So his non-response was *totally normal*. It had to be.

I surprised Rob again by asking him to drop me in front of Dr. Fine's building.

"I can't walk from the garage in this humidity. I'll barf."

I was still standing in line to check in when Rob entered the waiting room, made a beeline to a seat, and began reading something from his briefcase. It didn't occur to me until I recounted this moment to my therapist that he should have taken my place in line so that *I* could sit down. After checking in, I sat next to him and completed the "first prenatal visit" paperwork. Not a word passed between us.

Dr. Fine was running late; we waited forever. Rob was quiet and squinched. I tried not to look too often at the other expectant couples in the waiting room; they were all engaged with each other in some way. There was physical contact even between those who were reading or checking their phones. I reached for Rob's hand, but he only patted mine once.

Finally, it was our turn.

"So sorry—we were waiting for the ultrasound room," the nurse winked.

I hurriedly put on the paper gown and pushed past the angst on Rob's face. I was ready to get some jelly on my belly and see our mini.

"Zoe, you've had a positive pregnancy test!" Dr. Fine shook my hand and closed the door behind him. He next turned to Rob, who sat at attention in the guest chair. "Josh Fine," he said, extending his hand.

"Rob Baros. Nice to meet you." Rob's voice was strained.

Dr. Fine smiled knowingly at Rob and then at me. "I know you're probably both anxious. Let's have a look."

A couple of my friends had learned at this same, first appointment that their embryos had died. But I was calm, despite the possibility of imminent disappointment. I couldn't shake the knowledge that all was well. I climbed onto the exam table. I didn't understand why Dr. Fine put my feet in stirrups, though. To my horror, Dr. Fine grabbed what looked quite like an enormous dildo, slid an extra-long condom onto it, and lubed it up.[12]

"Relax. Deep breaths, Zoe," he said as he slid the dildo inside me. Only a man could instruct a woman with an oversized dildo in her vagina to relax. Rob was horrified.

A bunch of black-and-white static appeared on the screen. Dr. Fine manipulated the dildo, challenging my bladder to a duel, before pointing to a tiny flutter on the screen.

"Here's the heartbeat. That's what we were looking for." He smiled.

---

[12] All pregnant people should know about transvaginal ultrasounds before encountering one. Consider yourselves warned.

We all watched it for a minute. Even Rob leaned in for a better view.

"Wow," I said.

I had expected to see more recognizable stuff on the screen, but the smudge Dr. Fine promised was a healthy heartbeat worked for me.

"Everything looks right on schedule," Dr. Fine assured us. "Want to watch the heartbeat for a minute before heading to my office?"

"Umm, I'd love to—but I have to pee."

"Ah! The joys of pregnancy," Dr. Fine laughed. "I'll take some pictures for you." He clicked the mouse a few times and removed the dildo. I heard the printer whir as I darted to the restroom.

"This is great," I told Rob as I dressed.

"Yes!" he said, his voice shrill.

He looked at the ground as we walked to Dr. Fine's office to talk about avoiding alcohol, cold cuts, and the litter box. Our due date was March 9, 2008.

EVEN THOUGH OUR screening for a seemingly unending list of birth defects, thanks to my Ashkenazi Jewish heritage, wasn't scheduled until week thirteen, I decided I'd tell everyone at work about the baby at week twelve. I was getting more and more anxious to spill the beans because it was harder and harder to act as if everything was the same. It wasn't. My pregnancy permeated my every thought. I was constantly aware of the actual magic happening inside of me, but couldn't talk about it at home. "We're still in the first trimester," Rob would say every evening before clicking on the TV.

When I was nine weeks pregnant, I got two emails. The first was from the cheesy list-serve I'd joined:

> You are now **9** weeks pregnant and your baby is the approximate size of a **grape**!

According to the attached photo, our baby looked like a space-alien-guppy.

The second email was from Alex's mom, from whom I didn't usually hear directly:

> Dearest Zoe, Congratulations. What a blessing! I wish all good fortune to you, Rob, and your dear one. Please let me know if you are expecting a boy or a girl (Alex tells me you will find out!) so that I may start knitting him or her a blanket. I will leave the bottom part unfinished so that I may embroider the baby's name there. With love and best wishes, Anna

I couldn't deny that my reaction to both emails was unnatural. Excitement was my *secondary* reaction; the need to hide both messages from Rob was primary. While I had until then managed to squelch concerns about Rob's distant behavior, something about receiving those emails, reacting to them, and probably, on a subconscious level, knowing that the end of my first trimester was rapidly approaching, made me confront them. I had to tell Rob that his failure to acknowledge my pregnancy worried me. I believed that, because most people are good and do the right thing, he would soothe me. He'd regret that his fears about miscarriage or being a good dad were burdening me. I took a deep breath and reopened my laptop.

"Rob?" I called. "I wanna show you something." My heart throbbed in my chest.

"Hey." He stood in the doorway of the office/guest-bedroom/soon-to-be-nursery.

"I got a picture of a nine-week embryo. It's starting to look almost humanish. See?"

He didn't move.

"Come look."

He still didn't move, so I scooted the laptop toward him.

"Isn't this cool? No more tail. *Look!*" I commanded.

Rob glanced at the photo like it was a bomb. He threw his arms in the air, backed into the hall, curled his hands into fists, and yelled.

"DON'T SHOW ME THAT, ZOE! YOU KNOW THAT FREAKS ME OUT!"

A deep red color rose up from his neck and crept down from his forehead until everything was crimson. Spittle framed the corners of his mouth—angry tears filled his eyes. Bile rose in my throat and I struggled to breathe.

"Jesus, Rob!" I sputtered. Then I measured my words. "This is what our *baby* looks like. *We're having a baby.* That's why I'm showing you this picture."

Rob crouched down and cried. I was paralyzed by ambivalence: Half of me was disgusted by Rob's self-centeredness; the other half wanted to comfort him. Desperate to normalize a uniquely abnormal situation, I got up from my chair, bent over, and put my hand on Rob's back while lowering my face to his. He recoiled.

"Rob, please," I cried, twisting my hands after he rejected them. "What is going on? Just talk to me!"

"I TOLD YOU," he seethed. "This. All. Freaks. Me. OUT."

"Yeah, I got that part," I said, a little unkindly. I leaned against the doorframe and cried. Nausea threatened to over-whelm me, but I willed it away. I wrapped my arms protectively around my abdomen. "What specifically is freaking you out?"

Rob continued to cry in his squat, and with each passing moment, it became clearer that he was performing.

"Enough," I snapped. "I am nine weeks pregnant. If next week's ultrasound looks good, the risk of miscarriage is less than one percent. We can start telling people in three weeks." I hesi-tated before adding, "This baby is going to be born, Rob."

Rob increased the volume of tears, which repulsed me. My ability to remain sympathetic waned.

"We're *married*, Rob. We chose to have a baby *together*. Re-member? We called the doctor, got off the pill, had sex, and as a result of those joint decisions, I—not we, but I—am pregnant. For the first time. How do you think I feel?"

I was crying every bit as hard as Rob by now. He glared at me and made a guttural sound. His face contorted and swelled so that his tortoiseshell glasses sat askew on the bridge of his nose. His entire body was knotted, from curled toes to bulging face. I was terrified.

I tried touching him, as though I could physically pull him back to sanity. He resisted. I followed when he sprang to our bedroom and asked him to sit down. He ignored me and paced with his hands clasped behind his head. He looked like a far less endearing version of Dustin Hoffman in *Rain Man*. I tried to convince myself that this could still be fixed, although I sensed, in the same bedrock place that knew my pregnancy was healthy, that it couldn't.

"Listen," I said. Our conversation was physically awkward, with Rob pacing around our small bedroom and me trying to stay out of his way. "It's totally normal to freak about being a parent. *I'm* freaked. I've never done this before, either."

Rob grunted. His skin remained blood red.

"And since all of this is happening in *my* body, you probably feel even more out of control than I do . . . theoretically, I could smoke crack in the alley."

Rob avoided my eyes and said nothing.

"Baby. I know you've had a lot of family trauma," I said softly.

He shot me a look. I tiptoed toward Rob and put my hand on his back. He allowed me to keep it there, but his body went rigid and his gaze remained fixed on the wall. I let my fingertips rest lightly on his shoulder blade, hyper-aware of the physical strain between us. I hoped my voice didn't betray my despair.

"You will be an *excellent* father. You're not your dad, and I'm not your mom. We'll support each other and let our children forge their own paths. Our home will be different. OK?"

Rob didn't budge or look inclined to say a word. This rattled me.

"We have plenty of time to wrap our heads around this," I blathered on. "We have a great apartment, good jobs, my parents are nearby. Alex's mom is even working on our first baby gift, and—"

Rob whirled around. "What did you say?"

I retreated. Rob looked so deranged that I started backing away, slowly, like a victim in a horror film.

"I—that you'll be a great fath—"

"*No.*" Rob snapped. "The part about Alex." His crying, I realized, had stopped.

He kept walking toward me; I kept walking backwards. I forced myself to stop at the bedroom doorway.

"That's what you're upset about right now? That I told Alex I'm pregnant and tired all the time, and going through this whole thing *by myself*?" Tears poured off my chin. "A baby blanket is the least of—"

"*It is not*," Rob spat. "I told you it was *really* important to me that you didn't tell anyone. You lied to me."

I paused, momentarily speechless. We looked at each other. I wore an expression of disbelief, he one of hatred.

"This is where you usually turn things, isn't it," I said with a cold calm that shocked me. "Not today. Not with this. And if you think I'm going to beg forgiveness for sharing this huge thing that's happening inside *my* body with *my* best friend, because you won't even acknowledge it, then you're out of your mind."

For a split second, I wondered if Rob might actually hit me. But he sat on the bed, jammed his palms into his forehead, and silently screamed. *Of course he wouldn't hit me.* I sat beside him.

"Look, I'm just trying to reach you," I pleaded. "You never talk to me!"

"I'm just so scared," he heaved. *Now we were getting somewhere!* I rubbed his back before gripping his shoulders.

"We'll be OK. We *will*," I urged. "You've *always* said you wanted kids—with *me*."

His crying picked back up. I cradled him from behind while he remained hunched over, but it was as if I couldn't feel him. He sobbed for an eternity. Vomit crept into my throat again. I swallowed. And waited.

"I can't have kids," he said quietly. "I was just trying to make you happy."

"What?" I whispered.

This couldn't be happening. This was *crazy*. I involuntarily shoved his shoulder.

"*Rob*. What are you saying? *Please*, stop and think—there are some things you can't take back!"

I cried; my mouth filled with viscous saliva. Rob only looked at me for a split second. But in that split second, I knew without a shadow of a doubt what he wanted to do. It was so insane—so incomprehensibly cruel—that I didn't want to acknowledge it. But I had no choice.

"*You want me to abort our baby?*" I couldn't believe I was saying these words.

He looked me steadily in the eye for the first time.

"That's what I've been thinking."

"What the *fuck!*" I cried. "You agreed to this! I AM ALREADY IN LOVE WITH THIS BABY! DO YOU EVEN CARE THAT KILLING IT WOULD KILL ME TOO?"

He set his jaw and stared at me evenly.

"SAY SOMETHING!" I shouted.

But he never did.

When I could no longer stand being pregnant, nauseous, and primally vulnerable, yet doing all of the thinking, comforting, and talking, I fled to the bathroom. I sat there with the door closed, wailing on the floor, until I retched. When I emerged, completely dehydrated, the door to our bedroom was closed, and the light was off. With no alternative, I crawled into the guest bed where I shivered, awake, until morning.

♡

July 23, 2007

I disappeared in you/You disappeared from me/I gave you everything you ever wanted/It wasn't what you wanted./The [wo]men who love you, you hate the most/They pass through you like a ghost/They look for you, but your spirit is in the air/Baby, you're nowhere.

# Eighteen

At dawn, I caught a cab to my parents' place. I sat at the coffee shop across the street until it was late enough to call—I will never forget the looks on their faces when I told them what had happened. I called in sick to work for the first time and ignored Alex's calls. Dad went to the office for half the day but came home as soon as his meetings resolved. Mom cleared her schedule. I kept telling her I was worried about Rob; did she think he might hurt himself?

"I'm not worried about Rob," she finally snapped. "I'm worried about my pregnant daughter."

With good reason. Because, while I teetered on the brink of insanity, Rob was, apparently, fine—he went to work. I called him at his desk, after getting no answer at home or on his cell, to ask him if my dad, the consummate mediator, might help us have another conversation about "things" when he got home.

"Of course," Rob said in his fake, office voice.

This was my first exposure to Rob's chilling ability to separate his own actions, and their consequences, from his day-to-day life. He worked a full day and had us meet him at the apartment at six thirty. The second he walked through the door, Rob took off his work face—which looked disturbingly normal, as though nothing out of the ordinary was happening and he didn't hold my sanity in his hands—and clenched.

"Hi, Mr. Greene." Dad and I both flinched—Rob hadn't called him "Mr. Greene" since high school.

"Hey, Rob," Dad said. "Let's sit."

He nodded. We sat. Frankie and Basil were on edge. They paced the rug.

"I understand you're having a serious case of the jitters," Dad began.

Rob rested his elbows on his knees and his chin atop his clasped hands. He stared straight ahead.

"It's not jitters. I *cannot* do this."

My dad and I locked eyes. It was at that moment—when my dad read Rob exactly as I had the night before—that I lost hope. I struggled to breathe. Dad pressed on.

"Well, of course you *can*. You have everything you need and more. Rachel and I could take the baby every Saturday night if you wanted."

Rob ground his teeth while continuing to stare past us.

"You know that my parents divorced," Dad tried again. "They had a terrible marriage and weren't great parents. But I'm sure you'll agree that Rachel and I made a beautiful family of our own."

I couldn't stand it anymore. "Say something, Rob."

Rob dropped his forehead into his hands and tried hard, it seemed, to cry. He wouldn't look up. When he sensed us staring at him, he started whispering, "No, no, no, no, no."

"Son," Dad finally said. "The fact of the matter is that Zoe is pregnant."

Rob's heaving intensified.

"You're going to have to come to terms with that. Let us help—"

"NO!" Rob shrieked. "NO!"

Now he clasped his hands behind his neck and stuck his head between his knees, like he was demonstrating Crash Position on an airplane.

He briefly met my dad's eyes with the familiar determination that he was going to get his way. Then he threw himself down on the couch to weep.

I was sorry and ashamed that my dad witnessed Rob's theatrics, but also glad that I was no longer the only one interpreting them. Dad looked at me over Rob's trembling body. He didn't have to say a word. I jogged to our bedroom to pack a bag. One at a time, I picked up and kissed Frankie and Basil, who'd been circling me nervously. When I returned to the living room, Dad slowly moved toward the door.

"Make sure you remember the pets," I said hoarsely from the threshold.

Rob grunted affirmation into the couch and said nothing when we left.

Buckled into my dad's passenger seat, I pierced the silence.

"I can't have a baby with him. He already hates me just for being pregnant. He'd ruin my life, and the baby's."

Dad was quiet and pale. His face twitched as he processed our meeting.

"I'm afraid I agree with you," he said softly. "I would have sworn this couldn't be. But there was something in his face . . . he is resolute."

"Yes. He is."

Despite the painful moments I'd experienced during our

marriage, it had never occurred to me that Rob was anything other than sad. But he was—he was hateful. I couldn't have imagined being as disgusted by another human being, much less one I'd loved and married.

THE NEXT FEW days were surreal. I cried to Maddie, to Boone and Brooke, to Alex. I cried to my parents and to Zach. I vacillated between deciding that I couldn't possibly withstand an abortion and that I couldn't possibly bring Rob's child into the world. Twisted nightmares usurped my sporadic sleep. I sent a truth-bending email to Chip et al that I would be working from home for a few days due to illness. Alex brought me a couple of files. While I absentmindedly rifled through them, Zach came to sit with me. He hugged me tightly and let me cry into him.

"Oh, Zodo." Zach had been quiet and reflective thus far. Now, he spoke his mind. "Rob's an asshole, Zoe. You've gotten him through college, law school, the start of his career, and he hasn't thought of you *once*. We were all hoping he'd grow up and pull it together, but he hasn't. And now he's put you in an unforgivable position. So *fuck him*."

He had a point.

"Have the abortion. Get a divorce. Get out from under that guy's thick, miserable cloud. And don't look back."

I stared at Zach. Wasn't he too young to be so prescient? Everyone else had been so *appropriate*. When I'd say I needed to keep the baby, Alex, my parents, Maddie, and Boone would pledge their unwavering support. When I'd say I needed to terminate the pregnancy and leave Rob, they'd do the same. They were right and kind to say those things. But Zach was righter.

"I will," I eventually said. "I just needed to make sure there was no way I could have this baby—which would tether me to Rob forever—and survive." I caught my breath. "But there isn't."

Zach nodded and held my hand.

"I'm scared," I gasped. "Because I will miss this baby *so fucking much*."

"I know. But you'll get through it. We'll help you."

"It's moot," I said. "This is my only choice."

I called Dr. Fine's office first thing the next morning, cried my way through the story, and set the abortion for Friday.

♡

July 25, 2007

Guys: I'm sorry I haven't written — my life's been unraveling. Maybe I was worried you'd judge me if I told you what's been happening . . . although I'd like to think that you're too kind and have too many special women/girls in your lives for that. Mostly, I think I worried that putting the words on paper would make this nightmare real. I hoped that Rob would rise to the occasion, and I didn't want to reread something — or, G-d forbid, for our <u>child</u> to read something — that was too awful to really happen. (Wouldn't that be something? For my kids to find this crazy diary when I die, and know for <u>a</u>

<u>fact</u> that Mom was insane?) But the fact is, on Friday, I won't be pregnant anymore. I'm getting an abortion.

I am pulverized, destroyed, wretched. And I'm scared. For the first time, I understand what people mean when they say they feel "alone." Because the problem is, there's nothing the loving people around me can do. I'm sorry for fucking things up so badly, for disappointing you, for making you sad. Love, Zoe

# Nineteen

Physically, the abortion was a breeze compared to the "procedure" I endured the day before.[13]

"It'll be safer and easier," Dr. Fine explained via phone, "for me to use a laminaria to dilate your cervix. It's very quick."

"Huh?" I was picturing *lu*minarias—those paper bags filled with sand and votive candles that line walkways at weddings and Martha Stewart's driveway at Christmastime. (Why does everything come back to Martha Stewart?)

"Come in this afternoon," he said gently, ignoring my confusion. "But once the laminaria is in, there's no going back. So you have to be, like, ten billion percent sure."

I blinked.

"Zoe?"

"Yes," I said, clearing my throat. "I'm ten billion percent sure."

♡

---

13 I fucking hate the word "procedure." "Procedure" is code for "surgery without pain management." If a doctor recommends having a "procedure"—*especially* if said doctor is a man and said procedure involves your vagina—*run.*

July 26, 2007

Dear Edge: I loved a particular interview you gave
about the song "One." There's so much talk about
"One" because it's "the song that saved the band,"
"the sound of four men chopping down the Joshua
tree," "one of Rolling Stone's best pop songs of
all time," etc.

But you noted that everybody flubs the line, "We
get to carry each other." It's not, "We've got to
carry each other." We've talked about that line —
the correct line — right here in this diary because
it's profound. It's a privilege to carry the right
person. Not a chore.

That's the kind of marriage I want but fear I've
squandered my chance on the wrong person. Thus, I
hereby request a permanent position working for U2
in Ireland, far away from here. I can start Monday.
Love, Zoe

# PART THREE

---

# What the F*ck Do I Do Now?

# Twenty

At my post-op appointment with Dr. Fine, I: (1) asked him if he was *really* sure I'd still be able to have babies; (2) cried when he told me to expect bleeding for six weeks but forbade me from using tampons; (3) obtained a prescription for birth control because, even after I explained that I had no prospects of ever having sex again, he'd insisted ("think positively, Zoe!"); (4) used a quarter-box of Kleenex; and (5) begged for, and received, more Ambien.

So, you know. Just another Monday.

After my exam, Dr. Fine handed me a business card for Jane Raddick, LCSW, Ph.D.

"That's the best therapist I know," he said. "I know you have family support, but Janie specializes in women's loss. Call her."

So that was me now. A *women's loss* person.

"Zoe?"

"Huh?"

"Promise you'll call."

"Right. I promise." I stuffed Dr. Lady Problems' card into my pocket and left.

WHEN I WALKED into Dr. Raddick's office the next day, I couldn't avoid the books lining the waiting room shelves: infertility, miscarriage, stillbirth, postpartum depression, divorcing with children, mood disorders. Terrific! I chewed two Pepto Bismols and buried my head in an issue of *Architectural Digest* until Dr. Raddick opened her door. A beaming young woman strutted out. The woman looked about my age and wore a sapphire wedding band. Her brown hair gleamed with honey highlights; toned calves brushed the hem of her pencil skirt. *She* wasn't a women's loss person. I could tell.

For the first time since I'd begun practicing law, I became painfully aware of my ill-fitting L.L. Bean khakis, sensible work sandals, and middle-school-boy, polo-style tee. I knew that my hair had frizzed during my walk from the train. Suddenly, I wasn't sure I'd be able to pry myself and/or my giant maxi-pad out of the chair, much less explain the last several days of my life.

"Zoe," Dr. Raddick said kindly. "Please come in."

I managed to oblige. Dr. Raddick was petite—small-boned and five feet tall. I immediately guessed she was Jewish because of her pale-but-olive complexion and tight, black curls. She wore a maroon wrap-dress, nude ballet flats, thin gold hoop earrings, and plain gold wedding band. She had a handful of barely noticeable grays pulled back into her half-ponytail and big, soft, brown eyes. I guessed that she was in her late thirties. She didn't necessarily *look* like a Women's Disaster Doctor. She watched as I settled myself into the comfortable club chair to which she'd gestured, handed me a box of Kleenex, and reached for a pad and pen before sitting down across from me.

"I hardly ever take notes," she explained, "but like to jot things down during the first session. Is that all right?"

I nodded.

"Please tell me what brings you here. I'd like to help if I can."

To my surprise, I practically yelled, "I want a divorce!"

*My husband freaked out, spiraled into depression (and, perhaps, psychosis) and demanded that I get an abortion—which I got, like, five minutes ago—but remains in our apartment while I'm sleeping in my parents' guest bedroom and trying to act like a lawyer* would've been overwhelming, but more responsive.

Dr. Raddick didn't flinch. "I'm so sorry," she replied, and waited as if she had all day to watch me cry and blow my nose. And she did, actually, look sorry. I liked her.

Our first session was two hours long on the recommendation of the unlucky intake staffer upon whom I'd dumped the not-so-general nature of my situation. I spent the time bringing Dr. Raddick up to speed on the abortion, the complex morass of feelings surrounding the abortion, the heavy cloud of loss that had followed me everywhere since the abortion, and my psyche's decision to proceed as though Rob had never existed. She wrote a lot on her notepad, but mostly listened, interjecting periodically with sympathy, encouragement, and the occasional question.

When I finished, Janie—which she'd insisted I call her—didn't appear disgusted by a twenty-nine-year-old woman who'd aborted a planned pregnancy and couldn't wait to divorce her husband.

"There's something I feel you should know," I confessed as we were wrapping up.

Janie's forehead wrinkled with concern. "Please."

"Umm. I've had a crazy diary—and I mean *crazy*—for fifteen years."

"OK...."

I took a deep breath. "It's letters to U2. Do you know them? The rock band?"

She nodded.

"Some are letters to *some* of U2 . . . it depends on the subject. I don't *send* the letters. But I just . . . love them. U2, I mean. Not the letters. I love U2 and tell them everything. Which I know is bananas." I exhaled loudly. "I've never told anyone. But you're my therapist, and I thought you should know."

Janie shrugged. "Do you know someone in U2?"

"No." *As if!*

"And—"

"I don't know any of them personally. Only their music and public personas. And that's more than enough for me."

She looked satisfied. "Cool," she said.

"*Cool?*"

"Yeah. I'm glad you have a safe—and creative—outlet for your feelings."

I cried a little.

"Would you like to come back Thursday?" she asked.

"Yes," I nodded. "I would."

# Twenty-One

Thursday's session began similarly.

"How are you?" Janie asked.

"Fine. I mean, horrible, but—you know. Fine."

Janie nodded.

"And positive that I need a divorce."

"That may be," Janie said. "But I suggest letting the dust settle before you make such an important decision. You've been with Rob for nearly half your life."

"Yeah, but—I don't know how to explain it. I'm just *done*," I insisted.

Janie narrowed her eyes in thought.

"How about this. What if we pick a reasonable time to revisit that decision, and work on unpacking everything else in the meantime?"

"What's a 'reasonable time?'" I cringed.

"Let's say, three months? When you're not quite so raw?"

I flipped calendar pages in my mind and gasped.

"Oh, my God. I'll turn thirty in three months," I said.

Thirty! *Fuck fuck fuck.*

"Perfect. Let's reassess around your birthday," Janie said lightly, as though my eggs weren't drying up by the second and thirty was a great age to be single and broken.

I spent the rest of the session answering Janie's deft questions. By the end, she knew not only about my childhood and family, but also Rob's, The Birthright, the funeral–wedding, and the unrecognizable, joyless man Rob had become. I left exhausted but confident that I was in good hands.

I OPENED OUR third session with an epiphany: "I'm crazy."

"Zoe, I'm really not concerned about your diary—"

"No," I interrupted. "This isn't about that. It's about—well, why would I try to fix such an obviously broken person? And try to have a *baby* with him?" Humiliation overwhelmed me. "*I* did this. To myself."

Janie studied me for a moment.

"Amazing," she finally said.

"Umm." I rummaged in my bag for Pepto Bismols. "It's amazing that I'm nuts?" I whispered.

"No," Janie said. "It's amazing that you're already in the self-examination phase."

I looked at her with a question mark.

"My job is to help you figure out where you want to go and what skills you need to get there," Janie explained. "You can't do that without examining yourself, and your past, first. A crazy person wouldn't already be reflecting upon her own choices."

"Oh."

"Let's take a step back for the moment—I promise we'll get to plenty of self-examination later."

I nodded.

"You fell in love with Rob when you were *children*. Things are never as clear in real time as they are in hindsight."

"But I wish I'd listened to the voice that had to have been in me—once we were married, as grown-ups, certainly—that wondered whether he—we—could really make it."

"Let's play that out," Janie suggested. "If you *had* listened to that voice, what would you have done differently?"

I didn't know.

"When Rob finally seemed to be cheering up and said he wanted to have a baby, I don't see you saying to him, 'You know, there are things that worry me about you. So even though I love you, have dedicated my life to you, and really want children, I'm going to leave and start over with someone new, just in case you don't get better.' Do you?"

Woah.

"No," I admitted. I thought for a moment. "So you're saying that, even if I'd listened to that voice, I wouldn't have left Rob, and because I wouldn't have left Rob, I wouldn't have turned down the chance to become a mom?" I choked up.

Janie strategically not-talked—one of her many skills—and handed me tissues.

"You're right," I eventually said.

"Would it be safe to say," Janie pressed, "that wanting to keep your pregnancy is the only time you ever asked Rob to put your needs before his own?"

I nodded wordlessly.

"And Zoe," Janie added, "could it be that it was always going to take something extreme for you to leave?"

I nodded again. I chewed my lip for a solid minute while we sat in silence. I could hear the clock ticking on Janie's shelf.

"By *forcing* me to leave, did Rob actually do me . . . a favor?" I asked. It seemed so perverse.

Janie chose her next words carefully. "I'm *not* excusing Rob's cruel behavior. But, ironically, that may be what ultimately sets you free."

♡

August 6, 2007

Dear U2: You are magic, but also <u>lucky</u>. Bono: If you hadn't found your bandmates, you could have been Dublin's maddest street busker. Edge: You could've gone off to med school, as you once considered. Larry: You'd have grumpily auditioned a bunch of wannabes, none of whom would fit the bill, chucked your drum set, and opened a gym. Or started a soft-spoken motorcycle gang. Adam: You'd still be a bassist. You're too badass not to be. And have too enormous a wang.

This now sounds painfully naïve, but until I talked to Janie, I'd always thought that, barring freak accident or illness, I could control my life. But here's the thing: When faced with a decision, you may not be experienced enough to know it's a bad one, and the person you're deciding on might not have even become a bad decision yet. That so much boils down to luck blows my mind. That my own parents' marriage worked out is probably 50% luck!

They couldn't have known, at age 20, that they'd grow into adults who complement each other. Right?

Each of you committed to learning his part, working hard, and putting the band — both music and friendships — first. You're talented. You're not divas. (Well, <u>you</u> are, Bono, but you wear it well.) None of you ever felt better than the rest, or like you deserved more money or power. That's all critical. But a lot of U2 is just kismet, isn't it? Everything special is. Love, Z.

# Twenty-Two

The next night I stared at my cell phone, which I had placed like a live bomb on my bed, and sweated. Alex sat beside me, hair piled sloppily atop her head. I tried to take deep breaths, but they were shallow and trembly.

"You've got this," Alex whispered.

"What if Rob can't manage on his own?" I whimpered.

Alex sighed from frustration and briefly buried her face in the duvet. Then she sat up, closed her eyes, and clasped her hands. "Not your problem. *His* wellbeing is *his* problem."

"I know." I whispered. "But his parents both left him!"

"And you and your entire family—plus friends, teachers, colleagues, half of Greektown, and the therapist he rejected—have offered him support. Suffering is a part of life. Of course, we sympathize, but adulthood means figuring out how to cope, and in a way that doesn't harm others."

"But where will he go? What will he eat? He doesn't know how to clean."

Alex stared at me.

"Not healthy?" I offered.

"No."

"OK then." I picked up my phone. "Thanks for being patient with me."

Alex softened. "Of course."

I wiped each sweaty palm on my pajama pants and dialed Rob's number.

"Hello?" he answered awkwardly.

"Rob, I need a favor." It was a struggle to get the words out.

He hesitated. "OK. . . ."

"I need to move back into the apartment. I've been at my parents' for too long. They need space, and I need to recover at home with the pets. Just while we figure things out." A gush of stale air whooshed out of my mouth.

"What?" he squeaked.

"It's the least—please. I just want to be at home, alone, for now."

"But where will I go?" he asked. There was a small, childlike quality in his voice. Could his need to move out really not have occurred to him? By the disgusted expression on Alex's face, I knew she could hear both ends of the conversation.

"Maybe crash with a friend for a bit," I suggested.

The silence on the other end of the line thrummed with shock. I had never asked Rob to do anything momentous alone. Changing the rules felt scary but invigorating. Alex nodded encouragingly.

"Oh," he said.

"You'll be OK, Rob," I persisted. "And you've got to do this."

There was an uncomfortably long pause.

"OK?" I asked.

"Well . . . I guess I can stay at Meaghan's," Rob said.

Alex rolled her eyes before covering them with a pillow. I winced. Meaghan was a smart, kind, perpetually single friend of Rob's from law school; she'd had a crush on him since they met. He took advantage of this by borrowing her notes and eating her cooking. The jealousy I'd once felt had turned to sympathy; I wished I could warn Meaghan to run.

"OK," I said. "Let me know when I can move back in." My breath quickened with excitement as I sensed the call's imminent end.

"Wait, Zoe?" Rob asked tearfully.

Alex and I exchanged glances.

"You won't try to screw me, will you? Financially? You know I still have student loans."

Alex had to leave the room. An unsavory response sprang to my mind—*You're a fucking lawyer who actually makes more fucking money than I do so get the fuck out of the fucking apartment you fucking fucker!*—but I took another tack.

"Rob," I said slowly. "I won't screw you over." Barf.

Rob sobbed like a toddler trying to calm himself. Huh-huh-huh-*gasp*-Huh-huh-huh-*gasp*. "OK. But please, Zoe—I'm all alone."

*BY DESIGN!* And yet part of me still worried that I was abandoning him.

"Let me know when you've gone to Meaghan's," I said. "Thanks, Rob."

I cried as soon as I hung up. I was desperately worried about him; old habits die hard.

# Twenty-Three

Thanks to Penelope, Rob was only on Meaghan's couch for a few days. She knew something was wrong after neither of us returned her calls; I eventually made Rob tell her everything. Immediately after hanging up on him, she left me a brief message: "I take care of it." She wasn't kidding. From halfway around the world, she located a furnished apartment in the West Loop and shamed Rob into a six-month lease. She even reserved the freight elevator, rented a storage unit, hired movers, and told me when they were coming to get his stuff. Penelope was the only Baros to whom I would always feel connected.

I moved back to the apartment, which was a mixed bag. On the one hand, a sick, gray pall had descended over it in my absence. What had been an airy, cozy work-in-progress was now dark, dirty, and still. On the other hand, moving out of my parents' house seemed a good first step toward moving on with my (lame, pathetic, hopeless) life.

I arrived home on a sunny Saturday afternoon. The pets had never been happier to see me: Basil spun and jumped in circles while Frankie kneaded my jeans with her front paws. After loving on them, I loaded all five slots in the CD player with U2: *Achtung Baby*, *Boy*, a compilation of live tracks that Maddie and

Daniel had made, *A Sort of Homecoming,* and *All That You Can't Leave Behind.* I put them on shuffle and turned up the volume. Part of U2's magic is that they seemed to grow with me—or, rather, their albums waited patiently for me to grow into them. No matter what was happening in my life, U2 had a melody, bass line, or lyric to match it. They created joy. I walked over to the framed collage that Alex and I had taken when we stood impossibly close to the stage during the Vertigo tour. I touched it before kissing my fingers, like one would a prayer book, to thank U2—for everything.[14]

Basil, Frankie, and I made rounds. We raised all the blinds all the way. I opened every window that could open despite making the apartment too cool. I changed the sheets and towels, strained Frankie's litter box (this stung—pregnant people are supposed to avoid cat poop), washed and filled the pets' bowls, dusted every surface while I let the toilet bowl cleaner and Scrubbing Bubbles set in the bathrooms, and cleaned the kitchen.

And then . . . it was quiet. My *body* was quiet. There was no baby growing within. The apartment, instead of being imminently up one resident, was now down one and a half. U2 faded away; a dial tone filled my ears. My chest got tight, and it suddenly felt as though everything in the apartment, including me, was encased in cement. My heart raced, and I sweated through my clothes despite lying perfectly still. Only after it passed did I realize I'd had my first panic attack. Once I could breathe again, I called Alex.

"HeyLadyYouOK?" she sputtered loudly after answering on

---

[14] Except for ignoring the wedding invitation(s) and multiple resumes I'd sent from Yale. Maybe one day I'll let that go. But probably not soon.

the first ring. Actually, it was the third ring, but for Alex, that's as good as a first ring, because she usually couldn't find her phone in her puitcase (my term for her "purse," which was bigger than an FAA-approved carry-on) until after it had stopped ringing and would therefore have to call me back.

"Yeah," I said reflexively. I could hear Alex moving away from the loud, ambient noise that had caused her to shout her greeting.

"Yeah?" she asked at regular volume. She'd gone outside.

"No," I admitted. "I don't know why I said that."

"But you're back home. Alone. Right?" she asked.

I looked at the immaculate, empty apartment and my concerned pets. I inhaled lemony freshness and bleach.

"Yep," I answered. "Very alone."

"I'm sorry, Lady," she said. "There's no way this wasn't gonna suck." I heard her light a cigarette—something she rarely did anymore.

"Yeah, I know." My voice quivered. "But I wasn't prepared for everything feeling so . . . *bad*. It's *really* quiet. And the pets were flipped out." I wiped my dripping eyes and nose with a paper towel from my cleaning bin.

I heard a car horn honk as it sped by Alex.

"I'm sorry, it's a Saturday night, and you're standing on a sidewalk," I said.

"Are you kidding? Like I haven't been waiting for your call. I even had my phone in my pocket," she said proudly.

"You answered right away!" I laughed. "But I'll still be fucked up tomorrow. You can call me then. I just wanted to hear your voice."

"Oh, please, I'm at a political thing that hasn't really started— and the only person I know here besides Jimmy is that jerk-off from last year who hit on me constantly and then, when I finally agreed to go out with him, stood me up."

"Ah yes. Chad," I remembered. "He was . . . special."

"Right? I can be at your place in, like, fifteen."

"Don't leave Jimmy," I insisted.

"Ha! Jimmy has been all over some intern since we got here —he won't even notice I'm gone."

"Are you sure?" I asked lamely. I desperately wanted Alex to come over, which I'm sure she knew.

"Of course. See you soon."

"You're the best," I said, about to hang up. And then, "Wait."

"Yeah, Lady?"

"Where are you?"

I proceeded to give Alex directions to my apartment for the seven-hundredth time. Despite living in the greater Chicagoland area nearly all her life, our city's grid eluded her. Alex was so directionally challenged that her mother gave her a Garmin GPS —pricey at the time—that could detach from her car for on-foot use. Alex, my beloved study in contradictions, could talk like a Valley Girl and get lost in her own apartment, yet could reduce any cocksure Republican to tears and was also a standout at our firm. Without her, I couldn't have gotten through the last few weeks and surely wouldn't make it 'til bedtime.

I HAD TIME to shower, eat "dinner" (crackers and peanut butter), and find more things to launder before Alex finally arrived.

"Sorry, I made a detour," she said, handing me two paper bags. "For these."

Inside appeared to be dried-up weeds and tissue paper. The

scent of patchouli made me sneeze. Alex squished her hair, tossed her puitcase in the corner, and proceeded to make her usual fuss over Frankie and Basil.

It was strange to me that someone else could feel—and look —so normal. Alex had blown out her long, thick, black hair, which maintained that perfect combination of straightness and volume I would never know. She wore more eye makeup than she needed, given that her hair alone made her brown eyes pop, and her usual nude, sparkly lip gloss; huge hoop earrings that only she and JLo could pull off; a flowy, black top; tight black pants; and suede boots. I, of course, wore pajamas.

Alex was the only child of two Albanian immigrants who'd had Alex in their forties. This fact imbued her with a subconscious confidence that she could date around, work, and attend as many political functions as she pleased before settling down when she was good and ready. Alex was perfectly proportioned. Her five-feet-eight-inch height balanced out curves that drove men crazy. My ass looked like a sad, flat pancake next to hers. She almost never wore anything not black after seven at night, and I had seen her without big earrings precisely twice. Her clothes were usually big on top—cowl necks, bell sleeves, scarves —and tailored on the bottom.

Once she extricated herself from the pets, Alex gave me a too-tight hug. Then she put her hands on my shoulders and said, "So. You're back."

"Yes. Whatever's left of me."

She walked me toward the couch while humming along with "I Will Follow." When we sat down, she clapped her hands together and surveyed the apartment like she'd never seen it before.

"Exactly as I expected," she said.

Alex saw her parents' homeopath instead of a regular doctor and believed in things like Ayurveda and biofeedback. Despite my sincere desire to embrace this, it always made me a little nervous.

"We should get started," she said, heading for the bags.

"Started?"

She couldn't hear me over the rustling tissue.

"So I assumed that, given all of Rob's negativity—and, you know, *eww*—the apartment would feel bad. It really doesn't feel like you at all in here, to be honest," Alex said, as though breaking delicate news. "Even despite the cleaning products, which, of course, are very you."

I shrugged.

"I don't know much about Feng Shui," she continued, "but we need to get rid of . . . this." She gestured disapprovingly at the air around her. "So I asked my friend Marie, who's into all this amazing herbal shit, what to do when I broke up with Theo, and she sent me to this place on Belmont. I swear to God, after we smudged, the air was better. You'll love it."

She removed what looked like two miniature, dried-up brooms from the first bag and incense from the second. She let the tissue they were wrapped in fall to the floor. I scooped it up to prevent Basil from eating it. Alex held up the brooms, matches, and incense and waited for my reaction.

"Very cool," I ventured.

Alex was thrilled. "These are sage, and some other things— I'm not sure. This is definitely incense, though, which you should keep burning for twenty-four hours straight."

She handed it to me.

"You already took care of the music." She nodded with approval. Alex was almost as crazy for U2 as I. "OK." She handed me one broom and kept the other. "Now we light these and go around the apartment—with purpose—and let the smoke float through every inch of it."

I didn't love that this ritual involved parading fire through an enclosed space, especially since that enclosed space was my home. But I knew better than to say so.

Alex struck a match and lit the brooms. She was focused and serious, intense and lovely, in the match's temporary glow. Bas and Frankie retreated to their respective beds. (I couldn't blame them.)

Once our brooms began to smolder, Alex gestured for me to follow her and urged me to have faith. We wafted our smoky branches through the kitchen/dining room, hallway, living room, two bedrooms, and two bathrooms. Alex even opened the door to the apartment to smoke the threshold, stairs, and entryway. Next, we lit the incense in the kitchen, since Alex dubbed the kitchen the "heart of a home." I managed not to sneeze. I looked absurd. Alex looked like a Mistress of Ceremonies. Her flowy black top helped; my Cabin Five 1991 flannels did not.

Our work behind us, we returned, satisfied, to the couch to share a bottle of wine. Alex scrounged through my junk drawer, found some votive candles, and lit them. I had to admit that everything did feel better. I hugged Alex and thanked her.

Before long, my mom buzzed.

"Your mom's coming, Lady?" Alex asked.

"Yeah," I said, a little embarrassed. "She agreed to sleep over —just for tonight. And . . . maybe some other nights."

"Perfect," Alex said without judgment.

I opened the door. Mom too came bearing gifts, although hers were in a Pottery Barn bag.

"Hi, Mrs. G.," Alex said, scooting Frankie off her lap to hug my mom.

"Alex! It's so nice to see you. And one of these days, you'll call me Rachel," she said. "You look wonderful."

"Oh, thanks," Alex said, squishing her hair. "I was at a political event."

"You know how proud we are of your activism," Mom said. Alex beamed.

We sat around chatting for a few minutes; Mom declined a glass of wine because, as usual, I only had red. She accepted a nip of Bailey's. "The candles are nice," she said. "And what's that scent?"

"We smudged the apartment. And incensed it. Gave it a spiritual face lift," Alex explained.

"Ah!" Mom surely didn't know what any of this meant. But she breathed in and looked around. "It feels nice in here. It really does."

"So what's in the bag?" Alex asked.

"I almost forgot!" Mom brought it to the couch. "It's a housewarming gift—of sorts." She handed it to me. "Open it."

Inside I found the new duvet cover, pillow shams, and queen sheet set I'd commented on when flipping through the PB catalog in the hospital waiting room. My eyes welled up.

"Ooh!" Alex exclaimed. "Love those." She raised her glass. Mom and I followed suit. "To new beginnings," she said. We all drank to that.

# Twenty-Four

Although, after making some minor changes, the apartment felt comfortable to me, my newfound solitude felt uncomfortable pretty much all of the time. I had never really been alone, and this seemed too much alone at once. "The greatest growth potential lies in uncomfortable moments," Janie kept telling me. Which sounded very much like something Bono might say, so I knew it must be true. But I didn't have to like it.

Nobody in my family felt up to supervising Rob and his movers. So blessed Alex arrived one Saturday morning—before ten o'clock, so you see what a big deal this was to her—and watched two men remove the oversized TV Rob loved so much; the office furniture; Rob's suitcases; and the bankers' boxes into which my saint of a mother had placed the remainder of his toiletries, books, and junk. (In addition to packing up Rob, my mom had also sorted through my photos and memorabilia and discarded everything Rob-related. "It was cathartic," she'd assured me.) When Rob tried to hug Alex upon his arrival, she considered kicking him in the penis, but instead put a hand in his face and watched the moving team wordlessly. Thirty minutes later, she locked the door behind him the second his butt cleared the threshold and called me. I met her at the apartment with tears, hugs, a gift card for a mani/pedi . . . and the locksmith.

All of us breathed easier once Rob's stuff was out and the locks were changed. My dad happily recommended a new TV and the two of us painted the whole apartment in one weekend. Mom went on a tear: She rearranged my furniture, helped me redo the office, suggested new paint colors, and filled my empty picture frames with family, friends, and U2. My mom kept for me only one Baros photo, tucking it in the back of an album. It was a close-up Christos had taken of Penelope and me; we had stolen a moment to laugh while transforming the funeral parlor. In the letter that accompanied the photo, Penelope said we'd always be family. And although I had no idea if or how our relationship would evolve in the future, I knew she was right.

"Guys," I said somewhere in the midst of my parents' toil. "You shouldn't be doing all this."

"We want to," they said in unison. "We need to," my dad added.

I looked into their satisfied faces and remembered my mom's old adage: *You're only as happy as your unhappiest child.* I wiped away my tears of gratitude, nodded, and accepted their help, knowing full well I'd never forget it.

ON OUR NEXT sleepover night, Mom and I ate popcorn in our pajamas in front of a breast augmentation episode of *Dr. 90210.* Dr. Robert Rey was bouncing his patient's new boobies at her first post-op visit and earnestly explaining to the camera how gratifying it was to change people's lives.

"Shall we turn in?" Mom asked as credits rolled. Basil was already snoring in his crate.

"Sure," I said, but didn't move. "Mom, do you think—and I know what you *have* to say, because you're my mom, but also that you're a terrible liar, so I'll know right away whether you mean it."

She swatted my hand and rolled her eyes. "What?"

"Do you really think I'll be OK?"

"Yes," she said. "You're actually doing pretty fucking great already." She beamed with pride; she rarely swore.

"Question the second," I continued. "Do you think I'll find someone? Like, a good, normal man? Before menopause?"

She laughed before adopting a thoughtful expression. "Yes, I do. You're too special to be missed."

"But you have to say that!"

"That doesn't mean it's not true."

I wanted to believe her. She was an open book, and I was comforted by the sureness I saw in her eyes. Still, I wondered. Wasn't everyone taken by now? Even Dr. Rey, who had single-handedly cornered the market on douchebaggery, had a wife and kids.

"But, Mom?" I asked, preventing her once again from going to bed.

"Yes, my love."

"Who will it be?"

She stifled a yawn. "I don't know. Someone from the dog park. A bar, a party, through a friend. Who knows?"

I nodded. But try as I might to picture myself partnered, I couldn't. My future was, for the first time, opaque. I was too early in my recovery to contemplate that the benefits of being single (producing great work; nurturing interests, friendships, and other relationships; breaking molds) merited consideration.

"Or," she continued, "it could be someone who's had his eye on you since childhood. Someone who's been waiting for you."

We brushed, washed, peed, turned out the lights, and got in bed.

"Mom?" I couldn't help but ask.

"Zoe. What." She was practically asleep.

"The only man I know who had a childhood crush on me lives on Sedgwick with his male partner."

"Oh, Zoe," Mom managed before letting out a long, low snore.

# Twenty-Five

Five weeks before my thirtieth birthday, I sat in Janie's club chair.

I'd been living at my apartment for well over a month. People at the office respected my delicate aura and didn't ask about my week-long absence. Working felt good. At first, it was a numb distraction. But soon after the bleeding stopped, I took a deposition that ended up crippling the opposition's case (I even got a "not bad" from Chip after he read the record). The depo marked the first time I'd focused on something besides my pregnancy for more than a couple of minutes in a row.

The nights were harder, but my parents and I had dinner together most weeknights, and I either third-wheeled with them or hung out with friends who knew The Whole Truth on weekends. Of course, I'd told Alex, Maddie, Boone, and Brooke right away. I'd asked Alex to tell Jimmy so I wouldn't have to. A week later, I told Caren, my other best work friend who'd joined Alex's and my class at the firm. Each of them was exceedingly generous, spending ample time with me in person or by phone. Maddie even flew in to spend a weekend eating, drinking, and being irritated together in our sweatpants. My mom told her family, and, as usual, Aunt Steffi stepped up to the plate by plying me with dinners and dirty vodka martinis and doing her damnedest to get me to jog with her in the mornings. Learning firsthand the extent of my friends' and family's kindness was the ultimate silver lining to a very dark cloud. It was also a stark foil: Rob—my own husband—couldn't step outside of himself for a single second, but my support team did so repeatedly. There were extraordinarily good people in the world, and in my life.

"I just want to confirm," Janie said, "that, besides conversations about moving out, which you initiated, you haven't heard from Rob—at *all*?"

"Nope."

"Nothing?" she asked.

"Correct. Zero."

Janie not-talked. Then she said, "Zoe. Are you still sure you want a divorce?"

"YES."

None of my nebulous future or the foggy pictures I saw in my head included Rob.

"I think about the baby constantly," I said. "Sometimes, the loss of her makes it so that I can't breathe, like I've had the wind knocked out of me." My voice broke. "But I never think about Rob. Ever." This was weird, but true.

She nodded. "What's your take on not hearing from him?"

What I said next surprised me. I suppose my subconscious had formulated the answer while my mind was otherwise occupied.

"I think that Rob is forcing me to divorce him. He successfully manipulated me into absolving him of fatherhood, so why wouldn't he do the same with the marriage he obviously doesn't want? Since I technically 'chose' the abortion, he didn't need to take responsibility for it. And if *I* divorce *him*, he doesn't have to take responsibility for that, either. It'll be my choice. He can be the victim. *That's* why he hasn't contacted me."

Janie's eyes widened—so, I'm sure, did mine.

She eventually said, "Sounds right to me."

"Why he sees me as an obligation, when I've been spoon-feeding him for years, I don't know. But he does. He wants out, and he needs me to make it all happen." I squeezed the bridge of my nose and closed my eyes to ward off the headache I felt coming on.

"Zoe, we've had many sessions and talked almost exclusively about your pregnancy. Now that I know you better, I don't worry that you're repressing feelings about Rob. Rather, I think he broke the camel's back. You almost certainly mourned the Rob you thought you knew, or thought he was capable of becoming, as he unraveled over time. Right?"

"Yes."

"Well. If you want a divorce and feel ready to take that on, I'd hate for you to wait any longer." As soon as she uttered these words, Janie's office looked lighter and brighter. I probably did too.

We spent the next several meetings talking about the stigma of divorce and the horrors of revealing mine to people who might feel awkward, judgmental, or anxious about their own marriages. It's particularly difficult to concede defeat at marriage because marriage is one of society's most sacred "achievements." Besides, sixty-year-olds were *divorcées*: They dieted, had eyelifts, took up tennis again, and went on singles' cruises. That was supposed to be a divorcée. Not me.

But I could worry about that later. For now, I focused on the joy of jettisoning Rob for good. Divorce was my only way forward. I smiled for the first time in ages. My life was pathetic, but at least it would be mine alone. I wouldn't have to think about Rob or Arianna ever again. They could just fade away. I bounded out of Janie's office like a kid with a hall pass.

♡

October 11, 2007

Edge: I'm going to be like you. That is, I now realize, the world's craziest sentence. But I am getting divorced, which makes me like you, and millions of other regular people, in one, tiny way. (Now I just need to stumble upon a nice Jewish belly dancer, like you did, to remarry. That would really give us something in common.)

Sadly, I won't be a divorced male rock star who can look to his bandmates, piles of money, and throngs of groupies for solace. The demise of my marriage won't inspire tens of thousands of potential sex partners to vie for my attention. But shedding my toxic shell of a marriage is something — a BIG something — even if I'm just a regular person. Please pass along any advice you may have, and also my number to your single friends. Even if they're older and embarrassingly rich, I could probably manage. XX, Zoe

# Twenty-Six

"Rob, I've done a lot of thinking. I need a divorce."

Even though I wanted this, the words still sounded insane.

"Oh." Rob sniffed. "I understand your decision."

*My decision.*

"I think this can be easy," I said. "We can divvy things up ourselves and just hire a lawyer to record our agreement."

Rob was quiet on the other end of the line.

"I mean, you've got your car. We can split our checking and savings accounts down the middle. You have your 401(k), I have mine, and you're welcome to whatever wedding gifts you'd like. When can you meet to hammer this out?"

"Umm," Rob finally spoke. "Whenever?"

"How's Monday? I can research lawyers by then."

Now Rob cried for real. "Please, Zoe. Let's be amicable. You know I'm in a difficult financial position with my loans—I'm at your mercy to be fair."

I'd prepared myself for this. But gross. How could I so recently have devoted myself to such a sorry shell of a person?

"We'll *both* be fair. And, Rob—you'll be fine."

THE NEXT DAY, I zeroed in on a boring, rumpled, but hopefully competent associate at a decent divorce shop to represent us.

On Monday evening, Rob met me at the apartment after work. My dad waited at the Starbucks on the corner just in case. I'd wanted to meet somewhere neutral, but Rob needed to pick up a few things he'd accidentally left in the hall closet. He didn't seem to notice the many changes I'd made to the place.

He was wise enough to buzz instead of using his building key. I opened the door and went to sit at the kitchen table so I wouldn't have to greet him. As soon as he shuffled in, I pulled out my legal pad. Thankfully, he took the hint and sat down without trying to hug me. My guts churned.

"Do you know what wedding gifts you'd like?" I asked. My voice sounded nasal; I tried clearing my throat. It was then that I realized that Basil—who was seated on my feet with his back against my legs, and had never shown anything close to aggression, ever—was directing a low, rumbling growl at Rob that he would sustain for the entirety of our visit.

"I don't really need any and don't have enough room."

Of course not! *Of course* I would store all the crystal, china, and napkin rings we'd never used and neither of us wanted. Perfect! Maybe I could dump everything on eBay. I passed him a copy of the list I'd prepared.

"Up here is what we talked about on the phone—your car, the bank accounts, etcetera—and down here are the things we'll need to do—change beneficiaries on our insurance policies, take you off the apartment lease, get me off your car insurance. And I suggest we use the same accountant for our taxes this year, just so there's no confusion." I held my breath. I'd sandwiched the thing I cared most about—keeping the apartment—in the middle of my intro.

"Yeah, sure," Rob said. He sounded relieved. "I'm glad we don't have to break the apartment lease. I couldn't afford to stay here alone if you didn't want it."

"Mmm." My throat felt so tight. "Speaking of expensive, I figured I'd keep the pets," I said.

Basil had an astounding number of food allergies, eye and ear issues, and hip dysplasia. I likely didn't need to work the expense angle, given that Basil was growling at Rob as we spoke (which pleased me immensely), Rob's building didn't allow pets, he'd never taken care of them, and FRANKIE WAS MINE FIRST. But I couldn't take any chances.

"Oh—definitely," Rob said to our mutual relief.

"Great." I patted Basil under the table, put my notes aside, and stood up. "Now the lawyer just has to type this up."

Rob stood too. I had no choice but to finally look at him. He appeared the same as he had the last time I'd seen him: pale and wan with circles under his eyes. His temple vein stood at attention, and sweat stains crept out from the armpits of his blue work shirt. He wore the same black pants, belt, and shoes I'd seen him wear a thousand times, the same tortoiseshell glasses and haircut. He smelled of the same deodorant and aftershave. We stood in what had so recently been *our* apartment. And yet he was a stranger. I could barely remember him despite looking right at him.

I didn't know how to navigate our parting. Rob attempted the trick he'd tried at every juncture along our twisted road—to express the "right" emotions with his eyes. But he failed. Whatever emotions he actually felt, if any, were unknowable to me and, I'd have bet, to him. I went to the door. Rob followed me while Basil, still growling, followed him. Although I was dying for Rob to run down the stairs and out of my life forever, he turned around one last time. He reached for my arm which I reflexively pulled away.

"Zoe," he said, in his crying voice, from the threshold. I forced my eyes to meet his. Basil stood between us. "I just—"

I cringed. I didn't know how I'd handle it if he apologized, after all that had happened.

"Rob—"

"I just wanted to say thanks. For lining up the lawyer and . . . stuff."

"No problem," I said quickly.

After what felt like a year, Rob finally stepped toward the stairs. I lunged to close the door behind him. As soon as I did, Basil stopped growling, hugged my legs in a figure-eight, and trotted off to his dog bed as though nothing had happened. I called my dad before feeding Basil an extra-large piece of cheese.


ONE MONTH LATER, Mom and I went to the courthouse I frequented for work, but to a floor I'd never seen. She recoiled when we saw Rob pacing in front of the courtroom. Despite our body language, which screamed, *KEEP THE FUCK AWAY FROM US,* Rob approached and kissed each of us on the cheek. It happened too fast for us to stop him. I thought Mom might actually die, but she just kind of froze and looked nauseated. I *was* nauseated. Rob's kiss felt aggressive. I wanted to punch his stupid glasses off his stupid face for touching us. But I couldn't, so I hummed "Take Me Out To The Ballgame" in my head instead. You know. Like a psycho.

Our benign little lawyer met us five minutes before the judge began her docket. Mom and I sat on the petitioner's side of the gallery, since I was technically the petitioner, and Rob sat across the aisle. I looked at all the older people around me and couldn't believe I was there. As a litigant. In *Divorce Court*. It took extraordinary effort to quash my fight-or-flight response when "Baros versus Baros" was called. Mom squeezed my hand, and I floated, like a specter, out of my body and up to the podium. Yes, we had been separated for the requisite amount of time. Yes, we had irreconcilable differences. No, Mrs. Baros was not currently pregnant. (Seriously—I had to answer that question.) Yes, we understood our agreement. Yes, we wished the court to enter a divorce decree.

"The petition will be granted," the judge said. I exhaled for the first time in minutes. Rob stood stoically at his podium as a single, sickening tear slid down his cheek.

"You have also moved to reassume your maiden name, Zoe Ellen Greene, correct?" she asked.

"Yes please, Your Honor."

"That motion is also granted," the judge said nonchalantly before banging her gavel. The clerk called the next case.

The magnet that had been lodged in my chest, pulling my shoulders and lungs inward, disappeared. I turned to leave the courtroom and motioned for Mom to follow me. I was ready to Forrest Gump it out of the building and all the way to Wisconsin, but Rick the divorce lawyer stopped us in the hallway.

"Here are your copies of the orders." He turned to me.

"You'll need certified copies to change your name on your license and stuff." (I began this process immediately.)

"Thanks, Rick," I said. Mom and I each shook his hand and —finally!—turned to leave.

"Zoe, wait," Rob squeaked.

*God.*

I instinctively pushed my mom behind me with one hand— I could tell she was about to blow—and made a stop sign-gesture with the other. Rob looked astonished and self-righteous.

"Don't," I said. I wasn't prepared to let him feel superior for attempting a "proper good-bye."

Mom could barely keep up with me as I bolted from the building. The crisp air cooled our hot faces; being back among the city's hustle-and-bustle was good. We were rid of him. It was over. We embraced on the corner of Washington and Dearborn before heading to Berghoff's for celebratory bratwursts and beer.

# Twenty-Seven

November 10, 2007

Dear U2: Today is my 30th birthday. Divorce is an inauspicious start to a new decade. I was <u>supposed</u> to be on the precipice of motherhood. Instead, I'm at a very different crossroads, unpregnant and alone. It's hard not to dwell on this. I believe you would admonish me not to get "Stuck in a Moment," which is good advice. I know you wrote that song for your friend Michael Hutchence after he committed suicide, but don't worry — I'm not in that kind of place. Still, I take the song's point: Sometimes, when life threatens to gobble us up, we have to <u>decide</u> to survive. I can't control nearly as much as I once thought I could. But I <u>can</u> control whether I'm going to give up or fight to put my life back together. The latter is what I'm deciding, on this milestone birthday, to do.

I have no idea what 40 will look like (it was

supposed to be me, Rob, a duplex in the city, a 10 year old, a 7 year old, and a second career involving neither electronic discovery nor Chip, in case you were wondering). But it will look better. I will be wiser. I'll do everything I can to make it happier too. XX, Zoe

PS: I'm not afraid of anything in this world/There's nothing you can throw at me/that I haven't already heard/I'm just trying to find a decent melody/A song that I can sing in my own company.

I WAS IN no mood to celebrate my thirtieth traditionally. Instead, I made my first-ever appointment with Rabbi Feldman. I'd joined the temple alone after Rob and I got married. Despite its embrace of interfaith families, Rob wasn't interested in participating, which I respected.

I loved my temple. It emphasized the right things: engagement with life's big questions, community activism, gratitude, family, justice. I started going to High Holy Day services with my mom's parents, and when my grandfather died, about a year before my divorce, I began taking Bubbe to Shabbat services most Friday nights. We'd attended every week since Rob and I separated.

I imagined Rabbi Feldman to be about sixty. He hadn't lost much, if any, hair, which was now an attractive shade of silver. Although of average height, he was long-limbed, which made him appear taller than he was. He wore tan corduroy pants, a dark-green sport coat, and a green-and-gray button-down shirt beneath. Stylish, clear glasses framed his brown eyes. The glasses were too stylish for him to have picked out alone; his wife was an interior designer, and those glasses had her name written all over them. I smiled when I saw him.

"Zoe," he greeted me. After a short hug, he gestured to one of his two guest chairs—I was suddenly conscious of how many things always came in pairs—and sat behind his desk. "What can I do for you?"

I panicked.

"I . . . don't really know," I admitted. His expression changed to one of concern.

"I just turned thirty," I said, "and I've been through some—stuff." I took a deep breath. "I guess I wanted to share it with you."

"Please," he said.

I told him everything.

Maybe I wanted to test my religion: Would Judaism still accept me, despite what I'd done? Or maybe I wanted to test myself: Could I tell my story to a virtual stranger, whom I respected, without falling apart or feeling ashamed? My family had to accept me because they were stuck with me. Janie had to accept me because she was a Women's Loss Person, and I was paying her. This was different.

I *did* cry when I told Rabbi Feldman how much I missed the baby and being pregnant. But I mostly did OK. He offered me Kleenex and shook his head a lot. He even reached across his desk to pat my hand a couple of times.

"Zoe, I'm so sorry," he said when I'd finished.

"Thanks," I shrugged. "I'm not sure why I told you all that."

"It's good to talk to people you trust when navigating life's challenges. And, of course, Jewish history is replete with challenges." He removed his glasses before leaning back in his chair. "You know, I have a daughter your age. She just had her first baby."

"Oh."

Rabbi Feldman pressed his fingertips together while he thought, as a good rabbi should. I waited, wondering if I could withstand whatever he was about to say.

"I've spent a lot of time with Beth lately—I've watched her begin her life as a mother. She's fortunate to enjoy a good marriage to a wonderful man." He paused. "And Beth's a lawyer, like you—she's getting ready to go back to work. Part-time for now."

My chest began to ache. He seemed to sense this.

"Zoe. What I'm trying to say is that having a baby is *terribly* hard. Even for Beth, under ideal circumstances, it's been hard. I was too enmeshed in it, when I had my own children, to really appreciate the difficulty of those early months, and *years*. The entire household gets turned upside down. I thought it was crazy when my wife told me she was taking four weeks' vacation to help Beth, but now . . . I understand."

"I know it's hard," I said. And I believed, then, that I did know—I'd listened to friends' stories about episiotomies from hell, sleep-training, and hormones gone haywire.

"You were facing far less than ideal circumstances. There would have been incredible stress on you during pregnancy, and during those intensely vulnerable months after birth. Experiencing pregnancy, delivery, and newborn-hood while navigating the demise of your marriage would have been quite a lot."

My eyes watered.

"Of course, this doesn't make your loss easier," he continued. "But people do have a robust capacity for recovery. Loss is a part of life."

It's funny, I realized then, how we never fully accept this until loss happens to us.

There was a long pause before Rabbi Feldman said, "I have a thought."

"Oh?"

"Well, you know how we rabbis are always saying that Judaism focuses on temporal moments—not places or things?

"Sure."

Prioritizing time, and how we spend it, over everything else was actually one of my favorite things about Judaism. There are no idols in a synagogue. There is only the Torah—words that inspire us to think, live, and do. Shabbat, the Sabbath, isn't a real day of rest in the Reform tradition. Kids go to soccer practice; adults work, drive, and eat out. But Shabbat is still the holiest holiday, despite its frequency, because it is a placeholder in time. It is a moment to be present and assess.

"One marker in time that Jews have found healing, under all kinds of circumstances, is the mikveh. Have you ever been?"

Hell no. Wasn't the mikveh that weird, naked hot tub? For serious Jews?

"Erm, no. . . ."

"Many people who suffer a loss or face a challenge draw strength and comfort from the mikveh. I'll email you some material to read; you might find the mikveh to be a productive way to mark your birthday."

"Huh," I managed. The rabbi laughed.

"If not, that's perfectly fine. But—food for thought."

"Thank you," I said.

"You're most welcome. And, Zoe—I'm glad you came."

So was I. I had begun to suspect, on occasion, that I might ultimately be OK, but when others seemed unsure, I flooded with self-doubt. So it was edifying that Rabbi Feldman saw a future for me—one I had the right to define, free from Rob— and even suggested a concrete (if strange and naked) step forward. His confidence gave me new life. I hugged him a little too tightly before stepping out into the sunshine.

# Twenty-Eight

According to the link Rabbi Feldman sent:

> "Ritual immersion in a mikveh—a gathering of living water (*mayyim hayyim*)—marks a change in status. People immerse at *Mayyim Hayyim* to celebrate moments of joy, to heal after times of sorrow or illness, or to commemorate transitions and changes."[15]

This sounded pretty apt. Still, I worried I'd feel like a poser going to the mikveh, seeing as how I couldn't even read Hebrew. I didn't know what to expect and was hesitant to step out of my comfort zone because I'd already shattered it. So I ran the idea by Brooke, whose sister had been to the mikveh after a miscarriage. "Do it," she said without equivocation. The fact that the only mikveh in the entire Chicagoland area was nearby sealed the deal.

It was a beautiful day when I went to the mikveh. November is a wildcard in Chicago: It can be crisp, fall perfection . . . or arctic. I lucked out with sunshine and fifty-five degrees. Jitters set in as I found the mikveh entrance and knocked on the door.

---

[15] https://www.mayyimhayyim.org/what-to-expect/

"Shalom," said the solemn lady behind the desk. She looked like a middle-aged version of Tzeitel from *Fiddler on the Roof*. "Are you Zoe?"

"Uh, shalom. And yes, that's me," I whispered. I handed her a check—those waters don't heat themselves!—and signed a register.

Rabbi Feldman arrived a moment later. He grasped my hands warmly. "After you enter the bath, I will read from behind a wall through which we'll be able to hear, but not see, each other," he said. "And I'll be here when you finish."[16]

Tzeitel ushered me into a locker room of sorts and pointed to instructions framed by the sink.

"Please go through each step on this list—everything you'll need is on the vanity. When you're ready, or if you have questions, just knock on that door." She left the room.

I turned in a circle, feeling woefully out of place. Then I read the pre-mikveh to-do list and considered bolting. Boone was right: "Judaism is OCD," he'd argued on many occasions. "*This* can't touch *that*. You can eat *this* only if it's been exactly so long since you ate *that*. And if this *does* touch that, bury the dish! THINK ABOUT IT." I was to remove nail polish, clean my belly button, floss, swab my ears, clean each nostril, and even wipe my ass with a "cleansing towelette." All I'd known in advance was that I couldn't be menstruating, a rule I'd previously thought only applied to swimming near sharks.

By the time I'd prepped, I was weirded out and agitated. *Why had no one warned me?* But people were waiting, so I put on the shabby temple robe and knocked on Tzeitel's door.

---

[16] I fervently hoped that this rabbi-won't-be-able-to-see-me-naked bit was true. My therapy budget was not unlimited.

She was serious, quiet, and barely met my eyes; she clearly wanted to fade into the background so I would feel alone in the water that lay before me. The room was attractive and plain. The mikveh did indeed look like an oversized hot tub, complete with a handrail and steps. The room's walls consisted of light-colored wood slats connected by opaque, beige fabric. Tzeitel turned her back and instructed me to disrobe and descend the seven steps into the water. I did, feeling exposed and vulnerable. The water was pleasantly warm. I nervously awaited instruction.

"When you're ready," Tzeitel said, "completely immerse your body and hair in the water. The rabbi will speak, you'll immerse again, the rabbi will speak again, and you'll immerse for a third time. I'll let you know when you're finished. And take your time."

I cleared my throat. "OK."

I could sense Rabbi Feldman on the other side of the wall on my left. I closed my eyes, inhaled, and concentrated on dunking thoroughly, because I knew that Tzeitel would make me do everything again if I didn't submerge every hair on my head.[17] The water hummed. I turned my face toward the surface, emerged, and took a deep breath of humid air.

"The first immersion is complete," Tzeitel announced.

"*Baruch ata adonai eloheinu melech ha-olam asher kid-shanu b'mitzvo-tav v'tzi-vanu al ha-tevilah,*" Rabbi Feldman read in a strong, clear voice.[18]

At first, the sound of Rabbi Feldman's familiar, confident

---

17 Maybe Boone was right.

18 Translation: "Blessed are You, Adonai, Ruler of the Universe, Who has sanctified us with the mitzvot and commanded us concerning immersion." http://www.mayyimhayyim.org/Using-the-Mikveh/Immersion-in-the-Mikveh

cadence comforted me—I was not alone. But as I stood with my eyes closed, I became less aware of him, Tzeitel, or my surroundings. I was laid bare. All that came into the waters were my emotional, physical, and spiritual selves. They were a muddle, but they were there, and they were all that was there. The boundary between the water and my body blurred. I inhaled again before plunging back beneath the surface.

"The second immersion is complete," Tzeitel said.

"As water creates change, so women are often the agents of change. May we be witnesses today, not only to this transition, but also to women as change-makers in our larger world. As water cleanses the spirit, may Zoe be filled with renewal, energy, power, and direction. May the One who blessed our foremothers—Sarah, Rebecca, Rachel, and Leah—bless, heal, and renew Zoe. May the Healer give her support and strength, patience of spirit, and courage. Amen."[19]

The rabbi's words and the currents that my second immersion had created swirled around me. I stole an extra moment to stand and breathe. The power and responsibility that came with being a woman, and profound respect for all that women sustain, literally washed over me. I thought of my mom's miscarriages, a colleague's stillbirth, my abortion, and the millions of similar survivors who preceded, coexisted with, and would follow me. For my final immersion, I dove down the deepest and ascended the hardest.

"The third immersion is complete."

"Zoe, please repeat after me," the rabbi said. "*Baruch ata Adonai . . . Eloheinu melekh ha-olam . . . she-asani bat chorin . . .*

---

[19] Adapted from ceremony by Rabbi Geela Rayzel Raphael, posted to http://www.ritualwell.org/ritual/abortion-ritual.

Blessed are You . . . our Infinite Power . . . Majesty of the universe . . . Who has given me my freedom . . . Amen."[20]

He then added, "*Baruch ata adonai eloheinu melech ha-olam she-heche-yanu, ve-ki-y'manu, ve-higi-yanu la-z'man ha-zeh.* Blessed are You, Source of all Life, Who has kept us alive and sustained us, and enabled us to reach this day. Amen."[21]

I didn't realize that I was still standing in the water with my eyes closed until Tzeitel instructed me to dry off and re-robe. She then ushered me back to the locker room. I caught my reflection in the mirror. My hair was straight and heavy with water; my skin was pink. Breath coursed through my extremities. I dressed hurriedly. My hand hovered above the doorknob to the lobby when I decided to stay still. I had my own mini-Shabbat.

I closed my eyes. I realized that a monumental emotional fatigue had taken root deep inside of me. It was well-worn, like a backpack that gradually assumes the contours of your shoulders, the curve of your spine. The residue of prolonged physical fatigue persisted but had begun to lift. The loss that for so many weeks was too huge to bear or contain had begun to contract—it now left room for the rest of me. I wasn't "empty." I was fuller for having known the beginnings of pregnancy. My body's power was no longer abstract.

Uncertainty shrouded me, which I hated. Some are born to be wild—I was born to know what's what. But for one brief, magical moment, I accepted my uncharted future and was grateful for it. I was still a friend, daughter, sister, lawyer, klutz, and U2 fan—but now a wiser, more textured version of those things.

---

[20] Adapted from ceremony by Rabbi Burt Jacobson.

[21] http://www.mayyimhayyim.org/Using-the-Mikveh/Immersion-in-the-Mikveh

Sexuality and motherhood, though dormant, remained. I *was*, actually, still whole.

♡

November 19, 2007

Gentlemen: I was wondering about All That You Can't Leave Behind. I believe you can leave some things behind. But maybe it's better to keep some things — even painful things. To examine them, shrink them, or store them in a different place, but to keep them with us always. Love, Zoe

PS: See the Bedouin Fires at night/See the oil fields at first light/And see the bird with a leaf in her mouth/After the flood all the colors came out. . .

.

# Twenty-Nine

Although it may lack the profundity of the mikveh, I did get another impactful thirtieth birthday gift: a one-year membership to the East Bank Club from my parents. Janie suggested I exercise regularly for a host of reasons related to my precarious mental state.

The East Bank Club—or EBC, as it is known in my family—is not a regular gym. It's a Chicago institution. The huge, almost entirely indoor fitness facility was built in No Man's Land in the early '80s, but No Man's Land soon became prime real estate in the heart of River North. (Smart investors.)

The beautiful, Botoxed, and connected belong to the EBC. Political bigwigs breakfast there. *Barack Obama hoops there!* Jesse Jackson was a fixture on the most visible stair-stepper in the cardio room for years. Oprah's Stedman was an early morning regular (and breathtakingly handsome). There are lots of regular people too: My mom went in the mornings, my dad after work, and they both exercised and brunched at the EBC most Saturdays and Sundays. I dined with them a few times during Rob's busy seasons when we were married, and more often since our split. In addition to hundreds of cardio, weight machines, and classes, a Pilates studio, spin studio, basketball courts, indoor and outdoor pools, tennis courts, a driving range, tracks, a rock-climbing wall, and a dozen personal trainers and physical therapists, the EBC also boasts an on-site dry cleaner, ATMs, banquet rooms, bar, casual restaurant, formal restaurant, juice bar, take-away shop, coffee bar, full-service salon and spa, a barber. . . . It's a veritable city—kind of like the Vatican, but with non-Catholics and vaginas. I considered moving in.

I had previously been one of the snots who'd scoffed at the EBC's see-and-be-seeners. But when I got my membership, I fell quickly and shamelessly in love. I became fast-addicted to the endorphins, the Blue Crunch smoothie, and Inga Liepins, my mom's former-Soviet-Olympic-fencer-turned-trainer.

I'd sworn to Aunt Steffi that I'd never run with her "in the mornings" because her "mornings" were my middles of the night. But, when she learned of my EBC membership, she insisted that I start treadmill training "just in case" I wanted to do a race with her. Emphasis on *start*: For my first jalk (jog/walk), Steffi said to jog for one minute, walk for four, and repeat four times. Eventually, she assured me, I'd be able to jog five, walk one, and repeat ten times. When I could theoretically do *that* without dying, I was supposed to "work on speed." Hilarious.

"We'll run the Soldier Field Ten-Miler together in the spring, Girlie. You'll see," she'd said when I reluctantly agreed to try this nonsense.

Aunt Steffi was, of course, delusional—I'd never "run" anything, much less a race—but training would be good for me, and Steffi was so kind that I owed it to her to try. (A few mornings, when I was feeling gangster, we *did* jalk together—"late," at six o'clock.)

Soon after joining the club, I worked up the nerve to stand

next to a treadmill. After asking one of the ever-cheerful EBC staffers to show me how it worked, I completed my first jalk without myocardial infarction. I listened to U2 and let my eyes dart between the room's five TV screens. I drank complimentary, optimally cooled water and wiped my sweaty brow on optimally sized towels. I bought my first Blue Crunch smoothie. I showered using only free toiletries. I did it all again the next day. And I liked it.

My strength training sessions with Inga began similarly. Mom practically beat me into making my first appointment —"You can't start running without getting into shape!"—and although I wanted to run, not jalk, from Inga's five-feet-ten-inch, utterly fatless frame, it took me sixty seconds to like her. She had a knack for pushing me far enough to be sore, but not far enough to be dead. I took her Tuesday morning seven thirty slot. Two months later, I added Fridays. She was that good.

My body did change. I stood taller, felt sturdier, had more energy, and didn't think as often about sucking in my stomach. My arms assumed age-appropriate muscle tone, and I developed calves. The EBC opened up a new world to me—one in which people unapologetically invested in themselves. I began to appreciate the mind–body connection, and how nurturing one can help nurture the other. I also decided that jalking and Inga-ing justified more deep-dish and wine, so, yay. But the best part of this generous gift, I told my parents when I renewed the membership on the eve of my thirty-*first* birthday, was that, at the EBC, my head was empty but for U2 and the sound of my own beating heart.

# Thirty

At two o'clock the day before Thanksgiving, someone knocked on my office door. My body tensed; if Chip wanted to Scrooge me with a last-minute Thanksgiving assignment, I'd quit.

"Come in?" I ventured.

"Hey!" my friend Jonathan Sealy said, carrying a glass of ice and a Diet Coke can. "What's up?"

He sat down, popped his Coke, and poured. I could tell he'd given up on working too. I'd accomplished nothing except cleaning my office and worrying about not billing time.

"Hey," I said, relieved.

Jonathan had become like a big brother to me when I was a summer associate. Despite being an accomplished attorney on the verge of partnership, he was humble, fun, and always made time to dish. Jonathan's wife, Jessa, had become a friend of mine too. I'd told them The Whole Truth, and on D-Day, they'd sent me a bouquet with a card that said, "Congrats on the first day of the rest of your life!" They got it.

Jonathan smiled awkwardly and waited for the foam to go down in his cup.

"What's new?" I raised my eyebrow.

"OK, so," he began, turning around to make sure the door was closed. "I don't know if you're ready, but if you are—Jess and I want to set you up!"

He beamed; I froze. My thoughts and breath all slowed to a near-halt. I finally spoke.

"Like, what? On a date?"

He laughed. "Yeah!"

*Shit shit shit.* Lately, I'd been daydreaming about dating—probably because I'd become clinically horny—but the thought of actually going on one brought to mind Plan B (eternal celibacy). Because dating would be *complicated.* For instance: Let's say I actually *did* have a good date with an available, heterosexual guy. When should I sleep with him? What if my vagina was deformed, but I never knew it, because Rob's penis was *also* deformed, and I'd blown my one-in-ten-trillion-chance of finding a partner with whom intercourse was physically possible? Were single women my age all in better shape? Did they have six-packs? Because, if I were deserted on an island with only Inga, state-of-the-art-workout equipment, and small mollusks to eat, I *still* wouldn't have a six-pack. But these questions assumed that someone would want to sleep with me. It might all be for naught and I would JUST DIE ALONE.

Janie was constantly trying to disabuse me of the notion that all the nice guys my age were taken. But a desolate future kept flashing before my eyes: me on my couch, wearing an L.L. Bean, Victorian-style flannel nightgown, flanked by cats, watching PBS, eating ice cream, and cursing the latest agency to deem me unfit to adopt. I cleared my throat to interrupt the cacophony in my head.

"A date," I repeated.

Jonathan cocked his head to the side, likely wondering whether something was deeply wrong with me.

"Yeah. I mean, no big deal *whatsoever*, but we thought it'd be good for you."

I started to sweat.

I debated shouting, *I'M NOT READY!*, running out the door, and picking up a tub of ice cream and a second cat on my way home. But, involuntarily, another word came out: "Cool."

Jonathan grinned. "Awesome!"

My mouth went dry.

"So this guy, Tyler, is *totally* legit. He dated a friend of Jessa's friend, Claire, for a year, and she has nothing but good things to say about him. So we know he's had at least one normal relationship. He's Jewish, grew up in Evanston, went to IU (Indiana). Lives on the Gold Coast. Does something corporate. Tight with his family, and Claire's friend—God, what is her name. Dana? No, not Dana. But—"

"Jon. Do you guys like him?"

"Oh, one-hundred percent!" Jonathan paused. "I mean, we only see him a couple times a year. At parties. With IU people. But we have no reservations whatsoever."

"OK," I said, wiping my palms on my jeans.

"Great!" Jonathan said, slapping his knee before standing up to go. "This is *great*."

"Wait," I said.

"Yeah?"

"How does this work?"

He laughed. "We'll give him your number."

I nodded, embarrassed. "Hey, thanks. And happy Thanksgiving."

"You too," he said.

Holy shit. Maybe I was about to have my first date *ever*.

# Thirty-One

The Saturday after Thanksgiving—which we'd celebrated, as always, by consuming many starches—Aunt Steffi pulled up to my apartment at ten after ten. She was supposed to be there at ten o'clock, technically, but Aunt Steffi's ten-minutes-late was like most people's fifteen-minutes-early. She must have been really excited.

Aunt Steffi had been a later-in-life surprise to my grandparents, so she was still in her forties, but with an energy younger than that. Her most committed relationship had been the business she'd built from the ground up, until she tripped over Uncle Jake's foot at the old Emilio's restaurant when she was thirty-nine. They married a couple of years later and were child-free.

She did her first fashion intervention when I began practicing law. "You should dress the part," Aunt Steffi had said. She changed tacks when Rob and I split: "Do it for *yourself.*" I'd been meaning to accept her offer to go to her favorite boutique—the source of nearly every item in her closet[22]—for

_____

22 Urban legend has it that a frustrated Aunt Steffi spontaneously walked into Joie de Vivre in the late '80s. She came face-to-face with Sandy—the tiny, frizzy-haired, Diet Coke-slinging, gum-chomping, hyper-yet-endearing owner with a great eye for both fashion and fit—and said, "No one can dress me. Can you?" Three hours later, Aunt Steffi flagged a cab to ferry her and an entirely new wardrobe the two blocks to her apartment. I had vague ambitions for a similar experience.

months, but the mission became urgent when Alex tried to find a date outfit in *my* closet (in case Jonathan's guy ever called) and found nothing. We ended up donating 90 percent of my stuff; the other 10 percent I kept only so that I wouldn't have to shop naked.

This far into therapy, I knew that I'd spent all my energy and time on Rob, but being confronted with the fact that I hadn't purchased anything other than L.L. Bean online in years—and that it all looked dated and dumpy—was sobering. Even Alex looked a little shell-shocked. *How could I have let things get so bad?* I cornered Aunt Steffi at Thanksgiving dinner. "THANK GOD, ZOE, FINALLY!!!" she exclaimed. (Steffi talks like she emails: heavily punctuated.) She was on the case, and I was glad.

"Hi, Girlie!" she said as I opened her passenger door.

"Hi! I brought ammunition." I put two skim lattes in her cup holders.

"You know me well." She smiled, picking up her coffee as soon as I put it down.

When we found a parking space on Halsted almost directly in front of the store, we agreed that this was a good omen.

"Welcome to the beginning of the rest of your *li-ife*!!" Aunt Steffi teased as we ascended the store's steps. "Just remember, Sandy's. . . ." She made bug eyes and jazz hands.

"I'm sure it'll be great."

We entered. The store was empty—Sandy told Aunt Steffi we should come first thing to beat the rush—and tiny. Most of the inventory was stored in back. Joie wasn't designed for browsers; it was designed for Sandy. And here she was.

"Oh, my god, OK, this is Zoe."

Sandy walked briskly toward us as she talked—brown, spiral

curls flew in all directions from her little head. She was five feet tall and weighed about as much as one average woman's thigh. Her skin was a leathery shade of tan; a tapestry of freckles covered her chest. Despite having the energy of a kindergartner, I pegged Sandy at sixtyish. She wore a navy, tank-cut bodysuit, gray, wide-legged linen pants, and silver gladiator sandals on her tiny, pedicured feet. A skinny silver belt and yards of silver jewelry completed the look. Anyone else would have frozen to death, but the kinetic energy that Sandy emitted made *me* warm. And even though Sandy clanked when she walked, her outfit was, somehow, perfect. I was speechless. She didn't notice because she was already working.

"In here honey," Sandy said, zooming over to one of the store's two dressing rooms. "And STRIP! No. Let me look at you first."

I hadn't yet adapted to Sandy's dizzying pace. I finally sputtered, "Nice to meet you!"

"You too, Honey. You know I've only known your aunt a million years. So I've been hearing about you for nine-hundred-ninety-nine-thousand-nine-hundred-ninety-nine years and three-hundred-sixty-four days. Now turn, Zoe, please."

I froze. She made a twirling motion with her index finger.

"Oh." I turned awkwardly in a circle, feeling nearly as exposed as I had in the mikveh.

"Fab. You. *Lissssssss!*" Sandy marched away, snapping her gum as she went. She began snatching things off the racks the way frogs snatch flies. She never looked at a label because she knew the precise location of each piece in her store. "OK OK OK, *now* strip," she shouted over her shoulder.

I couldn't make out what Sandy was saying, but she talked

the whole time it took me to undress. "Now it is time to. Have. Some. *FUN!*" she concluded before whipping open my curtain without warning. I stood, like an idiot, in my skivvies and wool socks. Sandy's hair and the mound of clothing she carried pushed past me. She hung things around my dressing room with warp speed.

"Start with the dresses," she instructed, "and come out to the three-way after each one. That's my only rule. Everything goes on. No matter what. Start with this." She thrust a short, swingy, sleeveless black halter dress at me. "*Uch*, so fun," she added mostly to herself as she whipped the curtain closed behind her.

I heard the *pop* of a soda can while I stared at the dress in my hands. I didn't do dresses. The only one I'd worn since prom was my wedding dress. And how could she possibly know my size? *I didn't even know my size.* I'd been working within L.L. Bean online's S/M/L rubric for so long. Whatever. I pulled the dress over my head. It was *way* too short. I could tell by the breeze on my thighs.

"Umm," I started to protest.

Sandy alighted to my room. "Love it. Fabulous. Next!" she declared to her Diet Coke.

I looked at Aunt Steffi, who stood half-naked in the other dressing room.

"SO ADORABLE!!!" She clapped with approval.

*Are these people fucking blind?* I was about to call the whole experiment off when I caught my reflection in the mirror.

Wait.

The dress was cute, modern, and age-appropriate. It *wasn't* too tight or too short. It hit just above my knees! The fabric was so light, and I was so unaccustomed to not having pants on, that

I only *felt* naked. This dress would be in the Papal Visit section of Britney Spears' closet.

Sandy stopped short of Aunt Steffi's dressing room with twelve garments draped over each arm wearing an expression that insisted, *Next!*

"Real quick," I said. "What would I wear this to?"

Sandy stared at me. "Hon. You're single, yes?"

"Er, yeah."

"So you wear it on a date, you dress it down with tights in the winter, a wrap, a blazer, no-tights-no-wrap-no-blazer in the summer, chunky-funky gold jewelry, spiky heels, a big bag, wear it to dinner. Fancier jewelry, smaller-bag-satin-sandals to a wedding. It's a black dress. You wear it everywhere."

Aunt Steffi nodded in agreement.

"I'm actually just divorced," I said for no reason at all. "So I haven't been on a date . . . lately."

Sandy softened. "Hon. You have a darling figure. You're single now. Time to have some fun. So no more of those baggy clothes you came in here with. OK?"

"I'LL TAKE IT!" I declared, and slung the dress onto the counter.

"Chop-chop honey," Sandy ordered as she hung even more clothes. "We've got work to do."


THIRTY-EIGHT HUNDRED dollars, three hours, two trips to the parking meter, three date-night outfits, one complete professional wardrobe, one leather satchel, one clutch, two belts (astonishing—the last belt I'd worn came with Esprit jeans in junior high), one leather jacket, and some chunky-funky jewelry later,

Aunt Steffi and I emerged. We squinted into the sunlight, dumped our bags in the trunk, and rubbed the bag-handle marks on our forearms.

"OK, that *is* a lot of money." Aunt Steffi began rationalizing my binge by the time she hit the ignition. "But you will wear this stuff FOREVER!!! Like, look. This top?" she nodded to her shirt. "It's Joie. From *ten* years ago. A DECADE!!!"

"Steff, it's OK." I laughed. "I was prepared for this. I get my bonus soon." I'd still spend the next week anxiously debating whether to return everything. But Steffi didn't need to know that.

"Oy," Aunt Steffi groaned as she pulled away from the curb. "*Do not* tell your parents we pre-spent your bonus on clothes."

"I'm super happy with everything. Especially the dress you got me." (While I peed, Aunt Steffi had surreptitiously bought the dress I'd rejected in order to bring my total under $4,000.) "Thank you. For everything."

"Oy," she repeated. "But I *swear* you'll feel like a new person. And you haven't spent a nickel on *you* in years."

"True."

Aunt Steffi pulled up to my building. "I hope you're really OK with this. And for the love of God, do NOT tell your parents!!!!"

I hugged her. "Steff. Seriously. *Thank you.*"

I meant it. For the first time, I'd brought home gobs of new things, on which I'd blown an irresponsible fortune, just for *me*. This qualified as a profoundly uncomfortable moment; I suspected that Janie would applaud the growth potential within it.

# Thirty-Two

After I'd laid the last of my Joie purchases on the bed for Alex to review, my phone beeped. I had a voicemail from an unfamiliar local number.

"Oh, my God, Al. It's him." Heat leapt to my cheeks. I would need to get these date-sweats under control before actually going on one.

Alex looked up from the clutch she was examining. "Play it on speaker."

Hi, Zoe, this is Tyler Lewin. Jonathan Sealy gave me your number and I was hoping we could meet. Give me a call when you can—I look forward to talking with you. Have a great one.

I turned to Alex for her reaction.

"Normal voice, straightforward . . . I like it." She nodded.

"I DO TOO!" I squealed.

Alex laughed. "Let's look at your stuff. You can call him back when I leave."

She effortlessly turned her attention back to my new wares. "Ooh, I love this." Alex picked up the first dress I'd tried on. "Everything here is so versatile."

I said nothing and twisted my hands. I hadn't heard her on account of being in the early stages of a cardiac event.

"Zo. Hello?" Alex sighed, cleared some space on the bed, and sat us down. "So, dating," she said kindly, choosing her words with care. "It turns us all into idiots. Even Tyler probably felt impaired while leaving that perfectly benign message."

I didn't believe her but smiled anyway.

"And I think it's great that you're excited about this first date. I mean, shit, you deserve it, and I hope he's awesome." I waited for the *but* I sensed was coming.

"But—and I'm *really* not trying to be a dream-killer, because first-date excitement is one of the best parts—but—" She hesitated.

"Go ahead," I said.

"Well, most first dates are . . . anticlimactic."

"Oh."

"Like, you go out, and the guy's not a psycho or anything—he's just not *memorable*. So *I* think the worst part about dating, that no one warns you about, isn't the debacles. Those we can laugh about. It's the blah dates . . . and there are lots of them." She winced.

"Oh," I repeated.

Alex guarded her heart zealously. In daring times, she dated. In vulnerable times, such as after a big breakup, she avoided the enterprise altogether. She'd confided in me her dating trials and tribulations throughout our friendship. I'd wiped away her tears. It really was tough out there. I began to feel deflated.

"This is not to say," Alex continued in her closing-argument voice, "that you won't have amazing first dates. Because you *will*. The kind where you end up making out in a cab. That'll happen! But I guess I just want you to. . . ."

"Manage expectations," I finished.

"*Exactly*." She sighed. "I feel like an asshole for bursting your first-date-outfit-picking bubble, but you're my best friend, and I want to prepare you in case Tyler isn't, you know, The One."

"Thanks for always looking out for me," I said. Alex smiled with relief. "But *of course* I'm not expecting Tyler to be The One. That would be *ridiculous*."

Obviously, I *absolutely* hoped Tyler would be The One.[23] Karma dictated that the smithereens would be balanced out by meeting The One immediately. *Zoe,* my friends would say. *Isn't it weird to think, sitting here with your hot husband and gorgeous twins, that only a year ago, you hadn't even* met *Tyler? And felt like total dogshit?! Isn't that CRAZY?!* In my head, I'd already toasted Jonathan and Jessa at the rehearsal dinner and asked their kids to be flower girls at the wedding. And suspected I'd be unknowingly pregnant at the wedding, by happy accident and fate. But Alex couldn't possibly understand this, so I kept it to myself.

"Duh," Alex said, interrupting my reverie.

"Hmm?"

"We can't pick a date outfit. We don't know where you're going!"

"Big duh," I agreed.

We took pictures of each piece. I emailed them to Alex so that she could advise as needed.

---

[23] By this point in therapy, I had begun to contemplate the idea that women could be happy single. But this realization was still nascent.

"WE'RE HAVING DINNER on Saturday," I announced as soon as Alex arrived at work Monday morning.

I closed the door behind me; Alex's hair was still wet from the shower, and she wore her I've-only-had-half-a-coffee-Monday face.

"OK," she said breathlessly as she put down her Starbucks and doffed her coat. She sat and took a swig. "Dinner. Saturday," she repeated, waking up before my eyes. "*Oh!*"

"Oh? Why *oh*?"

"I'm just surprised is all. Most people just do drinks on a weeknight for first dates. But Jonathan's guy is going all out."

Alex saw my face fall.

"Which I think is really nice! Old school. Chivalrous."

"Yeah?"

"Totally. Where to?"

"Gibsons. Eight o'clock."

I willed Alex not to mention how much we hated overpriced steakhouses like Gibsons; they were touristy, crowded, and expensive, and Gibsons was located in the congested Viagra Triangle, where old bald dudes and twenty-something girls went to meet. I wanted to focus on the fact that Tyler had selected a restaurant, made a reservation, and emailed me the confirmation six days in advance. Rob had never planned anything for us. And I figured I had twelve hours to experience actual joy before fixating on what to wear, how to put on makeup, do my hair, and act like I'd been on a Saturday night dinner date before.

"Aww," Alex said, reading my mind. "He wants to make a good impression. I love it."

I smiled gratefully. "At your leisure, please consult my virtual closet. You are not only my second shrink but also my stylist."

"Of course."

"I love you and couldn't live without you. You know that, right?" I asked.

"The feeling is mutual, Lady. One hundred percent."

♡

November 26, 2007

Loves: You know that my life's been on a steady trajectory down the toilet. So tell me honestly: Do you think I'm ready to date? Or that I'll be eaten alive?

Has any of you even dated? Not Bono and Larry, who met their Forevers as children. And Edge, when you met Morleigh, you were a rock star, she was a hot belly dancer, you were on tour together . . . I don't see awkward early-stage dinners for you. Adam, we know that you and your giant penis don't have to worry about dating. Must be nice — all of you.

I have begun working out, purchased modern clothing

from a brick-and-mortar store, and started blow-drying my hair almost every day. So this seems as good a time as any. Right? Wish me luck! XX, Zoe

# Thirty-Three

S aturday arrived.

By three o'clock, I was at DEFCON PSYCHO: I'd already spent $25 on a wildly optimistic bikini wax, $35 (plus tip) on a blow-out, and $98.50 on concealer, tinted moisturizer, bronzer, and blush. The clothes Alex had chosen were already laid out on the bed: sleeveless white blouse, fitted black blazer, skinny jeans, and the black, patent-leather high heels my mom had insisted I buy when she took me shopping for dating panties. (I wore those too.) I'd borrowed Alex's thinnest silver hoop earrings and stacked three silver rings on my right middle finger.

At six o'clock, I called Caren. She was an experienced dater who adhered to strict dating rules, and I had a question.

"Hey," she answered. "Are you getting ready?"

"I'm about to." I wasn't about to divulge that I'd spent *all day* getting ready. "Can I ask you something?"

"Of course. I date by committee too."

This was a surprise: Caren always seemed to operate with such enviable confidence that I couldn't imagine her asking for dating advice.

"OK. I swear I don't usually drink alone, but I'm a little nervous—"

"One shot of whiskey or half a glass of wine," Caren said.

"Thank you."

"Thirty minutes before the date. A must."

"That's what I thought!" I was delighted. "Thanks, Care."

"Sure. And can I give you some unsolicited advice?"

"Please."

She paused. "You know that I am a one-hundred-percent feminist and believe in absolute free choice."

"Of course."

"But your dirty martinis. . . ."

"Oh!" I said, perking up. "Gibsons *does* have excellent dirties."

"So, actually, I'd skip the martini. On a first date."

"Really?"

Now, I *had* always been a lightweight. I couldn't drive after one martini, and on the rare occasion when, surrounded by my nearest and dearest, I drank two, I'd be completely shitfaced.

"Just to be clear, you should have *something*. I would never suggest that *anyone* go on a first date sober," Caren snorted. "But, even though this guy is a friend of Jonathan's, he *is* a stranger to you, so. . . ."

"Ah. I get it. This guy could be an axe murderer with human body parts in his freezer. So I should have my wits about me. Makes total sense."

"Also," Caren added, "please text when you're home safe. That's always a good idea."

"So smart! And sweet of you. I will."

Despite my fear of being dismembered and frozen, I saw no way around taking half a shot of whiskey. By the time I got into the cab, I had stopped sweating. (It helped that it was thirty degrees outside.)

Unable to manage my nervous energy, I called Jimmy.

"HI, DOLL!" he screamed from somewhere in Boystown. It was nice of him to pick up. And inconsiderate of me to spew my anxiety into the receiver while he was otherwise engaged.

"Jimmy, I am now one of those assholes who *totally* misrepresents herself to dates. Because I *look* like I know how to round-brush my hair and put on a five-minute face, but I don't, and I'm wearing clothes selected by others."

"CONFIDENCE!" he commanded. The Boystown din was deafening. "YOU'RE GORGEOUS!" he screamed.

"Aww, Jimmy." I rolled my eyes into the phone.

He laughed his wonderful laugh. I laughed back. The cabbie glanced at me in his rearview mirror.

"ZOE, *TEE-RUST* ME, THIS GUY WILL BE FALLING ALL OVER HIMSELF IF HE HAS ANY SENSE."

"Thanks. I'm a dork. Go—love you."

"FROZEN, WITH SALT!" I heard him say to someone unknown. "LOVE YOU TOO! CALL ME AFTER!"

As we joined the line of cabs trying to get to the restaurant, tiny droplets of perspiration dotted my hairline.

"I'll get out here," I said quickly, thrusting money at the driver. "Thanks."

Warm waves of nausea swelled in my gut. I stood stock still on the freezing sidewalk for a few seconds before panicking. I couldn't just walk in there! It was only 7:55, *and* I realized I hadn't a clue what Tyler looked like. His company website had no pictures, and Alex confirmed that Tyler wasn't on Facebook. OMG. I decided to walk around the block—slowly—in my too-tall heels. I stopped to read a text from Alex: No dirties, u get 2 drunk. Luv u, call me. XO.

Then my phone rang. "Hi," I answered. Tyler called just as I was rounding the last corner. I could tell from the background noise that he was inside the restaurant. I checked my watch: 8:02. Love it! A grown man who's not afraid to be punctual. My first date was off to a promising start.

"HELLO?" Tyler shouted. I cleared my throat, closed my other ear with my gloved hand, and said loudly, "Hi, Tyler, can you hear me? And—"

"HI, ZOE!"

"Tyler, I'm almost there—and I'm wearing a red wool coat."

"OH, OK, GREAT. I'M IN GRAY PANTS AND A NAVY SWEATER... HEADING TO THE DOOR."

"SEE YOU IN A SEC!" I shouted back.

I paused for a last breath of cold air before shuffling through the revolving door. My heartbeat momentarily drowned out the chaos of Gibsons on a Saturday night. I quickly spotted a short, bald man wearing gray pants and a navy sweater. He waved and walked toward me. I smiled at him, but my heart sank: We would not be raising twins together in a townhouse in the city. Shame overwhelmed me—about my runaway imagination, the bikini wax, and most of all, judging another human being so harshly on appearance alone. I rearranged my face as speedily as I could and bent down to hug Tyler. I silently cursed the too-tall heels.

"Zoe, it's so nice to meet you," he said effortlessly. His eyes darted quickly up and down my body—he probably wasn't even aware he'd done it. Our knee-jerk physical assessments of each other marked my official entry into the dating world. It's strange that one can live right next to this world in blissful ignorance of its existence.

Tyler helped me out of my coat—how sweet, and foreign, this felt—and smiled wide. I relaxed. I didn't know what I was doing and wasn't attracted to Tyler, but this "totally legit," normal-message-leaving male found me attractive and Gibsonsworthy. Me! Zoe Greene, of llbean.com infamy.

We were shown to a noisy table as soon as Tyler checked our coats.

"Please," he said, gesturing for me to lead the way. Tyler waited for me to sit first. I found each of these everyday dating rituals both exciting and nerve-racking: I was starved for attention, but while Tyler had clearly been on many, many first dates, I was approximately ten years late to the party. We smiled at each other.

"So. How was your Thanksgiving?" Tyler asked loudly across the table. I was about to answer when our waitress was upon us.

"Good evening and welcome to Gibsons. I'm Jenny," she said.

"Hi," I smiled.

Tyler looked up politely, but said nothing.

"May I offer you something to drink?" Jenny asked.

"Zoe?" Tyler gestured to me.

Right. Even short people can have body-part freezers, so I ordered a nice, safe glass of cabernet.

"Lovely," Jenny nodded. "And for you, sir?" I winced at the formal address—Jenny had at least five years on Tyler. And two inches.

"I know this is nuts." Tyler laughed before extracting something from his wallet. "But I like a particular cocktail that's well known in London, but not here. Your bartender will have the ingredients. Here are the instructions."

Tyler handed Jenny what looked like a business card. I saw the words "dash," "parts," and "twist" embossed on thick card stock before Jenny slipped the recipe into her pocket. *Now* perspiration trickled into my armpits. I peeled my elbows from my sides in a futile attempt to air things out.

Jenny expertly gathered herself. "Shouldn't be a problem." She turned to leave. I was startled by the sound of my own voice calling her back.

"Umm. Sorry. But do you have bleu cheese olives?"

*What the FUCK?*

"We do," she nodded.

"Oh good," I said mostly to myself. "Then may I please have a dirty vodka martini? Instead of the cab?"

"Of course."

*Jenny, I swear I didn't know about the drink card*, I tried to tell her with my eyes. *I don't even know this guy!* But she was gone. I may have seen her stifle a tiny grin before she left me alone with Sir Piccadilly Circus.

"I swear I'm not an ass," Tyler said. He looked appropriately chagrinned. Maybe the drink thing was a singular quirk. "I just love this cocktail that this *fantastic* bartender made for me in London. And whenever I used to order it in the States, there'd be a ten-minute back-and-forth between the waitress, bartender, and me, so. . . ."

"This is easier," I finished, wanting very much to leave the topic.

"Right." He leaned forward and rested his forearms on the table. "I'm thirty-five." He shrugged. "I like what I like."

"Sure," I said, trying to convince us both that bringing embossed recipe cards to a restaurant was, you know, whatevs. We stared at each other for one second too long; I reached for something to say. "Were you in London recently?"

"Last year. It was my parents' fortieth wedding anniversary, so my sisters, their husbands, and I all went with them to London and Paris."

"That sounds amazing," I said sincerely.

"It was. My folks really did it up. I think they were kinda like, how many opportunities are there to take a family vacation, when all the kids"—he made air quotes—"are grown-ups, with busy schedules and whatnot?"

"Not many," I agreed.

OK, the guy loves his family, and they're functional enough to vacation together. Gotta applaud that. I started thinking about how Rob's *dys*functional family made us miserable, and how we couldn't make a functional family of our own. And that maybe I was broken. Or that dates would *think* I was broken, once they knew The Whole Truth, whether I was or not. I snapped myself out of it by asking Tyler all the questions I could think of about his trip—where they went, what they saw, his favorite attractions—which kept him talking, and freed me to recover, until Jenny returned with our drinks. Thankfully, Tyler didn't say a word about whatever was in his glass—he just tasted it and nodded. Jenny and I were relieved. She took our order: crab claws to start (his idea), white fish for me, filet for him. My armpits were 90 percent dry when Tyler continued.

"In London we stayed at the *Dorchester*."

He waited for my reaction. Christ. I knew that the Dorchester was a swanky hotel because it was oft mentioned in *Us Weekly*. Jen and Brad used to stay there before Angelina killed America's dream. But I was curious to hear Tyler's answer, so I asked, "What's the Dorchester?" and took a delicious sip of 'tini.

"Oh," Tyler smiled in an *isn't-she-cute?* kind of way. "It's a five-star hotel."

"Cool," I said casually. He may as well know upfront that I wasn't impressed by five-star hotels (or Gibsons). He positioned his slender little hands daintily around his cocktail glass.

"I know this may sound snobby, but I'm at a point in life where I'll really only stay in nice hotels."

Forgetting my manners, I said nothing and cocked an eyebrow. He didn't notice.

"I mean, I work really hard. So if I'm gonna take a trip, I'm gonna take a *trip.*"

I toyed briefly with telling him that, when I was twenty-two, I'd backpacked through Europe, stayed in hostels, bathed sporadically, and loved every minute of it, and that I'd take that kind of freedom and spontaneity over a stuffy hotel any day. But it didn't seem worth it. So I just said, "Totally."

Tyler smiled, satisfied.

The rest of the dinner was harmless. The food was good, the martini exceptional, and all of it overpriced. We talked easily—about the suburbs, Tyler's desire to relocate to Lincoln Park, and our jobs. We each offered a funny story—his about accidentally wearing a pair of his sister's flats to his first summer internship, mine about falling down the firm library's staircase—and shot the shit without incident. I didn't resist when Tyler insisted that we each have a post-cocktail glass of wine. He graciously refused my offer to split the bill. I thanked him profusely and hated that this exercise cost him $200. By the time we left Gibsons, I was unscathed but exhausted, moderately drunk, and knew I'd never see Tyler again.

Once outside, I veered away from the logjam of people, cars, and taxis by the front door, figuring I'd catch a cab past the fray. Tyler walked with me. The open space and cool air were heaven.

"Are you walking me home?" he joked (I think). I smiled and pulled my coat to my chin to thwart the wind.

"The great thing about living on the Gold Coast is that you really can walk everywhere. I'll grab a cab up there," I said, pointing north.

Tyler put his hands up as if to say, *allow me*. Like a less-dashing, more-Jewish Zorro, he sped ahead to flag down a car. Suddenly, I was desperate to be home—alone—before the muck of emotions simmering inside of me boiled over.

"Here's one!" I said, stepping into the street. I opened the taxi door before turning around to thank my first-ever first date. "Thanks so much again for the great dinner," I said. "I had *a lot* of fun." Why I added the insincere superlatives, which sounded annoying even to me, I couldn't tell you.

"Me too," Tyler said. "You're welcome."

He smiled. The poor guy was oblivious to the hot mess lurking beneath my blow-out and five-minute face. No matter. I was literally one step away from going home. But when I turned toward the cab, I felt Tyler close behind me. Did he want a hug? I looked just in time to see his puckered lips coming toward me. Instinctively, I whipped my face in the other direction. His mouth may have grazed my cheek and definitely my ear before eating a wad of my flat-ironed hair.

I loved the cabbie for creeping away from the curb before I'd actually shut the door. I wondered how many women he'd rescued from bad dates. "Thank you," I said before giving him my address.

I texted Jimmy, Alex, and Caren because I didn't have the energy to call them. I climbed gratefully into my L.L. Bean flannel PJs,[24] de-spackled my face, threw on my coat, and stuffed my feet into the L.L. Bean winter boots[25] everyone thought were Uggs (suckers) to walk Basil. I read one and a half pages of *Us*, briefly grieved the Dorchester's now-lost appeal, and fell deeply to sleep.

BY DINNERTIME SUNDAY, I'd resolved never to tell anyone if I went on another date; I'd spent the entire day recounting Tylergate, from bikini wax to curbside-cheeking, to approximately one thousand people. I took Boone and Brooke's call that evening despite my hoarse voice. Rob and I had attended their beautiful New York wedding eighteen months after ours.

"What if he calls you again?" Boone echoed. He had me on speaker.

"Did you not hear me? I flicked my hair into his mouth before jumping into a moving taxi. He won't call," I said.

"Uh-oh," I thought I heard Brooke mutter.

"Hold on," Boone said. "Brooke wants to talk to you."

"Hey," she said.

"Hey. You may have gathered that my single life hasn't started well."

"It's not so bad," she said, laughing. "But. Umm. I just want you to be prepared . . . he might call you."

"No," I assured her. "You probably didn't hear that I cheeked him. So."

---

[24] I'M NOT SORRY.

[25] SAME.

"I did hear," she said to my surprise. "But he tried to kiss you, which means he likes you. And I'm sure you were nice to him—"

"Of course I was *nice* to him. But I left in a getaway car!" Geez.

"Yes, but he's a man. And men sometimes. . . ."

"We don't get it," Boone interjected.

"Exactly. You went out last night, right?" Brooke persisted.

"Yep."

"Did you contact him today?"

"No! I mean, of course, this morning, I texted a thank-you. It's a really expensive place," I explained.

"He'll call Tuesday or Wednesday," Brooke decreed.

"Jesus. This is a thirty-five-year-old man we're talking about. He's not gonna wait three days to—he won't call."

"OK, OK," Brooke relented. "Just—if he *does* call, what will you say?"

"Huh," I considered. Who could resist obsessing about a situation that would undoubtedly never arise? "I have no idea."

"DON'T GO OUT WITH HIM AGAIN!" Boone yelled from somewhere in the apartment.

"I agree with that," Brooke said.

"Was he really *that* bad?" I wondered aloud. "He was chivalrous, his family sounds functional. Snobby, perhaps, but—"

"Zoe, please don't take this the wrong way. But is there any chance you'll sleep with him?" Brooke asked.

"Oh, good God, no. Definitely, *for sure* not. Uh-uh. No way."

"That's what I thought," Brooke said.

"ME TOO," Boone yelled again.

"Why are you so far away from the phone?" I asked him. "If it's because you're on the toilet, don't say anything—I don't wanna know."

"THIS IS ME NOT SAYING ANYTHING."

"Adam!" Brooke barked.

"Boone! Eww. You're a grown man. You shouldn't still be like this."

"LIKE WHAT?"

I had spent entire study sessions outside Boone's bathroom door while he was on the crapper. When we first met, I'd assumed that he had Crohn's or similar; turns out it was just a grave lack of boundaries.

"Anyway," I continued. "If he calls—which he won't—couldn't we just be friends?"

"*No*," Brooke said at the same time Boone yelled, "NO!"

"Adam," Brooke said. "Stop yelling. Zoe, he doesn't want a friend. He's looking for someone to sleep with, fall in love with, and marry."

"WHAT SHE SAID," Boone agreed. "YOU HAVE FRIENDS. HE HAS FRIENDS. NEITHER OF YOU NEEDS ANOTHER FRIEND."

"Wow. That's cold," I said.

"Wouldn't it be colder to let him take you out for another expensive dinner when you're not interested?" Brooke countered.

She had a point.

"MEMORIZE THESE WORDS," Boone admonished. I could not believe I was taking advice from a man who conducted half his life from the toilet.

"I. Didn't. Feel. A. Connection," Brooke recited.

"THAT'S WHAT *I* WAS GONNA SAY!"

"Ouch," I mumbled.

"I mean, you can obviously thank him for the invitation and tell him you're flattered first," Brooke clarified.

"BUT HE DOESN'T WANNA BUY YOU ANOTHER DINNER IF YOU'RE NEVER GONNA TOUCH HIS PEEN. YOU CAN'T CHEEK A PEEN, ZOE." He paused. "ACTUALLY, YOU *CAN* CHEEK A PEEN—I CAN THINK OF SEVERAL SCENARIOS IN WHICH THAT COULD HAPPEN."

"Adam," Brooke said. "Get it together."

"Yeah, OK, thanks, guys. This has been . . . helpful. I love you both, but I've gotta go."

I hung up, even more agitated, if possible, than I'd been in that cab.

# Thirty-Four

On Wednesday evening, I felt empowered. Chip had been on a particularly bad tear at work—he buzzed me twelve times, often summoning me back to his office right after I'd left. The twelfth time Chip demanded I return because he'd changed his mind again, I found him angrily clipping his toenails over his desk. Without looking up, he barked that the case law I'd sent him was "all wrong!" When I replied that I'd sent him exactly what he'd asked me for two visits ago, and pointed out that he hadn't given me enough time to research what he'd changed his mind about, he snapped, "WELL THEN, WHAT ARE YOU DOING IN HERE? PLEASE GET WORKING ON WHAT I CHANGED MY MIND ABOUT."

One year earlier, I would have kept my mouth shut and stayed late to do a bunch of work I knew Chip would forget about by the time I finished. And fretted about it endlessly. But the shit smithereens had depleted my tolerance. (So had the toenails.)

"Chip," I said. "I'm here because you buzzed me. Which you've done twelve times today."

I might get fired, but hey. Why not add that to the list of Awesome Things That Happened To Zoe In 2007? He looked up, speechless. I waited. To my astonishment, his lips relaxed into a smile before opening with laughter.

"I'm an asshole!" he chuckled.

Now *I* was speechless.

"I am!" he continued. "You kids think I don't know this, but I do."

"Oh," I said dumbly.

He sighed, swept his toenail clippings into the trash, and crossed his bare feet on his desk.

"Let's call it a day and regroup tomorrow." He chuckled again. "I've obviously worked myself into a frenzy. I think I'd best go play tennis."

"So—stop?" I asked.

"Yes!" He logged off of his computer. "Goodnight, dear."

I bristled at being called "dear," but had the good sense not to look a gift horse in the mouth. I finished a couple of things at my desk, recorded my time, and left the office at 5:45. By 6:20, Basil had been walked, my face washed, and sweatpants donned. Then I saw Tyler's voicemail on my phone.

> Hi, Zoe! It's Tyler. I was hoping we could find a time to go out again. Call me so we can mesh schedules. Talk soon. Bye!

I spent the rest of the evening in a panic and Thursday in an obsessive loop. I crept down the back staircase to jalk things out at the EBC[26], but it barely helped. When I climbed into my new RAV-4 (grocery shopping had gotten too cumbersome to do on

---

[26] Four minutes jogging, two minutes walking, repeated seven times, zero heart attacks.

foot), I knew that my nervous system would implode if I put off returning Tyler's call any longer. I inserted my earpiece. *Thanks so much,* I'd say. *I'm flattered, but I just didn't feel a connection.* I'd close with, *But thanks again for a great evening.* I practiced this twice in my head as I backed out of my parking space. At the red light at Grand, I took a deep breath and dialed. My hands became so slick with sweat that it took effort to steer.

Four rings. After each one, I silently prayed for his voice-mail.

Hey, this is Tyler. Leave me a message.

*Yesssssssssss.*

"Beep."

*Shit! What was I supposed to say again?*

My lungs overfilled. I couldn't breathe. That I could (and should) simply hang up didn't occur to me. I'd lost my mind.

"Hi, Tyler, this is Zoe," I said in a hysterical tenor I didn't recognize. "Thank you so much for your message—and—and for dinner Friday. I mean, ha! Saturday."

*Nice.*

"Umm. I had soooooo much fun, I really did—". I paused to choke on my own saliva. "Yikes, excuse me! *ACH-HEM.* My divorce"—*What? OMG why are you talking about your divorce?* —"just recently went through. So...."

*Oh my fucking God.*

"... uh," I continued. "I'm just not ready to date. I'm really sorry. You're great and I hope we can be friends. Maybe we'll run into each other? And if you were serious about moving to Lincoln Park, I think I know one. A realtor, I mean. I think I know a realtor. I *know* I know a realtor. So . . . yeah. Thank you so much for dinner. *So much.* And—umm. Bye!"

I hung up and dropped the phone on the passenger seat. I was drenched and, apparently, hopeless.

THE NEXT DAY, after reluctantly recounting my heinous voice-mail to Janie, I confided in her several things: (1) my humiliation; (2) my exhaustion; and (3) my unrelenting fear that the longer I delayed dating—which I planned on doing, because I hated everything about my first date—the lower the scant number of available men would dwindle, leaving me alone. Forever.

She handled my first two beefs deftly. The third took her a minute. "Let's take a scientific approach," Janie suggested.

"OK."

"What percentage of your friends are in committed relationships?"

I thought. "Almost all of them. Ninety percent."

"And your colleagues?"

Hmm. Even Chip was married. "Same," I admitted.

"The majority of adults want partners and children," Janie said. "Of course, there are exceptions—and thank goodness, because our society depends upon them in so many ways. But, for the majority, the search is biological."

I liked this. Darwin with the save! I was still certain that, like the Hotel California, I would never be able to *leave* my worry. But maybe I could check out of it for a minute.

"If most people are wired to partner and procreate, though, doesn't that support my concern that they've all done that by now?"

Janie shook her head. "You're so *young*. The data doesn't support your concern. At your age, it's highly unlikely that all the men with whom you'd be compatible are partnered. And life doesn't move in a straight line. Things happen. Look at you: You're a catch, and you're single."

Calling someone who'd left that diarrhea of a voicemail "a catch" was a stretch.

"Zoe. Give yourself some time to regroup. You'll get back out there when you're ready, and really open to receiving someone."

I winced. Was "out there" some kind of purgatory? And what if I were *never* ready? Janie seemed to believe that I would be a spouse and parent. But I couldn't tell if that's just because I was paying her.

# Thirty-Five

The holidays sucked nuts.

The distraction Tylergate provided had worn off by Christmas.[27] I had *planned* on being OK. Zach slept over on Christmas Eve so my apartment didn't feel empty and we could stay up late watching *National Lampoon's Christmas Vacation* and *A Christmas Story* without apology. That was great. Then we were to head to Mom and Dad's to open gifts Christmas morning. *La di da*, I thought, as I waited for Zach to finish his Christmas morning dump. I opened my laptop to troll for sales. That's when I found this spam message:

Ho ho ho! Take 25% off Premiere Pregnancy Photography! Book your shoot today!

I deleted the message immediately but couldn't un-see it. I slammed my laptop shut and vowed to be *JUST FINE*. But compartmentalization isn't my strong suit. It didn't take long for me to plunge down the drain I'd apparently been circling. I sleep-

---

[27] My Jewish family rocks an impressive, secular Christmas: decorations, ornaments, cookies, stockings, carols, presents, and a party at my parents' every Christmas night. Between Thanksgiving and New Year's, the Greenes present like olive-skinned WASPS.

walked through the day at my parents'. I needed to go home to shower and dress for dinner but couldn't bear being in my empty apartment alone. I was supposed to waddle up the stairs laden with baby blankets and toys, not new running shoes and a case of wine. But Basil couldn't hold it forever so, eventually, I went home.

The unusual quiet didn't help. My building was always empty on Christmas; most of its young residents went to older relatives' homes. My favorite parking spot right in front was open, but what used to elicit joy now only highlighted my solitude. After walking Bas, to avoid being still, I decided to go for a jalk. It was unusually warm and would kill just the right amount of time.

I laced up my new shoes and clipped on my iPod. I jalked faster than usual all the way through the zoo, to the lake, and back, but couldn't outrun my panic—about premature menopause, flannel nightgowns, cats, ice cream, and eternal solitude. Sorrow, loneliness, self-pity, and neuroses trumped whatever endorphins I'd generated. So I was already teetering on the edge when I approached my apartment and saw Tina Sorensen, her adorable husband, Matt, and their adorable baby, Maggie. All three of them were blond, blue-eyed, rosy-cheeked, and barfishly gorgeous. And Tina was fucking pregnant. Again. Already.

Tina was three years younger than I and lived on the south side of the building. She was one of those girls who looked airbrushed during pregnancy. When I bumped into her at the coffee shop down the street—God, just over a year ago—she wore a fashionable cowl-necked sweater that I'm sure wasn't even maternity over leggings and boots. Her bump was so perfect that I wanted to pat it, but the rest of her body appeared unaffected by growing a human. When I asked how long she had to go, I figured at least three months, but instead she'd chirped, "I'm due Tuesday!" *Vomit.*

I made Tina and Matt brownies when they brought Maggie home. When I asked Tina—who apparently left whatever weight she'd gained at the hospital—how she was holding up, she said, "I'm sooooo tired! Mags is up like every hour!" Then she looked at the sweet babe in her arms and added, "But she's so amazing that I don't mind."

I was so jealous that I told myself Tina was full of shit. That, actually, her vagina and perineum were irreparably shredded, and she was in the throes of postpartum depression—she just wouldn't admit it in order to make regular women, like me, feel small. But she was lit from within. I knew she was for real.

Maggie must've been only fourteen or fifteen months old, and Tina looked five or six months along with number two. Maybe she was due Tuesday! Tina and Matt held hands as Maggie, in a cozy winter coverall and bunny hat, bounced contentedly against Matt's back in the baby carrier. They held steaming to-go cups in their free hands.

While this perfect little family reveled in a stolen Christmas moment, I began to unravel.

I shook and got dizzy. My stomach cramped, and I had to pee. Tears popped from my eyes. Every time I thought I'd finally shed the last one, they regenerated. Like Gremlins. I *had* to get inside before the Sorensens saw me. Now in full nut-job mode, I frantically isolated my building key and plunged it into the door.

I flew up the stairs, burst into my apartment, locked the

door behind me, peed, and sobbed—right there on the toilet. I eventually hauled myself to the couch without bothering to pull up my pants. Bas and Frankie paced nervously. What kind of lowly person had I become? A bitter, selfish one who finds misery in other people's happiness. That's who. I filled the bathtub with hot water and submerged, hoping to burn out my tears—and my thoughts.

It didn't work. I would never be pregnant again. I would never have a baby in my belly and another in my arms—much less in my adorable husband's baby carrier. I *knew* it. The Sorensens and I might as well have been living on different planets. I lay in the tub until the water turned cold. It was dark, and I was late for Christmas dinner.

MY REWARD FOR surviving Christmas? Enduring New Year's! I decided to spend the holiday in hiding at my parents'.

"Hi, Sweetie!" my mom shouted from the second floor as I let myself in. Bas raced upstairs to see her before I could get his coat off. "Hi, Zo!" Dad echoed. They were listening to Motown—Dad snapped his fingers to "Heard It Through the Grapevine"—when it occurred to me that they were the cutest people alive. I found them in the kitchen working on appetizers. Mom unwrapped a wedge of cheese while Dad emptied a container of olives into a bowl.

"Hi, guys," I said and kissed them both. Basil was glued to my mom's leg, his eyes locked in on the cheese. He didn't notice when I shimmied him out of his coat. "Yum," I said after stealing an olive. Zach had headed to New York to celebrate New Year's with friends before school resumed.

After Dad added salami and pita crisps to the cheese board, he stood still for two seconds—about as long as he can tolerate—before asking, "How about some champagne?"

"Lovely idea," Mom said. She found three flutes while Dad pulled the champagne from the fridge. I surveyed these people who were still saving my life. They looked much better than they had a few months earlier. Thank God. I was out more now, between yoga, jalking, temple, and enjoying my girlfriends in a way I guiltily realized I hadn't when I was married—and Mom didn't spend the night anymore. Their healing sprang from mine. *You're only as happy as your unhappiest child.* I hated that I'd hurt my parents and that I needed them so. But I did and was profoundly grateful for them.

Dad popped the cork. I couldn't help but smile. We passed glasses around and held them up for a toast.

"This year has been rough[28]," Dad began. "Life can be relentless, and it certainly has felt that way lately.[29] But Zoe, your grace and fortitude, frankly, amaze me." My eyes watered. He turned to my mom. "And Rachel?" he said softly, "We did good too." She mouthed a kiss. "To a new year," he finished.

"Cheers," said Mom.

"Cheers," I said softly. "I'll never, ever be able to thank you enough."

If the phone hadn't rung, I probably would have lost it. I answered upon seeing Zach's number on the screen.

"Hey, Dude," I said.

"Zodo! What are you doing there?"

---

[28] "Rough" is Steve Greene for "tremendous clusterfuck."

[29] One of my dad's best friends died of leukemia a month before my abortion. So yeah, 2007 was "rough," and could fuck itself.

"I'm spending the holiday in hiding," I explained. Zach knew how brutal Christmas had been for me.

"Maybe you shouldn't," he ventured. "Maybe you should do something fun. Celebrate the year *ending*."

"Oh, I'm celebrating that for sure," I said. "Just in my own way. What are you up to?"

"Obviously, I'm going to a weird party in Brooklyn."

"Obviously."

"Hey, love ya," he said.

"Ditto. Happy New Year, Zachy. Have fun."

"I will."

"And be careful!" my mom shouted.

I passed the phone to my parents.


MOM AND DAD soon headed to the suburbs for their friends' annual NYE party, which famously ended at precisely 12:01 a.m. They invited me to join them, but I recognized that celebrating New Year's in the burbs with a bunch of baby boomers was not good for my morale. My plan was to sleep at my parents' so that I could hide out but still have company on New Year's morning.

So I popped *Tenenbaums* into the DVD player, pulled Basil onto my lap, and turned up the volume to drown out his snoring. By the time A.B.'s monologue ended, I felt great: The holiday had come, it would go, I was comfy as could be and had a glass of wine and a slice of pizza nearby. No sooner had I shimmied down to the sweet spot on the chaise than my phone rang. I had planned not to pick up, but it was my friend Anna, and I realized I'd forgotten to return her Christmas voicemail.

"Hey," I said.

"Hi, Doe." She was so congested I'd never have recognized her voice.

"Oh, no! You sound terrible."

"Ugh, I know. Hode on." She honked into a tissue. "Cwoe's pwee-schoo had all kinds of stuff. I got stwep, wiff ear 'fections. Started Z-Pak today."

"Aw, that sucks! Sorry, Anna Banana."

"I'm not contagious anymow," she honked again. "But not weddy to go out."

"No kidding."

"Cwiff is out, tho. I'm home wiff Cwo."

"What can I bring you?" I asked.

"Oh, nuffing. I'b fibe." She sounded pathetic.

"Don't be absurd," I said, standing up. I looked longingly at the dogs, none of whom flinched when I transferred them from lap to couch. "Have you eaten today?"

"Well, not weally," she admitted. "I mean, soup. En tea. Ech. I'm tho thick of soup en tea."

"I'll bring leftovers," I volunteered. "I made pizza."

"Doe, are you show?" She sneezed. "You totally don't have to. Weally I just wanted to say Happy New Yiss."

"I'm at my parents." I told her. "Be over in two." Anna lived in the next complex.

I grabbed the pizza from the fridge, bundled up, and trudged down the block through the snow. Anna was a friend from high school. We'd lost touch until we discovered that she was one year ahead of me in law school and rekindled our friendship there. She was already married by then—she and Cliff started dating their freshman year of college—and I was visiting Rob a lot on the weekends, but we always enjoyed grabbing a beer when we could. Anna practiced at a sweatshop firm, and despite going "part-time" when Chloe was born, she billed sixty hours most weeks. Nowadays, we saw each other either at professional events or around the neighborhood. I knocked quietly so as not to wake Chloe who, it just occurred to me, must have been nearly three.

"Oh, my God," I said when Anna opened the door. Her bright red nose matched the rims of her eyes.

"Fanks a wot," she snuffled before waving me inside.

"No," I tried to recover. "I just feel bad—"

"I'll be otay. Just not weally sweeping cuz Cwo's been up en down at night."

After unbundling, I handed her the pizza. "I'll only stay a few minutes. You should go to bed after you eat."

"No, no," she said as she transferred the pizza to a dry frying pan. (Chicagoans know how to properly reheat pizza.) "Have a gwass of wine wiff me. It's depwessing being awone on New Year's." She stiffened. "I'b sorry, Doe. I just meant it's depwessing to be home *sick* on New Year's." I'd told Anna I'd divorced but not exactly why.

"No worries," I assured her. "I'm alone tonight by choice." I sat on a kitchen stool. "Are you sure you want to drink with that cold? And meds?"

"Definitwee!" she said as she reached for a bottle. I laughed. "It's just one gwass."

We moved to the couch while she ate and we drank. It was nice to catch up; I always enjoyed our conversations. Anna was clearly starved for human interaction after being stuck on the sick ward for a week. Happily for me, our discussion gravitated toward things other than a) New Year's or b) Rob. But the more worn out Anna got, the more serious she became. I was about to send her to bed when she looked straight at me.

"Are you OK, Doe? I mean, *weally* OK?"

Frick.

"Yeah," I shrugged. "Generally speaking."

"You're so *bwave*," she shook her head.

"Umm. . . ."

"No, *sewiouswee*."

"Nah," I said and stood up. "Easy to be brave when you don't have a choice."

"But you're *awone*," she said gravely. "And you're doing *gweat*."

I shifted my weight and regretted letting Anna drink. "Eh, you should've seen me on Christmas, bawling my eyes out."

"Of cowse you get sad," she continued, still seated. "But dat-uhl pass, en even now, you, wike, do stuff. Wowk. Dwinks wiff gurlfwends. Yoga. Duh gym." She paused. "You wook uh-*mazeen*, by duh way."

"Thanks. . . ."

"And anyone could wok froo the doh!" Her sick eyes got big. "You never know who you'll half sex wiff next!"

"This is not a good thing, Anna. . . ."

"It's exciting! Duh best sex of yoh life is ahead of you!"

Ah. I'd heard the *there's-something-to-be-said-for-not-limit-ing-yourself-to-one-lover* spiel from other married girlfriends too.

"Theoretically. But I think my vagina has taken early retirement."

"Doe?" Anna looked serious and ignored my joke.

"Yeah?"

"Cwiff en I haven't had sex since Cwo was bohn."

*Fuck.* I sat back down.

"I haven't tode anyone that," she said, bringing her hand to her mouth.

"I won't say a word," I promised. I was shocked. I put my arm around her when she started to cry.

"We don't hate each other," she explained. "We don't *fight*. We just don't . . . fink that way anymoh. Oh weally talk about, wike, *weal* fings." She sighed heavily. "We're wike woommates."

"Have you shared any of this with Cliff?" I asked after debating what, if anything, to say.

"No. We do our fing—watch TV, go out wiff fwends, talk about wowk, the house, Cwo. Reguluh stuff. And dat's *it*."

Anna stared into the distance, a little drunk, a little stoned on cold meds, and utterly exhausted. I took our glasses and her plate to the sink. She didn't notice.

"Anna," I said gently. "What do you need for bed?"

"Oh," she said, refocusing her eyes. "Just anuh-ver Sudafed and some watuh." She forced the corners of her mouth into a smile. I got her Sudafed and water, clicked off the hallway light, and turned down her bed while she washed up. When she emerged from the bathroom, Anna's eyelids struggled to stay open. I hugged her, told her I was sure everything would work itself out, and left. I was stunned as I shuffled home. I'd always thought that Anna and Cliff had exactly what I wanted. That they didn't felt like a loss. Janie had helped me realize that it was better to live alone than with a toxic partner. But Anna revealed a rather terrifying middle ground. The further I progressed into singledom, the more nuanced it all became.

♡

December 31, 2007

Dear U2: I like that YOUR New Year's Day is about mass murder and despair. Fuck "Auld Lang Syne." A friend whose marriage I envied just told me it's a sham. Is there any hope for any of us? Happy Fucking New Year. Love, Zoe

# PART FOUR

# Dating in the Internet Era

# Thirty-Six

During the pallid, pasty bleakness of February, I marched into Janie's office with unusual purpose.

"I'm getting on J-Date," I announced.

"Great!" she said. "What's changed?"

What had *really* changed was that eight months of celibacy was enough—I had begun to resent the vibrator Alex gave me for my thirtieth. I figured that now was as good a time as any to end my born-again virginity: I wore at least one form of makeup most days. I had proper dating panties and new clothes. I was confident that my heart was "healthy enough for sex," as they say in the ED commercials. And I NEEDED TO GET LAID.

But I said, "I just think I'm ready."

"Wonderful."

"I mean, I have no idea how Internet dating works. But if Boone did it, so can I."

"Of course," Janie agreed.

I started to worry while Janie not-talked. "I've got one over-arching concern, though. Besides the whole I'll-never-find-any-one thing."

"Which is?"

"Well, if I *do* find someone . . . how will I know he won't be another disaster?"

Janie nodded.

"I chose wrong the first time—*very* wrong, with someone I'd known forever. So what if I go through all this effort—write the stupid profile, choose a photo, message people, all that crap —just to screw up again?"

"Ah. . . ." Janie twisted a hair elastic between her thumb and pointer finger while she thought. "You briefly considered breaking up with Rob for a spell at Yale. Why?"

"Well, there was John Hutton. . . ."

"Right. But why do you think you were suddenly open to the idea of dating someone else?"

I shrugged. "I don't know. I mean, Rob was having such a hard time adjusting to law school and kind of expected me to fix it all, even though I was far away . . . I guess that got exhausting."

"So this was during your first year?"

"Right."

"You must have been surrounded by really talented, interesting people."

"Yeah. The awesomest bunch of nerds ever. So freaking smart." I laughed. "To this day, I'm convinced I got in by accident."

"Why would you say that? You had an almost perfect college grade point and helped build a charter school."

"No, you don't understand—my LSAT score was *so* low for Yale. And the charter school is my mom's friend's."

"But she chose *you* to help her."

"I guess, but—"

"Yale Law School doesn't admit students by mistake. And your mom's friend was not obligated to hire you." Janie stared at me. I didn't know why. "Zoe," she continued. "Have you ever heard of 'imposter syndrome'?"

"Uh, no?"

"It's extremely common among women. Especially successful women."

"OK...."

"I've noticed, during our time together, that you describe each of your accomplishments as an 'accident.' But that's a lot of accidents."

"Huh?"

"And you *still* talk about your appearance as if you're in middle school—I know all about your orthodonture, feeling too tall, having frizzy hair, and not feeling noticed by boys."

I felt smaller than I'd ever felt in Janie's office.

"You seem genuinely not to have noticed the physical transformation you've undergone since I've known you. Zoe, I can see biceps through your sweater."

I looked at my sleeves. I could see biceps through my sweater, too! YAY!

Janie not-talked.

"Oh, my God," I finally said. "After what felt like a real disaster with Parker Owens, Rob was the first boy to notice me."

Janie raised an eyebrow.

"I stayed with Rob through college, and didn't break up with him in law school because I thought I couldn't do better."

"I just wonder," Janie said, "when you were finally on your own, surrounded by intriguing people, and even experienced mutual attraction with a classmate, if you didn't break up with Rob not only because you felt obligated to him, but also because you simply lacked confidence."

I swallowed. "I didn't have the guts to fully immerse myself at that school," I nearly whispered.

"Why not?"

"Because I wasn't smart enough. I *thought* I wasn't smart enough." I looked at my lap. "Do you know, it wasn't until I got my final transcript in the mail, and looked at the legend on the back, that I realized I'd *just* missed graduating with honors? I was in the top 20 percent of my class. But my whole time at Yale, I'd assumed I was somewhere in the middle. Or worse."

Janie looked sad. My eyes welled up.

"You're right. I thought that John Hutton—and everyone else—was out of my league."

"You thought you were impersonating a beautiful, smart, successful woman," Janie said softly. "But really, you were one. You still are."

♡

February 5, 2008

Dear Edge: As it turns out, I wasted half my life on a loser who abandoned me and our unborn child all because Justin Murphy told me I was too tall, too smart, and not pretty enough in fifth grade. I paid a Women's Loss Doctor a lot of money for this epiphany. I should bill Justin Murphy.

My rational self knows that I <u>am</u> worthy of someone great and shouldn't settle for less. But waiting for that someone feels scary and hard.

As for my confidence, unlike you, seventy thousand
fans aren't screaming my name or throwing
undergarments at me on any given night. So I guess
I'll just read the Imposter Syndrome book Janie
recommended and fake it 'til I make it.

Oh, also. I signed up for guitar lessons at the Old
Town School of Folk Music. My motives are not pure:
Setting up my jDate profile was so humiliating that
I wanted to do a normal activity, one that might
attract normal guys whom I might meet normally.
My screen name is "Edge'sGirl," by the way. Zach
says that's gross, but Alex says to be myself, so
I'm keeping it. I love you, Zoe

I SPENT THE next several days in jDate hell. Its many dings,
flashing icons, and neon lights called to mind a fucked-up ar-
cade. The site appeared dominated by men seeking women half
their age and people who placed no value upon proper punctua-
tion, grammar, or spelling. The former group sent messages I
found nauseating. The latter group sent messages I could barely
decode. Nondescript guys abounded. And on Day Three, I re-
quested that jDate block "Scotty2Hotty," who repeatedly blasted
me with: "ill mak u cum so hrd." I began to approach my laptop
as though it were a live bomb. Some days, I wished it actually
were.

♡

February 13, 2008

U2: My guitar class is comprised predominantly of middle-aged lesbians, and I _loathe_ jDate. Please let me come work for you. Maybe my One is sitting in a Dublin café, just waiting to forgive me for spilling tea on his copy of _Ulysses_. Send for me tomorrow — for Valentine's Day? Please? Love, Zoe

# Thirty-Seven

Lisa, the legal recruiter I'd contacted in 2006 after a particularly crap week with Chip, called after a week of jDating. We'd kept in touch despite my Chip Stockholm Syndrome; I considered her a friend. Lisa had even cooked dinner for Caren and me once (Caren didn't love Chip either). Lisa was fifteen years older than I, but it never felt that way.

"Lisa, thank God you called."

"Uh-oh. Why?" she asked.

"Because I was obsessing about dating stuff instead of working. What's up?"

"How apropos! I bumped into Caren on the El, and she told me how great you're doing, and mentioned that you're dating." Lisa knew I'd gotten divorced, but not why.

"More like *trying* to date." I left it at that.

"Ha! So, I don't usually do this. . . ."

"Buhhhhtt?"

"But," she said, laughing, "I just placed someone at Bates & Finnegan—it's a trial boutique—"

"Sure, I know it." And heard it was an overpriced sweatshop.

"Oh, cool. So anyway, he's thirty-three and really funny. And," she lowered her voice, "he's cute. *Really* cute. Like, *gorgeous*, actually."

Ooh! I sat up straighter. Lisa was a dating veteran and not easily impressed. She'd dated for ages before marrying at thirty-eight. If she thought someone was funny and gorgeous, he was.

"He's not Jewish, though."

"Not an issue," I said.

"Great! I didn't know. Caren mentioned jDate, so—"

"Yes. But I'm open to heterosexual, age-appropriate, non-serial-killers of all—or no—faiths."

She laughed. "Sean made some joke about being 'hopelessly single,' I pressed a little, and he's definitely available. So I thought we could do something low key. Like, maybe you two could meet Jack and me for a quick drink. How does that sound?"

"Umm." My stomach began roiling the way it did whenever I spent more than three minutes on jDate. *Growth potential lies in uncomfortable moments.* "Sounds perfect. If he's down with it, I'm down with it."

"Oh, yay! How about I email everyone?"

"That'd be amazing. Thank you so much."

My intercom buzzed. It was Chip. "Zoecanyoupleasecomeup."

"Go ahead," Lisa said.

"ZOEPLEASECOMEUP!"

"Maybe we should talk about professional stuff sometime too. . . ." I said apologetically.

I grabbed a pen and darted up the stairs.


BY THE TIME I'd returned from Chip's office, Lisa had already emailed. Her message—entitled "Introduction"—was addressed to me and one seanokelly@hotmail.com. It cc'd her husband, Jack:

> Hello! Sean, meet Zoe. Zoe, meet Sean. Jack and I would
> love to meet you for drinks one evening. Why don't you
> two shoot us some dates? Looking forward to it, L.

Lisa's message had been sent two minutes ago. I'd need to repress my instinct to immediately Reply All to (1) accept Lisa's invitation and (2) inform the group that any night but Mondays (yoga) and Wednesdays (guitar) worked for me.

It was going to be a long day.

♡

February 18, 2008

Gentlemen: It is obviously not a coincidence that I'm being set up with an Irishman. He's probably not actually Irish. But wouldn't it be great if he were? Love, Zoe

I MANAGED NOT to check Gmail until *eleven o'clock* the next morning. My cool indifference paid off, because this was in my inbox:

> Hi, All, I'd love to have drinks. I look forward to seeing
> you, Lisa, and to meeting you, Zoe and Jack. I'm finishing
> a trial, but how's next week? Take care, Sean

Alex had not one cautionary word. She just encouraged me to write back before floating out of my office. (I'd have to see what was up with her after responding to Sean—she'd been very floaty lately.)

> Hi! Next week works great. How's Tuesday? Looking forward to it. Zoe

Everyone replied quickly. Tuesday it was.

ON FRIDAY, BUBBE and I went to services before I met Alex for dinner. We hadn't talked all week, thanks to depositions, briefs, and, of course, Chip. Finally, we were nestled into a corner table at Tarantino's, each with a 'tini and bowl of pasta in front of us. Heaven.

About fifteen minutes into our evening, Alex gave me my opening. "You look great, Lady," she said. "As relaxed as I've seen you in a long time."

"You know, I've actually been thinking that about *you*! You're very glowy." I stole a glance at her. She blushed; I persisted. "So either you're pregnant, in which case, I need to know what I've missed since your last menstrual period—and to confiscate your 'tini—or you're in love. In which case I *still* need to know what I've missed since your last menstrual period, but you keep the 'tini."

She laughed. "I am *definitely* not pregnant. *Or* in love."

"But?" OMG her face was so red.

"But I . . . kinda met someone." She tried so hard to suppress her smile. I couldn't believe she'd cracked so easily.

"You *kinda* met someone? Alex, you're so cute right now, it's ridiculous. Spill!"

"It's so early," she tried. "It might be nothing. It's *probably* nothing."

It was obviously not nothing, but I knew better than to say so. "Fine. But tell me anyway."

She hesitated.

"Al," I said. "I *want* to know when something great happens to my friends. So c'mon!"

"OK!" she said, assuming the aura of a thirteen-year-old girl. I'd never seen Alex like this. "A couple of weeks ago, the boys dragged me out to the Green Mill for jazz. And it was kind of like a movie—this shit *never* happens to me—because when Jimmy came back from getting drinks, he said this hot guy was checking me out. I look up, and said hot guy—tall, broad, totally my type—is leaning on the bar, looking right at me."

"Oh, my God."

"I know."

"I'd have no idea what to do. What did you do?"

"I smiled, I think. And he smiled back, and kind of tipped his glass toward me. Like we were in Casa-fucking-blanca."

"Oh, my God," I repeated.

"And then the guys started poking me, like juveniles, and I wanted to die."

"Natch. Now get to where you meet." She held up a finger while she sipped her drink; I slurped some pasta.

"So he went back to his table, and when it was time for our next round, I went up to the bar, wondering if he'd notice. He did, and came up to talk to me."

I squealed—loudly. So, of course, our waiter, whom we

didn't recognize, chose that exact moment to check on us; he raised an eyebrow and sped away.

"DID YOU GO HOME WITH HIM?" I asked.

Alex looked smug. "I totally wanted to . . . so I did."

"*Please* tell me you had amazing sex."

"No sex, but great making out. After talking to him for literally hours at the Green Mill."

"I would never have pegged you as the type to close down the Green Mill. But continue."

I wanted all pertinent intel immediately. I knew that something big had happened and didn't have the patience to wait out Alex's new-boyfriend-reticence phase. She approached every new relationship with extreme caution because of past heartbreak. Few knew this because it belied her confident aura.

"At first, I assumed it was a one-night deal, which is why I didn't say anything about it," she said. (Translation: I *wanted* it to be more than a one-night deal but told myself it wasn't so as not to be disappointed.)

"Mmm."

"But he made me text to let him know I got home OK, and then he called me the next day—like normal people used to do. We actually *spoke*. He asked me out for coffee that afternoon."

"Yay!"

"But I said no."

"*WHY?!*" I accidentally spat noodle at Alex. "Sorry."

"That's OK."

"So, WHY?" I asked again, after chewing and swallowing.

"Oh, because that's a little much for the day after a first hookup. I made up some excuse, but we ended up talking for an hour—"

"About what?"

"Lots," she shrugged. "He asked about Jimmy, my job, my parents . . . and it turns out he's progressive too, so he was really complimentary about my volunteer work for the campaigns, for Planned Parenthood. . . ."

*HE LOVES YOU!* I thought but didn't say. "This is fabulous."

"Yeah, it was nice. I asked a lot about him too, obviously. And we've done two dinners, two happy hours, and," she lowered her voice, "one sex and one overnight since."

I clapped my hands like Mike Myers' Phillip the Hyper-Hypo from SNLs of yore. I think I knew, right then, that this was The One for Alex. Something about this man made her let him in and be her full self.

"What's his name?" I finally asked.

"Brian," she said sweetly. "His name is Brian."

What would I wear to the wedding?

# Thirty-Nine

first seriously considered quitting jDate on Day 12. But that's when, on a Sunday night, I got this:

> Hello Edge'sGirl! My name is Aaron. I think your profile is fantastic. You have a sense of fun about you (and aren't hard to look at, either). I'd love to learn more about you and tell you more about me, if you're interested. To start, I consider myself a novice U2 fan. I hope you have a great week and also to hear from you soon. Aaron

This message was both complimentary *and* punctuated. It contained no emoticons and only one exclamation point. I clicked on Aaron's profile. He looked sweet, cute, and Jewish. Aaron was forty and divorced. And *WOAH*—he was a rabbi. I dialed Maddie.

"Whatcha doin'?" I asked.

"Daniel's playing video games and I'm reading a cookbook about chocolate, I'm afraid."

"Sounds right," I said.

"Yep. So what's up?"

"Well, I got a jDate message. A good one."

"Oooh! Read it to me," she commanded.

I did.

"Sounds great!" Maddie said. I was quiet. "So . . . is he an ex-con or something?"

"What? No. He's a *rabbi*."

"Oh."

"So." I waited.

"So?" Maddie asked.

"*So?* What do I do?!"

"Write him back!"

"But I eat bacon and celebrate Christmas."

"Who cares?" Maddie said. "This is a nice, educated guy. He sent you a thoughtful note. Write him back!"

"You don't seem bothered by the rabbi thing," I marveled.

"I'm not." Maddie sighed. "We're not kids anymore, Zo—people are complicated. You said yourself that your main takeaway from 2007 is that people don't fit into neat little boxes."

Touché.

"You're a sage," I said. "Thanks."

"Glad to be of service."

"G'night, Mads."

AFTER YOGA ON Monday night, I decided that obsessing over my response to Aaron would be a great way to avoid obsessing about Tuesday's double-non-date-date with Sean. Here's what I sent:

Thanks so much for your message, Aaron. My name's Zoe. I'd love to find out more about you and to bolster your U2 knowledge! My email address is: zoe.e.greene@gmail.com

if you'd rather communicate that way. Hope your week's
off to a great start. Zoe[30]

I laid out my double-non-date-date outfit before going to
bed. I wanted it to say, *This Isn't a Date Outfit, I'm Just Naturally
Very Stylish So I Wear Things like This to Work Every Day.* Or,
even, *This Isn't a Date Outfit—I'm So Busy with Dudes, I Forgot
We Were Meeting Tonight!—But I'm Just Naturally Very Stylish So
I Wear Things like This to Work Every Day.* It took me until midnight to achieve satisfaction. Hopefully, the mess I'd made of my
closet would be worth it.

♡

February 25, 2008

Dear U2: Pigeonholing is appealing because it gives us
a false sense of control. But people are
complicated muddles of nature, nurture, experiences,
and relationships. Maddie's right — you can't box
all that up. Yet that's precisely what jDate aims
to do: subdivide Jews into even smaller boxes. So I'm
quite sure that it and all dating websites are
hopeless, and that I am most likely doomed.

But I'm feeling very Wide Awake in America,

---

[30] These messages deserve their own Oscar category. That five-sentence message took
22 minutes to draft, or 4.4 minutes per sentence. Really, it took more like 3 minutes per
sentence, plus an extra 7 to remove and replace, over and over again, the one
exclamation point I ultimately left in.

corresponding with an Irishman one day and a rabbi
the next. Edge, you married Aislinn O'Sullivan . . .
and then Morleigh Steinberg. So maybe I, too, am on
the right track. Love, Zoe

# Thirty-Nine

S ean O'Kelly Tuesday was a rare, uninterrupted day despite Chip being in the office. I even had time to put more mascara on before setting off.

Lisa was brilliant at setups: She texted to tell me where she and Jack were seated twenty seconds before I arrived at the bar and ten seconds after I'd begun worrying about how to find Sean if he arrived before Lisa. I was surprised when a bouncer asked for my ID at the door. Warmth returned to my face as I climbed the stairs.

"Zoe!" Lisa called and waved. It was 5:46 p.m., and the place was packed.

"Hey!" I waved back. Jack and I arrived at the table at the same time; he was carrying a basket of popcorn from the bar.

"Hi, Zoe," he said. "Good to see ya."

"You too. Thanks for doing this—I'll bet the last time you agreed to set someone up, you didn't have to hire a sitter."

"Please. I get to have drinks with my beautiful wife! I'm thrilled." Jack was so kind and sincere that I wanted to both high-five Lisa and weep for the rest of us.

We all unbundled and small-talked for a few minutes before Jack got down to business.

"I'm thirsty," he said. "Ladies? What are we having?"

"A glass of red for me please, Babe," Lisa said.

This was an Irish pub crawling with people under twenty-five. I wondered whether they even *had* wine. "I'd love a Guinness. Thanks, Jack." I reflexively reached for my wallet.

"Nah. You get the next round," Jack said, waving me off before returning to the bar.

Could I even do a next round? It was already six o'clock and we'd agreed to meet at five forty-five. Lisa must've seen me check my watch.

"I'm sure Sean'll be here soon," she said.

"It's all good. I just need to walk my dog eventually." Lisa pulled out her Blackberry; she must not have had any messages from Sean because she put it right back down. "I'm not worried," I lied.

Late people were my kryptonite. Greenes arrive five minutes early *to everything*. My entire bloodline (minus Aunt Steffi) was afflicted with the need for life to march to the beat of our synchronized watches. But I resolved to suppress all outward signs of the Tardiness Tizzy I felt coming on and not check my watch for ten more minutes.

"I've never been here," I said. "It's—unusual."

"Yeah. Me neither. Sean picked it, said his colleagues come here...."

*Why?* The place felt like an upscale frat house. Why would a grown man choose it for a double-non-date-date with two forty-five-year-olds? I could tell Lisa was wondering the same thing; a hint of discomfort wafted across her face. Just then, Jack returned with our drinks, happily oblivious to it all.

Lisa, Jack, and I chatted and sipped. They told me stories about their kids and the latest home improvement project they couldn't seem to finish. I told them about Chip's toenails. At six twenty, our glasses were empty. Lisa checked her Blackberry.

"Aha," she said, relieved. "Sean got tied up but is on his way."

"Oh, OK," I said as calmly as I could.

*WHO* arrives this late to a *first* double-non-date-date? I pressed my hand to my knee to stop my foot from tapping.

"He's literally across the street. Should be here any second," Lisa mumbled.

Soon, she grinned and shouted over my shoulder. "Sean!"

She leapt up to hug him. Jack stood to introduce himself. I was blocked in but turned around in my chair. When Lisa (finally) released Sean, I froze. If Alex was living *Casablanca*, I was living *Sixteen Candles*—only Sean was even hotter than Jake Ryan. Something I hadn't previously thought possible.

Sean was not the guy you pass on your way to work and think, *prrrrr!* before resuming your debate about going grande or venti. This was a guy you know has never once waited for a table or unhooked a woman's bra (because she did it for him first). I'd never seen someone who looked like this outside the pages of an Abercrombie catalogue. But he was an actual *man* with a sex appeal the Abercrombie boys couldn't match. I wanted him to lift me out of my seat so that I could wrap my legs around his waist.[31]

Sean was six feet two inches but looked distinctly Irish: ice-blue eyes, porcelain skin, a smattering of perfectly nut-brown freckles, and not-too-styled thick black hair. He had a chiseled jaw, masculine cheekbones, and, obvious even from underneath his still-buttoned coat, a strong, athletic body. *Holy fuck.* Lisa

---

[31] This is not my usual reaction to strangers.

flashed me an *I-told-you-so!* grin. I determinedly rearranged my face when Sean's eyes met mine.

"Sean, this is Zoe," Lisa said. Still blocked in, I stood up as much as I could to extend my hand, knocking my bag off my chair in the process. Sean wore an expression I couldn't read. When I retrieved my bag from the floor, his eyes flashed so quickly, and the corners of his mouth turned up so briefly that I may have imagined it. "And this is my husband, Jack."

"Nice to meet you both," Sean said.

I couldn't help but lean slightly toward him while he unbuttoned his coat. Lisa did the same. Sean was the center of some kind of magnetic field. His formal work attire fit him flawlessly but looked out of place; he belonged in rugby shorts and a long-sleeved Henley. *Unbuttoned, so I could rub his chest.* Sean jolted me back to reality by sitting next to Lisa. Jack and I exchanged an *oh-kaayyyyy* look. Jack regrouped by offering to get another round.

"Nope, my turn," I said.

Going to the bar would buy me a minute to gather myself. But, obviously, Sean would insist on getting this one to apologize for arriving thirty-nine minutes late. Right? Jack hesitated briefly to give him a chance. But Sean didn't budge; he just smiled his irresistible half-smile while Lisa and I stared at it.

"Nah, I'm up," Jack said graciously. "Another cab, Baby?" Lisa nodded. "Zoe?"

"Jack—" I started.

"It's my pleasure." Jack held my gaze and nodded toward Sean. *Stay. The whole point is for you to meet this shit who just sat next to my wife,* his eyes said. I nodded.

"Another Guinness sounds great," I said. "Thank you, Jack."

"Sean?" Jack clapped his hands together. "What can I get you?"

"I'd love a Harp," he said. "Thanks."

I inexplicably knocked over my (thankfully empty) beer glass. Jack scooped it up like a pro before departing. I picked at my cuticles to occupy my hands. Sean looked at his Blackberry before tossing it on the table in front of him. He sighed. At the end of a stressful workday, my breath smelled of kennel. But Sean's smelled of fresh spearmint, plucked from a field in the Alps. (I don't know if spearmint really grows in the Alps, but Sean's breath made me think that it must.)

"Long day?" Lisa asked. She patted his back. I stifled a laugh.

"Nah," Sean said. "I'm never out of the office this early—I'm great."

We all looked at each other for a minute. Just as things began to feel awkward, I spoke. "Lisa said you come here often?"

"Yeah. It's so close to my building. . . ."

When Sean looked at me, I thought something passed between us. In hindsight, I'm sure it did—if we'd been depicted in a comic book, there would have been a dotted line drawn from our eyes to a bubble between us that said, *ZAP!* He held my gaze a split-second longer than required, and his beautiful blue eyes sparkled a little extra. But at the time, his mixed messages—arriving late, not apologizing, sitting next to Lisa—were tough to decipher. Before I could suss things out, Sean was reading his Blackberry, and I was sure I'd imagined it all.

This—plus lust, irritation with Sean's tardiness, and preoccupation with Basil's bladder—flummoxed me completely. So I started talking.

"Your new job!" I said. "Congratulations. On that." Sean looked up, wearing a question mark on his impeccable face. "Sorry." I laughed nervously, "I just meant—Lisa said she placed you recently." The right corner of his mouth turned up again.

"Yeah, she kept me off the dole." Sean finally looked squarely into my eyes before turning his attention to Lisa. I worried I might pass out. He was unfazed.

Jack returned with more popcorn. A cute, blonde waitress arrived with our drinks a minute later. Her lips parted when she saw Sean. I was elated that Sean didn't appear to notice her.

The conversation flowed easily between Jack, Lisa, and me. We all asked Sean questions: "Where are you from?" (me); "Do you have a big Irish family too?" (Jack); "Are you still enjoying the new firm?" (Lisa). He answered politely but didn't ask us anything. I could sense him looking at me only when I wasn't looking at him. At seven ten, I put on my scarf. Basil would be crossing his legs by now, and trying to banter for forty-six minutes with someone so aloof had worn me out.

"This was great," I said. "Who doesn't love a two-Guinness Tuesday? Thanks so much, guys," I told Jack and Lisa. "Sean, I've gotta run. I have a pup at home who needs a walk."

"But I just got here," he said, looking bewildered.

His bewilderment bewildered me. He was late, and my dog needed to pee! And then it hit me: Sean wasn't used to being left. I wondered if I was the first woman ever to walk away from him. Hmph. I hoped so.

"I know, I'm really sorry," I said as I bundled up. "It was great to meet you, though." He nodded, took a sip of beer, and ran his tongue along his lower lip. The arrogance! I wanted to slap him. And also to run *my* tongue along his lower lip.

"We actually have to relieve our nanny pretty soon, too," Lisa said.

"But we can stay while you finish your beer," Jack offered.

"OK," Sean said.

The right thing would have been for me—the childless, nanny-less one—to let Jack and Lisa go first. But I was becoming unhinged. I hugged Lisa and Jack, gave Sean an awkward wave and smile, and closed with the elegant, "Sean, I know you're crazy busy so . . . yeah. Thanks for coming out."

"It's cool, Zoe." His half-smile was sexy as hell. "Nice to meet you."

"You too." I stuck my chin in the air and headed out.

Something compelled me to look back when I got to the top of the stairs. I caught Sean's eye; he'd been watching me walk away. Although I'd never admit it, this sent shivers of excitement down my spine.


"WHAT A DOUCHE," I huffed into my cell as I raced home to Basil.

"Fuck, your date!" Alex remembered. "What happened?"

"Well *first* of all, he arrived almost *forty minutes LATE.*"

"Uh-oh," Alex whispered. She knew me well.

"*I know.* And he was totally unapologetic once he showed up."

"Rude!" Alex agreed.

"Right? Like, these people have kids they're paying someone to watch while they do us a favor."

"Yeah," Alex said.

"I get the impression he's not just flighty, but really *up his own ass*, you know?" I continued. "And when Jack offered to get us drinks, and I said he'd already bought the first round—which we finished *while we were waiting*—Irish just sat there."

"Irish?"

"Oh. His name is Sean O'Kelly so, you know. Irish."

"Ah," Alex said, sounding like she knew something I didn't, which made me mad.

"Oh. *Annnnddd*, he picked the cheesiest place EVER. It's an under-age meat market posing as an upscale Irish pub."

"Kilkenney's!" Alex said.

"Yeah! You'd hate it."

"I've been there—once. And you're right, I hated it," she recalled.

"Well. Guess who's a regular there?"

"Patrick. Aiden? Er—Irish."

"Yup! And he's thirty-three, by the way. So. Way too old for that place."

Neither of us spoke for a minute. Alex was still at the office; I'd probably interrupted her.

"Well," she ultimately said, "it's over. So who cares?"

"Oh, I *definitely* don't care. I dismissed him right away, and now that I'm running it down to you, he's an even clearer *no*."

"Mmmmmmm-hmm."

"What," I snapped.

"If he's a clear no. . . " Alex was enjoying this, ". . . then why are you out of breath?"

Damn her. I was, actually, out of breath. And knew I sounded like I was on speed. I had no choice but to come clean.

"Before I tell you, I want to emphasize three things: Irish is *so* entitled, *so* selfish, and *so* rude."

"Noted. But?"

"But. . . ." I sighed.

"What."

"He is crazy—and I mean *crazy*—hot."

"Ah."

"And. . . ." I trailed off.

"*What?*"

"Well, I might be totally wrong. . . ."

"*BUT WHAT?*"

"But I think that we have—maybe—a little . . . chemistry. Or something. But I probably imagined it."

"Oh, God."

"I know."

"The hot, maybe-asshole. I know this guy. I've dated this guy." She lowered her voice. "I've *slept* with this guy."

"YOU HAVE?!" I shouted.

"No! Not this *actual* guy. This *type* of guy. The guy you want to jump so badly that you ignore that little voice inside, screaming at you to run." She sighed. "But what can you do?"

"Nothing, because I'll never hear from him again," I swore. "After all, I am me, and he is sex personified."

"Mmm."

"Stop doing that," I snapped.

"Whatever you say, Lady." Alex laughed. "Whatever you say."


I COULDN'T FACE jDate that night. Basil had his nose out of joint about being left 'til after seven o'clock and refused to cuddle. Gmail had a nice surprise in store, though.

Hi Zoe! It's nice to know your name. I hope this isn't too forward, but I always prefer talking face-to-face. May I take you out for a drink or coffee one night this week? Your profile says you're a lawyer, so I'm not sure what your schedule's like, but I'm generally open on weeknights, except for Wednesdays. Let me know. I'll look forward to (hopefully) meeting you. Aaron

Before I knew it, we were on for Thursday. Irishmen, rabbis, and an invitation to go on a real date, all in four hours. When it rains, it pours.

# Forty

I made it to March. March is a tricky month for Chicagoans. Your calendar may show a field of spring flowers, but the city's encased in immovable gray ice. Still, when I woke up Wednesday morning, I wondered if maybe *my* spring had arrived. The upside of my interface with Irish was that I was attracted to a real, live human. And even though Aaron and I were an unlikely long-term match, I bet he'd be on time. So maybe shit was turning around.

I'd also really started digging my guitar lessons. Although they'd almost certainly prove useless in my quest to find a lover, I was psyched to be learning "Blackbird," and always enjoyed my weekly post-lesson beers with the two lesbian couples I'd befriended. Paula and Lynn were in their early forties, and Julie and Debra were in their late forties. I fed off their steadfast belief that I would end up a happy, one-cat person, and loved listening to their wise perspectives on how complicated adulthood can be. By the time I got home from the guitar Wednesday immediately following Jewish–Irish Tuesday, I had some intel waiting for me.

Naturally, Boone gave me merciless shit about The Rabbi. Most of the messages he sent were nonsense—*Papa can you hear me? Do you tell him about your bacon cheeseburger fetish before or after you do it through a hole in a sheet? What's the Talmud's position on oral?*—but one was helpful:

> Zees: Reb Tevye is an associate rabbi at a Conservative synagogue in Oak Park—has been for a while. So, if you become Mrs. Reb Tevye, you'd better be down with hoofing it to shul in the burbs. Adam

*Rabbis are people, not boxes. Boone is an idiot and also mean,* I told myself. Besides, for all I knew, Reb Tevye[32] was on the verge of leaving the rabbinate to take his jam band on the road. I'd have to wait and see. I managed to fall asleep after undressing Irish in my head a time or twelve.

ON THURSDAY, I considered wearing the same outfit to meet Reb Tevye that I'd worn to meet Irish. But I ultimately opted to change into skinny jeans, tall black boots, and a loose black sweater. I took a full shot of whiskey because I kept picturing Reb Tevye with a long beard, forelocks, and a black hat. Shortly thereafter, Reb Tevye called to tell me that he was around the corner.

"Wish me luck," I said to Basil, who cracked one eye before going back to sleep.

Reb Tevye did not arrive in Topol's horse-drawn buggy; his Honda Civic Hybrid pulled in front of my building just as I stepped into the cold night. I liked his car. Driving a hybrid in

---

[32] Unfortunately, Boone's nickname for Aaron stuck. ("Reb Tevye" is a reference to the character so brilliantly portrayed by Chaim Topol in *Fiddler on the Roof*.)

2008 said, *I care about the planet, I'm not afraid to try something new,* and *I don't need to drive a BMW to feel like a man.* The sky was clear; I could easily see the blinking lights atop the Hancock building. Rebbe put the car in park, saw me, and waved. I walked to his passenger door in a nervous fog and eased into the eerily silent vehicle.

"Hi, Aaron," I said over the racket of my racing heart. "It's so nice of you to pick me up."

We both started speaking at the same time, then laughed at the mutual interruption. Reb Tevye apologized and hugged me over the gearshift. He was taller than Tyler—maybe five feet ten. His body was thin and wiry, like John Hutton's (although the similarities stopped there). His brown eyes, although unremarkable in shape or color, were welcoming and kind, and rosy cheeks warmed his olive skin. His teeth appeared perfect when he opened his thin lips into a wide, easy smile. The Rabbi radiated both confidence and goofiness, a combination I found endearing. He wore a puffy, black coat, Gap jeans, and hiking boots. The Kansas City Royals hat covering most of his curly brown hair was the only blemish on an otherwise perfect first impression.[33]

Reb Tevye slapped his thighs after we released our hug. "Well," he said, sounding nothing like Topol, "It's nice to put a face to your emails." Rebbe smiled ear to ear and looked straight into my eyes. I could see the outline of his contact lenses.

"Yeah, absolutely. It's *so* great to meet you." Dammit. I made everything superlative when nervous, and The Rabbi's eye contact was intense.

---

[33] I was born and raised a Cubs fan.

"So where to?" he asked. "Shall we grab a drink?"

"*Definitely!*" I winced. I must learn to speak normally. "I thought of two places—one has better food with regular drinks, the other, a wine bar, has great wine but so-so food."

"How about the wine place?" he asked without breaking his smile.

"Excellent." I directed Reb Tevye to Webster Wine Bar.

He drove deftly. *This shouldn't surprise you, Zoe. He's not Tevye the oxcart driver.*

"Are you a big wine connoisseur?" Rebbe asked as he came to a stop sign.

"Oh, no." I waved my hand dismissively. "I mean, I *definitely* like to drink it, but don't know much about it. You?" I wondered if he'd noticed my speech impediment.

"Same. I'm trying to learn more, though—my neighborhood wine guy has kind of taken me under his wing, which is fun." He smiled and lightly tapped the steering wheel.

"That's cool," I nodded, noticing for the first time the dimple that appeared on Reb Tevye's right cheek when he smiled. "Oh—you'll want to turn left at the light and then grab any space you see."

"Perfect," he said as he approached a parallel spot right in front of the bar. Reb Tevye parked easily while I yammered on about wine, probably sounding like a hardened alcoholic.

We met on the sidewalk after he insisted on opening the door for me. I couldn't help but look down while we walked; when The Rabbi looked at me, it felt like his eyes bored into the darkest corners of my soul. I decided to focus not on this but on his pleasant stature. I imagined nestling into him while we walked side-by-side.

We were shown to an actual table, which was one of my favorite things about Webster Wine Bar. Aaron gently touched my back for a second so that I'd know to walk ahead of him. Rob would never have performed this type of unconscious chivalry, and neither, I'd bet, would Irish. The Rabbi never did remove his Royals cap, but I could still tell that he was cute in an accessible, appealing kind of way. He wore a black pullover sweater.

"I am so ready for a thaw," I said, rubbing my freshly ungloved hands together. I wondered what percentage of Chicago's first dates didn't begin with weather talk.

"No kidding," Aaron nodded, sliding a big leather menu toward me. "But I like that it's starting to stay light a touch longer . . . gives us hope, right?"

"Totally. And the air *has* taken on that great muddy smell . . . the snow's about to melt."

"I love that! What a great observation," Reb Tevye enthused. "That is *so true*."

His excitement over my throwaway comment startled me. But his genuine enjoyment of small pleasures, easy posture, and natural smile counterbalanced his intensity. Our server arrived just when I needed a break.

"Hello there," she said. She wore a short Afro and thick-rimmed glasses.

"Hi," Aaron and I said simultaneously.

"I'm Darlene. May I help you select some wine?"

"Geez, sorry. We haven't even looked," Reb Tevye apologized. I liked the way he gave Darlene his full attention. Tyler would've been thrusting business cards at her by now. And Irish might not have looked up from his Blackberry.

"You know," I told him, "I never even look at the wine list

here. It's too big. I usually just ask the expert." I gestured toward Darlene. She smiled.

"What a relief!" Reb Tevye said happily. "We're in your hands."

Darlene recommended a flight of whites for The Rabbi and reds for me. Caren would have given Reb Tevye two strikes for drinking white wine, but I couldn't have cared less; it wasn't Manischewitz. When Aaron laughed at something Darlene said, I suddenly realized that I could, actually, see myself kissing him. Which was both exciting and sweat-i-fying.

When Darlene left, Reb Tevye's face turned serious. He leaned forward. I braced myself.

"At the risk of sounding too—I don't know, something—I'd really like to get to know you. How about we start with this U2 obsession of yours?"

I laughed, relieved. His interest in me was flattering. "You're sweet to ask. But," I imitated his serious expression, "I need to correct you."

"Oh," he said with concern.

"It's not an obsession. It's true love." I smiled.

"Ha! I stand corrected. Tell me, then, about this true love."

So I did. I told him how I fell in love with *The Joshua Tree* at summer camp in 1987, when I first realized that music could really say something. I told him about listening to *Achtung Baby* on repeat on my neighbor's new CD player and recognizing, around one in the morning, that it might be even better than *The Joshua Tree*. I told him about catching the live bug—bad—at a PopMart show. He listened with rapt attention, interjecting thoughtful questions at the right times.

An hour later, when we each ordered another glass of wine, I realized that Reb Tevye knew about Zach, my parents, my job, where I went to college and law school, and several of my friends' names, in addition to U2. I, on the other hand, knew only that he was a rabbi with a gift for getting strangers to talk to him.

"Aaron, I've been talking about myself for, like, ever. Why don't you tell me about *you?*"

"Sure, OK," he said, leaning back in his chair and stretching his arms behind his head. "Where would you like me to start?"

"I'm not as good at this as you are, but how about something easy. Like, where did you grow up, and do you have any siblings?"

"Ah. Columbus. But my dad hails from Kansas City." He pointed to his cap. "And I've got one brother, three sisters."

"Wow, five of you!"

He laughed. "I know! I *loved* growing up in a big family."

After prodding a little, I gathered that his family wasn't particularly religious, so they were surprised when he chose to go to rabbinical school; that his brother was a sports writer, two of his sisters were lawyers (although one stopped practicing after having her second child), and his other sister was an OB/Gyn; that the thing he liked most about being a rabbi was comforting people in crisis; that he was crazy for his eight nieces and nephews; and that he'd been officially divorced for nine months.

"You're divorced too, right?" he asked. My wine buzz evaporated.

"Yep." I searched for the right words to add but didn't find them.

"How did you find that—the divorce process?" Reb Tevye asked with now-familiar earnestness.

"Uh." I decided, for lack of a profound or graceful alternative, to be honest. "I found it soul-sucking, humiliating, and discombobulating in every way."

"Well put. Me too," he said quietly. He smiled again. "But this isn't first date material! Why ruin the good wine?"

"Agreed!" I smiled back.

Reb Tevye shifted easily into telling me about the poor kid he was tutoring for his bar mitzvah. "Thirteen is a tough age for a young man's voice," he explained. "When we started working together, it was all singing—he had a cherubic voice. But now he has to speak a lot of the singing parts. I really feel for him."

Eventually, I realized that I was tired. The one thing I'd already learned was that, good, bad, or indifferent, all first dates were exhausting. At 10:25, the bill came. Reb Tevye grabbed it.

"Let me contribute," I offered.

"No. It's my pleasure. You can get the next one. How about that?"

"Sounds great," I said. "Thank you very much."

On the way to the car, I thanked Reb Tevye again for driving into the city.

"Oh, I love the city! That's really my only complaint about my current synagogue. The city is so vibrant."

"You could always move," I suggested as I ducked into the Civic. "I mean, if you avoid rush hour, the commute from Oak Park really isn't bad."

Reb Tevye looked momentarily uncomfortable. "The way I practice my religion right now . . . I need to be within walking distance of the synagogue."

*Fuck.*

"I'm sorry, Aaron. I'm an idiot."

"No, don't be silly," he said, laughing. His relief was palpable. While I'd been focused on my foot-in-mouthiness, he'd been focused on his religiosity not freaking me out. When we pulled up to my building, Reb Tevye thanked me for introducing him to Webster Wine Bar.

"Hey, thanks for treating me," I said. "I had fun."

"So I can take you out again?" Reb Tevye asked. His eyes bored a hole into my forehead.

"No, but I can take *you* out. That was our agreement, right?" I looked down. Inga always knew when I needed a "spinal break" to stretch—I wished that Reb Tevye knew when I needed an eye-contact break.

"Yes! It was." Reb Tevye laughed. His smile took up half his face. "You know," he said, looking suddenly contemplative, "I've had five dates in the last ten days. I probably shouldn't have said that. . . ."

"No, it's fine," I said. "We did meet on jDate, after all."

"True." He laughed again. "What I'm *trying* to say," he searched my eyes again, "is that I was getting a bit fatigued. But I *really* had a great time tonight. I feel like we connected."

"Yeah!" I hoped I didn't sound as awkward as I felt.

When Reb Tevye reached for a hug, he brushed the left corner of my mouth, ever so briefly, with his lips. I smiled, and then he was gone.

# Forty-One

was surprised to have an email from Reb Tevye waiting for me
at 7:07 a.m.:

Hi, Zoe! Thanks again for such a wonderful evening—I'm
enjoying getting to know you. I don't use my phone
during Shabbos, so I wanted to write well before sunset
(and to let you know I was thinking of you first thing this
morning!). Also, I was wondering, can I see you Sunday? I
could bring kosher Chinese to your place and prove that
it's delicious! Let me know. I'll be thinking about you 'til
then. A.

I forwarded the email to Alex. She came right to my office—
with bedhead.

"Brian's last night?"

"Oh, no! You can tell?" She patted her hair.

"Well *I* can, but Chip won't. How are things?"

"Good." Alex smiled and looked down, demure.

"I LOVE THIS!" I said too loudly. "Sorry. I'll be cool. Er.
Cool*er*."

She laughed. "How was *your* night? Looks from his email
like Mr. Rabbi is smitten."

I said nothing about her change of subject. "It was good. I'll do the full debrief later, but this was by far my most enjoyable first date. Of two-point-five, but still."

Alex sat in one of my guest chairs. "Yeah?"

"Yeah. I mean, the Shabbat stuff and kosher Chinese is a little, you know, *wow.*"

"Right."

"But otherwise, he's great. Smart, kind, cute. Just . . . intense."

"Seems so, writing that early to ask you out again."

"What should I do?" I asked anxiously.

"Well," Alex leaned back and stifled a yawn. "Honestly, whatever you want. If you want to see him—and make out, because you know that's what asking to come over means, right?— then go for it. If not, then tell him you're busy to slow him down."

I nodded.

On the one hand, I wanted very badly to make out with somebody. On the other, Reb Tevye's pace was nuts: At this rate, we'd have toothbrushes on each other's sinks by April. My libido won, as libidos tend to do. I accepted The Rabbi's offer and got to work.

SUNDAY MORNING HIT like an emotional Weedwhacker. Everything was humming along fine . . . until I turned my New Yorker page-a-day calendar while waiting for my pre-EBC toast to pop. March 9, 2008. My due date. I was supposed to be having a baby today—not choking down kosher Chinese. I dropped my gym bag and sank to the floor. *You think you're doing so great because you have a second date with someone you* might *kiss? You were supposed to be a fucking parent!*

When I didn't pick up their calls, my parents parked and let themselves in. I didn't even notice until I saw them sitting on the floor with me. Unable to speak, I gestured to the calendar. They exchanged a knowing glance, wrapped me in a Zoe sandwich, and let me cry.

When the sobs abated, my dad asked, "Zodo. What can we do?"

"Name it," Mom added.

I took a breath. "The problem is, there's nothing more you *can* do. I want to be a mom *and* have a husband, and I was supposed to have all of that today, but instead I have nothing. I'm totally lost."

"You've got a lot more than nothing, and you're not lost," Mom said. "The world is at your fingertips, Zoe. I know you can't see that today, but it is."

"Everybody always tells me that I'm young, I've got time, things will work out, blah blah blah. But I don't feel young—I feel exhausted." My throat caught again.

"We know," Dad whispered as he hugged me. We sat quietly for a few minutes.

"Zoe." My mom's voice was firm. "If you'd had that baby—today, next month, next year—you'd be in a lot more trouble than you are now."

I'd heard some version of this more than once before. But, for whatever reason, that day, it clicked. I instantly catapulted three stages ahead in my recovery. Mom was right: Being a wife and mother—the way I wanted to be—wasn't an option I "gave up." It was never on the table. Rob would never have let a baby's needs supersede his own. He would never have stopped demanding more than I had to give. I knew this on a primordial level when I'd ended my pregnancy, but now this knowledge became conscious.

So no. I didn't have what I wanted, and didn't know when or if I ever would. But, even though the chances of being a whole person *and* parent *and* spouse, simultaneously, seemed pretty fucking remote at that moment, if I had had Rob's baby, there would have been no chance at all.

"You're right," I said. I grabbed my mom's hands and looked directly at her. "*Thank you.*" I stood up, slapped some peanut butter on my cold, hard toast, and grabbed my bag. "Sorry I made us late. But let's go—I've got five miles to do today."

I wrestled with my feelings as I jalked. I began to vaguely recognize that the freedom to mold my life as I saw fit, regardless of social norms, was worth a lot more than I'd previously thought. When I got off the treadmill, I postponed Aaron until Tuesday in order to spend some time alone in my new skin.

♡

March 9, 2008

Dear U2: Today was supposed to be my due date. But I'm OK. Mostly. I think. Love, Me

PS: I'm not the only one/Starin' at the sun/ Afraid of what you'd find/If you took a look inside/Not just deaf and dumb/ Staring at the sun/Not the only one/Who's happy to go blind.

# Forty-Two

Monday, March 10, 2008, 9:26 a.m.:

Hi Zoe! I'm writing on the off chance you have time to check your email. Just wanted to tell you that I'm thinking of you and rooting for you as you work through your big project![34] I'm also counting the minutes until I can see you, yummy Chinese takeout in hand! 😊A.

Caren would have given this email three solid strikes for the exclamation points and emoticon alone. But like any woman who'd just survived her due date divorced and alone, I ignored every red flag in Reb Tevye's email and told him to come Tuesday at seven.

His Tuesday morning confirmation email said outright that he couldn't wait to kiss me.

So I had *two* shots of whiskey before buzzing him in at 6:54. Reb Tevye wore the same Royals hat and hiking boots as last time, a collared shirt, sweater, and khakis. He held a bag of takeout in one hand and a bouquet of grocery-store carnations in the other. He wore a huge smile. I envied how easily he managed to summon unvarnished happiness.

---

[34] A fiction that allowed me to push him from Sunday to Tuesday.

"Hi! Come in," I said. "Let me help—you're so nice to bring dinner." I darted to the kitchen for a break from Reb Tevye's yearning stare. I felt him close behind me when I put the food on the counter.

"Wine?" I suggested.

"Sure, of course."

I summoned the courage to turn around when I felt him step back to remove his coat.

"Can I hang that up?" I asked.

"Nah—I'll just put it right here," he volunteered, draping it over a chair. He played with the flowers in his hands while I opened and poured the wine. I handed The Rabbi his glass.

"Thanks," he said. I didn't think he'd stopped smiling once. We clinked and laughed after he said, "L'chaim!" and I said, "Cheers!"

"I love your place," he added, looking around. "It's very warm and comfortable. How very you."

"You're sweet." Ugh—I blushed.

"I'm *so* happy to be here with you!" He was suddenly inches away and handed me the carnations. "I wanted to get you some flowers and kind of ran out of time, so I'm sorry—this is all they had left."

"They're perfect," I said. And because he thought to buy them, they were. "Let me just put these in some water. Then, we can eat." As I reached for a vase, I felt something shift in The Rabbi. I heard him put his glass on the counter. When I turned around, he enveloped my hands in his.

"Actually," he said, "there's something I was hoping to do first."

"Uh," I wheezed.

"Zoe. Can I kiss you?"

I tried to subtly exhale the extra air that always got trapped in my chest when I was nervous. Thank God I'd had the whiskey. I did want to kiss him, eventually, but was discomfited by his timing. Still, I felt obligated to respect the direct-but-gentle way in which The Rabbi cut to the chase.

"Of course," I managed.

He pulled me close and lifted my face to his. I closed my eyes to escape the overwhelming drama of the moment. Reb Tevye's lips were soft, save for the little bit of stubble around them. His hands sent swollen currents of heat to places that had been dormant for too long. For a moment, I just enjoyed being kissed again—in that exciting, imploring way that couples who've been together for a while don't kiss anymore—and focused on the taste of Altoids and Crest on The Rabbi's tongue. His chest pressed into mine; his breath became heavier until he pulled away.

"Sit with me," he said.

"OK." I took him to the couch.

As soon as our kissing resumed, so did the tongue war that had begun brewing in the kitchen: He kept pushing his tongue into my mouth, and I kept pushing it out. He paused.

"Is this working for you?" I asked, sounding more confident than I was.

"Oh!" he said, surprised. He grasped both my hands again. "It's *so nice*. I just think we have . . . different styles." He sounded so assured—like he was *certain* that beating my tongue into submission was the "right" way to kiss—that I crinkled my nose.

"OK. . . ." I said.

"I like more tongue," he informed me before smiling again.

*Ew, ew, EWW!* My eyes widened in disgust before I could stop them. *Maybe he's not a rabbi at all. Maybe he's a lothario and a con man. Maybe that Chinese food isn't even kosher.* Unlikely. But still. His critique, so early in my dating career, hurt my feelings—and ticked me off. When Rob and I started dating, he liked my style just fine. This emboldened me.

"Well. I like a little less," I replied, as politely as I could.

He lips resumed a grin. "I'm sorry! I can be too bossy." He laughed at himself, totally disarming me in the process. "I love kissing you. And I'd love to get back to it if you'll let me."

I took control of the situation by kissing him first. And after a minute or two, we'd found our groove. It wasn't the best making out I'd ever done, but it felt desperately good at the time. We kissed faster. I heard myself moan softly as his hands drifted from my shoulders to my breasts. Possessed a little by confidence and a lot by desperation, I wound up on his lap.[35] He exhaled and started pressing himself into me. The hardness beneath his khakis confirmed that my style worked just fine for him too.

"I'm taking my hat off," he breathed, which he did in a snap before he wrapped his body around mine. His chest was strong and his arms were lanky but muscular. Unconsciously, I ran my hands up the back of his neck to his wiry hair. I felt pins holding a yarmulke in place. This shouldn't have surprised me, but it did. I wondered: *Do I say anything? And if so, what? No. Don't say anything. But you stopped kissing him, so now you* have *to say something.*

"Umm. Is this why you wouldn't take your hat off?"

---

[35] There should be some kind of Divorce Club in which members make out with each other biweekly to keep skills fresh, desperation at bay, and self-respecting women from straddling rabbis mere hours into their relationship.

"I didn't want to freak you out," he said sheepishly.

"I'm not freaked!" I lied, desperate both to put him at ease and avoid the obvious ways in which we didn't fit. None of my friends or family wore yarmulkes outside of temple. Neither did Rabbi Feldman! Reb Tevye gently kissed my ears and neck. I groaned and, without even thinking about how my stomach would look where it met the waistband of my jeans, took off my shirt.[36] He pressed his chest into me in appreciation and gripped my back as we lay down on the couch. I helped him take off his shirt and my bra. For a blinding moment, I thought I'd never need anything more than this feeling of skin on skin, chest on chest, to be happy. Neither of us ventured a hand below belt. When I could no longer ignore the dry-humping—I *really* didn't want to usher in my post-divorce sex-life with an in-khaki-ejaculation—I pulled away. The Rabbi appeared unfazed.

"Zoe," he said. "You're incredible."

"Me?" I said, which made us both laugh.

We stayed lazily entwined and talked about how nice it felt to be together. Well, really, he did most of the talking. I silently marveled that, apparently, dry-humping wasn't just for high school. Neither of us seemed ready to have sex that night, so we just sort of . . . stopped. After a while, I felt overexposed.

"What time is it?" Reb Tevye asked mercifully. "You must be starving!"

I looked at the DVD clock. "Eight thirty."

"I should feed you," he said, not quite at ease.

"Perfect. Let's eat!" I lifted my head from the couch with one arm pressed clumsily across my boobs. He stood up. While

---

[36] Fine. It may *briefly* have crossed my mind.

he looked for and put on his shirt, I hurriedly dressed. This *really* felt like high school.

We ate kosher Chinese—which, I had to admit, *was* pretty good—straight from the cartons at the kitchen counter. We sipped our wine. We laughed and talked about nothing in particular, both awash in the glow of our first physical connection. We made out for a minute more at the door before he left. I was a muddle of emotions—excitement, discombobulation, bashfulness. But intimacy was intimacy, and the fact that I'd now officially experienced some felt like a significant post-Rob win.

I LOVED KNOWING I'd have something from Reb Tevye when I opened my laptop Wednesday morning.

> Good morning, Beautiful Zoe! I could hardly sleep last night. I can't stop thinking about you—or smiling! You're very special . . . thank you for sharing your night with me. When can I come over again? Love, Aaron

*This* email would have sent Caren to the asylum. She wouldn't have known where to start between the exclamation points, mush, and signature line. (She'd totally start with the signature line.) Embarrassed, I archived it immediately. But once again, what Reb Tevye's unreserved crush did for my spirits trumped all else. The frantic need for sex also impedes higher brain function. So what if he barely knew me? So what if I liked pepperoni on my (non-kosher) pizza? So what if I was vehemently opposed to moving to Oak Park and going without electricity for one seventh of my life? So what if the last time I succumbed to my need to be needed, I wound up gutted and bleeding into an adult diaper? I couldn't survive another month of abstinence. That was all I could see.

After class, the guitar ladies and I treated ourselves to margaritas at the Local Option. As usual, we began the cocktail portion of our evening by laughing at the young, perma-stoned guy who always sat front and center, only to sleep for the majority of class. My cell phone interrupted us.

"Shit, sorry," I apologized as I rummaged through my bag. The Rabbi's number flashed on the screen.

"Who is it?" Lynn asked.

"It's The Rabbi, which is weird, because he knows it's guitar night, usually stays late after Hebrew school on Wednesdays, and knows we're hanging out tomorrow."

"Go ahead—take it," Paula said.

All four women stared at me. I shoved the phone back into my bag.

"I'm sure it's a butt-dial. I'll talk to him later."

They were all too kind to say anything about my red cheeks.

It was ten fifteen by the time I took Basil out. We were almost back home when Reb Tevye called again. Something must be wrong.

"Aaron?"

"Hi! It's so good to hear your voice." He sounded fine—I was relieved.

"You too!" I said. I held my phone between my ear and shoulder while I unleashed Bas, took off my coat, and went to my closet to change. "Sorry I missed you earlier—I may have mentioned that I take guitar lessons on Wednesdays."

"You did indeed." He laughed. "I wasn't sure what time your

lesson was, or when you'd be done. I couldn't resist giving you a try."

"How sweet," I said as I pulled off my socks and jeans.

"*Well,*" he said before taking a dramatic pause. "I was actually calling to see if I could come by, just to kiss you goodnight."

"Come . . . here? From *Oak Park?*"

"Yeah!" He laughed. "Is that OK?"

"Umm. Of course! I'm just sorry that guitar buggered up your plan." I stepped into my Yale Bulldog flannel pants.

"Well *actually* . . . it didn't. I'm in front of your building!"

Holy crap. I was half-PJed and wore no makeup but for the mascara remnants I'd missed when washing my face after work. It was 10:33 *and* I had to draft a brief the next day. "Uh," I said.

"I know it's late," his said breezily, "but don't worry—I'll just kiss you goodnight and head out. Promise. I couldn't wait 'til tomorrow." The buzzer sounded, which sent Frankie under the bed and Basil into barking circles.

"Umm. Is that you?"

"Yep!"

"Oh, OK. . . ." I hung up and spun in a few circles of my own. I didn't have time to indulge the panic attack threatening to put me in a full body bind. WHY WAS HE HERE? Was he going to cut me into pieces and put me IN MY OWN FREEZER? Would my parents even think to look for my remains in there? I fumbled with the buzzer and made my discombobulated way to the door. In seconds, Reb Tevye stood before me. He'd ditched his Royals hat and also his contacts. His retro, black glasses were super-cute, as was The Rabbi in sweatpants and two Henleys. We smiled at each other . . . and then he was on me. I walked blind and backwards to the bedroom while we kissed. Suddenly, we were down to our underwear. Reb Tevye's hands were everywhere. Part of me surrendered to his touch, but most of me was still trying to process that he'd driven all the way from Oak Park, on guitar night, without warning. Twenty minutes later, The Rabbi's dry-humping had become literally painful. I rolled away.

He apologized. "I guess I got a little carried away."

We lay two inches apart, our hands still resting on each other's bodies, absurdly aroused from more foreplay than I'm sure either of us had had in years.

"This is getting ridiculous, right?" I ventured. He wrapped himself around me and closed his eyes.

"Mmm," he said. We were still for a minute.

"So. Umm. Aaron? Should we, like . . . talk about. . . ."

"Yes!" he practically shouted. "We *should* talk about it—about taking the next step." He became serious. "But I don't want to rush you."

"We're adults." I laughed. "We can't go on like this forever."

"No," he replied. "And I really do want to apologize—I *swear* my plan was to kiss you on your doorstep and go. But then I saw you and. . . ." He shrugged. It was impossible not to be flattered to bits.[37]

"No worries," I said as I leaned back into him. "I've been told, by the *many* jDate suitors who've been in this bed, that I have that effect."

He laughed heartily. "You're too much!" I laughed to make sure he knew I was kidding. He pulled my face closer and kissed me. The kissing had gotten *good*. Soon, I was desperate, and he was standing at attention again.

---

[37] Before you judge me too harshly for this, remember that I had been involuntarily celibate. And that my soul had been recently beaten to a pulp.

"Aaron. I don't have any condoms."

"Me neither," he said. "I really wasn't planning this."

I sat up. "OK. I'm on the pill, but we should use condoms."

"We should," he said before pausing. "I haven't used a condom in years . . . I haven't had many partners."

"Me neither," I admitted. "But we need to use condoms."

"Yes."

"And because we women do the heavy lifting when it comes to birth control, I'll let you buy them!"

"Fair enough." He laughed before kissing me.

I couldn't stand to let things escalate again and told him so. "And you still have to drive home!"

"I know," he sighed. "It's just hard to leave you. But I have to be at the synagogue early and don't have a change of clothes, so I can't stay over."

*Stay over?!*

"Thanks for the spectacular tuck-in," I said as I threw on my clothes and handed him his glasses. I walked him to the door where he started kissing me.

"Aaron!"

"OK, OK! I'll be back tomorrow, and better supplied."

I suspected even then that the situation wasn't quite healthy. But I would've overlooked Mt. Everest in order to JUST. GET. LAID. So I smiled, shut the door, and dragged my frustrated lady parts to bed.

# Forty-Three

I went to work at seven o'clock the next morning for two reasons: (1) anticipating my impending Sex Appointment made sleep impossible, and (2) I was concerned I wouldn't be able to finish my brief before said appointment. Alex thought The Rabbi was being pushy and objected to scheduling sex on principle. "But you need to bone. So proceed," she ultimately advised.

Chip spent the day at the racquet club, so I was able to complete a first draft of my brief by five fifteen. I texted Reb Tevye that I should be home by eight o'clock and dashed to the floor's kitchen for some well-deserved Oreos. I was ready to begin editing when my Gchat pinged. This was usually Caren—I maximized the chat box to tell her I was on deadline. But it wasn't Caren.

Sean O'Kelly: Hey stranger.

What in the ever-living fuck? I was paralyzed. But my green chat light was on. He knew I was there. FUCK AND SHIT.

Zoe Greene: Hey! How are you?

Sean O'Kelly: Not so good.

Zoe Greene: Oh no—why?

Sean O'Kelly: Well. I got set up with this hot little number —she's super cute—but she only stayed for, like, 5 minutes before she bolted. So I don't know what to do.

OMG. I reread these sentences five times to confirm their existence. This kind of thing did *not* happen to me. Ever. I instantly forgot about Reb Tevye, the Sex Appointment, and how rude and late Irish was. I stared at my frozen fingers, willing them to write back. I needed time! To draft a pithy response. To find Alex. To finish my brief. To *think*. But I had none.

Zoe Greene: Geez, I'm sorry to hear that.

*SHOULD I SHOULD I SHOULD I?!*

Zoe Greene: But I think I can help.

**OMG.**

Sean O'Kelly: I was hoping you'd say that. 😑

**YESSSSS!**

Zoe Greene: My guess is that this girl has a dog she needed to walk after a long day at work.

Sean O'Kelly: God, you're good. That's exactly what she said.

Sean O'Kelly: I didn't believe her, though, because who runs from a guy she might like?

**I suddenly remembered my conflicting emotions about Irish.**

Zoe Greene: And did she really stay for 5 minutes? Or—I don't know—were you super late, but she stayed for 45 minutes anyway?

Sean O'Kelly: Naw. I was 10 minutes early.

**This made me laugh out loud.**

Zoe Greene: Love it.

Sean O'Kelly: Love what? I have no idea what you're talking about.

Sean O'Kelly: Hey, I've gotta run—thanks for your help. But one last question for you.

*OMG OMG OMG.*

Zoe Greene: Shoot.

Sean O'Kelly: Do you think that if I asked this girl out, she'd say yes?

Zoe Greene: I think you should give it a try.

**Oh, was I bad. I was about to have sex—with a *rabbi*. *That night*. Bad, bad, bad.**

Sean O'Kelly: Great, thanks. Bye!

*Ohmyfuckinggod.*

Sean O'Kelly: JK. Will you have drinks with me? I *promise* I'll be on time. Scout's honor.

Sean O'Kelly: And I actually *was* a scout (Eagle—snap!). So take that to the bank.

*One-potato. Two-potato. Three-potato.*

Zoe Greene: I'd love to.

Sean O'Kelly: Purrr-fect. Chat soon, Mizz Z.

**Umm.**

Zoe Greene: Sounds great.

Sean O'Kelly: Oh, Mizz Z?

**Do I ignore all these Z's?**

Zoe Greene: Yessir?

Sean O'Kelly: Maybe you can wear the same jeans you wore to Kilkenney's. Because maybe I've been thinking about them.

I put my head in my hands and nearly died of embarrassment right there at my desk.


"LISA, PLEASE DON'T hate me," I gushed into my phone while frantically picking up my apartment, changing, and walking Basil in anticipation of Reb Tevye's arrival.

"I could never! What's up?"

"OK." I took a deep breath. "You were so nice to set me up with Ir—Sean, but I didn't hear from him, and thought he didn't like me . . . and so . . . I started seeing someone else." I exhaled.

Silence. Eventually: "And?"

"And that someone else is a *RABBI*. Who's also recently divorced. But I *may* have just accepted a date with Sean. And I know you stuck your neck out, and now I'm all over the place, and—"

"Zoe," Lisa interrupted calmly.

"Oh, my God, I'm sorry—I probably called at the worst possible time!" I didn't know exactly what happened at seven at night in a house with young kids, but figured it was a lot.

"No worries—Jack's overseeing showers," she said before changing her tone. "Zoe? Please forgive me. I'm about to mother you a bit."

"I feel like I could use five extra mothers, so fire away."

"You're *seeing* someone?"

"Right."

"How many dates?"

"Let's see . . . Can this be right? We're on our third. But—but he's a rabbi, and a *very* serious person. So it feels like things are, you know. Serious." I wasn't about to tell her that we'd scheduled a Sex Appointment for THAT NIGHT.

"Three dates?!"

"Umm, actually, two . . . the third's tonight," I confessed.

"I suspected as much."

"But like I said—"

"Sorry, but has this man asked you to be his girlfriend?"

"Well, not in so many *words*—" If only she'd met Reb Tevye, she'd understand.

"Are you engaged?"

"What? No!"

"That's all the information I need," she said.

"But he's a *rabbi*," I insisted.

"Zoe. You can't turn down invitations—from people you might *like*—just because you've been on two-slash-three dates with somebody else. I dated Jack for *months* before I stopped accepting other offers."

I was too busy processing the conversation to respond.

"You're *just* starting to date," Lisa continued. "You're entitled to meet *lots* of people before taking yourself off the market. And you *should*."

"Huh."

"Look. You could always just *tell* The Rabbi that you're seeing other people, if it'd make you feel better. But, at this point, it's not necessary."

"Really?"

"Really. And, incidentally, you should assume that this rabbi is dating around too. I mean, what—you're both gonna settle down with the first person you meet?"

"No, that would be crazy!" I cackled, sounding deranged. Because, of course, that is *precisely* the scenario I suspected Reb Tevye and I had both been hoping for. Only after listening to

Lisa did I realize exactly how shortsighted we'd been. I sighed. "I am *so* sorry I bothered you with this."

"No worries," she said kindly. "Dating's hard. I just happen to be a grizzled veteran. You can always call me."

"Thank you endlessly. You're a saint."

"Hardly!"

"So you're *sure* I'm not messing anything up for you?" I asked. "By maybe seeing Sean *and* The Rabbi?"

"Zoe, just take a deep breath and enjoy yourself. You're not messing anything up."

"You're literally the best ever."

I BREATHED THE biggest, guiltiest, sweetest sigh of relief when Reb Tevye called to cancel three minutes later.

"I am *so* sorry, Sweetie," he said, "but that family I told you about? They're going to take Hazel off life support. I'm on my way to the hospital now."

I shook off the "Sweetie" to focus on Hazel, her family, and the kind man I still felt I was two-timing. "Oh, my gosh. Aaron —I'm so sorry. I'll be thinking of all of you."

"Thank you. She's had an amazing life. But for her family, saying good-bye will be difficult." He sounded tired.

"Of course," I said. "What an incredible legacy Hazel will leave—seven great-grandchildren, right? They're lucky to have you."

"You're so special. So good," he said. I winced. "I'm really sorry our evening got disrupted. And it's Thursday, isn't it?"

"Yep. Oh! Shabbat tomorrow." An even deeper relief enveloped me.

"Zoe, can I come over on Saturday night? I'll hop in my car the second the sun sets."

Alex had just bailed on Saturday 'tinis and dinner to go to a wedding with Brian. "Of course," I said.

"Oh, good! *I can't wait to see you.*"

I giggled nervously. "Oh. Umm. Me neither. My best to Hazel and her family, and—good luck."

"Thanks, Sweetie. Goodnight."

Oof.

♡

March 13, 2008

Adam: You know when you're about to sleep with one person — who may think you're in love with them, or that they're in love with you — but you can't stop thinking about sleeping with someone else? (Of course you do.) Question: What if the first person is a rabbi? What would you do <u>then</u>? Please advise. And also, I love you. (And would have sex with you with no strings attached. By now I realize that's been made abundantly clear. But still. I would.) XX, Zoe

# Forty-Four

A seven-mile jalk at the EBC passed a good chunk of my Sabbath. Three o'clock pre-wedding pizza and wine with Alex passed another. When I'd broached the subject of eating out with Reb Tevye—because going out, like normal people, instead of jumping straight to Sex Appointments would, it seemed to me, be healthier—he'd said that he doesn't eat in non-kosher restaurants (*OUCH*), but *had* started eating sushi *at home*.[38] I tried, and likely failed, to mask my disappointment, and promised to have sushi waiting for him that night. I knew he wouldn't be interested in eating it before consummating our fledgling relationship, and Alex hated how seven o'clock weddings meant no dinner until ten, so our midafternoon meal benefited us both. Also, sharing three o'clock pizza and wine is a sign of a sound friendship.

Alex stashed three condoms in my nightstand and helped me choose an *I Look This Cute Even When I Stay Home* outfit. While she was concentrating on the outfit, I convinced her to let me meet Brian over drinks. The fact that this didn't take much convincing confirmed my suspicions that Brian was The One. As

---

[38] I didn't have the nerve to ask why someone would eat non-kosher food from a non-kosher restaurant, but only at home. What about eating the non-kosher food *in* the non-kosher restaurant made it worse than eating it in my non-kosher home?

the sun set, the song "Sunrise, Sunset" tormented me—I couldn't shake it. So I chased one shot of whiskey with two Pepto Bismols, and, in record time, the buzzer sounded. *Holy fuck.* I opened the door and tried to look normal.

"Hi, Sweetie!" *Ew. Why* did he have to co-opt the pet name heretofore used solely by my parents? I didn't call Rob anything other than "Rob" for three years. Aaron beamed. He wore a dress shirt under a fleece, navy blue slacks, a black belt, and black dress shoes. He'd come straight from synagogue. He kissed me before unloading the many items in his arms.

"Hi!" I said shrilly. "What's all this?" He relieved himself of another bunch of grocery store carnations, *two* gym bags, and a pink, Cubs teddy bear. I forced my lips into a smile while he slid the gym bags off his shoulders.

"A cutie for my cutie," he announced as he offered me the teddy bear. Thank God for Pepto.

"Aww," I managed. It was unreasonable to expect The Rabbi to know, so soon, that I didn't do cuties. And the gesture came from the right place. I kissed and thanked him.

"I keep coming here with lame flowers." He handed me blue carnations and laughed. "But I'm always in such a hurry to see you."

"It is totally the thought that counts, and I love them," I said. He followed me to the kitchen for a vase.

"Oh, and the Boy Scouts were selling those teddy bears the other day." He smiled anew. "I love spoiling you."

I tried and failed to swallow. "Thank you."

We smiled at each other for a minute before he assumed his Lust Face and lunged at me. The first ten make-out minutes always felt like Reb Tevye was cruising at a hundred miles an hour while I was still backing out of the driveway. But by the time we were down to just underwear, I felt warm and soft and transported. When he took off my bra and pressed against me, I was desperate to move things along. I thought of the condoms in the drawer next to the bed, but never had to mention them.

"Let me grab my bag," Reb Tevye said before peeling himself off me. He leaned down and was able to reach and drag the bag to him without leaving the bed. What all was in there I couldn't begin to guess. After rummaging for a minute, the dear man then pulled out a jumbo box of brand new condoms.

"That should do it," I said. He laughed.

"Zoe, you are too wonderful." And then on a dime, the color drained from his face, his usual kinetic energy evaporated, and he lay there, still.

"Here," I volunteered. My hormones were screaming—I couldn't wait for him to wrestle with the plastic wrap. So I reached into my nightstand and handed him a Trojan. We made out some more before awkwardly removing our undies under the covers. Then he pulled away, gazed deeply into my eyes, and said, "You're very special."

"You too." I coughed. I was singularly focused on *finally* getting laid; my groin throbbed like a cheap romance novel. The disgusting sound of crinkling lube confirmed that Reb Tevye had put on the Trojan. I reached down, but he pulled away.

"Zoe. . . ." He laughed nervously. "I just have to—I—I'm concerned about premature ejaculation."

Ick.

*Actual* premature ejaculation, I was prepared for. Discussing it in advance, in clinical terms? Not so much. I wanted to empathize with his nerves but really was desperate to have sex. Now. So I reached behind his neck and pulled him close.

"Aaron. It's just me. Let's have fun and not worry. OK?"

"OK!" he said excitedly and planted a wet one on my lips.

The tip of his penis then started poking me. Maybe it was some sort of pre-entry ritual.

"*Ohhhhhh*," he groaned in my ear as he flapped his torso against me with the rapidity of a hummingbird. "*UHHHHHH-HHHH!*" He was beating against me so fast that my hip and pubic bones began to hurt. Should I say something? What, exactly, was he doing? All I knew is that every body part surrounding, but not including, my vagina was getting beaten to a pulp. Reb Tevye—who was really sweating now—dug his fingernails into my shoulders and moved even faster.

"Oww," I said.

He must not have heard.

"Shit! Oh *SHIT!*" he yelled before letting out a soft "*Ahhhhh*." He opened his eyes to search mine, shuddered, and lay down on my chest. I could feel his heart hammering. "Oh, Zoe. That was amazing."

*What? What was amazing?*

*Oh, no. NO.*

"Umm. Aaron?" I finally brought myself to ask. "Did you just—come?"

"YEAH!" he yelped.

He rolled off of me before I'd really grasped that whatever had just happened was . . . it. That was the sex. If I didn't know he'd been married, I'd have thought that this was a very unfunny reenactment of the *40-Year-Old Virgin*. How could he dry-hump me, come, and think his job was done? Just then, a passing headlight illuminated The Rabbi's body and explained everything. I looked closely to make sure my eyes weren't playing tricks on me. But yes: Reb Tevye had the world's smallest penis. *That wasn't the tip tapping my outsides. That's as far inside as it goes.* My poor, unsuspecting vagina had been penetrated by something so miniscule, it hadn't even noticed. Size wasn't everything, but one needed *something* to work with. Even if that something was finding a way to get me off. FUCK.

"Oh," I stammered.

"I know," he grabbed my hand. "It was so fast! We were *so amped.*" He scooched closer and waited until I reluctantly met his eyes, which were now one Rabbi's penis length from mine. "I love you, Zoe."

I sucked air as if I were having that nightmare where you're trying, but unable, to scream.

"You don't have to respond. I just wanted you to know." He buried his face in my neck.

"I—Sorry—" I stuttered.

"You felt *incredible,*" he whispered directly into my ear. My entire body began to shake as The Rabbi fell right to sleep.

♡

March 15 / March 16, 2008

Adam: Hi again. I can barely see — I'm using the streetlight outside my bedroom window to write, because I wouldn't want to wake the FUCKING RABBI — or, more accurately, the NON-FUCKING RABBI — who appears undisturbed by the awfulness that just

happened right here in this very room. I'm writing to
(a) calm myself; (b) enjoy the irony of consulting
one of the world's biggest cocks while lying next
to one of the smallest; and (c) to say goodbye,
because I don't see how I'll make it 'til morning.
You all have meant everything to me. Love, Zoe

# Forty-Five

"I don't understand," Caren said for the seventeenth time since we'd begun our walk Sunday morning. "*Did* you have sex—or not?"

"Technically? I don't know." I couldn't stop shivering.

"How is that possible?"

"I feel bad for saying what I'm about to say, but . . . it's relevant."

"Go ahead."

"So—"

She nodded for me to continue.

"The Rabbi has such an incredibly small penis—and I mean *incredibly* small. Like, there has to be a medical term for it—that I can't be sure whether it was inside me or not."

Caren chewed her lip. "Oh, God," she whispered.

"So maybe it was in there—or just near there? At the time, I thought he was kind of . . . poking my outsides with it."

"Oh, God," she said again. "I'm so sorry." Now *she* shivered.

We walked for a minute before she broke the silence.

"Is it possible that, because you've never had sex with a Jewish man before, you just weren't . . . prepared? For that?"

"Absolutely not. Procreation wouldn't be possible for any

subset of the population with that median penis size," I reasoned. "And, although the last several months have made me doubt myself in many, many ways, I'm reasonably sure that I don't have a huge, gaping vagina." *Or did I?*

"Of course you don't," Caren said. We crossed the street. "Exactly how small are we talking?"

"Fully erect? Maybe three inches tall."

"*No!*"

"*Yes.* And so *thin!* One and a half fingers thin." I needed reassurance. "That can't be normal for Jewish guys, or *any* guys. Right?"

"No, *definitely* not. I mean, three inches—hard—is crazy small. And that really is thin." She lowered her voice and mouthed the words "hard" and "thin" because we were passing two old ladies on a bench.

I nodded. The combination of nausea and exhaustion I felt must have showed, because Caren stopped and clutched my shoulders. "Look. I've seen enough penises to know that you'll *never* have another run-in like this again. This was just bad luck."

"*Terrible* luck," I corrected.

"Terrible luck," she agreed.

We walked in silence for a few minutes.

"I have another question, Zee."

"Uh-huh."

"What did he offer to do for you? He must've been mortified."

"That's the thing! He was *not* mortified!" Caren was now mortified. "He seemed almost proud, when he woke up from the catnap he enjoyed during my massive panic attack. My satisfaction clearly never crossed his mind."

"That is beyond disgusting," she said.

"Beyond."

"Seriously. I've been with guys who haven't been so well-endowed, but they knew how to get the job done. This guy . . . I mean, he could have *tried*."

"*Exactly*."

"So please help me understand how he didn't leave your apartment until two hours ago," Caren said.

"Well, buckle your seatbelt. Because things got even *worse*."

"Fuck."

"Yep. Where was I—his post-splooge *I love you* and the sudden death of my sex drive?"

She nodded.

"Well. I'd picked up sushi—and fucking paper plates, since he won't eat off of my dishes. Sorry—that was mean."

"You're entitled," Caren said.

"So he wakes up from his nap and says he wants to eat, and I think I had an out-of-body experience. It was like I was watching myself put sushi on paper plates from afar. I must have looked like death—sushi is one of my favorite foods and I managed three bites—but he didn't notice. He wolfed down everything I'd bought, told me he couldn't wait any longer, and went to get one of his gym bags."

"WHY DID HE HAVE A GYM BAG?"

"Caren. He had *TWO* gym bags." I ignored her tortured expression. "So he gets one, pulls his chair next to mine, and says he wants to tell me all about his family."

"No," she whispered.

"*Yes*." I sniffed the air—I could have sworn that, despite two showers, The Rabbi's scent was still on me. "So then he pulls two huge photo albums from the bag. One from childhood, and one of him as an adult with his nieces and nephews."

"So he's *literally* insane. What did you do? I think I would've screamed at him to get out."

She probably would have. I probably *should* have.

"I was paralyzed. I just sat there, looking at the pictures, but not really seeing them."

I started to cry. The rest of the story gushed out, fast and furious, like The Rabbi himself. "And he has this horrible stare —I didn't tell you about it, but he does—and he stares into my eyes after *every single picture* of his nieces and nephews, and I can't stand to look at him, and after the eighth or twelfth one, he says, '*Aren't they delicious?*' and then I died.'"

"*Delicious?*"

"Yes."

"Repulsive."

"*I know.* At this point, I start thinking about how desperately I need him to leave, so that I can shower and wash everything around me, or alternatively slit my wrists—"

"No—"

"—but then he hits me with—and I quote, because it has been ringing in my ears ever since—'*I ache for children. I'd love five. What about you, Sweetie?*'"

Caren recoiled. "I don't understand."

"He wants five kids, Care. He *aches* for *five* kids. And less importantly, but still an issue, is all this 'Sweetie.'"

"I would have had a psychotic break," she said.

"I may well have. I think I jumped up to walk Basil right around then...."

"Nicely done."

"When I got back, he'd moved his overnight bag—which, if you've been paying attention, you will remember was his *second* piece of luggage—into the bedroom, changed into PJs, and put the Cutie on my pillow."

"I forgot about the fucking Cutie!" Caren cried. "And I'm outraged that he packed pajamas. In a *bag*."

"He wouldn't leave, and wanted to hold me while I lay awake on the wet spot, and he snored, and I shook, maybe with some kind of trauma-induced fever, until I could finally wake him and shove him out the door. Thank God for nine o'clock Sunday school! I can't see him again—I literally *cannot*—and he thinks we're in love and are going to have a million children and that I'm going to move to Oak Park and walk to temple. . . ." I was beginning to hyperventilate.

Caren sat me on a bench. "Look. You're not moving." I nodded and tried to breathe evenly. "This was a bad experience—really bad—but you know what? You'll end it and move on."

"But how do I end it when I can't even look at him?"

"Why would you have to look at him?" Her eyes widened with understanding. "Honey. You do *not* have to dump him in person."

"I *don't?*"

"No!"

"But he's a *rabbi!*"

"So the fuck what? He's nuts! I mean, he thinks he fucking loves you already? Who jizzes all over someone and then says that? And crams family photo albums and five hypothetical children into a *third date?!*"

I knew I shouldn't have told her it was only our third date.

"Given how delusional he is, and how traumatized you are,

it would actually be a terrible idea for you to meet in person."

"So what do I do?"

"You call him," she said. "The sooner, the better."

The thought of having to talk to Reb Tevye turned my stomach, but talking was a whole lot better than enduring his stare ever again.

# Forty-Six

Monday finally arrived. I'd let Reb Tevye go straight to voicemail twice on Sunday—he didn't leave a message either time—so I knew I'd have an email waiting for me at the office that morning. Decency required that I respond, and soon. I was sure The Rabbi's anxiety was through the roof, and also that I was a terrible person.

> Good morning, Zoe! I thought about you all day yesterday but sensed that you wanted some distance. Spending a day processing taking our relationship to the next level is probably wise. But you know me . . . I couldn't resist reaching out 😊. Also, I've been thinking: You mentioned a few times that it'd be nice to go out, and I agree! So may I take you to a movie tonight? It'd be wonderful to spend the evening together. Love, Aaron

I responded:

> Hi Aaron, Thanks so much for the kind invitation—I love the movies! But I really try not to miss yoga. I have a full day at work (I'm sure you do too), but how about I call you as soon as I leave the office? I'll look forward to chatting then. Zoe

Stuck in rush-hour traffic on my way home from the world's longest and least necessary deposition, I felt compelled to call Reb Tevye despite not knowing what to say.

"Hi!" he answered. His voice was strained; he'd intuited that all was not well, which made me feel even worse about hurting his feelings.

"Hi," I said. "Sorry I've been out of the loop today—I was literally out of the Loop, at a deposition. And, umm, yesterday I had to prepare for it," I lied. A partner took the dep and brought me along only because I'd organized the exhibits.

"So," he said after a brief pause. "I know the movies are out, but can I come kiss you goodnight after yoga?"

*NO YOU MAY NOT.*

"Somehow I end up going to sleep at one in the morning when that happens." We both tried to chuckle. "Aaron," I said. Boom. Suddenly, I had the words I needed. And a plan. "Can I talk to you about something?"

"Of course," he said seriously.

"OK. So I think you're the best—smart, kind, cute, interesting—and I know the right person is out there waiting for you *right now*. But I think that you and I are on different timelines." My heart raced.

"I freaked you out, with the pictures. Right? My sister told me I shouldn't have done the pictures. But I just wanted to share my family. . . ." His voice trailed off.

I probably would've liked his sister.

"No, no," I lied again. "I just—I think I rushed into a relationship too soon. I realized, after you left, that—"

"Your divorce is too fresh," he interjected. He sounded relieved. I ran with it.

"Yes! Exactly." I hoped I was doing the right thing, lying repeatedly to a clergyman. "I'm not ready to be intimate with someone else just yet."

"I understand."

"And you're way ahead of me—ready to move on, get married, have kids, right now. But I think I just need to. . . ."

"Slow down," he finished for me again. "I totally get it. So. Let's slow things down!"

*Sigh.*

"Aaron—"

"It won't take you long. I mean, you want kids, right?"

"I do—"

"And," his voice rose a register, "you *are* in your *thirties*. . . ."

*EW.*

"As of a few months ago, yes," I said as evenly as I could. I considered adding that one's eggs don't all die at the stroke of midnight on one's thirtieth birthday, but decided to stay focused on ENDING THE CALL. I cleared my throat.

"Aaron. We're on totally different timelines. You deserve someone who's right there with you."

"Well," he said in a tone that told me that he was about to negotiate.

"I haven't healed," I interrupted him. "I need more time—"

"But—"

"And I don't know if that's a year, or two, but this kind of thing can't be rushed." I knew I'd put the nail in the coffin as soon as I'd uttered the word *year*; he couldn't delay his future children for a *month*. "And now, *NOW* is your time!" I held my breath.

"You know, I really *do* feel like now is my time," he finally said. "I just—" he choked. "I wanted my time to be with *you*."

Fuck. My heart swelled. I wished he had a Janie. "Oh, Aaron —I'm so sorry." He didn't seem to hear me.

"I *really* thought this was *it*, you know? That I was finally on my way. . . ." he said.

"I know," I interrupted. He'd hate himself later if I let him keep talking. "But I also know that, by the time I start dating again, I'll hear through the grapevine that you're either married, or getting married, and you'll be exactly where you want to be, with exactly the right person. I *know* it. You'll see."

He sniffed.

"We can still talk. Right? We can still be friends," he insisted.

*Of course*, I almost said. But then I stopped myself. "Honestly, Aaron? I think you need to be fully available to receive Mrs. Right. You deserve that."

"You're right." He sighed mightily. "You're right."

*YES!*

"Take good care, Zoe. I have to go and, you know . . . process everything. Good-bye, my love."

*Ew, ew,* and *ew.*

"Umm. Good-bye, Aaron."

"Zoe?"

"Yes?" I retracted the sigh of relief sitting at the top of my throat.

"You really *were* wonderful the other night. . . ."

*STOP.*

"The way you make love is so—giving."

I submitted to one whole-body shiver before squeaking, "Take care" and snapping my phone shut.

# Forty-Seven

I reveled in my freedom—from piercing stares, painful dry-humps, and worse—for the rest of the week. I kept a regular schedule. I slept in freshly sterilized bedding. I got back down to one shower per day. I was breathing again. Until Friday morning, when this happened:

Sean O'Kelly: Hey, hot stuff.

I began sweating into a dry-clean-only top at eight thirty. *Hot stuff? How did someone so gorgeous speak this way?* I shut my door to give this non-billable non-client my undivided attention.

Zoe Greene: Hey, how are you?

Sean O'Kelly: Jesus. So swamped. It's been murderous over here. :0--:

I laughed. Even Caren would approve of the corpse emoticon. Maybe.

Zoe Greene: Sounds brutal. So sorry!

Sean O'Kelly: It's cool. Cuz one way or another, this hearing's donezo by close of business. And you maaayyyyy recall that you, sexy thang, promised me a date.

The angel on my left shoulder advised me to avoid men until my pubic bone healed. The devil on my right shoulder knocked her unconscious.

Zoe Greene: That does ring a bell. . . .

Sean O'Kelly: So how about tomorrow? Dinner. Wear the jeans ;).

**I froze.**

Sean O'Kelly: Chickadee?

*I mean.*

Zoe Greene: I have dinner plans tomorrow—can you do drinks instead?[39]

Sean O'Kelly: Oh boo. C'mon. Whoever he is can't possibly be as punctual as me. Ditch him 😑.

Zoe Greene: Ha! I never ditch girlfriends.

Sean O'Kelly: Well well. Far be it from me to interfere with a GNO! Drinks it is.

Zoe Greene: Deal.

Sean O'Kelly: Not so fast—I'll need confirmation on the jeans.

*Creepy? Flattering? Both? Regardless, I should write Sandy a thank-you note for the jeans.*

Zoe Greene: Confirmed.

Sean O'Kelly: Gaslight, 5:00?

Zoe Greene: Perfect.

⟅ℯ⟆

---

[39] Lie. Caren, Alex, and I only had loose plans to drink Caren's book club leftovers at some point Saturday night.

I DECIDED TO tell Alex and Caren about the date. (But not the jeans, *hot stuff*, *chickadee*, or my recurring Irish sex dreams.) I was about to grab my leather jacket and head to Gaslight—a good pub-slash-sports-bar within walking distance of my apartment—when my phone buzzed.

SO: Don't hate me. Can we do 5:30? Stuck at work 😩

I wiped my sweaty hands on The Jeans and waited a minute before writing back.

ZG: Of course.

SO: Know what ur thinkin, but Ill b on time

ZG: No worries!

I'd already had my shot of whiskey. There was nothing to do but wait.

I walked into the bar at 5:32. Noise overwhelmed me when I opened the door; the place was packed. The season's first baseball games were on the bar's many TVs. Gaslight was a marked improvement over Kilkenney's in that there was no unnecessary bouncer, and a substantial portion of patrons were over the age of twenty-five. I shimmied toward the bar to wait for Irish. But he was already there, leaning against it. He made no effort to hide the fact that he'd been watching me since I walked in. A wool peacoat was draped over his arm. His jeans, though slightly dated, fit perfectly, as did an old, gray, long-sleeved Holy Cross baseball tee. A pair of Puma sneakers completed his Saturday look. He cocked a half-smile before reaching for me.

"Hi," I stuttered, as he gave me a lingering hug and kiss on the cheek. His body was broad, his arms were strong, and his blue eyes even more brilliant up close. I worried I might pass out, so I pulled away.

"Sorry I'm *late*," he said with a flourish I ignored.

"All good! Sorry you had to work," I managed. His physical presence was a lot to get used to. He reached for the beer the bartender had just hurriedly placed at his elbow. We were quiet. I began to remember how conversation hadn't come easily at Kilkenney's.

"So," I tried. "Crazy hours notwithstanding, how's the new firm?"

"It's great." He took a drink. "Conservative. Church-going. Lots of Catholic-school alums." He misinterpreted my raised eyebrows as a request for elaboration. "So they're good guys— they know right from wrong. Know what I mean?"

*Fuhhhhhcckkkkkk.*

"Not really," I heard myself say. "I'm liberal and Jewish, as are several of my colleagues—male *and* female—and we all seem to know right from wrong."

He stared at me, beautiful and speechless, until he stuttered, "Oh, God. Of course they do! I don't know why I said that. I think—sorry." He shook his head and laughed nervously.

I felt a twinge of pity. "Don't worry about it," I said, even though I wondered if I should find a nice way to leave.

"Can we please start over?" Irish asked. His freckles stood out amid the pink that had washed across his gorgeous face. "Here—I'll get your jacket. Let's start there."

He managed to graze both my shoulders as he slid my jacket off. And fuck, he smelled amazing. Then he *full*-smiled at me and looked so worried that I couldn't help but smile back. I also suspected that my response to his inane comment may have been the teeniest bit obnoxious.

"What would you like to drink?" he asked as he pulled me

next to him at the bar. He left his right arm around me. His coloring was incredible . . . I had the sudden urge to lick his face. He motioned ever so slightly to a cute, young bartender in a tiny tank top. This was all it took to steal her undivided attention from the crowd.

"Hi there. This beautiful lady needs a drink." He looked at me. "Guinness, right?"

*Yes, please*, I should have said. *Sounds great.* But the way Irish's T-shirt draped over his muscled shoulders, the feel of his arm across my back, his scent, the craziness that came out of his mouth . . . I ignored good advice for a second time and asked the pretty girl for a scotch. Irish cocked his eye and turned up the corners of his edible lips. I struggled to remain upright.

"Scotch," said Irish, grinning. "I need to up my game."

I shrugged with what I hoped looked like nonchalance. And almost had a heart attack when Irish leaned even closer to look me in the eye. "I thought sexy little things like you got cosmos." He half-smiled. "Drinks with umbrellas in 'em." His crystal blue eyes danced as he nudged me. And fuck all if I didn't giggle like a schoolgirl.

"Nah. The Guinness should've put you on notice," I wheezed. I was *freaking out* that he'd called me a *sexy little thing*, which I suspected he knew.

"I'm just givin' you shit," he said amiably. And *may* have glanced at my lips, but I couldn't tell for sure. I was in very real danger of kissing him when he looked over my head.

"Ooh—they're about to leave." He pointed behind me. "How about I wait for your drink while you grab the table?"

"Sure," I said, grateful for a moment alone. I managed to beat two young, appletini-toting girls to the table and sat down.

Then I got to watch Irish walk toward me. He flicked his head gently to one side to move a lock of hair from his forehead. I took our drinks from him so that he could dump our jackets over the back of his chair. Even his beer breath smelled good.[40] We smiled at each other.

"Thanks so much," I said. "For the drink."

"Absolutely. Least I can do, after making you wait for me—twice."

*Sexy little thing! And he finally apologized!*

"Your shirt," I yelled over the noise. "Did you play?"

"Oh—yeah," he looked down to remind himself what he was wearing. "I did." He half-smiled. Probably because he'd just busted me looking at his chest. I glued an unimpressed expression onto my face. "I actually played professionally for a couple of years. Before law school."

*"You did?!"* I squealed, now looking *very* impressed.

"Yep. But don't get excited—it doesn't mean what you think it does."

"Really? Because I think playing Single A for five minutes is amazing."

"Nah, not the minors. I played in a separate league not affiliated with Major League Baseball."

I didn't know there was a separate league. But it was still *professional*, which explained his professional body. "What position?"

"Catcher," he said through a smile. His baseball days were obviously happy ones.

"For how long? And how'd you end up in law school?"

He leaned back and rested his fingers on the table. "Well, I

---

[40] How is this possible?

was a solid hitter but never had a strong enough defensive arm. So just two years." He paused. "As for law school, I always knew I'd have to get a real job eventually. That baseball wouldn't last forever."

*But the square shoulders might!*

"But if you were a great hitter, why didn't they try putting you at, like, first base?"

His eyes gleamed. I started to wonder if I might literally die.

"That's a great question. But my team was stacked with first basemen. So time to hang 'em up and start earning money." He folded his arms across his sculpted chest. "How do you know so much about baseball?"

"How'd you know I know about baseball?"

He laughed. "You knew that a first baseman doesn't need to throw runners out at second from his knees, but could use some of his catcher's skills to scoop balls from the dirt." He looked me up and down over the rim of his glass as he sipped. "Impressive, Miss Zee."

"I've picked up a few things." I was *sure* my face was beet red. "My dad took me to my first Cubs game when I was two."

"Cubs?"

"Born and raised," I said.

He grimaced and pointed to himself. "Cardinals."

*Gross.*

"So listen," Irish said as he sat up straight and furrowed his milky brow. "I wanted to say something. About earlier."

*Please don't. Let's forget all about it so I can continue enjoying your hotness.* "Oh, don't wor—"

"No, seriously," he insisted. "I offended you, and I want to apologize."

"It's really not—"

"—I didn't mean anything by my comment." He looked at his hands for a second before continuing. "I think what I meant was that, I think religious people—*not* just Catholics—tend to be more . . . ethical. Than other people."

*Shite.*

"Some of the most ethical and important people in my life aren't religious at all," I snapped. *Why did I keep biting his head off?* His comments *did* offend me, but I could have responded more graciously.

Irish hung his head. "Maybe I should just stop talking," he said. I tried to think of something to say, but couldn't, so he went on. "I don't know why I keep . . . I really am trying to apologize." His blue eyes met mine as he deadpanned, "Now begins the silent portion of our evening."

I couldn't help but laugh.

We were interrupted by our waitress. Irish ordered another round of drinks and some snacks. I still couldn't think of anything to say, so I tried to just smile—without slapping *or* licking him. He knocked back the rest of his beer.

"Honestly? I think you've got me a little flustered, Miss Greene."

He blushed. He couldn't be serious. His *T-shirt* got me flustered.

"Huh?"

He laughed, and with good reason. I was totally flummoxed. "You heard me! And I'll bet you've heard it before."

I'd heard this precisely zero times before.

"Umm, no. But I'm sorry for snapping at you."

He laughed heartily. "No! I'm not flustered because you're

spicy. I *like* that you're spicy." We were both leaning toward each other now; even I couldn't deny the chemistry between us. "I'm flustered because I haven't gone out with many girls who are so outspoken, smart—*and* hot."

OMG.

"Pfft. . . ."

He walked his fingers across the table and nudged my hand. "You were fiery the second I met you." He whistled. "Hoo-boy, were you pissed!"

"No, I seriously just had to walk my dog. You were *very* late."

"Oh, please, you were *totally* pissed. *Firecracker.*"

I threw up my hands in exasperation. "Just because I had to leave doesn't make me—whatever—"

"Spicy," he finished. "A spicy firecracker." He was really enjoying this.

"Fuff." I gave up.

"It didn't matter," he said. "I thought you were so friggin' cute. And knew you were a spicy firecracker before you even opened your mouth."

"You did not." I finished my drink to buy myself time and then changed tacks. "Honestly? I thought you were totally uninterested. You hardly looked at me."

"Well it was kinda weird," he shrugged, "with Lisa and Jack there, and you hating me by the time I arrived."

My mom always said I had no poker face. Apparently, she was right.

"I wasn't mad!" I said anyway, which only made Irish laugh harder.

"Yes, you were! Flames were coming out of your eyes, and your mouth was all scrunchy. Like this." He leaned across the table and pushed the sides of my lips into a pout with his right thumb and index finger.

"Stop it!" I giggled again. Jesus. My breath was shaky from feeling his fingers near my mouth.

"It was sexy. In a pissy way."

We flirted recklessly over my second, and his second and third, drinks. Part of me was still trying to parse the troubling things he'd said, but most of me just gave in. The situation felt dangerous but also strangely empowering. Despite being confused and a little drunk, and despite Irish's otherworldly gorgeousness, I felt, somehow, in charge.

"So you really won't have dinner with me?" he eventually asked with mock incredulity.

"I can't." I looked at my watch.

"Your dog?" he asked. I rolled my eyes. "Sorry, it's just so easy," he smiled.

"No, my girlfriends."

Alex and Caren were, of course, indifferent to when I showed up, but Irish didn't need to know that.

"Tell them something came up. Let's order dinner and a bottle of wine."

"I really can't," I said.

Which wasn't a total lie, because I'd *for sure* mount him if I ingested one more drop of alcohol. And have a stroke. And die. He begrudgingly motioned for the bill.

"Rain check, then," he said. He looked me up and down and, this time, made no effort to hide it. The energy between us thrummed.

"You know I'm divorced, right? And Jewish. And also a Democrat."

This all flew out of my mouth without my permission. My face fell—*why in the fucking fuck am I always such a SPAZ?*—but Irish just leaned in closer.

"I *didn't* know you were divorced, but I *did* learn, about two minutes after you walked in here, that you're Jewish and a Democrat." He grinned. "*Liberal* is, I believe, how you described yourself."

My mouth literally hung open.

"Which is funny," he continued, scooping up my hands and skimming my wrists with his thumbs, "because divorced, Jewish Democrats, who are super cute and sexy, are kinda my thing."

*Oh my fucking God.* This cheesy line, coming from him, slayed.

"Oh, please." I coughed.

He released my hands to sign the bill. He winked at me before standing up and handing me my jacket. As we walked out of the bar, he rested his hand on my lower back. I urgently fumbled for mints in my purse.

"Are you *really* serious about this no dinner thing?" he asked when we stepped out into the quiet.

I nodded and smiled at him. "Another time," I said.

His face totally changed. Only then did I realize he'd been sure, until right then, that I'd be going home with him. Once he accepted that it wasn't happening, he was ready to end our date.

"I'm that way," he said, pointing back over his shoulder.

"Oh. OK—I'm gonna grab a cab."

"Cool." He kissed me on the cheek. He looked awkward and beautiful at the same time.

"Thanks again," I said.

He smiled and turned toward home.

"YOU REALIZE THAT you will totally have sex with this guy," Caren announced over Thai takeout and wine. "The dirty kind."

"Oh, *totally*." Alex laughed. She put her hand out for a high-five from Caren, which Caren hit without having to look away from her food.

I rolled my eyes. "Despite his intermittent rudeness, I hope you're right."

"You deserve some functional sex," Caren said.

I turned to Alex. "You're seriously OK with this?" Where was the guarded, liberal, feminist atheist we all knew and loved?

She considered. "Yeah. I mean, what's the harm? Even if Irish isn't boyfriend material, he might make a *great* rabbi-eraser."

We all shuddered. "Agreed," I said. "Now can we please talk about literally anything else?"

"Actually," Caren straightened up, "I've got something."

"Thank God," I said.

"OK. So you've both inspired me. To get back out there. I signed up for Match.com."

"Amazing!" said Alex.

"Yay!" I squealed.

Alex and I had always suspected that Caren's many, many dating rules were one big defense mechanism. Like Alex, she'd taken a couple bad breakups to heart.

"All right, all right. Let's not get ahead of ourselves—I just made my profile today."

We knew better than to say a word more about it. So we drank wine and talked about Brian, the office, my slow and steady jalking improvement, and other normal life stuff, before Alex and I shared a cab home at midnight. It occurred to me when I put my key in the door that, for the first time in months, my shit smithereens hadn't even come up.

# Forty-Eight

I usually appreciate clear, direct communication. But when I awoke (mildly hungover) on Sunday morning to an unambiguous text sent by Irish at 1:34 a.m., I panicked. I guess I'd been expecting him to disappear again. Or maybe I just had morning-message PTSD from The Rabbi.

SO: divorced+jewish+dem=sexxxy

I had literally never received a text message containing any variant of the word "sex." I had no idea what to do. But after a painful jalk,[41] I decided to respond.

ZG: You're hilarious. Thanks again for a great happy hour.

I heard nothing back, and convinced myself I never would. So, of course, *TWELVE* days later, I was rushing to meet Bubbe for Shabbat services when my computer dinged.

Sean O'Kelly: heyyyyy, good lookin'

I briefly succumbed to my usual Irish-induced paralysis.

Zoe Greene: Hey!

Sean O'Kelly: Whatcha up to tonight?

I debated telling him the truth, and then did. May as well get real.

---

[41] Note to self: DRINK LESS.

Zoe Greene: Actually about to take my grandma to
temple.

To his credit, only a few seconds elapsed before his next
communiqué.

Sean O'Kelly: Awwww. So maybe you're sweet *and*
spicy ;).

And Jewish.

Zoe Greene: Maybe so.

Sean O'Kelly: A *sweet* firecracker.

Zoe Greene: What's up with you?

Sean O'Kelly: Nice segue, Counselor.

Zoe Greene: I try.

Sean O'Kelly: Something fun, I hope, cuz I just finished an
arbitration that kicked my ass. Call me after Granny's in
bed. We'll have dinner.

Sean O'Kelly: (Dinner is this thing normal people do after
drinks. You'd love it.)

OMG.

Zoe Greene: Ha. OK, I'll call you. Gotta run!

I hightailed it to meet Bubbe's bus with my cheeks on virtual
fire.


I CALLED IRISH right after I dropped Bubbe off. He didn't answer, so I left a voicemail. An hour later, I ate a burger with my
parents. By eleven o'clock, I was frustrated, horny, and pissed. I
washed up, popped in my mouth guard, donned my oversize U2
*War* T-shirt, and climbed into bed. I was just settling in with *Us*

*Weekly* when my phone dinged. *Don't even look at it,* I told my-self. But I was already out of bed and halfway to my charger.

SO: Come see me.

What nerve! *One Mississippi. Two Mississippi. ThreeMissis-sippiFourMissi-Five.*

ZG: Figured you got tied up so already in bed.

SO: Tied up . . . bed. Dirty gurl 😏.

ZG: G'night!

SO: Come see me.

ZG: Dinner is this thing people do before 11:00. Turning in.

SO: Unturn! @ Twisted Lzrd.

My Irish fantasies had reached such fever pitch that I proba-bly *would* have walked over to Twisted Lizard, a DePaul spot with mediocre Mexican food and strong margaritas—if I didn't have zit cream smeared across my T-Zone and suspect that Irish was the bad kind of wasted.

ZG: Literally in bed. Have fun, talk later.

SO: Mmm, bed. I'll come2u 😏.

Visions of Reb Tevye's unannounced visit danced in my head.

ZG: Ha. G'night!

SO: Ur always leavin me hangin 😔

I typed and erased eighteen versions of *ARE YOU SERI-OUS?!* before going with:

ZG: Oh please. Congrats on the arbitration. Talk soon.

*But please don't have sex with any cute DePaul girls tonight,* I prayed as I turned off my phone and tossed it across the room.

♡

March 28, 2008

Dear Manager McGuinness — Paul, if I may.
Honestly? I think you bear some responsibility for
this — my Irish fetish, that is. It's become
unhealthy. And if you'd never brought U2 to the
world, then maybe I wouldn't be as fixated on this
guy . . . but then the world would be shittier.
(And U2 would've found their way onto the world
stage anyway, don't you think?) So never mind. Even
though you and I don't talk as much, I wanted you
to know that I love you too. XO, Zoe

"YOU'RE PISSED BECAUSE Irish lost track of time while celebrating an arbitration finishing?" Boone asked while I ran errands Saturday morning.

"*No.* I'm pissed because he asked me to dinner, told me to
call him when I was ready for dinner, and then stood me up. I
can't believe I have to explain this to you."

"Zees. I know you're gonna go all '*Boonie, you pig!*' on me, but
women are too good at mindfucking nothings into somethings."

I groaned. I heard Brooke groan in the background too.

"OK, first, I wouldn't call you a *pig.* I'd call you an *asshole.*"

"Noted. Second?"

"*Second*, he blew off dinner *and* my call."

"*God*," Boone said. "He didn't miss your call *on purpose.*

When he realized the time, he texted. So now you know for sure that he wants to do it with you."

"Oy," Brooke said.

"See? *Brooke* knows he's playing games," I said.

"Zo. As the only party to this conversation with a penis, I say this guy slept a total of six hours last week, asked you out with best intentions, but ended up getting drunk with his colleagues and didn't check his phone. He reached out, even though it was late, because he likes you. Period."

An hour later, I got a text from Brooke:

Didn't want it going to A's head, but he may b right. Have fun w/this 1! XO

If only I could figure out how.


AT TEN THIRTY that night, Jimmy ordered drinks for a bunch of Alex's friends, including *moi*, at Bluebird, the cute bar next to Hot Chocolate (still my favorite restaurant). I loved when Al's college friends came to town: They were irreverent, boisterous, and fun. We'd had a fairly raucous dinner next door and now Jimmy was bringing me my third glass of wine. Halfway through it, I felt my phone buzz through the clutch I was holding under my arm.

"Oh, my God."

"Who is it?" Alex and Jimmy asked simultaneously. I could tell from Alex's expression that she feared it was Rob or The Rabbi, and from Jimmy's that he hoped it was Prince William or similar.

"Irish," I said before turning to Alex's friends. "The guy you all decided at dinner is either commitment-avoidant, closeted, or a garden-variety asshole."

"OOH! GIVE IT," demanded Jimmy, before wrenching my phone from me. "IT SAYS, *WHERE R U, HOT STUFF?*" he squealed with delight.

"Tell him to come here!" Nina pleaded. Nina had gotten married right out of college and, at this point, experienced all romantic excitement vicariously. Now she and Jimmy were both hopping around and clapping.

"Yeah!" Scarlett seconded. (She got married young too.)

I looked to Alex.

"Here's the deal," she said. "This is a booty call. Straight-up. So only go for it if you're OK getting action with *no strings attached.*" She studied me carefully. We'd talked often about *wanting* to be Samanthas but *really* being Carries (an improvement for me, because I used to be a Charlotte)[42].

"I'm good," I assured her. "It's time to put up or shut up."

"I HOPE HE PUTS *WAY* UP!" Jimmy hollered. The girls roared. Alex was quiet.

ZG: Bluebird in Wicker Park.

My heart pounded. "Someone give me gum," I commanded. Scarlett retrieved and placed a piece of Trident on my open palm. All of us were relieved by Irish's quick response.

SO: Perf. At map room. Meet me!

"But we want him to come *here*!" Scarlett cried.

"HE *SHOULD* COME HERE!" Jimmy insisted.

"Fuck it," Nina said. "If she wants to get laid, *who cares*

---

[42] I hope this footnote is gratuitous, but please watch *Sex and the City* in its entirety if you haven't already.

who goes where? Feminism means not worrying about shit like this."

"I actually agree with that," Alex said.

"YARSE!" shouted Scarlett in a guttural tone.

"For the love of *God* please go," said Shireen, wringing her hands. "I can't even remember my last good sex." Shireen was in a dry spell.

"I'M GOING!" I shouted.

I drank the rest of my wine, plus half of Jimmy's, and bummed another piece of gum.

ZG: See you in a few.

"Come right back if he sucks," Alex whispered when she hugged me.

"TAKE THIS," Jimmy did *not* whisper before pressing a neon green, glow-in-the-dark, watermelon-flavored condom into my hand.

"Jesus, Jimmy!" I handed it back to him. "I'm not going to a carnival." I kissed him on the cheek.

On the short cab ride to the Map Room—a Chicago institution with an infinite beer list—I received Irish's one-word response:

SO: Cool.

I briefly considered bolting as I approached the Map Room's front door, but I was buzzed enough to proceed. And then I saw my Jake Ryan at the bar. Our eyes met when he looked up from his beer. He half-smiled, and I was officially toast. I planned to kiss him, right there at the bar . . . until I noticed this guy with him. I settled for a lingering hug before Irish introduced me to Doug, his boring dude-friend.

I loved how Irish found ways to keep bodily contact while we waited Doug out. But by the time I'd finished my beer, I was seriously hating Doug. Would he ever leave? Should I just go back to Bluebird? But then Irish pressed his chest into my back, wrapped his arms around me, and rested his hands so that his thumbs touched the skin right above my jeans. Somehow—I wasn't really paying attention, since Irish was *LITERALLY TOUCHING ME*—he got rid of Doug, and we were alone. He spun me around, clasped his hands behind my back, and looked down into my eyes. I wobbled slightly.

"My li'l firecracker. You finally came to see me."

"I tried to see you last night. Don't be hyperbolic."

"I love how your vocab's still major, even when you're drunk."

Our lips were millimeters apart. No matter what, my body *always* responded to him.

"You're a Republican, aren't you?" I asked boozily.

Irish laughed uncomfortably but held his grip on my waist. His eyes drifted to my mouth.

"Betcha voted for Bush," I slurred. Were there actual ice crystals in his eyeballs? "Don't answer that. . . ."

He kissed me. It was amazing.

"It wasn't a question," he replied when we stopped.

"Huh?"

"You said not to answer a statement."

"Right," I whispered.

We kissed again.

"Where'd you go to law school, anyway? Didn't Lisa say it was fucking Harvard or something?" He pressed my entire body into his. The way his arms fit across my back was killer. The room started to spin.

"*No way!*" I said, as if Harvard were preposterous. "Yale." I grinned.

"Well la-dee-fuckin'-dah," he crowed, loosening his grip on my waist to throw his head back. I teetered; he caught me easily. "An Ivy League girl," he said before lifting me onto Doug's vacated bar stool with almost no effort. I draped my arms around his neck. "Ivy Leaguers talk too much," he said.

Before I knew it, we were making out like college kids.

The next day, I could barely remember the cab ride to my apartment. But I knew that: We made out for a couple of brilliant, sweaty hours; undies stayed on (rightly, given how drunk we were); and Irish looked as good mostly naked as I'd imagined. I woke up at eight o'clock on Sunday morning to find him—in all his chiseled, Celtic splendor—sleeping soundly next to me.

If I hadn't felt like death, I probably would have stared at his perfect form before jumping him. But I *did* feel like death, and didn't want to barf on Irish.[43] So I slipped on the shirt nearest the bed (his) and weaved my way to the guest bathroom. I splashed water on my face, took two Peptos, and brushed my teeth with the spare toothbrush I was thrilled to find under the sink. When I got back to my room, I heard Irish taking an interminable whiz in my bathroom. I raced out of his shirt and into a bra, T-shirt, and shorts. Getting dressed so fast made me nauseous; I clamped my eyes shut and leaned against the closet door.

"Hey," Irish half-smiled when he emerged. He wore only boxers but seemed totally at ease.

"Hey," I smiled awkwardly as I fell back into bed. "Are you as hungover as I am?"

---

[43] Seriously, Self. Please drink less.

"Kinda beat up," he said. "But I'll survive."

Despite my misery, I enjoyed watching him dress. "I think I'm gonna walk home," Irish said. "Shake off these cobwebs."

We moved toward the door. I was relieved to see Basil in his crate, which meant I must've walked him and put him to bed. When we faced each other, I felt seriously sick, and also mortified about how I must've looked. Irish, of course, looked perfect—he was impervious to alcohol. He pulled me toward him.

"Do all Yalies have such hot little bodies?"

Overwhelmed, I looked at the floor. When I looked back up, he kissed me. He'd found the Scope in my medicine cabinet. His breath was minty, his hands were sure, and then he was gone.

AT TEN THIRTY, the buzzer woke me. (My body and I had reached an accord after Irish left: In exchange for not vomiting, I would allow it to lie very, very still on the sofa.) "Crap!" I stood up too fast. My down-the-street neighbor, Hannah, and I were supposed to do an eight-mile jalk, and I'd forgotten all about it.

Inga had introduced me to Hannah a couple of months earlier because we were both "runners." Although Hannah was an *actual* runner, Inga wanted her to jalk to get her strength back after a hip injury. We'd gotten to know each other over several jalks. Hannah and her husband, Joe, had met in college and had an adorable toddler, Abigail. I guiltily opened the door.

"Well hello," she said, smiling knowingly before laughing. "You look like shit, Dude! No offense." She was bright-eyed and adorable in leggings, long-sleeved running shirt, and mesh baseball cap. She was a green-eyed, natural redhead who, she swore, "would manage to burn on the North Pole."

"I'm so, *so* sorry," I moaned as I walked gingerly back to the couch. She closed the door behind her. "But . . . Irish just left."

"He *did*?! Ooh!" She clapped her hands and stopped abruptly. "Wait—isn't he the asshole?"

"Most likely."

"Ah." She unlaced her shoes.

"Suffice it to say, I was not expecting to get irresponsibly drunk or have Irish spend the night. I'm *so* sorry I spazzed on our run."

"Oh, please," she said generously. "I've got my iPod so I can run solo. After you tell me *everything*." Her demure, sweet face broke into a mischievous grin. She sighed wistfully after I delivered the details as best I could remember them.

"So my first sex was actually with this football player at Notre Dame," she said conspiratorially.

"NO!" I had been *sure* that Joe was her one and only.

"Do not say a *word*," she cautioned. "He was totally aloof, and I never heard from him except to have sex three times. But it was good, and I don't regret it."

"*No,*" I gasped again.

"Don't look at me like that!"

"I'm sorry! I'm just surprised—but actually love meeting this side of you."

"I was eighteen, we had this *huge* chemistry . . . and didn't really even talk. It was a purely physical relationship." She shrugged. "I loved it for what it was."

I was speechless. She laced back up, smiling to herself, lost in memories. Because she was a real runner, eight miles alone didn't intimidate her.

"When you're an old fart mom like me," she added, "you'll be really glad to have had some hot sex in your life."

Her belief that I would, in fact, be an old fart mom one day made me forget my nausea for a whole minute.

"Enjoy it. Seriously," she said before gently suggesting that I shower.

# Forty-Nine

I slept and slugged Gatorade for most of the day. That night, I finally got to meet Brian—fittingly, at the Green Mill, for some live jazz. Our lovebirds had clearly already found their groove: Alex accompanied Brian to jazz clubs, Brian accompanied Alex to political events. I arrived first (shocker), so I saw them walk in together. Their faces glowed, their body language was relaxed—they'd obviously just had sex. Sigh. Brian's hand rested gently on Alex's back; she looked down, smiled, and tucked some hair behind her ear. I'd never seen her look prettier.

If I'd been told to design the perfect man for Alex based solely on her physical preferences, Brian would've been it: He was tall and broad—six-three, 240—and in good-but-not-intimidating shape. His skin was the shade of my optimal suntan; I'd forgotten that Brian was half Persian, one-quarter White, and one-quarter Black. His short black hair was flecked ever-so-slightly with gray; his expression was open, his eyes were kind. He walked like a man at ease with himself and happy as a pig in shit. I worried for a moment that I might cry at their beauty.

"Hi!" I said as normally as I could when they arrived at the table. I hugged Alex.

"Zoe, Brian—Brian, Zoe," she said. I hesitated, wondering how best to greet him.

"I'm thrilled to finally meet you!" I said, and held out my hand like an idiot.

"*The* Zoe? The pleasure's all mine. Bring it in, girl!" Brian let out a big belly laugh and pulled me in for a hug.

"He's great!"

I'd *meant* to mouth this to Alex, but accidentally said it out loud. Thankfully, Alex just laughed and said, "I think so too."

"She's ridiculous, right?" Brian asked. He pulled Alex close. "Us not meeting 'til now?"

"I know!" I agreed. I looked at Alex. "Now is when we gang up on you."

"With good reason," Brian said. "She's been keeping me locked in her closet—only lets me out for conjugals."

"Stop it!" Alex laughed like a tween.

We spent the next five minutes riffing on Alex's secrecy before Brian bought drinks. He sat close enough to Alex to touch her but not so close that I'd feel pathetic. We then turned right to the looming 2008 election. Obama Fever had gripped the City. Although Alex had been a staunch Hillary supporter, she was now fully onboard the Obama Train. None of us was comfortable with McCain; all of us were desperate to say good-bye to W and his cronies. The way Alex and Brian refined each other's points and fed each other details called my parents to mind. I enjoyed watching them interact at least as much as the conversation. Brian was an Obama guy but respected all of the reasons Alex had so fervently supported Hillary, and when she went all Alex on him—talking faster, cursing more, becoming more impassioned by the second—Brian ate it up.

"So this is foreplay for you guys, huh," I quipped before the band took the stage and the show began.

I don't remember who played that night or whether I liked the music. But I'll not likely forget how Alex was. Brian seemed to amplify all of her best qualities while imbuing her with new confidence. He made his love for Alex known without announcing it. He understood her. He loved her as she was. I was thrilled. And maybe a hair jealous.


AFTER BARELY SURVIVING my jalk[44]—outside, since the Soldier Field ten-miler[45] was only six weeks away, and I had yet to get off the treadmill—I stuck with the morning's masochistic theme by plunging back into jDate. After willing myself *not* to gouge my eyes out, I noticed someone new had joined the fray. It was his screen name—LloydDobler—that caught my eye.[46]

"Lloyd" was a thirty-two year-old divorcé and father of one who lived in Northbrook. He actually looked kind of like John Cusack—same body type, brown, unkempt hair, and basset-hound eyes. He wore a sweet, goofy smile in his picture. He worked in commodities and seemed educated, given his ability to spell, capitalize, and punctuate. The way Lloyd worked his three-year-old son into most of his profile answers was charming. Take, for example, his Favorite Hobby: "Making ice cream sundaes with my little man." Dating someone who (presumably)

---

[44] Body to Self: Drink less, sleep more. OTHERWISE I CANNOT HELP YOU.

[45] Aunt Steffi swears that I agreed to this race when I was of sound mind, but she must have put something fishy in one of my 'tinis.

[46] If you don't know who Lloyd Dobler is . . . I don't know what to say. Watch *Say Anything* at once! John Cusack stars as loveable misfit Lloyd Dobler, who successfully woos Ione Skye's beautiful valedictorian, Diane Court. Every girl who came of age in the '80s/'90s has held Lloyd Dobler in her heart since meeting him via VHS or Betamax.

wanted to be a dad and was (presumably) able to be a dad was
attractive. *Northbrook*—a stereotypical white suburb a solid thirty
to forty minutes from the City—was the problem. Lloyd was
also a Conservative Jew who kept kosher, something I would
have blown by but for my ill-fated rabbinical encounter. Still, I
messaged him:

> Dear Mr. Dobler: I'm sure your inbox is overflowing with
> messages from other *Say Anything* fans . . . You're
> probably blasting "In Your Eyes" to some lucky lady as I
> write. But I wanted to compliment you on your inspired
> screen name and tell you that I really liked your profile.
> Have a great weekend, Zoe

I smiled and shut my laptop. (That John Cusack. He'll do it
to you every time.)

My phone buzzed just as my usual Sunday depression was
creeping in.[47]

SO: hullo, Sweet T's

OMG. I hadn't heard boo from Irish since we were naked
together seven and a half long days ago, and he'd just abbreviated
the word "tits." I should ignore him. I should.

ZG: Hey! What's up?

SO: umm, me—thinkin bout you

ZG: Get outta here, Irish[48]

---

[47] Sundays are when I'd most enjoy cuddling with someone on the couch or, better yet, in bed.

[48] I'd apparently started calling him "Irish" to his face when I was hammered. He seemed to think it was cute when he teased me about it Sunday morning. As in, *last* Sunday morning. As in, the last time I'd heard from him.

*(Painfully long pause of approximately three minutes.)*

SO: so what r u up to, lil biscuit?

And I'm smiling at this shit! I'm supposed to be a *grown-up*.

ZG: Unfortunately I'm coding dep transcripts in front of reality TV.

ZG: You?

SO: similar—organizing exhibits @ office

SO: we suck, don't we

ZG: Yep.

ZG: Shouldn't have gone into client services.

SO: i quite like servicing YOU 😊

And then he disappeared back into the ether, as he was wont to do.

# Fifty

When I logged into jDate after yoga at ten thirty Monday night, I wondered if Chicago might have been under the influence of an eclipse, or similarly rare barometric event, because I found this:

> Hey, Zoe! Thanks so much for writing me! I think I need to come clean and admit that I've never seen *Say Anything*, but my sisters have always thought I look like John Cusak (sp?). My real name is Elliot 😊. I'm new to jDate and find it kinda overwhelming. But I love your profile. Plus, you sent me an actual message, instead of a "hot list," "like," or other embarrassing jDate communication I don't understand! So am I totally behind the times, or can I skip the rest of the jDate stuff and ask you out for a drink?! I'm at elliot.g.stern@gmail.com 😊.
> Have a great night! Elliot

WE ACTUALLY ENDED up meeting for drinks that Thursday. When contrasted with Irish, the ease with which this occurred felt otherworldly. He was coming from work and didn't know much about the city, so he'd first suggested a tourist-trap restaurant. I panicked and countered with Tarantino's—a seriously selfish move, considering its proximity to my apartment, but also a great local spot for Northbrook Dad to try.

The Dad was by far my most normal first date. (I know that four first dates does not a veteran make, but still.) For starters, Elliot was the right amount of awkward. Unlike Reb Tevye, he grasped the need to blink. Unlike Irish, he arrived on time. And unlike what's-his-name, he had no drink-recipe cards in his pocket.

He was obviously relieved to see me—I looked something like my profile picture and nothing like a serial killer—and super-psyched about finding a great parking spot. I found all of this endearing.

And speaking of cute, it really did look as though John Cusack had time-traveled from 1989 to have drinks with me. The Dad's vibe was at least as goofy and charmingly disheveled as Lloyd Dobler's. His hair was slightly mussed and his black leather jacket outdated. His jeans were perfect and of-the-moment, though. Something about them screamed, *My sister took me shopping!* He wore a "dress-up" black T-shirt—the kind with subtle ribbing and sheen—underneath. Rob had never worn those T-shirts and I'd always found them hard to pull off by guys not living in New Jersey. But somehow, on The Dad, it worked. I was flattered to be dress-up-tee-worthy. His brown eyes were mahogany with twinkles in them. They were more interesting than I imagined John Cusack's to be.

"Hi, Elliot," I said after he emerged from a Nissan Maxima with a car seat containing a Marvel lunchbox.

"Hi, Zoe," he said cheerily. He hugged me without thinking about it. He was a great height for a hug. This reminded me briefly and regrettably of The Rabbi. "So," he said. "Shall we?" When we walked into the restaurant, I gestured toward its small bar.

"Wanna grab a drink?" I asked.

"It's really cute in here!" he said as he looked around. "And I'm starving. Do you mind if we sit? Have you eaten?"

I didn't hesitate to respond. "No, and the food here is great."

"Oh, good!"

We were seated immediately.

"I hope this is OK," I said as we settled in. "I couldn't really think of anywhere downtown where I knew we'd be able to hear each other, and this is three blocks from the highway, so easy for you to get home."

"No, this is great!" he said. "I love eating in the city and I've never been here before."

"Excellent," I said. He really was adorable.

The twenty-something, muscle-bound guy who'd waited on Alex and me a few times approached our table.

"Oh, hey," he said with an up-nod of recognition.

"How are you?" I asked.

"Yeah, it's all right." He pulled the list of specials from his apron, then snapped and pointed at me. "Martini, right? Where's your girlfriend?"

Sheesh. I blushed. "She's . . . not here. And, umm, I'll just have a glass of red wine."

"Nah, go on!" The Dad teased. "Have the martini! Pretend *I'm* your girlfriend." I hesitated. But The Dad didn't seem to think I was a lush or a lesbian. Or both. "I'll have something too," he added gently. "Please."

"OK," I told the waiter. "I'll have the dir—"

"Dirty vodka martini with *extra* bleu cheese olives. Got it. Two?" he asked The Dad.

"Oh, no," The Dad said, reaching for the drink menu. "I'll need something more manly than that." He perused the offerings with dramatic flair before looking up. "*I*," he began, "will have a watermelon appletini." I giggled in appreciation.

"Coming right up," said the waiter with a good-natured laugh before walking away.

"I drink girlie drinks," The Dad said gravely. "You may as well know this now."

He seemed very much at ease. This impressed me.

"Good women know that it takes a *real* man to order a fruittini," I said.

"And on a first date too. What can I say? I'm a renegade." He winked and rested his forearms on our romantic table-for-two.

"I can see that. You're dangerous, but in a good way."

"Exactly!" He laughed and brushed his hair absentmindedly across his forehead. I saw the bartender pull out two martini glasses, one bottle of Grey Goose, and two neon-colored liqueurs.

"Was this an OK time to meet?" I asked.

"Perfect. I usually leave the office by five thirty, but we had a snafu today. So the extra time was handy."

A man with a humane work schedule was straight-up sexy at this point. I could already tell that The Dad would never ghost me during trial.

"Uh-oh. An end-of-the-day snafu sounds bad," I said.

"No big deal, we got it fixed. It was a great day." The way he said this was so matter-of-fact and sincere that it charmed my socks off.

"I'm embarrassingly ignorant about what working in commodities means," I confessed. "So I won't even pretend to guess what kind of snafu you had."

"I'm still trying to figure out what 'working in commodities' means myself." He laughed. I knew this wasn't true, but it was a graceful segue to something more interesting. We chatted easily. And The Dad's willingness to eat out, regular working hours, and way of occasionally looking down to break eye contact all made him extra appealing.

"A watermelon appletini for the lady—er, gentleman," our waiter said as he served our drinks. He was very pleased with his lame line, which was clearly not spontaneous. "And a *real* cocktail for my friend here."

"Yeah, no *way* could I handle that real cocktail," joked The Dad. I got the feeling he'd been through this routine many times before. I could only imagine the shit his guy friends gave him for drinking fruit-tinis . . . assuming divorced Northbrook Dads met guy friends for drinks.

We talked and sipped. Or, rather, *I* sipped—he gulped. His glass was empty in sixty seconds. ("Tastes like a Jolly Rancher!" He shrugged.) We polished off the polenta fries we'd asked for as soon as the drinks arrived and then ordered dinner: salad and rigatoni for me and, he decided, the same for him. I debated pointing out that the rigatoni contained cream *and* prosciutto, making it the opposite of kosher, but figured he was capable of reading a menu. And that he might have accidentally checked the wrong box on his jDate profile.

By the time The Dad ordered a second neon cocktail—I waved off his invitation to join him, since my glass was still nearly full—he was telling me that his parents had moved to the San Diego area several years ago to be with his sisters and their kids.

"That must be such a bummer, having them so far away," I said. "You could probably use the help with your son."

The Dad was bent over his pasta, which he attacked with the same gusto he applied to the appletinis, but I thought I saw him tense up. I had violated an unwritten rule by mentioning his child before he did and felt like an asshole. But he just shrugged and said, "Oh, it's OK. I'd love to have them here, but SoCal's a great place to visit. And Evan's becoming quite the surfer dude." He smiled at the thought of him.

I appreciated his grace regarding my mistake. "That's adorable!"

"It'd be nice if Evan's mom would be just a *teeeeensy* bit more reasonable and let me take him there for Memorial Day. But reason isn't her strong suit." He laughed dismissively but didn't look quite as easygoing as when we'd arrived.

"Yuck. She's still being difficult, huh?"

"She's always been difficult. Difficult's kind of her thing. But I shouldn't be boring you with that on our first date!"

"It's totally fine," I said. We ate in silence for a few seconds. "How long's it been since your divorce? Sorry," I added quickly. "You don't have to tell me." I shouldn't have ordered a martini.

"I don't mind," he said before dabbing his mouth with his napkin. "The divorce was final on March twenty-first."

"March twenty-fist. . . 2008? Like, a couple weeks ago?" I blurted.

"Yep! But we were separated for a year and a half. So it feels like a *long* time."

*WOW.*

I tried to recover. "Ah. I'm really sorry you had to go through all that."

"It would've taken one-twentieth the time if I'd had control over the process, but she dragged it out and made it as unpleasant—and expensive—as possible."

I couldn't think of a graceful way to change the subject. "That's awful," I said.

"Yeah, it sucked for both of us. Evan and me, I mean. I can't speak for *her*."

"I'm so sorry. And so happy for you that it's over."

"Yeah. I love Evan, but you're lucky you don't have kids with your ex."

I knew that I was. But also that I wasn't. I was relieved that I'd never have to wrestle with Rob over custody—or, God willing, anything. But I was also sorry not to have someone at home whose name alone could make me smile. I guzzled ice water to chill my discomfort.

"But anyway. Now I get to be here with you." Elliot smiled his best Lloyd Dobler smile, and I took a deep breath. It worked. I'd started to recover quicker from moments like these—moments that used to make me feel lacking and empty. But regaining my equilibrium required all of my focus; I therefore dismissed Elliot's thorny ex-wife, his hatred for her, and the trauma their animus might be causing their son for the moment.

I soon became distracted by the fact that Elliot's plate was clean; his lonely fork sat in a quarter-teaspoon of tomato sauce. I came from a long line of fast eaters, but this guy was a machine. He cocked his head to the side and checked me out in a flirty way. After so many years with Rob, I wondered if I'd ever get used to simply being noticed.

"So who's this girlfriend you drink martinis with every night?" The Dad asked with a twinkle in his eye.

"Ah—thank you for raising this. Actually, Alex—Alexandra, my best friend—and I come here once a month, tops." I nodded back toward the waiter. "I'm not the hardened booze-hound he'd have you think I am."

"He's amazing, right?" The Dad whispered conspiratorially. "Like a twenty-two-year-old stoner trapped in a WWF wrestler's body."

"Totally amazing," I whispered back. "Alex described him almost exactly the same way. Although I think she said, 'in the body of a linebacker.'"

"Eh, you want a piece. Admit it." The Dad smiled.

"OK, fine, he's totally my type. Which is why I joined jDate."

He liked this one and rapped the table as he laughed. When he looked at me again, he said, "You have really beautiful eyes."

"Oh—thanks." I toyed with my hair and tried to find somewhere to look.

"You're welcome," he said before taking a long drag from his water glass. I'd decided to take most of my pasta home so that The Dad wouldn't have to wait for me to eat it. He must have read my mind. "I'm sorry I'm such a fast eater," he said. "My mom would be mortified!"

"Oh, please," I said as though I hadn't noticed. "I'm glad you liked it."

"Hated it. Obviously," he said, leaning back. "Please take your time—I'm enjoying the company."

"So am I." We smiled at each other before I asked, "So what do you think of jDate?" I tried to focus on eating while listening to him.

"Oh, God," he said. "I don't know. It's great, on the one hand, because it puts you in touch, potentially anyway, with so many people—like you." He paused to Lloyd Dobler me.[49] "But on the other, it's just so—" he wrinkled up his face while considering how to articulate the horrors of jDate.

"Juvenile? Embarrassing? Absurd?" I suggested.

"Yes!" he said. "Those things." We laughed. "I cringe when someone 'hot lists' me. Like, is this really what it's come to? I'm a grown man!"

"Yep," I sympathized, loading another bite onto my fork. "The blinking lights, the flashing hearts—all that shit's the worst."

"The *worst*," he echoed.

I knew my martini had gotten to me when I failed to censor the profanity I usually reserved for family and friends. But he didn't flinch.

"Of course she'll take it," The Dad said when the waiter offered to box things up. Then he turned to me. "I love leftovers."

"Me too," I said, unable to suppress a smile. Rob refused ever to eat leftovers, and it drove me insane.

The Dad smoothly picked up the check after we lingered at the table a while. When we ambled back to his car, I managed to peek at my watch: It was 9:47. Two hours and seventeen minutes for a first blind-date "drink" seemed promising.

"Shall I walk you home?" he asked.

"Oh, that's OK. I'm literally right there." I pointed at my building.

The Dad stifled a yawn. "Are you sure?"

"One hundred percent." I started to wonder how we'd end the evening. "Hey, thanks for a great night."

---

[49] Smile in a singularly charming and irresistible way. You *must* see this movie.

"Oh, same here," he said, smiling. "My pleasure." He had his hands in his pockets and rocked subtly back and forth on his heels. OK, we would not be kissing—the poor guy clearly had no idea what to do. So I hugged him.

"Thanks again," I said as I turned to walk home. I waved when I realized that The Dad was watching me turn the corner toward my front door. He waved back and then headed toward the highway.

♡

April 10, 2008

Lads: Maybe there's hope for me and jDate.
*Maybe.* XO, Zoe

# Fifty-One

boldly decided to write to The Dad on Friday morning.

> Hey, Elliot! Just wanted to thank you again for a great
> dinner. Have a relaxing weekend and enjoy this nice
> weather. Zoe

I spent a long day at my desk coding the same effing dep transcripts I was pretty sure would stalk me for the rest of my career. So, obviously, I checked Gmail every hour. At five thirty, I finally got this:

> Hey Zoe! Thanks for your sweet note. I've got just a
> minute before Evan and I dig into our pizza. I had a great
> time too! Wanna do it again? How's next Thursday? Have a
> great night, Elliot

I promptly accepted The Dad's invitation before hightailing it to meet Bubbe at temple.

"IT SOUNDS QUITE lovely, really," said Paula in her awesome British accent after guitar on Wednesday night.

"It does?" I asked.

"Yes!" chorused the other ladies.

"The Dad's speed seems a nice medium between Rabbi and Irish," Lynn said.

"It's *Normal Speed*," said Debra.

"Huh." I hadn't heard from The Dad for five days and had therefore convinced myself he'd forgotten all about me and wouldn't show for our date the next day. But everyone around me seemed unconcerned. "So this is what normal dating looks like?" I asked.

"Indeed," Julie said.

God, I hoped so.

MY FRIENDS' POSTMORTEM of my second date with The Dad was harsher than I'd expected.

Jimmy began the discussion during the next Friday evening's happy hour at Smith & Wollensky.

"DID YOU FINALLY GET LAID?" he asked.

"No. There was nothing." I whispered this in a futile attempt to encourage Jimmy to lower his voice.

"KISSING?" he shouted.

"Jimmy—shush," Alex said. "Zo, start at the beginning. Where'd you guys go?"

"We met kind of late, cuz we both had a lot of work . . . so, Webster Wine Bar."

"Oy." Caren rolled her eyes.

"WHAT IS IT WITH YOU AND THE WINE BAR?" Jimmy asked.

"I swear it was his idea," I explained. "He said he'd been dying to try it—I didn't have the heart to tell him I'm a regular. Especially since he probably thinks I'm an alkie already, thanks to that beefcake waiter at Tarantino's." Alex shrugged.

"OK, FINE, BUT GET TO WHY THERE WAS NO TOUCHING," Jimmy said before waving at the waiter. He ordered two baskets of truffle fries for the table.

"I don't know! The conversation was good, I thought he was cute—I *think* he thinks *I'm* cute—we stayed a while. . . .'"

"Did he pay?" Caren asked.

"He did, but I felt bad about it."

"LET IT GO," Jimmy insisted. "IT'S A MALE-EGO-PRIDE THING."

"But you never pay on dates!" I said.

"TOTALLY DIFFERENT."

"Whatever. I still felt bad because his ex is basically taking all his money."

"Umm. *What?*" Caren asked.

"So we'll definitely come back to that," Alex interrupted, "but first I wanna know why Caren asked if he paid."

"Oh—I was trying to see, given the no kissing, if he'd put Zoe in the Friend Zone."

"EXACTLY," Jimmy shouted.

"That's sexist," Alex responded over her 'tini.

"I agree with you," said Caren, "but I do think that whether or not a man pays is a good indicator of his interest. Unfortunately." She paused. "Or maybe I'm just oversensitive about the Friend Zone because of Head Pat guy."

"HEAD PAT GUY?" Jimmy asked.

"The med student—" I began.

"*Resident*," Caren corrected.

"The *resident* who took Caren out, like, three times—"

"Four," she said.

"—and acted crazy about her—"

"And was *thirty years old*," Caren added.

"—but who wouldn't touch her, even when she invited him to her apartment to 'watch a movie'—"

"WHICH EVERYONE KNOWS IS CODE FOR '*HAVE SEX*,'" Jimmy said, rolling his eyes.

"Thank you," Caren said.

"—and actually ended up patting her on the head when she tried to kiss him after the movie."

"GAY, OBVIES," Jimmy said.

Caren considered. "Hmm. Maybe."

"DEFINITELY," Jimmy yelled right as the waiter dropped the fries and sped away.

"Uch," Alex sympathized with a shiver. "A *head pat?*"

"Literally. Like this." Caren demonstrated an arm's length double-pat on Jimmy's head.

"Eww," Alex said. She grabbed some fries. "But I just have this feeling that Zoe isn't in the Friend Zone. My gut says The Dad's just rusty."

"That's definitely true," I said. "He got with his ex in college and wouldn't date until the divorce was final—even though she remarried that afternoon."

"WHAT?" *Everyone* shouted this time.

I avoided their raised eyebrows by staring at my 'tini. "She apparently started dating their couples' therapist, and it got serious as the divorce dragged on."

"STOP IT," Jimmy yelled.

"Oh, it gets worse. She had his baby—the therapist's baby—

fourteen months after therapy began. Which means she conceived while she and The Dad were still in counseling. With the
therapist. The Therapist New Dad."

"Shit," Caren whispered.

"He *told* you all of this? On a second date?" Alex asked.
Everyone stared at me.

"Yeah," I said, feeling like an idiot. I hadn't fully processed
how crazy this was until I'd said it out loud. "He also told me that
every little thing—like switching a visitation day for Evan—has
to go through the lawyers. Which is why he sends everything he
earns to the lawyers."

"Jesus," Jimmy mumbled—quietly, for once.

"But here's the kicker," I said.

"There's more?" Caren asked.

"He has to live in the Northbrook School District until the
custody agreement expires . . . when Evan goes to college. In fifteen years." I put my head in my hands, unable to meet Caren's
eyes. She'd already rejected six first Match.com dates over email
formatting alone.

"Oh, my God, forget him. *Northbrook?*" Caren said this like
a dirty word.

"Hold on," Alex said, mostly to Caren. "First of all, they're
only two non-physical dates in. Second, Zoe likes this guy. And
third, *Zoe* should decide if Northbrook, or any of the other way
more serious stuff, is a deal-breaker."

Everyone looked chastened.

Jimmy finally broke the silence. "I'D LIKE TO KNOW
HOW ALL OF THIS CAME UP."

"I don't know," I shrugged. "He just kind of dropped details
here and there."

"Did he ask you about *your* divorce?" Alex asked.

"Hmm. I know he asked when it was finalized. . . ." I said. Concern wafted across Alex's face.

"BUT HE KNEW FROM YOUR PROFILE THAT YOU DON'T HAVE KIDS, SO WHY WOULD HE ASK YOU ANYTHING ABOUT YOUR DIVORCE SO EARLY?" Jimmy asked. "MOST OF HIS DIVORCE TMI IS ABOUT MANAGING HIS SON."

"True," I said.

Jimmy sighed. "YOU KNOW, TWO OF MY BROTHERS ARE DIVORCED WITH KIDS. ONE WAS AMICABLE, BUT THE OTHER WAS A NIGHTMARE," he said. "DAN'S A GREAT GUY, BUT I COULD *TOTALLY* SEE HIM LETTING TOO MANY DETAILS SLIP, ESPECIALLY IF HE WAS NERVOUS." He paused. "SO MAYBE, *MAYBE*, WE SHOULD GIVE THE GUY A MINUTE."

That shut everyone up. Until Alex said, "Jimmy's right. Mercy is important in dating—and in life." She looked directly at Caren.

"Well, it is early," Caren said, chastened. "But I still say proceed with caution."

"STILL," Jimmy said, "IF YOU WANNA SEE IF THERE'S ANY *THERE* THERE, INVITE HIM OVER TO WATCH A MOVIE."

"And be prepared to make the first move," Alex added.

"YES," Jimmy added.

"Yes," Caren said. "There's no use worrying about the divorce drama if he's a head-pat guy."

"A movie makes sense," I said. "Done." I thanked my friends for their advice and eagerly changed the subject.

♡

April 18, 2008

Adam: I'm sure you've been with hundreds — maybe
thousands — of women who've made the first move.
My question for you is: Which move is your favorite?
I'd like to know because The Dad might like it too.
Luv, Z.

ONCE THE SEED was planted, I was desperate to know whether
The Dad was a Head Pat Guy or not. So I broke our email proto-
col and called him after my long jalk Saturday morning.

"Hey!" he answered. He sounded happy to hear from me,
which took the edge off.

"Hi there," I said. "Listen, I know this is totally last minute,
but seeing as how I own it and you haven't even seen it—which is
tragic, by the way—do you wanna come over to watch *Say Anything* tonight?"

I held my breath. To my delight, he pounced.

"I'd love to! But—sorry, just one sec." I waited. "OK, I
stepped away. I have Evan this weekend." My heart sank. "But we
have a busy day planned—he'll be out cold by eight o'clock. Is
there, uh, any chance I can convince you to bring the DVD
here?"

Yikes. It hadn't occurred to me to go to his house when Evan
was there. Did he plan on actually *watching* the movie? *Was* he
Head Pat Guy? Something in his tone made me think not. But

still—how could this work? I had no idea, but now I had to say yes—he knew I had nothing else to do.

"Sure," I replied. "There's just one problem."

"What?"

"This movie is old school. It's on VHS."

"Well," he sounded relieved. "I'm an Old School guy. So we will watch this movie in my Old School basement on my Old School TVCR."

"I love that you have a TVCR. I had one in college." The TV and VCR combined in one box was a 1990s dorm room staple. "I'll be there," I said.

We arranged for him to text me directions after he put Evan to bed.


I FURIOUSLY CHOMPED spearmint gum all the way to North-brook.[50] Not too long after exiting the highway, I pulled up to a lovely house on a lovely street. The Dad had a smallish colonial that presented like a home in progress: bags of mulch and soil, and three one-gallon paint cans, leaned against the garage. A swing hung from a tall tree in his front yard just as they did in each neighboring yard. A miniature red bike and a dinosaur helmet lay on the front walk. Manual sprinklers drizzled newly planted impatiens.

I parked on the street instead of pulling into the driveway; I didn't want to be presumptuous or wake Evan. I stepped over some sidewalk chalk on the front stoop, put my grocery bag down, and texted The Dad. (I'd been instructed not to ring the bell.)

---

[50] My drive was actually thirty minutes. It just *felt* like "all the way to Northbrook."

"Hi!" he greeted me. He took the grocery bag and kissed my cheek. A good sign. I smiled.

"Hey!" The Dad looked a little sunburned—from planting the impatiens, I guessed—and wore the same designer jeans I saw on Date One with a retro *Happy Days* T-shirt. The shirt looked like one of those faux-vintage tees popping up in department stores, but The Dad's actually *was* vintage.

"Come on in," he said. "What'd you bring?" He looked in the bag.

"I'm a Jew." I shrugged. "I brought food—brownies. And a bottle of red and a bottle of white."

"You're really thoughtful. Thanks."

I smiled; my long debate about what to bring had worked out. I followed him to the kitchen. He gestured to a stool by the island—I sat while he searched for glasses. The room had white Kitchen Aid appliances, original wood cabinets, and newish cream-colored granite countertops. Preschool artwork and letter magnets covered the fridge. It was exactly what I'd hoped my fridge would soon look like; I felt a twinge in my chest. The front room had an old big-screen TV, leather sofas, a coffee table, and 1990s lamps with the hammered metal and big clear domes over the light bulbs. Framed posters—one from the Met, one from a New Orleans Jazz Fest—adorned the walls. Little boy shoes lay beside grown-up flip-flops next to the stairs. The house felt lived-in and warm, if a little sparse. Someone walking in cold would be unsurprised to learn that it was evolving after a divorce.

"Your house is beautiful. I love the new flowers," I said, and meant it.

"Oh, yeah, thanks," The Dad said in his breezy way. Larger-

than-expected biceps became evident when he rummaged for a
corkscrew. "We did a *lot* of planting today. Ah! Here it is." Given
how long it took him to unearth two wine glasses and a corkscrew,
I suspected that The Dad didn't often entertain. I wondered if he
was lonely, especially when Evan was at his mom's.

"Was Evan exhausted?"

"Oh, totally," he said as he poured red for us both. "I may
have overdone it . . . I just always feel like we have to maximize
our time together. He crashed out *hard*." I liked that he always
smiled when Evan's name came up. "Cheers."

"Cheers," I replied. We clinked glasses. The Dad looked
adorable.

"Shall we?" He held up the VHS tape after looking unsure of
what to do for a moment.

"Sure," I said.

He took me to a den behind the kitchen. It was very 1950s
with log-cabin-type walls, burnt-orange carpet, and an old-fashioned recliner. It also had yet another leather loveseat that
echoed the sofas in the living room. The Dad had rigged up the
TVCR on a card table, which charmed the shit out of me.

"This is a room in progress," he apologized. "But it's better
than the basement, which still smells too painty."

"I'm impressed. New landscaping *and* finishing the basement?"

"Eh, *finish* isn't quite the right word . . . I'm just trying to get
it un-scary. As for the den, I promise that orange carpet is not
part of my long-range plan."

"I love it," I said. It looked exactly how a den in a suburban
fixer-upper should look. "And I'm sorry you had to lug the
TVCR upstairs!"

"It was no problem. I *just* painted down there—we would've been poisoned by noxious fumes."

He cued up the movie. I sat on the loveseat. He hesitated before sitting a foot away from me.

We laughed at the VHS quality and cheesy, dated previews. A subtle warmth radiated from The Dad, from his day in the sun, nerves, or both. I thought I smelled cologne but then decided it was Degree deodorant. By the time the actual movie began, I couldn't concentrate at all. I wasn't going to jump a man whose child slept upstairs, but this was tortuous.

Just then, The Dad took my wine glass out of my hands and placed it next to his on the table. He bit the inside of his lip, looked at me, and froze. *Could* I jump a man whose child slept upstairs? I summoned courage from somewhere and pulled him to me.

That was all it took—we synced right up. In record time, we were lying down, he kind of sideways on top of me. Just as I started to panic about Evan, I felt an erection against my leg and heard The Dad's breath quicken. Off came my carefully chosen black tank, my bra, his tee. He playfully pulled me onto the floor with him.[51]

So there I was, getting after it on a 1950s den floor, with a guy I'd recently met, whose unsuspecting kid lay one flight of stairs away. And then my jeans were off, his jeans were off, and he was on me like white on rice with only two pairs of underpants between us. Were *we going to have sex*? *No, wait—I was on my period. And I'd bet a million dollars this man didn't have con-*

---

[51] Why always shirt-bra-off-pants-on? This combo is rife with love-handles and unflattering angles. It would take me many more years of therapy and maturation to let this preoccupation go.

doms. *Did they even sell condoms in Northbrook? HIS KID WAS UPSTAIRS!*

He pressed his chest into mine and kissed me like a man who knew exactly what he was doing. I got a little dizzy (the good kind). *Oh my God and shit.* I shimmied myself out from under him, turned over, and rug-burned my own boobs in the process.

"Elliot—" I started.

"Oh, God. Am I going too fast? You're on the floor! I'm so sorry." He panicked.

"It's OK! I'm fine." I put my hand on his shoulder to reassure him. "It's just that," I attempted to prop myself up while still using the carpet for nipple coverage, "I think we probably shouldn't have our clothes off." He looked at me blankly. "Because of Evan."

"Oh! God, no, he's fine," he said easily. He pulled me close again. "I'm just really sorry we can't be in my bed, like normal people." I said nothing, but my face must have given me away. "Listen. I know my baby," he added, as he ran his fingertips up my spine, "and he is *out*." I smiled. He kissed me hungrily. So naturally. . . .

"Dah-*deeeee!*"

My stomach fell through my feet as if I were on the plunge portion of a roller coaster. The Dad jumped up, pulled on his T-shirt, and ran to the bottom of the stairs—stubbing his toe on the loveseat on his way—with superhuman speed.

"Coming, Buddy!" he yelled.

I'd never felt dirtier than I did right then, hastily dressing on The Dad's plush carpet. I contemplated running for the door, but didn't to want to risk Evan hearing me—or, worse, *seeing* me

—so I stayed put. I heard his muffled whines from above followed by The Dad's low, soothing replies. Then there were footsteps on the stairs; I strained to make sure they were his alone. I peeked around the loveseat and spied The Dad filling a Playtex race-car cup with water before heading back upstairs. I barely breathed during the five minutes it took him to return. He frowned when he saw I'd dressed and put on my shoes.

"Don't go," he pleaded and sat down next to me.

"Oh, I really think I should." He put his face in his hands. "It's OK," I said.

"No, it's not. But I swear—he never, *ever* wakes up! He was thirsty. Maybe from all the gardening. . . ."

"He didn't—I mean, he doesn't—"

The Dad looked at me, puzzled, before understanding. "Oh! No, he has no idea anyone's here."

"Thank God!" I said. I started to stand up. He grabbed my hand and Lloyd Doblered me into sitting back down.

"You know, he was practically sleepwalking," he said as he leaned in close. He bit his lip again. I sympathized with how good it feels to finally get some after a divorce . . . and knew that, at that moment, I'd have to think clearly for the both of us.

"Elliot. I really should go."

"But—"

"Listen. The *last* thing I could have handled, when *I* was three, if my parents had just split up and my mom had a new baby, would be catching my dad with a naked stranger."

He finally nodded. I hugged him. "I'm around," I added. "We'll raincheck." He nodded again and walked me to the door.

"Wait, lemme grab your movie—and the brownies," he said.

"No, keep both. We'll need them soon, right?"

"I'm really sorry about this, Zoe."

"Don't be. It's all good," I said, hoping he couldn't see how weirded out I was. We slipped out the front door and onto the stoop. "Actually?" I ventured. "I'm kind of relieved. I wasn't sure if you wanted to. . . ."

"Are you serious?" he asked. "I wanted to the moment I saw you."

I smiled because I knew he meant it.

# Fifty-Two

"You need a drink, Lady," Alex announced when I called her on my way home.

I'd made it until the end of The Dad's block before wigging out about our near miss. Brian was celebrating his dad's birthday in Indianapolis that weekend, so Alex was getting ready to meet Jimmy & Co. at the Kerryman. She invited me to join. It was only 10:20 when I pulled into my parking space, and sitting home alone with my shame was unappealing. So I touched up my makeup, grabbed a wrap, hopped in a cab, and walked into the Kerryman at 10:40.

"UMM, HELLO, DADDY'S GIRL." Jimmy laughed.

"Shush!" Alex scolded. Jimmy's expression dissolved when he read mine.

"I'm disgusting," I said.

"NO, YOU'RE NOT." Jimmy hugged me. "I'LL GET YOU A DRINK."

"Bless you," I said, when he slid a 'tini into my hand.

By twelve thirty, I'd had *three* 'tinis, which I knew was a huge fucking mistake even before I'd ordered them. Goddamn this drinking. But I needed to laugh with Alex, Jimmy, and their fellow politicos in order to stop obsessing about how I'd almost been caught diddling a little kid's dad. If it took three martinis to make that happen, so be it. Alex and I were in the middle of laughing hysterically at the latest outrageous thing Jimmy had said when I felt a light pressure on my waist. I twirled around, expecting to see another of Alex and Jimmy's politicos. But it must have been a full moon or something because, Ladies and Gentlemen, it wasn't a politico—it was Irish.

I stopped and stood perfectly still, as if he were my Gchat window, for I don't know how long. Pleasantries I no longer remember were exchanged. And then, somehow, Irish and I were nose to nose with his arms around my waist and my arms around his neck. He leaned his head back to survey me; he was fucking gorgeous. And then, out of nowhere, I was *mad*. Every frustration from my short dating career came to a head. That Irish had wronged me, and was singularly responsible for my not having a stable romantic life, all seemed so clear in that vodka-soaked moment.

"My li'l firecracker," Irish said, trying to read my pouty face while maintaining a firm grip on my waist.

"HOLY SHIT, THAT IS TOTALLY FUCKING IRISH," I heard Jimmy say from somewhere outside our bubble.

Irish and I stared at each other for a second more before he kissed me. And damn him, it felt *great*. This too was a man who knew what he was doing, although in a totally different way. But I wasn't about to let some *guy*—who'd ignored, insulted, and booty-called me only when convenient for him—get his way. I pulled away; he lightened his grip.

"No," I said more harshly than I'd intended.

"No, what?" he countered.

"Just *no*," I replied, ever so coolly.[52]

"Hey, simmer down, Hot Pants." Irish sounded uneasy and looked confused.

"Oh, *please!*" I said.

He pulled me closer, although a little less surely this time. As I relaxed involuntarily into his arms, I felt his confidence rebuild. *I got this,* his subconscious was saying. That our sexual chemistry was combustible pissed me off.

"Listen," he whispered into my ear. "I'm sorry. I've been busy. But you *know* I've been thinking about you." His breath sent goose bumps down my neck; his body melted into mine. "A lot."

"Whatever," I managed—lamely, seeing as how my face was still pressed to his. He kissed me again. His hand slid over the curve of my butt, like he owned it.

"Come on. Let's get out of here," he said.

"NO!" I heard myself yell like a psycho. I peeled my body from his. He looked stunned. "That's right," I sneered, "*I* am telling *you* NO."

"OH, SHIT," Jimmy said from somewhere within my personal space. Irish glanced at Jimmy for a split-second before turning back to me. "DAMN, HE *IS* HOT!" Jimmy said before Alex yanked him away.

"What the hell, Zoe?" Irish asked, his voice aggravatingly calm. He folded his (rippling, alabaster) arms across his chest.

"What do you mean, '*What the hell?!*'" I stammered. "When I didn't hear from you—for weeks, and weeks, *annnnnddd* weeks, I . . . I. . . ."

---

[52] Not at all coolly.

"You *what*," he challenged.

"I started seeing someone," I sniffed. I pulled myself up to full height despite my complete lack of composure. "Someone who actually *talks* to me, and gives two shits, and not just at last call."

Irish looked stung for a beat before plastering an aloof expression on his beautiful face. "OK, wait a minute. I work like a *dog*, Zoe. I'm not gonna apologize for that." He lowered his voice and ventured a step closer. "I like you. But I work."

"What, and I don't? I'm not a lawyer, too?"

He shook his head; he was at a loss. We were nose to nose again, but I was determined not to move. I had no idea how much, if any, of what I'd said (or felt) was deserved. But I was irate—I was *sure* Irish still thought I'd be going home with him —frustrated, drunk, and embarrassed. I'd kissed Irish only hours after kissing the kind and vulnerable Dad. I pushed him away.

"Calm down," he cautioned.

"Oh, I assure you, I am *perfectly* calm." That this was a lie was painfully obvious to everyone but me. "And I'm not going home with you."

"Yeah, I think I got that part." He made a show of taking a big step backwards. "You're totally freaking out—and claiming some 'boyfriend' I seriously doubt you have, based on how you kissed me forty-five seconds ago—all because I was *busy*."

"He's not my *boyfriend*. We're *seeing each other*. AND *YOU* KISSED *ME*!" I shouted like a lunatic.

This is when Alex intervened. She grabbed my hand. "C'-mon, Lady," she said firmly. Then Jimmy pulled himself up to his full height and stepped between Irish and me. He ushered both Alex *and* me a few feet away, into the demilitarized zone, before turning back to Irish to stare him down. Irish strode to the door, stopping only long enough to indicate to his friends that he was leaving. The politicos had made themselves scarce as soon as the drama began, so Alex and Jimmy were the only ones left to see me burst into tears.

"WHAT'S WRONG? THAT'S THE MOST ACTION THE KERRYMAN'S SEEN IN *YEARS*!" Jimmy said before Alex knocked him upside the head.

"Let's go, Babes," she said.

I nodded and we left.

♡

April 19, 2008

I don't know you/You don't know the half of it/You can't even remember/What I'm trying to forget/It was a dirty day. . . .

I SPENT THE next three days avoiding human contact. And jDate. I felt wretched.

That Tuesday night at six o'clock, I got a call from The Dad.

"Hey, hi!" he said sweetly. The poor man had no idea I'd gone 'round the bend.

"Elliot—hi." I gulped.

"I'm so glad I caught you! I wasn't sure I would."

"I'm still at the office, but really glad to be caught." It was hard to feel wretched with Lloyd Dobler on the other end of the line.

"I'm sorry. I shouldn't be bothering you at work," he said hurriedly.

"No! I was actually just getting ready to leave."

"Oh," he said with a lift in his voice. "So, actually, I threw your movie and brownies in the back seat this morning, just in case. I know you have a busy schedule, and I didn't know what *my* schedule was going to be like, but I'm winding down, too, and . . . can I come over?"

I wondered. Could I dig myself out of the dumps in time for things not to be weird? Was it even ethical to have The Dad over when I'd just drunkenly kissed—and nearly punched—somebody else? When I opened my mouth, I didn't know what would come out.

"Totally," I said.

"Oh, umm. Cool." I loved the bashfulness in his voice. "Do you like pizza? Because I'm bringing dinner."

And just like that, the clouds parted. I pushed my potentially deteriorating mental health aside and hightailed it home.

AT SEVEN THIRTY, I took a shot of whiskey—even though the weekend's post-martini pain was still very much with me—because I was as nervous as a pimply-faced teen about to play Spin the Bottle. The buzzer sounded at seven thirty-two.

"Hi!" said The Dad.

He was trying to balance the plate of brownies in one hand and a Malnati's pizza in the other, all while squeezing the VHS tape under his arm.

"Hi! Let me get these," I said, rescuing the brownies and pizza and walking them to the kitchen. "You should've called me," I said over my shoulder as I put everything down. "I could've met you at your car—"

I experienced a chilling sense of déjà vu when I felt him right behind me. I turned around cautiously. But it wasn't Reb Tevye with his searing stare. It was The Dad, who now looked at me with as come-hither an expression as someone that Lloyd-Doblery can have.

"So, hi. . . ." he said as he ran his hands up my triceps.

"Hi," I said.

"I'm really sorry—about the other night."

"No, don't worry," I said. Without thinking about it, I laid my hands on his chest.

"I—well. Anyway," he trailed off before kissing me.

In that first second, I knew he'd been waiting since Saturday to be like this again, which really got me. I let myself melt into his kiss. Which took a little doing, because honestly, what was it with these people, not eating or drinking before diving in? My mind drifted to the similar, but distinct, ways that Irish and The Dad kissed. Both were confident, firm but gentle, and used an appropriate amount of tongue. And yet, I felt like I was on a different planet with each.

I soon found myself pressed against the counter. The Dad was breathing heavily; there was a palpable, deep-seated yearning in him. I pressed my hands gently into his chest. He responded to my nonverbal request by backing up far enough to free me from the counter. When we locked eyes, he looked more masculine, animal, and un-goofy than I could previously have imagined him. I briefly debated whether to slow him down, offer dinner, start the movie, or *something*, before impulsively wrapping my arms around him and yielding to his pace. The way he held my face up to his when we kissed was killer. He looked up just long enough to see the hallway to my bedroom and started guiding me there, not taking his body off of mine. I let him take off all of my clothes; we jumped under the covers where he ditched his boxers in a hot second.

Finally, yet also suddenly, it was Go Time. "Condom," I sputtered, pointing to my nightstand.

"Oh, right," he panted. I diverted my eyes as he executed this awkward necessity under the covers. *This is horrible. Condoms are horrible.* And then he was on me again. I will pause to relieve those of you in suspense: The Dad's penis was of normal size. Most importantly, it was ready. I closed my eyes and tipped my head back in anticipatory pleasure, and then . . . nothing. I opened my eyes. The Dad looked gray and clammy. His whole body—minus the one part that mattered—was stiff. He sank down next to me.

"I—geez. Sorry," he muttered, removing the condom his body had ejected.

*FUHHHHCCCCKKKKKKKKKKK!*

"Oh," I squeaked. "Don't worry."

I prayed that he couldn't sense the intensity of my disappointment. My body didn't start and stop as quickly as The Dad's; my nether regions hadn't yet processed the evening's sad turn. But my brain was already beginning to wonder if something was terribly, terribly wrong with me.

"I swear, this has literally *never* happened before," he said. *Just like his son never, ever wakes up,* I thought.

Then, as if things couldn't get any worse, he turned away . . . and went to town. On himself. OMG.

"Elliot?" I ventured. "It's OK. It happens."

He kept going, not even turning around, and panted, "No—it's—*not*—O—*K!*"

It felt as though I was no longer even in the room. It was one man against himself—literally. I couldn't stand it. "*Elliot*," I said. "Look—can you please just turn around?" He sighed, let go of himself, and rolled onto his back. He reluctantly turned his face toward me.

I touched his chest. "I'm guessing that, as a recently-married person, you haven't used a condom in . . . approximately ever?"

"That's approximately right." We both laughed.

"So I say, don't worry about it." I shrugged. "Fuck it."

"I tried," he deadpanned.

We laughed some more, talked for a few minutes about nothing, and soon were making out again. Uncharacteristically, I didn't worry too much about what was or wasn't going to happen. I enjoyed the sense of intimacy I inexplicably felt more with The Dad than . . . OK, fine, than with the only other two guys I'd hung with since Rob. In a moment of idiocy, I didn't resist when he came at me without a condom. And then we fucked all night long, like Tom Cruise and Kelly McGillis in *Top Gun,* and I had the best six orgasms of my *life*!

Sadly, no. The Dad stopped just short of the target and thwarted my aching loins once again. He barely had time to mutter an apology before throwing on his clothes and fleeing my apartment.

# Fifty-Three

"I see," Janie said quietly as I sat across from her just over three weeks later. I'd seen no way around divulging to her the more pertinent and painful details of my encounters with The Dad. "I'm sorry—that's tough."

"I think I didn't mention it 'til now because I really wanted it to be just one of those things. Like, a fluke."

Janie not-talked.

"But it isn't a fluke," I forced myself to continue. "The Thursday after Terrible Tuesday, I forwarded Elliot an *Onion* article, just to break the ice. I didn't know if I'd hear from him again, but he called that Friday."

"And?"

"He was giddy—bursting with news."

"Really."

"He said he was so upset about Tuesday that he'd called his doctor. The nurse had finally gotten back to him and told him that a medication he's on can . . . have that effect."

"Mmm," Janie said. She sounded as if she already knew this story's end.

"He seemed so relieved, so happy, that even though I'd deduced from our conversation that he'd been on this medication a long time—which made me skeptical that it would suddenly cause, you know—he seemed *sure* that he had the answer."

Janie waited.

"So, by the time he tells me he wants to come over, I'm excited too. I *did* insist that we go out to dinner, just so that sex didn't become, like—" I fished for the right words.

"The sole objective," Janie offered. "That was smart."

"And we had a great time! He was totally relaxed—drank two espresso-tinis—and talked less about his ex-wife than usual."

"Ah." Janie's concern about The Dad's allegedly problematic ex-wife had been written all over her face during our last couple of sessions. But she knew better than to dive too deeply into that unless or until necessary.

"So we go back to my apartment, we make out, everything seems fine . . . and then it happens. Again."

"Oy." Janie winced.

"Yup."

"And—sorry—but when you say, 'it,' do you mean, he couldn't . . . start? Or finish?"

"Start. He's always *ready* to start, but when he gets to T-minus one millimeter, it's over."

Janie sighed sympathetically. I shook my head and felt my eyes well up.

"Zoe. You have to know, this isn't you—"

"Wait. It gets worse," I whispered. "He tried, like, two more times. Same deal. He finally left at two in the morning. It was miserable."

"I'm sure," Janie said.

"And I've started to wonder—I can't help it—if something about my physiology is, you know. Repellent."

"Zoe—" Janie started.

"It's hard not to wonder. . . ." I didn't want to have a confidence talk just then, so I quickly continued. "So anyway, we did the same thing, where I sent him some meaningless email, and wondered if maybe I just wouldn't hear from him—"

"But you did," Janie said.

"Yes. He called on Thursday. And again, he sounded like a different person—totally fine—like his regular self. And I guess I'm a glutton for punishment, because I agreed to meet him for drinks that night. What I was thinking, I don't know. I knew I'd made a mistake when I saw him because I thought, wow, he just looks so tired." I paused. "Now that I say that, I wonder if he's always looked so tired, and I just hadn't noticed."

Janie nodded.

"Anyway, he tells me he's been off that medication for the right number of days, that the nurse said he should be good to go, blah blah blah. Eventually, we drive to my apartment, we make out, and—like a truly insane idiot—I get my hopes up, again—"

"It's hard not to, in the moment," Janie offered.

"—but problems don't evaporate for no reason, so the exact same thing happened. Of course it did, right? So this time, I short-circuited his usual 'let's try again' stuff and asked—once we were dressed—if he was OK, and if there was anything he wanted to talk to me about, because if so, he could."

"That was sweet of you."

"He didn't seem to think so. He said that *he* was just fine, but that he was furious at his doctor. Then he said he had to go, and I let him."

Janie exhaled and sat back. "Wow," she said. "How are things now?"

"We've been emailing a little, about nothing. But there are longer pauses between messages . . . I just can't imagine there's anything more for us to say. I'll bet he fades away."

"Hmm," Janie said. "And if he does reach out, and wants to try again?"

"I can't." I realized this was true only after I'd said it. "I worry it's me—deep down, in my neurotic place. Because it just doesn't feel great to have someone insist, over and over, that never in the history of his sexual life has he not been able to get it up—er, keep it up—*except with you*. But I also know, in my sane place, that it's him. He has a lot to work through that he's studiously avoiding."

Janie smiled, which I found strange.

"What?" I asked eventually.

"You recognize that The Dad has a lot of work to do, and that you can't, and shouldn't, do it for him. You've come a long way. Good for you."

Against all odds, given that session's topic, I walked out of Janie's office feeling infinitely better than when I'd walked in. Even though I did worry, on some level, that there was a pox on my vagina—some kind of voodoo curse that neutralized men's penises—I suspected that, in time, I'd get over this. Now I just had to figure out how to end things with The Dad without adding yet another scar to his collection.

"HI!" THE DAD answered the phone in his usual way. I called him after my jalk Tuesday night. There was no embarrassment in his voice, which made me feel both better and worse.

"Hey," I said. "You'll be proud of me—I think I might actually survive this race."

"Of course you will," he said. "How far'd you run tonight?"

"Just four miles," I said. "I'm tapering down, since the race is Saturday. But for someone who thought she'd never combine the words *just* and *four miles*, it's kind of a thing."

He laughed. "Nice." The Dad was the kind of runner who did five seven-minute miles before work.

"What about you?" I asked. "Lay it on me—you've done ten miles since we started this call, right?" I was starting to get nervous about what lay ahead.

"Right." He cleared his throat. "Listen, Zoe—I'm glad you called," he said in a more serious tone.

"Yeah," I started. I was about to tell him how fabulous I thought he was, how attractive, etcetera, before suggesting that we take a break—to let him get his feet under him after his divorce. But he didn't give me the chance.

"Because—Well. You know how I was on jDate for, like, five seconds, before we met?" he asked.

"Yeah. . . ."

"And you're *so* great, and smart, and sexy, so we just kind of jumped right in?"

Oh. No. *Way.* The man with the depressed penis and more baggage than Santa Claus was breaking up with *ME.*

"Well, I was with Jodie for so long that I think I just—I think I owe it to myself to see who's out there. To date around a little."

I struggled to get my wits about me. Finally, I said something like, "Oh. *Totally*," and tried very hard not to sneer. I mean he was kind of doing my work for me. But *come on!* This impotent, traumatized, Northbrook-shackled man—who freely shared that (a) he gave every dollar he earned to lawyers to fight his (b) crazy ex-wife who (c) had their marriage counselor's baby while (d) still married to The Dad, thereby (e) possibly devastating their young son—was now telling *me*, ever so earnestly, that he needed to give all the other ladies banging down his door a chance? I. Could. Not.

"You're *amazing*," he said.

Gross. I was determined not to let this turd-burger ruin Lloyd Dobler for me!

"Mmm," I replied.

"OK! Well . . . I hope you have a great rest of the week."

"All right. . . ."

Actually, no. This was *not* all right. I was tired of men working out their problems on me. And done sacrificing my own dignity in favor of theirs. "Wait. Elliot?"

"Yeah?"

"This is so random, but I've been meaning to ask—your profile says that you keep kosher."

"Umm, I do." He sounded confused and worried I might be rattled. This, of course, emboldened me.

"Oh, weird. Then why'd you order pasta with prosciutto— that's Italian ham—and cream sauce on our first date?"

There was a long pause before he yelped. "Ohmigod. I did? I ate *TREIF*?"

"Yep. It said so on the menu." He was speechless. And I hate to tell you that I reveled in his misery. "But anyway, good luck— with the dating."

"Oh—thanks," The Dad said meekly.

"Good-bye, Elliot."

I hung up with a smile.

♡

May 20, 2008

Dearests: What in the everliving fuck is wrong with you fucking people and your fucking penises? Love, Zoe

PS: Nothin' much to say I guess/You're just the same as all the rest/Been tryin' to throw your arms around the world/And a woman needs a man, like a Fish Needs a Bicycle/When you're tryin' to throw your arms around the world.

# Fifty-Four

The Soldier Field Ten-Miler turned out to be a (rather painful) blessing: My training distracted me from things like my outburst at the Kerryman, being dumped by The Dad, and the paucity of punctuated messages in my jDate inbox. When the Saturday of Memorial Day weekend arrived, I was ready—if unhappy about waking up at five o'clock. Aunt Steffi's cheery chit-chat as we stretched in the predawn light was obnoxious.

The weather was perfect: sixty degrees, dry, and sunny with a light breeze at start time. Aunt Steffi used her enormous sports watch to time our jogging and walking intervals. Yes, we were slow, but we completed the race with confounding ease. When we entered the stadium—the finish was located, awesomely, at Soldier Field's fifty-yard line—I felt an unfamiliar peace. The race couldn't have come at a better time: This particular journey had been challenging, but doable—and finite. To succeed, I had only to show up and do the work.[53]

By the time I arrived at Hot Chocolate for a celebratory dinner with Alex, Brian, and Hannah—as a race day gift to Hannah, Joe sent her out to dinner while he stayed in with Abi-

---

[53] It occurs to me that being a world-class runner may *actually be easier* than online dating. Doesn't seem fair.

gail—I was convinced that I needed to incorporate more achievable, short-term goals into my life. I pledged to sign up for another race and to perform "Blackbird" at the Old Town School of Folk Music's next recital. They were milestones I could actually reach while the rest of me floundered and felt increasingly deflated.

"I love the race and recital ideas," Hannah said when I shared my epiphany with the table. "And think you need a Dating Hiatus."

Alex and Brian nodded. I waited for an explanation, but they all just kept eating and drinking, as if everyone knew about this "Dating Hiatus" but me.

"What's a Dating Hiatus?" I finally asked. "And how do you know about it, Hannah? You've never had to date!"

"I have three sisters. And it's exactly what it sounds like," she said. "When dating feels like nothing but a chore, you just take a break."

"Huh," I said. I reached for my milk stout. Even though I could practically hear Janie insist that I *wasn't* running out of time by the second and *wouldn't* necessarily die alone if I took a dating break, I simply could not kick the feeling that it was me against the clock.

"It's not *forever*," Alex said, reading my mind like always. "It's just a pause. A reboot."

"Exactly," Hannah agreed.

"We've all done it," Brian said.

"I can't just, like, stop *trying*," I said. "Aren't I too old, and also too young, to give up?"

"Don't be ridiculous," Hannah said. "Taking a couple months off to focus on things you actually like isn't 'giving up.'"

Hmph. Easy for her to say.

And then, Alex and Hannah started talking among themselves about other things—as if the next step on my path were so obvious. But they had no credibility. Because *they* were partnered. *I* was single, alone, without prospects, and getting older by the day. As were my finite quantity of viable eggs. There was no time to waste! I wondered if any of these people, including Janie, could really empathize with me from the greener pastures of coupledom. Then I noticed that Brian wasn't talking—he was thinking.

"Zoe," he eventually said. "I took a long dating break right before I met Alex."

"You did?" I asked.

"Yeah. I didn't consciously decide not to date. But I *did* consciously decide to stop forcing it." He looked at Alex. "Because the kind of authentic connection I was looking for can't be forced."

My stomach squirmed uncomfortably. I was a habitual forcer of most things.

"When I finally accepted that, my life got better. I stopped fixating on meeting someone and just kind of . . . lived my life." He shrugged. "Ironically, I think that made me more likely to meet the right person. I mean, I met this *amazing* woman—" he leaned into Alex, who leaned back into him—"when I went to hear some jazz. I love jazz, so I went to hear some jazz. And then, boom."

"*I* actually don't love jazz, and was at the Green Mill only because the boys dragged me there." Alex smiled. "But it all worked out."

"You will come to love jazz in time, honey," Brian joked.

He drank his beer nonchalantly, but we were all impressed. I was touched not only by Brian's wisdom, but that he would share it with me. If Alex didn't marry him, I'd kill her.

"My therapist always says that. 'Live your life, the rest will come. You'll meet like-minded people organically.' And my yoga teacher is always talking about being present in the moment. But *not* pushing for something I really want—the thing I want most —is totally counterintuitive. I'm not sure I buy it, and definitely not sure I can do it, to be honest."

I usually didn't talk about this kind of thing with men other than Zach. But Brian was unfazed.

"Honestly, girl? I think you need to find some peace—and *confidence*—just being with yourself. Like when you run. Once you can tap into that, you'll be ready. And he'll be one lucky dude."

Alex could no longer help herself. In incredibly un-Alex-like fashion, she grabbed Brian's face in her hands and kissed him, square on the mouth, for all the restaurant to see. I wanted to follow Brian's advice, because I was pretty sure it was right. But I also wanted to scorch the earth to find the Brian to my Alex, and it's hard to take a hiatus from that.

♡

May 24, 2008

Guys: I'm going to take that Dating Hiatus because I have to. Even I can't deny that I am F.R.I.E.D. But how can "just living my life" not include doing everything I can to be happy? If I give up on dating and end up alone, won't I have only myself to blame? Thank you for being so easy to love. I'm finding the rest of the penis-toting population to be a lot harder. Or, softer. Or, just — you know. Difficult. XO, Zoe

Sean O'Kelly: Hi there. I know I owe you a real date, so please respond if you'll let me take you on one. (But don't if you're gonna knife me ;0!)

I stared at this chat on a Monday afternoon, more than two months after I'd last seen or heard from Irish, for I don't know how long. It was July—July, people!—and I was eight weeks into my Dating Hiatus. So far, it was going OK. Of course, I had my panicky moments. But when I finally stopped forcing myself to log onto jDate night after night, the unvarnished joy I felt made it impossible to ignore the benefits of the break.

I'd gone to temple every Friday since my hiatus began. The sermons were more impactful because I no longer worried that I should be "out there" instead of sandwiched between Bubbe and her old lady friends. Yoga was more restorative because I no longer wondered what lurked in my email, jDate inbox—or, in the bad old days, on my doorstep—after class. I enjoyed learning more about the guitar ladies now that my dating issues no longer dominated our conversations. I also bought myself an electric guitar and could play "Stairway to Heaven" almost all the way through. I decided not to tell anyone that I *did* keep my jDate profile up, and *did* check messages once in a while; since I didn't go on any dates, what did this matter?

Ironically, I'd also found closure on Irish. He wafted through my dreams on occasion, but I'd come to accept two things: (1) as Miranda said on *Sex and the City*, "he's just not that into me"; and (2) this fact—and really, everything relating to Irish—was moot, because only a crazy person would talk to me after the way I'd behaved at the Kerryman.

So maybe Irish was crazy. My finger hovered over the mouse.

Zoe Greene: Hi. I won't knife you.

The second I hit *Enter*, I knew I shouldn't have. My sex drive was a real asshole.

Sean O'Kelly: That's a great start.

Zoe Greene: I'm sorry about the Kerryman. I was really drunk.

Sean O'Kelly: Um, yasssss, you were.

[Nerve-wracking pause.]

Sean O'Kelly: You still seeing someone?

Zoe Greene: Nope. That didn't work out.

Sean O'Kelly: If I said I'm sorry, I'd be a-lyin'.

Zoe Greene: Thanks, Irish.

Sean O'Kelly: You're a cute drunk. A real f*ckin pistol, but kee-yuuuuuute. 😊

*Help me, help me, HELP ME.*

Sean O'Kelly: Pistol Annie? You still there?

Zoe Greene: Yep! Just got a call from dreadful partner, tho. Talk later?

Sean O'Kelly: Roger, Sweet T's. Holler at me and I'll take you to dinner. For real this time.

No one had called me. I raised my arms above my head to let the firm's overactive A/C dry out my pits.

"THIS REALLY SUCKS, but I need to tell you something because I don't want you to be blindsided," Caren said as soon as we sat down to a pre-yoga bite that evening. I had been ready to tell her about the amazing fact that Irish had chatted me of his own volition, but could tell the second I saw her face that she had something else to discuss.

"OK, what?"

She looked down and fiddled with her fingers.

"Care—you're freaking me out. Are you OK?"

"Yes. Sorry, I'm fine." She took a deep breath.

"OK, good."

"But I bumped into Rob today. And he cornered me."

Christ. In a way, I'd been waiting for this moment. It was kind of weird that it hadn't happened already. Once in a while, I gave spontaneous thanks that *I* hadn't seen Rob.

"Ick," I said. "Sorry. But you know what? I like your delivery, because compared to the catastrophic health news I was expecting, running into Rob sounds like a nothing."

Caren guzzled some water. I'd never seen anyone get an enema, but her expression called exactly that scenario to mind.

"I debated all day about whether to say anything, but decided I had to."

"Of course," I said.

"Just remember: The real moral of this story is that you're *done* with that weirdo. OK?"

I shifted in my seat. Now *I* probably looked like I was getting an enema. "OK," I said.

"Apparently, his firm moved to the building next to my bank. He stopped me in the bank lobby."

"I'm so sorry for inflicting him on—well. Everybody."

"It's OK. He did make me hug him like we were long-lost friends, though. That was sick."

I nodded. "He's always been like that. He thinks that observing everyday pleasantries makes you a good person. He used to call it 'acting classy.'"

Caren grimaced. "Well, it was weird. And *then,* when I made it clear that I wasn't going to stop and chat with him, he literally grabbed my arm to prevent me from walking away."

"Oh my God."

"And before I could even turn all the way back around, he starts telling me—just, like, spilling—that he's living in Morton Grove now—"

"Morton Grove?! Why?"

"Umm. Because that's where his pregnant fiancée lives." Caren held her breath. So did I. We stared at each other for what felt like a while.

"Are you OK?" she asked, reaching across the table to grab my sweaty hand.

I closed my eyes and forced myself to inhale. "Yes." I exhaled. "Go ahead."

She trembled but continued. "He told me the baby is a 'happy surprise.' Total non sequitur. And that's really it."

"I should hope so," I said. "That's quite enough."

I tried to laugh but it didn't work.

"I was so rattled by the conversation. Most of it, I think, is because I had *no* idea what a freak this guy was when you were together—none of us did. Not that we didn't believe you, because of course we did, and he certainly acted like a freak at the end . . . but anyway. I'm just *so glad* that you're free of him."

"Yeah," I said, although I wasn't feeling particularly free of him at the moment.

"What I can't shake is that he's supposedly engaged and *having a child*, but what matters most to him is that you know about it. He couldn't get the information out fast enough. I wonder how his fiancée would feel if she'd seen him."

"Gross."

"You have no idea," she said.

"I mean . . . I kind of do, though." We laughed. Then Caren's face changed.

"I haven't gotten to the weirdest part yet."

"*You haven't?*" God, how I wished I no longer gave a fuck. But I did. I gave a seriously large fuck.

"No. The weirdest part was when he finally took a freaking *breath* so that I could say 'good-bye' and bolt, and he yelled my name across the lobby—like, loudly enough that other people turned to look. So I said, 'Yeah?' And that's when he said, 'Do you have any pets?'"

This I was not expecting. "What?"

"Exactly. I said 'no' and tried to leave again, but then he shouts, 'My fiancée and I just bought a Frenchie!'" I accidentally swallowed an ice cube. Caren patted my hand while I coughed.

"So he wanted me to know that he's not only replaced me and our unborn child, but also our dog," I said.

Caren's naturally beautiful features contorted with concern. By the time I caught my breath and took a sip of crisp, cold water, I realized that, improbably, I was less shaken than she.

"Do you even think he's telling the truth?" Caren asked. "Or did he make it all up?"

"It's true."

"How do you know?"

"I just know." I shrugged. "I told my therapist, right at the beginning, that Rob would find someone to take care of him *fast*. I actually predicted that to my mom on our way home from my abortion. But Janie shored up the idea when she explained his type." *Charming, manipulative, singularly focused on his own needs.*

"Wow."

"I didn't necessarily think he'd do it this fast, but I knew he'd have his own kids because *that* would mean, in his mind, that the problem was never with him. It was with me."

"No," Caren whispered.

"Yes." Now angry tears began to fall. "Fuck," I complained. I pressed the heels of my palms beneath my eyes to try to stem the flow. "I don't know why I'm crying."

"Dude, *I* almost cried after seeing him! But now I've upset you, which is exactly what I didn't want to do."

Her lip quivered. I took her hand back. "Care Bear. Thank you for telling me. I needed to know."

She nodded, but tears escaped from the corners of her eyes.

"I'm OK," I said. "I mean, this'll sting for a minute, but I'm OK. I don't want what he's patched together. Not with him. And not in Morton Fucking Grove!"

She laughed through her tears. We both did.

"Get your shit together, man," I told her when I'd composed myself. "We can't *both* be crying in public. Look. Our waiter's freaked out."

I pointed to our young, wary-looking server who turned back to the water station as soon as we made eye contact.

"You wanna screw yoga and get a bottle of wine?" she asked.

"One hundred percent yes," I said.

We got a little drunk and split an obnoxiously large dessert before sharing a cab home.

AFTER TOSSING MY pristine yoga mat in the closet, I marched my wine buzz over to my laptop and opened Gchat.

Zoe Greene: So when's dinner?

*Please respond please respond please respond.*

Sean O'Kelly: Friday. Book it. 😊

Zoe Greene: Deal.

♡

July 23, 2008

Dear U2: It's been a weird few days. What I feel most, now that Rob's news has sunken in, is . . . gratitude. Bizarre, right? It was upsetting to hear about Rob. But I only had to <u>hear</u> about him — from one of my best friends, whom I genuinely love, and who genuinely loves me. I don't have to <u>live</u>

with him, or his problems, anymore. Thank G-d I got out. I do wish the script had been different. But still. Thank G-d. Love, Zoe

PS: And if the nights run over/And if the day won't last/And if your way should falter/Along the stony pass/It's just a moment, this time will pass.

THE SUN HAD begun to bake my office on Thursday afternoon, so I poured a Coke over ice before logging onto Westlaw. I had just typed my password when Alex knocked.

"Hey, Lady," she said, and shut the door behind her.

"Thank God you're here. I'd just run out of excuses not to start Chip's latest dead-end project."

She sat down. "Oh good! I just wanted to say hi. And check on you."

"I really am fine," I said. And meant it. Alex had been checking on me lots since Caren dropped her Rob bomb. Everyone had. But, just as Rob had so eerily exited my consciousness after the abortion, he'd done so again now. I changed the subject. "You look so pretty lately, it's kind of disgusting."

"Aww," Alex said, embarrassed.

"You're stinkin' happy, and it shows." I couldn't keep up my facade of revulsion any longer. I grinned. "And being bashful about it only makes it cuter."

She laughed my favorite guffaw. Then she picked at her fingernail polish.

"What's up?" I asked.

"So," she began. "Brian asked me to move in with him. And I said *yes*." Alex was smiling so big I thought her face might split in half.

"Oh, my God!" I squealed way too loudly. "Alex Alex Alex: I am *so* proud of you."

I sprang up to hug her. She beamed. Her body was relaxed. This was a totally different Alex than the one I'd seen every other time she'd faced a romantic commitment. I squelched the urge to ask why they didn't just get engaged; if Brian could respect Alex's pace, then so must I.

"I feel like I'm watching a flower bloom!" I teased after we'd finished doing our office version of jumping up and down (extra quiet, light on the toes).

"Shut it." She laughed. We sat back down.

"So when's moving day?"

"Saturday the thirtieth—next month."

"I'll help, obviously," I said.

"You really wouldn't mind?"

"Hell, no! You oversaw the removal of my crazy ex-husband's stuff from my apartment in the presence of my crazy ex-husband. This is the least I can do."

"God," she said with a twitch. "That feels like forever ago, doesn't it?"

"In a lot of ways, it really does," I nodded. "So, the thirtieth. I can't wait." And I couldn't.

# Fifty-Five

Friday night arrived. I was supposed to meet Irish at Twisted Lizard at seven thirty. I showered, blow-dried, and *did* squeeze in a bikini wax after jalking at the EBC. But at seven fifteen:

SO: F me, Sweet T's. At office, will be a little late.

Will I ever learn with these bikini waxes? I think it was Helen Keller who said something about there being nothing without hope, but still. I should have known.

ZG: OK.

SO: Don't b mad! Call u soon.

I hung up my clothes and tossed my chunky funky jewelry back in its box. I ate beef and broccoli in my pajamas and walked Bas. The pets each claimed a thigh while we watched TV. I washed my face and admired my bikini wax in the bathroom mirror before climbing into bed with *Us Weekly*. It was déjà vu all over again when my phone buzzed at eleven o'clock.[54]

SO: come over.

ZG: What?

SO: please?

---

[54] The fact that I left my phone on likely means exactly what you think it does.

ZG: No.

SO: c'mon. horrible day.

SO: really sorry about din. promise i'll make it up.

SO: let's salvage this friday night.

ZG: I'm in bed.

SO: oooooh

ZG: Stop.

SO: throw on some jammy pants and come over.

ZG: Why.

SO: because we're adults and we want each other.

SO: that's why.

[Long, fraught pause.]

ZG: Where do you live?


I WORE A Joshua Tree shirt, cotton pajama pants, dating panties, and a scowl to Irish's apartment. I rinsed off my zit cream but didn't bother with makeup.

Irish lived on the top floor of a three-flat one half-block from Damen. There was no buzzer, so I texted him to let me in. My heart raced on his doorstep, for so many reasons. Through the front door's large window, I watched Irish jog down the stairs with an athlete's gait. He was still wearing his work clothes, although he'd ditched his shoes and tie and undone the first couple buttons on his shirt. His hair was mussed—ideally, of course—and his poreless skin showed no signs of his long, trying day. He was smooth and rosy in the right places; there was light in his eyes. He scooped me up into an easy hug and tried to hide the smile he always wore when I was pissed; my body melted into his and, after a few seconds, I stopped instructing it not to. He smelled of fresh deodorant and mint.

"C'mon, hot thang," he whispered into my ear before taking my hand and leading me upstairs.

His apartment threw me. Of course it was dirty—he was a single, male workaholic—but it was also dingy and dull, which are the last two words I'd use to describe Irish. The walls needed painting, the appliances were ancient, and the kitchenette's linoleum floor was cracked. The only light came from a dim floor lamp and the underside of the microwave. A small drab couch sat between two plastic deck chairs, all of which surrounded one sad card table. An ancient A/C unit wheezed from a window. It saddened me that someone with such je ne sais quoi lived in this depressing place. But I guessed he was never home.

Irish was oblivious to his apartment, or at least my reaction to it. As soon as he shut the door and took a swig of just-opened beer, he pulled me to him. Shouldn't he at least *say* something about dinner? So that we could pretend like he actually intended to take me out—ever? If I went along with this, wasn't I complicit in being jerked around? Alas, he was a pro; he held me as though we were slow dancing and whispered, "I'm sorry about work. You know I'd rather have been with you."

The way his chest and arms fit around me was magic. I contemplated bucking up. But as he began to touch me and nuzzle my ear, I finally realized: Why bother? I'd gone to his apartment because I wanted him. So I pulled back, looked at his amazing face, and kissed it. We picked up as though no time (or near fisticuffs) had passed. I let everything go.

So, yeah. We finally had sex. Functional sex, with a condom—two, actually, because we did it twice—that resulted in two climaxes (both his). It was decent sex. But it was first-time sex. Irish's *body* was every bit as spectacular as I'd imagined, but he didn't know me; he didn't know where I liked to be touched, or how, or when. Nor did he ask. After he finished, he fell immediately and deeply to sleep. I must have dozed off too. (That week, in addition to abiding Irish's standard bullshit, I'd logged fifty-five billable hours, two sessions with Inga, and two substantial jalks.)

I opened my eyes at 2:11 a.m., according to Irish's digital clock. He was sound asleep. I seized the opportunity to pee, clean up, and dress. Then I sat down next to him. Irish looked so perfect, lying there, even in the worn gray sheets. I don't know why I decided to wake him; I'm not sure what I'd hoped he'd say or do. But I shook him anyway.

"Hey—Irish," I nudged.

"Hmm." He grunted without opening his eyes.

"Irish." I nudged him again, harder. "I think I'll go—OK?"

"Mmm, stay." He said this mostly into his pillow and pulled me toward him. Then he flipped over and went back to sleep, his back against mine.

"I really have to go," I said into his ear.

"Aww. Nkay. Bye, Sweet T's."

As seemed to happen when I was with Irish, I freaked. "Wake up! Walk me out."

He groaned, yawned, and threw on gym shorts and, to add insult to injury, a Cardinals T-shirt. We stuffed our feet into our respective flip-flops and walked wordlessly to Damen. I wasn't sure if he was really awake. At the corner, he gave me a sleepy hug, whispered that I had a hot body, and turned toward home.

"Irish," I called to the back of his head. He looked over his shoulder. "Stay with me until I get a cab."

"Oh, OK," he agreed. He stood with his eyes closed.

I flagged a taxi ten seconds later. Irish opened his eyes to half-mast and managed a quick smile, but walked away before I'd even closed the car door. He didn't look back once. I cried the whole way home.

♡

Wee Hours of July 26, 2008

Don't check/Just balance on the fence/Don't answer/ Don't ask/Don't try to make sense/I feel numb.

# Fifty-Six

briefly hesitated to answer when Penelope called Sunday night. I didn't want to discuss Rob's engagement, especially on the vulnerable heels of my ill-fated rendezvous with Irish. And during the months Penelope and I had been out of touch, I'd wondered whether the divorce had erected some kind of boundary between us—one I shouldn't breach. But seeing her number made me realize how much I'd missed her.

"Penelope?"

"Zoe, hello!" We giggled at the sound of each other's voices. "It has been long time!"

"Too long! My fault."

"Not 'fault.' We are busy women! We *both* make new lives."

She sounded giddy, and international calls were expensive, so I cut to the chase. "What's going on?"

"I have happy news. But also maybe surprise."

"I love happy news!" The surprise—maybe Rob was having twins?—could wait. "Tell me."

"I found love of life!"

I'd never heard even a whisper of her dating. "Wow! Penelope, that's amazing!" I tried to focus on my happiness for her rather than on everyone around me finding love while I seemed to actively repel it. "How long have you—"

"Zoe. My love is woman."

*Click.* It felt like I was watching a film reel come into focus; meanwhile, poor Penelope was holding her breath.

"Tell me *everything!*" I squealed.

So she did. Penelope met Vittoria when Penelope's newspaper sent her to Milan. Vittoria worked in fashion, it was love at first sight, and Penelope was moving to Italy, where she'd work a different beat. The couple communicated in English. After we gushed for several minutes—Penelope about Vittoria, me about Penelope's bravery taking on a new partner, country, language, and job all at once—I sensed there was something more. But she changed the subject before I could probe.

"How is Asshole?"

I deflated like a balloon. "Busy. I assume you've heard."

"No," she said warily. "We hear little from American Baroses now. What?"

"Well . . . he has a pregnant fiancée."

There was silence on the other end of the line.

"HE IS SHIT!" she shouted. Then sighed. "But makes sense. Father? Shit. Mother? Shit. Uncle says she goes to hospital for everything except her real problems." Chills crept up my spine. "Robert had little chance of being good person."

Something about Penelope's tone—or timing, or perspective—helped reshuffle Rob in my brain. Janie and I had begun discussing his childhood wounds and their consequences at length, which helped not to excuse, but to contextualize, his behavior. Penelope now planted the seeds of something more. Something like acceptance. Pity. Maybe even a kernel of forgiveness.

"No, he didn't," I agreed. And in that moment, I let something heavy go.

"Zoe. I want to marry Vittoria. But my family are avoiding . . . it is difficult."

"I'm so, so sorry."

"My mother I think will adjust. My father . . . I hope. But Vittoria and I, we want to marry—not to wait."

"Good for you. Life's too short to postpone joy."

"We go to Netherlands—where woman can marry woman —but want to make party in Italy." Penelope sounded cheerful again. "Vittoria's family will come. I would like support too. I know it would be long trip for you, but I wondered. . . ."

"I'll be there," I said without hesitation. "I'm honored."

"This means very much."

"As has everything you've done for me. And I have to tell you—I'm looking forward to a Baros wedding without a corpse."

She laughed. "We make good family, yes?"

"Yes," I said. "We always will."

After we hung up, I pulled out the photo Christos had taken of the two of us, laughing in the funeral parlor, and marveled at how far we'd come.

# Fifty-Seven

"C'mon. Let us buy you dinner," Brian urged after guzzling half a liter of water. We all sat on the couch in, as of thirty minutes ago, Brian *and Alex's* apartment.

"Oh, I'll get a 'tini out of this eventually," I promised. "Besides. That was the easiest move ever."

I knew that Alex had always been nomadic but still couldn't believe how little stuff she had. One professional Sherpa could have completed her entire move in an hour. I stood and stretched.

"Stay," Alex said. "We'll order in."

Clearly all they *really* wanted to do was have sex in every room and go to sleep. But they also wanted me to know that, even though Alex was now coupled, I was welcome in her life, in *their lives*, and in their home. They were so kind. I couldn't lie to them.

"I actually can't stay," I said, "because—Bri, since you've been officially indoctrinated into the Life of Alex, you too now have to listen to this shit—I have a date. A stupid, stupid jDate."

"What?" Alex asked in her alarmed-but-still-kind-of-even-keeled Alex way. "I thought you were on hiatus."

"Yeah!" Brian added. His concern made me smile.

"I was. But I caved. I've just gotten through some shitty an-niversaries. Rob's moving—or, I guess, has moved—on with his life. Irish is done, no one else was on the horizon . . . I was having a moment. So I accepted an invitation for a drink from Nonde-script Guy the Zillionth."

"Oh," Brian said.

"Umm, that—anniversary?" Alex asked in distinctly break-able code.

"Yes. That anniversary," I said.

"Are you OK?" she asked.

"Yeah. Of course." I played with the top of my water bottle.

"This date—it's just a drink. Right?" she asked.

"Right," I echoed.

"So no big deal," Alex and I said in unison.

I hugged them both. Alex followed me into the hallway.

"Al, the abortion-iversary—I'm in a little funk, but just have to get through it. I'll be fine."

"Are you sure?" she asked while wearing her Most Worried Face.

"I am. And this is your first night as a Domestic Partner. Enjoy it, OK? Go show Bri how happy you are to be here. He's *so* excited."

She nodded, gave me a huge hug, and hovered in the hallway until the elevator doors closed behind me. By the time I got to the lobby, I had a text from Alex saying that she was rallying the troops to celebrate her move at the Burwood Tap. She wanted me to know about it "just in case." I loved her so much.

FALL WAS COMING. Even though the sun was still pretty merciless at five o'clock in late August, I enjoyed the walk to the Wanna-Be Pretentious Bar my date (Blake) had chosen. (It couldn't really be pretentious because of its proximity to Costco and the 24-hour CVS, but it was trying. Hard.) It had been a while, but my first-date-butterflies reemerged. I smoothed the maxi-dress that Sandy convinced me to buy and opened the bar door.[55] I spotted Blake immediately. He was seated at the bar, his sweater draped over the next stool to save it. He wasn't unattractive—just as utterly plain looking as his profile picture suggested. He really *was* a Nondescript Guy.

"Blake?" I inquired.

"Zoe," he said, looking up from the wine list. "Nice to meet you." He stood and shook my hand.

"Thanks for saving me a seat." I lifted my cross-body bag off my shoulder and over my head before sliding onto my stool.

"Of course," he said, sitting back down and angling his stool toward mine. His eyes were a dark hazel. He wore khaki Dockers, a plain brown belt, and a white-and-light-blue-striped Polo shirt; his outfit was exactly what the boys wore to parties in junior high. It was a strange choice, I thought, for a first-date drink on a Saturday afternoon.

We each ordered a glass of wine. Because the glasses started at $15, on principle, I chose their cheapest one.

"How was your day?" I asked.

"Oh, good. Any day out of the office is good."

"So true."

We sat in silence. Blake bowed his head just low enough to

---

[55] Damn right I went back to Joie after The Dad Dump + Rob Weirdness + Irish.

expose a receding hairline; the thin, delicate tufts in front formed a V. He kept the V long so that he could comb it straight back, but it didn't work—there was plenty of scalp on display. The futility of his 'do made me sad.

"Umm. Remind me. What do you do again?" I asked.

"I don't think we talked about it. Or, you know, IM'd about it." He laughed a nervous laugh. "I'm in IT, in Schaumburg." He told me the name of his company, but I couldn't quite hear him, and it didn't ring a bell. "We're in a corporate park out there."

"Oof. That's some kind of commute."

"It's not too bad," he insisted.

I didn't believe him. Fighting the reverse commute all the way to Schaumburg every day—to a corporate park, no less—was my idea of a recurring nightmare. We looked at each other and bobbed our heads. Right before our wine arrived, I noticed a faint ring around his collar.

While the bartender fussed with cocktail napkins and water glasses, a loud bus pulled away from the stop across the street. The bus vestibule displayed an Obama campaign sign declaring, "YES WE CAN!" I was grateful for the conversation starter. I cleared my throat.

"So, are you as ready as I am to just go ahead and have this election? It's crazy exciting, but I'll be on pins and needles 'til it's over."

"Oh, yeah! The election. For president . . . right?" Blake asked.

I cocked my head and tried to read his face. But his languid smile remained the same. "Right. For president," I eventually said.

I watched him uneasily.

"I really don't know much about either of those guys," he mused. "And isn't the election, like, soon?"

"Yeah. . . ."

"I totally forgot to vote last time." He winked.

Now, why, out of *all* the crazy things that had happened over the last year, this was the one that pushed me over the edge, I'll never know. I'd been splooged on by a rabbi, dumped by an impotent suburbanite, and tossed out onto Damen Avenue like an empty keg. I'd been on dates so nondescript that, when I sat down to tell U2 about them, I had literally nothing to write—and cheeked a man whose favorite drink recipe had been embossed onto card stock. My delusional ex-husband was engaged and poised to procreate—even his *dog* was newer and younger than mine. Poor Blake just happened to be with the wrong girl, at the wrong bar, at the wrong time.

My hands began to sweat. My breath quickened. I tried taking a large gulp from my glass. *It's just a drink. You can do this.* But my body was getting away from me.

"You forgot to *vote*?" I asked.

"Yeah. Doh! Bad, right? I wanna do it this time, but I'm blanking on their names. The candidates."

"Barack Obama and John McCain."

"Right! Thanks," Blake said. My stomach began to cramp. "The one guy—the old one—he was a senator or something. Wasn't he?"

My face burned but my fingers went cold. Maybe I was getting sick. "Both of them *are* senators," I said quietly.

The entire city of Chicago had been whipped into Obama Frenzy for a full year—arguably two. Sarah Palin had just made her loud, crass, terrifying entrance onto the national stage.

*Everyone* was talking about it. (Jonathan Sealy, Alex, Caren, and I were, anyway—we wasted at least one billable hour per day on the subject.) I caught *the audacity of hope* in a groupie-style way when I happened to walk into the EBC at the very moment Obama's security detail was ushering him to the front door. There was something so normal about him, but also magnetic. That kind of star quality and relatable humanity didn't often occupy the same body. Every bus stop, billboard, newspaper, local news outlet, TV ad—the entire Internet—bombarded Chicagoans with election coverage every moment of every day. *Could he do it? One of our very own?* The city felt like it would burst. I wasn't sure we could make it until November.

But, somehow, all of it had passed Blake by.

"What do *you* do?" he asked.

"I'm an attorney," I squeaked.

"So *that's* why you're up on all this election stuff!" He rapped my knee.

"Uh. . . ."

I tried to change the subject, and get control of myself, but fog filled my head, and a high-pitched noise filled my ears. I didn't know what was happening, but I knew I had to leave. Now.

My hot, spasmy insides floated up toward the bar's vaulted ceiling. Floating Zoe then heard on-the-ground Zoe utter things she might sometimes think, or tell her weird U2 diary, but never, ever—usually—say.

"Blake?" I grabbed my bag, stood, and retrieved two twenties from my wallet.

"Uh, yeah?" he asked, uncertain.

"I'm sorry." I placed the twenties under my glass. "I'm so sorry," I repeated. "I'm an asshole. But I have to go."

"Oh—OK," Blake said nervously, wondering whether he'd done something wrong. And he *had* done something wrong—he was a moron with no sense of social responsibility—but that was neither here nor there.

"*You're* fine," I said. "*I'm* the asshole." I felt compelled to come up with some kind of explanation, but couldn't. "I'm sorry," I finally said again, and left.

Worse, I smiled before turning away. I couldn't help it. To be so candid, open, and reactionary was both scary and impolite—but, also, exhilarating. A voice from somewhere inside told me not to run out on a date, but that's exactly what I did. I ran. In a maxi-dress.

The fresh air felt amazing on my cheeks. I slowed to a brisk walk only when I needed to; I hadn't taken a full breath in ages. I forced my lungs to open and close, haltingly at first. I shook my head a few times, pried open my jaw, and moved it around. I walked some more. And eventually my muscles, revived by fresh oxygen, began to feel pleasant. Awake.

It wasn't until I saw a young gay couple survey me with concern that I considered what I must look like, alternately shaking my head, laughing, clenching and unclenching my hands into fists. I had even turned around to aim both middle fingers toward the bar—not at Blake, not at the other Nondescript Guys, but at *all* of it. The whole thing. The nice gay gentlemen probably assumed I'd gone off some critical meds. So, probably, did everyone else. But I didn't care.

I was still working it through—guilt about Blake, frustration that I'd agreed to go out with him in the first place, the excitement and terror of facing the unknown, openly, for the first time —when I arrived home. I spontaneously passed my front door and cut up Webster. I watched the red and orange sunset bounce off the building windows. With each new breath, I relaxed. My scalp, forehead, cheeks, throat, shoulder blades, and ribcage— they all began to melt. My arms and legs swung free.

I pulled out my Blackberry and logged onto jDate, looking up frequently to bob and weave through pedestrian traffic. I steadfastly clicked past each obstacle jDate erected: *Are you SURE you want to give up? Are you SURE you're ready to descend into single oblivion? You KNOW this site may be your last hope, right? And also that you won't be refunded for the remainder of this billing cycle?*

By the time I rounded the corner to Wrightwood one block from the Burwood Tap, my jDate profile was officially down. I laughed. It was by far the most satisfying breakup I'd ever had.

I stopped short of the Tap. I could see my friends through the picture window. Alex was holding a martini laden with extra olives in one hand and gesturing animatedly with the other. Brian leaned on the bar behind her, holding a pint glass, admiring not so much what Alex was saying, but Alex in general. Jimmy threw his head back to laugh. Caren broke her smile only long enough to snare some popcorn with her tongue. She covered her pop-corn-mouth with her hand to thank the bartender for the beer he'd placed in front of her.

This was one of those rare moments when I could tell—not after the fact, but in the moment itself—that something seismic had shifted within me. I had no husband, no boyfriend, no crush. No baby, no fetus, no embryo, and no idea when, or if, I would ever have any of those things. There was no telling when there'd be a man in my bed again, much less my heart. Every-thing I'd wanted, everything I'd clawed and scraped and tried to coerce into fruition over the past year—it all hung out in the ether as one big, vaporous question mark. I, Zoe Greene—the goal-oriented, order-loving woman who likes her gas tank full and her hamper empty—the woman who always, *always* had a plan—had absolutely no idea what was next. I took a breath. I let it out. I walked into the bar.

## PERMISSIONS

Many thanks to the artists and entities who have granted permission to quote their material:

HarperCollins Publishers, Ltd. (US and Canada) for permission to quote Rabbi Joseph Telushkin and Caitlin Moran

Carrie Bornstein and Elizabeth Eggert at MayyimHayyim.org for permission to quote their mikveh-related prayers, and for making them publicly available

RitualWell.org for permission to quote Rabbi Geela Rayzel Raphael's pregnancy-loss blessing

Rabbi Burt Jacobson for permission to quote his divorce blessing

U2 (eek!) and Hal Leonard LLC for permission to quote lyrics from these songs:

## Lemon

Words and Music by Paul Hewson, Dave Evans, Larry Mullen and Adam Clayton
Copyright © 1993 UNIVERSAL MUSIC PUBLISHING INTERNATIONAL B.V.
All Rights Administered by UNIVERSAL – POLYGRAM INTERNATIONAL PUBLISHING, INC.
All Rights Reserved Used by Permission
*Reprinted by Permission of Hal Leonard LLC*

## Tryin' To Throw Your Arms Around The World

Lyrics by Bono and The Edge

Music by U2

Copyright © 1991 UNIVERSAL – POLYGRAM INTERNATIONAL MUSIC PUBLISHING B.V.

All Rights for the United States and Canada Controlled and Administered by UNIVERSAL – POLYGRAM INTERNATIONAL PUBLISHING, INC.

All Rights Reserved Used by Permission

*Reprinted by Permission of Hal Leonard LLC*

## Numb

Lyrics by Bono and The Edge

Music by U2

Copyright © 1993 UNIVERSAL – POLYGRAM INTERNATIONAL MUSIC PUBLISHING B.V.

All Rights for the United States and Canada Controlled and Administered by UNIVERSAL – POLYGRAM INTERNATIONAL PUBLISHING, INC.

All Rights Reserved Used by Permission

*Reprinted by Permission of Hal Leonard LLC*

# ACKNOWLEDGMENTS

Writing and publishing this book required me to cultivate patience, a thick skin (the book business is neither fair nor kind—to all of you aspiring authors, just keep going), courage, confidence, and trust, and to not give too many fucks. Literally none of this comes naturally. I depended upon and will be forever grateful to these generous souls:

Josh, who either really believed I could do this or did an outstanding job faking it, and who both pushed and loved me through the entire process.

Jacob and Wyatt, for believing that moms should have dreams too.

Frieda Rich Wolf, for showing me what female power is and helping me to find my own.

Otto Thelonious Wolf, for infusing me with everlasting joy.

Mike Wolf, for gamely copyediting his daughter's novel, despite the sex scenes; Leslie Wolf, for raising me to question the patriarchy; Nate Wolf, for tolerating me as a child; Miranda Wolf, for finally giving me a cherished sister; and to all aforementioned Wolfs for your love.

The skilled, patient, neuroses-indulging women at Ladderbird Literary Agency, especially Katelin Spector, and *doubly* especially Beth Marshea, who took a chance on this book and on me. May every author have champions like you.

Ditto Deborah Brosseau of Deborah Brosseau Communications AKA The World's Best Publicist.

Bettina Elias Siegel, for her sage advice, giving nature, steadfast support, vision, kindness, and mad web skills; Stacey

Aaronson for her attention to detail, great taste, and generous heart; Lea Särnblad, for teaching me social media; Mary Shannon Tompson for nailing it; Jen Maconochie for being my Chicago team; Shira Zemel and 73Forward for joining forces; Jade Dressler and The Pixel Dust Sisters, Carol Morgan-Eagle and Barbara Davis, for their creativity; and She Writes Press, for determinedly amplifying female voices.

My writing compatriots and the authors who so kindly shared their knowledge—Mimi Swartz, Kay Kendall, Carla Powers, Andrea White, Ami Polonsky, Jen Waite, Jasmine Guillory, Allyn West, Beth Whittemore, Helen Mann, and, most especially, Catherine Devore Johnson, who has generously helped to untangle my gnarliest writerly webs, shared her brilliance, and been my author-anchor for over a decade.

My best friends, true friends, old friends, and extended family (especially Shari Wolf and Tom Dobrinski, who give me a loving home whenever I need one), for caring about me, my writing, and my survival of this book's birth. You know who you are.

The members of the Let's Burn This Shit Down text chain, formed during That Terrible Night (Election Night 2016)—Ellyn Josef, Phillip Winston, Kellianne Hill, and Hubby. Together, we survived Trump. Kind of. So far. Your support has been a ballast.

My Village: Tabitha Rice—my boss knows no equal, and I am lucky to call her a friend; Leslie Viswanathan, for covering umpteen VERY EARLY carpool runs and still making time for real talk; and Karlie Middleton, who cares for my kids in a way that belies her young age.

My mental, emotional, and spiritual health crew: Dr. Carrie

Feig, Steve Katzman, Dr. Amy Robbins, Elyse Cathrea, and Glennon Doyle, Amanda Doyle, Abby Wambach, and the *We Can Do Hard Things* podcast. I don't know where I'd be without you, but it'd be nowhere good.

All the women who've said the things that need saying; your work has sustained me since childhood. Especially Caitlin Moran—when I read your words, it's like I have a (smarter, funnier, English-accented) sister living in my ear. PLEASE DO MORE IN AMERICA.

Neil McCormick, for writing *Killing Bono*, which fell into my hands at just the right time, simultaneously validating both the agony and virtue of being a creative.

The professors who encouraged me: Maud McInerney, Rebecca Pope, Christine So, Margaret Stetz, and Maureen Corrigan.

The feminists, for holding up the sky, pushing us toward the light, and being honest, often at great personal expense. Extra gratitude to the women of color, for whom the stakes remain the highest.

Finally, the reproductive justice crusaders. From the OGs, like the magnificent RBG, to Justices Kagan and Sotomayor, and, I pray, Jackson, the healthcare professionals and activists who put women first, their allies, and all those who fight for bodily autonomy and integrity and to change the abortion narrative to align with truth. I owe my life to you.

# ABOUT THE AUTHOR

Credit: Al Torres Photography

EMILY WOLF is an ardent feminist, U2 fan, and native Chicagoan. She now lives in Texas (the politicians are mostly terrible, the queso is mostly excellent) with her family of humans and dogs. She is working on her second novel and has published several essays in the *Houston Chronicle* and at www.emilyvwolf.medium.com. Although she is tech illiterate, she tries to do things on Twitter at @EmilyWolfAuthor, Instagram at @emilywolfpaperbackwriter, and her website at www.emilywolfbooks.com.

SELECTED TITLES FROM SHE WRITES PRESS

She Writes Press is an independent publishing company
founded to serve women writers everywhere.
Visit us at www.shewritespress.com.

*A Better Next* by Maren Cooper. $16.95, 978-1-63152-493-6. At the top of her career, twenty plus years married, and with one child left to launch, Jess Lawson is blindsided by her husband's decision to move across the country without her—news that shakes her personal and professional life and forces her to make surprising new choices moving forward.

*Appetite* by Sheila Grinell. $16.95, 978-1-63152-022-8. When twenty-five-year-old Jenn Adler brings home a guru fiancé from Bangalore, her parents must come to grips with the impending marriage—and its effect on their own relationship.

*Cleans Up Nicely* by Linda Dahl. $16.95, 978-1-93831-438-4. The story of one gifted young woman's path from self-destruction to self-knowledge, set in mid-1970s Manhattan.

*Montana Rhapsody* by Susanna Solomon. $16.95, 978-1-63152-361-8. When thirty-something pole dancer Laura Fisher reluctantly goes on a canoe trip with a man she just met in order to escape the three thugs after her, she is challenged in ways she never expected.

*Wishful Thinking* by Kamy Wicoff. $16.95, 978-1-63152-976-4. A divorced mother of two gets an app on her phone that lets her be in more than one place at the same time, and quickly goes from zero to hero in her personal and professional life—but at what cost?

*Vote for Remi* by Leanna Lehman. $16.95, 978-1-63152-978-8. History is changed forever when an ambitious classroom of high school seniors pull the ultimate prank on their favorite teacher—and end up getting her in the running to become president of the United States.